PRAISE FOR GREG RUCKA'S
FINDER

"If you're looking for a private eye with hard-edged skills and a soft center, try FINDER."
—*Alfred Hitchcock Mystery Magazine*

"The action is nonstop."
—*The Boston Globe*

"FINDER moves with dizzying speed. It is gritty, profane, violent, and sometimes profound. . . . Rucka has a talent for burrowing under the surface and exposing the vulnerability we all know is there in each of us. . . . FINDER offers great rewards."
—*Statesman Journal,* Salem, Oregon

"A fast-paced and very contemporary thriller with a plot, as they say, that will not let you go. Suspense fans will finish this in one satisfied sitting, only to find themselves impatient for Rucka's next offering."
—*American Way Magazine*

"Fine cliff-hangers, well-executed violence, and skillfully sketched characters. Superior."
—*Kirkus Reviews*

"A fast-paced mystery charged with humanity and love."
—*The Ottawa Citizen*

Also by Greg Rucka

KEEPER

and coming soon in hardcover:

SMOKER

Look for it at your favorite
bookstore in November 1998

FINDER

GREG RUCKA

BANTAM BOOKS
NEW YORK TORONTO LONDON SYDNEY AUCKLAND

This edition contains the complete text
of the original hardcover edition.
NOT ONE WORD HAS BEEN OMITTED.

FINDER

A Bantam Book

PUBLISHING HISTORY
Bantam hardcover edition published July 1997
Bantam paperback edition / September 1998

ISBN 0-553-57429-9

Published simultaneously in the United States and Canada

Bantam Books are published by Bantam Books, a division of Bantam
Doubleday Dell Publishing Group, Inc. Its trademark, consisting of
the words "Bantam Books" and the portrayal of a rooster, is
Registered in U.S. Patent and Trademark Office and in other
countries. Marca Registrada. Bantam Books, 1540 Broadway, New
York, New York 10036.

PRINTED IN THE UNITED STATES OF AMERICA

OPM 10 9 8 7 6 5 4 3 2

This is for Jennifer

ACKNOWLEDGMENTS

Thanks go out to the following people for their assistance and aid in making this book possible:

As always, the President of Executive Security and Protection International (ESPI), Inc., Gerard "Jerry" Hennelly, for service above and beyond the call of duty *and* friendship.

Jonathan Rollins, for telling me more than I could ever want to know about the clubs of Manhattan, both for firearms and B/D; Officer William "Bill" Conway of the NYPD, for legal points and procedural accuracy; Elizabeth Rogers, NY EMS Paramedic, for advice about wounds; Paul Biddle of Dorsett, for fact checking and accuracy via long distance.

Benjamin Toro, for telling me that who dares wins.

Special thanks to: Kate, Peter, Amanda, Mike, Nic, Daria, Nunzio, Joaquin, Veil, and Tut. The debts are great, and the thanks not nearly enough.

Some kill their love when they are young,
And some when they are old;
Some strangle with the hands of Lust,
Some with the hands of Gold:
The kindest use a knife, because
The dead so soon grow cold.

Some love too little, some too long,
Some sell, and others buy;
Some do the deed with many tears,
And some without a sigh:
For each man kills the thing he loves,
Yet each man does not die.

Oscar Wilde, *The Ballad of Reading Gaol,* st. 8 and 9

CHAPTER ONE

She was lost.

I only saw her because I was doing my job, just looking for trouble, and I must have missed him when he came in, because I didn't see him enter. He was a white male in his early thirties, neat in his clothes and precise in his movement, and he clearly wasn't with the scene, the way he lurked in the corners of the club floor. The Strap had been built in an abandoned warehouse, the walls painted pit-black and the lights positioned to make shadows rather than eliminate them. For people who were serious about the scene, The Strap wasn't a club of choice, and if they showed at all, it wasn't until after midnight, when the wannabes had gone to greener pastures or to bed.

Bouncing is a people-watching job, a process of regard and/or discard. You look for potential trouble; you isolate potential trouble; then you wait, because you can't react until you're certain what you've got really will be trouble.

I was waiting, watching him as he looked for her, as he weaved around the tops and bottoms playing their passion scenes. It was after two now, and the serious players had arrived, a detachment of leather- and PVC-clad types who took their playing very seriously indeed. Now and again, over the industrial thud of the music, the slap of a whip hitting skin, or a moan, or a laugh, would make it to my ears.

Trouble stopped to watch a chubby woman in her fifties get bound onto a St. Andrew's Cross, black rubber straps twisted around her wrists and ankles, making her skin fold and roll over the restraints. His hands stayed in his coat pockets, and I saw that he was sweating in the party lights.

Maybe cruising.

His manner was wrong, though, and when the woman's top offered him his cat-o'-nine-tails, Trouble fixed him with a level stare that was heavy with threat. The top shrugged a quick apology, then went back to work. Trouble cracked a smile, so fast it was almost a facial tic, then turned and headed for the bar.

It wasn't a nice smile.

Hard case, I thought.

I followed him with my eyes, then let him go for a minute to watch two new entrants. As the newcomers came onto the floor a woman cut loose with a pathetic wail, loud enough to clear the music, and the younger of the two stopped and stared in her direction. Both men were dark brown, with skin that looked tar-black where the calculated shadows hit them. The younger looked like a shorter, slighter version of the older, right down to their crew cuts. Both were dressed for watching, not for playing, and the younger couldn't have been much over twenty-one, just legal enough to get inside. His companion was older, in his forties. He shook his head at the younger man's reaction, said something I couldn't hear, and as they began moving off again, I looked back to the bar.

Trouble had ordered a soda from Jacob, the bartender. The Strap was a licensed club, and since there was nudity on the premises, it couldn't serve alcohol. Trouble paid with a wallet he pulled from inside his jacket, and when he put it back, the hem of his coat swung clear enough for me to see a clip hooked over his left front pants pocket. The clip was blacked, the kind used to secure a pager, or perhaps a knife.

So maybe he's a dealer, I thought. Waiting to meet someone, ready to make a deal.

Or he really is trouble.

He sipped his soda, licked his lips, began scanning again with the same hard look. A man and a woman crawled past me on all fours, each wearing a dog collar, followed by a dominatrix clad in red PVC. She held their leashes in one hand, a riding crop in the other, and gave me a smile.

"Aren't they lovely?" she asked.

"Paper trained?"

"Soon," she said.

Trouble had turned, looking down at the other end of the bar, and I followed his gaze, and that's when I saw Erika.

She wore a black leather miniskirt, torn fishnet stockings, and shiny black boots with Fuck-Me heels. Her top was black lace, also torn, showing skin beneath. Her hair was long, a gold like unfinished oak. The club lights made it darker and almost hid the stiff leather collar she wore, almost obscured the glint from the D ring mounted at the collar's center.

She was brutally beautiful.

She was just like her mother.

She was only fifteen.

Trouble and I watched her light a cigarette, tap ash into her plastic soda cup while watching the scenes play around her. She looked carefully bored, meeting gazes easily as she found them, no change in her expression.

The pitch and yaw in my stomach settled, and I took a breath, wondered if it really was Erika, wondered what the hell I was supposed to do now.

Trouble finished his soda and moved, settling beside her, his lips parting in an opening line. She didn't react and didn't look away, and he spoke again, resting his left arm on the bar, his right in his lap.

Erika cocked her head at him, then turned away on her stool, tossing her hair so it slapped him in the face.

He responded by grabbing her with his left hand, taking hold of her shoulder and spinning her back to face him, and that's when I started moving.

Erika tried to shrug his hand off, but he didn't let go, and I was close enough now to hear her saying, "Fucking fuck off, asshole."

"We're going," he told her.

Jacob had turned behind the bar, figuring maybe to break them up, but Trouble's right went to his pocket, and it wasn't a pager he'd been carrying, but a knife. He thumbed the blade out and it left a trail of silver in the light, like water streaming in a horizontal arc, and he casually swiped at the bartender's eyes. Jacob snapped his head back, both hands coming up for defense. Trouble kept the point on him over the countertop, his other hand still on Erika, and I arrived to hear him saying, "Don't be a hero." He had an accent, British and broad.

His back was to me, but Erika saw me coming, her mouth falling open with surprise and recognition as I brought my left forearm down on Trouble's wrist, pinning it to the bar. The surprise of the blow made him lose the blade, and it skidded over the edge, landing in a sink full of ice. It was a nice-looking knife, with a chiseled tanto point, the blade about three and a half inches long, and Jacob went for it immediately as Trouble started swearing. I felt him shift to move, and I snapped my right elbow back as he was bringing his free hand around for my head. I hit first, catching him in the face, and I came off his pinned arm, turning, to see him staggering back. He had released Erika, and had one hand to his nose.

She said my name.

"Erika," I said, still looking at Trouble. If he had reacted with any pain or surprise, I'd missed it, because now his hand was down and he was smiling at me. He looked at Erika for an instant, then back to me, and I took the opportunity to check his stance.

He knew what he was doing. He knew how to fight.

Blood flowed over his upper lip, and the smile turned bigger, and I could see dark pink around his teeth.

"You want me to show you out?" I asked him.

Trouble shook his head, and the smile blossomed into a grin.

"You took my knife," he said. The lighting made the blood from his nose look black. "That's a fucking precious knife, and you took it."

"You didn't have a knife. If you had a knife, you would have just committed a felony, and we'd have to call the cops."

"Fuck that," Jacob said. "I *am* calling the cops." I heard the rattle of plastic on metal as he reached for the phone.

Trouble shifted his weight, settling and coiling, wanting the fight, and I took a step to the side, putting myself between him and Erika, figuring that if I was about to get beaten, at least he'd walk away without her. His hands were up and ready, and his breathing was under control.

If he was a serious martial artist, I was deep in the shit. Despite my chosen profession, I don't like pain, and at seven-fifty an hour, I'm not getting paid enough to change that fact.

"You've no idea the world of hurt you've bought," Trouble said, showing me his teeth. His eyes moved from me to see beyond my shoulder, and then everything changed. His glee vanished with the grin, face turning into a battle mask, and he spat blood onto the floor.

I wondered how much this was going to hurt.

His hips began to torque, and I thought he was starting with a kick, prepped myself to block it.

But the leg didn't launch.

Instead he turned, breaking for the fire door, pushing through the people who had stopped to watch this different scene being played, knocking over the PVC woman with the leashes. She went backward, falling onto her slaves, crying out, and he kept going.

I went after him, trying to be more polite about my pursuit, but the fire door had already swung shut by the time I reached it. I slammed the release bar down and pushed, stepped out into the alley, checking left and then right, spotting him as he reached Tenth Avenue, then turned the corner.

By the time I could make the avenue, he'd be gone.

I thought about going after him anyway, then decided I'd gotten off easily and had better not push my luck. My breath was condensing in the mid-November air, and it was cold out, and getting colder. There was a wind blowing, too, floating the smells of alcohol, urine, and exhaust down the alley.

I heard the rubber seal at the base of the fire door scraping the ground, saw Erika stepping out to look past me to the avenue. The door swung shut slowly, and I heard the latch click.

"You broke his fucking nose," she declared.

"Probably," I said. "What'd you do?"

"Me? I didn't do anything."

"Something scared him off," I said. "What did he want?"

"He wanted to top me."

"With a knife?"

She shrugged, faked a shiver, and said, "I'm going back inside."

"The hell you are."

Erika stopped, turned her head and tossed her hair much as she had done to Trouble. "What?"

"You're fifteen, Erika. Isn't that right?"

"Twenty-one," she said immediately.

"You got some proof of that?"

"Atticus. You know who I am."

"Exactly."

She waited for more, and then realized that was my whole argument.

"Fuck you," she said, finally, then spun on one of her too-high heels, making to go back inside. I let her, because she couldn't get far. It was a fire door, after all, and there was no handle on the outside. Great for exiting the building in a hurry, not so good for a return trip.

It took her a second to come to the same conclusion. "I'll go through the front. No problem. I've done it before." She brushed past me, heading down the alley.

"I'll make sure you're carded."

"I've got ID."

"I'll tell them it's fake," I said.

That stopped her once more. Without turning, she said, "I fucking hate you."

"Nice to see you, too."

"Go to hell," Erika snarled. She turned and pointed a finger at me. "Where the fuck am I going to sleep tonight?"

"At home."

"You are so wrong." She threw her hands out as if to ward me off, then began shaking her head and muttering. The wind kicked up, gusted down the dark street, and I felt its teeth through my jacket. Erika had goose bumps on her skin, and the cheap lace of her top made her pale breasts stand out in contrast. I looked toward Tenth Avenue, feeling like a dirty old man.

She certainly wasn't dressing fifteen.

"Why the fuck are you doing this?" Erika demanded.

I took off my jacket and offered it to her.

She ignored it. "Where the hell do you get off telling me I can't go back in there? What's your fucking problem, huh?"

"You're underage, Erika," I said. "Will you put this on?"

"So fucking what?"

"So it's illegal, that's so fucking what. How'd you get in there?"

"None of your business."

"Will you please put this on?"

"Why?"

"Because I can see your nipples and they're erect and I embarrass easily," I said.

Erika checked her front, then grabbed a breast in each hand and looked at me. "That's the point, asshole," she said, squeezing, her thumbs and forefingers pinching flesh.

"Put on the goddamn jacket, Erika."

She grabbed my coat and put it on.

"Thank you," I said.

"You're a fucking asshole," she said.

I began heading toward Tenth Avenue, walking slowly, hoping she'd join me. After five steps, she did, falling in on my left.

We were almost to the corner when Erika asked, "How you been?" She asked it like I'd seen her yesterday and we'd maybe just caught a movie, then done some window-shopping at Macy's.

"I've been better. Why aren't you at home? Why aren't you in D.C.?"

Erika laughed. "The Colonel retired, lives in Garrison, now. I don't even live with him."

"So where do you live?"

"Wherever I find a bed, dipshit." She stopped, checked her tone, then continued, more patiently. "That's why I need to get back in there, Atticus. That's where I'm going to find my shelter for the night."

This time, I stopped. "You're tricking?"

"Sometimes, I guess. Sure."

"What the hell's happened? Why aren't you living at home?"

Erika took an impatient breath and looked off past my shoulder, shoving her hands into the pockets of my army jacket. The gesture revealed her age, the jacket much too big for her, the miniskirt almost entirely swallowed by its hem. The light on the street wasn't fantastic, but I could see her eyes clearly, and they looked

fine, her pupils equal. She didn't seem to be on anything. I waited.

Erika said, "They got a divorce, you know that,
right?"

"I heard a rumor."

She ran a knuckle over the bridge of her nose, wiping
imaginary club grime away. "Yeah, well, the rumor is
true. Maybe a year after you left, Mom took off. They've
been fighting since then, over money, over me, you
name it. It all went final about a year ago. I don't even
know where she is these days, and frankly I don't fucking care. So, I live with the Colonel, just him and
me . . . and he doesn't go out much anymore, you
know?" She was still watching something beyond me,
keeping her gaze distant. "He sort of sees me . . . he
sort of sees me as in-home entertainment. So I don't
like to be around the house that much."

In-home entertainment. I swallowed, felt a little sick
as all of the implications of that phrase hit home.

An NYPD sector car turned off the avenue and
headed down the street, passing us. Erika watched its
progress, and when it stopped in front of the warehouse, she said, "Guess somebody called the cops,
huh?"

"How long has it been going on, Erika?"

She shrugged, picking a spot on the pavement that
interested her. "He retired a little before it went final,
brought me home from school; I was going to boarding
school in Vermont." She rubbed her hands against her
upper arms, making friction for heat. "You going to
take me home now? I'm fucking freezing my tits off."

CHAPTER TWO

After my old apartment in the Village had been trashed in a fire, I'd spent a month searching for a new place to live, trying to reconcile my love of space with the real estate prices in Manhattan. The same friend who'd found me the bouncing job at The Strap had hooked me up with a rental agency, and the end result was that I now had a four-room apartment in Murray Hill all to myself. In exchange for this, I handled the building's security and did consulting for the realtors, pro bono. I couldn't complain. I had a home, which is more than a lot of people in this city can say.

More than Erika could say, it seemed.

I unlocked the door to my apartment, hit the lights, and let her inside. She took a few steps in, looking around.

"Cool," she said.

"Glad you like it."

I'd had the apartment for two months and her approval mattered simply because I still wasn't certain what I thought of the place. Everything I owned had been turned to ashes, and with the arrival of my insurance check, I'd begun the process of rebuilding the trappings of my life. My shopping so far had been haphazard. The kitchen and bedroom were pretty much furnished, now. Both the spare and living rooms still needed work.

I locked the door as Erika began walking through the space, exploring her way through the bedroom, then the kitchen, then the bathroom, the spare room, and finally the living room. She shook her head at the cheap couch I had backed against one wall, opposite the radiator. It had been left by the previous tenants, and I hadn't bothered to haul it outside and down the four flights of stairs to the street yet. Besides, it was a surprisingly comfortable couch.

"That is pathetic," she said.

"But comfy."

In another corner were some painter's supplies, three rolled canvases, a folded easel, two stained palettes, and a box of paints. I had shared the apartment in the Village with a friend, Rubin, and all of his belongings were ash now, too. He had kept a studio in Chelsea, though, and when I had cleared it out, Rubin's things had come home with me. The only other object worth attention in the room was an oil painting that hung on the wall opposite the window, almost cartoonish, done in two frames. The first depicted a well-kept hand holding a ridiculously complex semiautomatic pistol. It had been painted in the act of firing, complete with the ejecting shell. The pistol pointed to the second frame, showing a frontal view of a very surprised face. The bullet exited on the opposite side of the frame, a wake of gaudy blood and matter following. Most of my friends thought the painting was morbid, but I sort of liked it. The expression on the victim was one of frustration more than anything else, as if he was saying, well, this is *just* what I needed.

Sometimes, I knew that feeling exactly.

Erika stopped in the center of the empty room and shrugged my jacket off, tossed it down and sat on the couch, curling her feet beneath her. The skirt climbed a bit, but she didn't move to adjust the hem. She looked at the painting. "That is so cool."

"Hungry?"

"Sure."

I brought the jacket to the kitchen and hung it off the coat hook I'd put in the wall earlier that week, then began foraging in the refrigerator. I found a container of cold chicken chow mein and a soda, got a fork from the appropriate drawer, and carried them back to the living room.

"I don't have a whole lot of food," I told her. "Need to do some shopping."

She took them, saying, "Thanks," and began to eat. I went back for a paper towel so she could use it for a napkin. After she took it, I sat down on the floor by the radiator, facing her.

Erika wiped her mouth with the paper towel, then pointed at the painting with the fork and said, "Rubin do that one?"

"Yes," I said. It surprised me that she remembered him. She hadn't met him more than once, and that would have been four years back.

"How's he doing?"

"He's dead," I said.

She gave me a look like she thought I was joking, then dropped it when she saw my face. "When did he die?"

"About three months ago. Closer to four."

"How?"

"We were on a job, protecting a woman. Some guy put a bomb under a car, and when it went off, Rubin took most of the blast."

It wasn't something I wanted to talk about, and Erika seemed to understand, hunting the carton with the fork for a minute in silence, spearing pieces of chicken and chewing on them thoughtfully. "He was a nice guy," she said.

"Yeah, he was. I'm surprised you remember him."

She smiled into the carton. "He made an impression."

"We need to talk about you."

Erika shook her head, and her hair swung from side to side, coming dangerously close to meeting the chow mein.

"Erika, if your father's molesting you—"

"I don't want to get into this right now."

"We need to find a place for you to stay. I don't want you on the street, and I don't want you tricking for a place to sleep."

"I'll stay here." She looked at me and, before I could respond, asked, "You don't want me to stay here?"

"No, you can stay for as long as you need to, Erika—"

"Why that look, then, huh? You don't want me?"

"I'm not sure this is the best place for you to be," I said. "That's all I meant."

"This is as good a place as any, Atticus. Come on, it'll be like in Maryland. You and me, that big brother, little sister thing we had going. It'll be fun, just like before, except no Mom. But that's okay, right? We don't need her."

She was so earnest and she again seemed so young that her words made me smile, made me realize how glad I was to see her again. She saw it, and that led to one in return, generous and warm, much like I remembered her mother's.

"See? You like the idea. You and me. Think about how much fun we could have."

"There's this little thing called life," I told her. "As in, you have one. Minor things like school, and so on."

"We can work that out."

I shook my head. "This is serious shit, kiddo, you know that. All the fun you and I might have, it still won't make your problem go away. We're still going to have to deal with the Colonel."

"The Colonel doesn't matter," Erika said. "He's doing his own thing, he's the same as always, and you know what that's like. Anyway, what the fuck are you going to do? Break his nose like you did that guy tonight? Let me stay here, Atticus. It'll be fine." She peered into the empty carton, set it on the floor, and took a drink from the can of pop, looking around. "You look like you could use the company."

"Do I?"

"We'll have to get some furniture in the spare room of yours. It's fucking empty in there."

"There's a desk," I said.

"And no chair. No, we'll fix that one up, and it can be my room. Get a futon or a bed in there, a decent sofa out here. God, you don't even have a television, do you?"

"As a matter of fact, no, I don't."

"And we can move the stereo in your room out here so we can share it. Is it a good one?"

"It's a good one," I admitted.

"All right, so we're not totally fucked up, then. And we'll get a TV and a VCR."

"And some clothes for you."

"You don't like what I'm wearing? Oh, yeah, I forgot." She pinched her nipples once more.

I shook my head.

"What do you think? Pretty nice, huh? Just like Mom's." She stood and planted her feet in a broad stance, raising her hands over her head, and then cocking her hips. She did it as if stretching, showing off her muscles, her body. Beneath the lace, her breasts looked crushed. "Just like Mom," she said again. Her eyes were hazel, flecked with gold, and they watched me the whole time.

I reached for the empty carton and the paper towel, then got up.

She dropped the pose, asking, "Are you blushing? Is Atticus blushing?"

"Atticus is going to put this stuff in the trash," I said, heading back to the kitchen. "And you are going to get some sleep."

"You *are* blushing." She came down the hall after me. "Why?"

"Because I'm a prude. You want a glass of water or something before you go to bed?"

"You are so not a prude. That's not it." She hopped up on the counter while I dumped the garbage in the trash can under the sink. "Do you think I'm pretty?" She probed a tear in her fishnets with an index finger.

I rolled my eyes at her.

"No, I'm serious. Do you?"

"Yes, I think you're pretty, Erika."

"Do you want to fuck me?"

I put the can back and shut the door, straightening up to look at her. Sitting on the counter, she was about my height. The look in her eyes was stone serious.

"No," I said.

"Why not?"

"Aside from your age?"

"Sure, if that's an excuse."

"I don't think of you in that way."

"You could."

"No, I couldn't."

She considered, then slipped off the counter and stepped to the middle of the room, turning her back to me. She pressed her ankles together, as if she were standing to salute, and then knelt. Once on her knees, she crossed her wrists at her lower back, her palms facing me, tossed her hair over her shoulder, and then pressed her left cheek gently against the hardwood floor. Her leather collar looked hard in contrast to her hair and skin, and the D ring had turned on its mount, easily accessible. "I'm told I'm pretty good," Erika said.

"Not funny," I said.

"You could just take me like this." She pulled her knees in tighter, raising herself up another inch or so.

"Get up." It was a position of absolute submission, of one animal awaiting the entry of another, and I didn't like her in it at all. I especially didn't like her using it on me.

She licked her lips as if in a movie, looking at me over her shoulder and upturned rear. "Is that an order, Master?"

There was a knock at the door.

"I'm making you hard, aren't I, Master?"

"Erika, get up."

"Make me," she requested. Her leather skirt was secured with a button and zipper at the waist. She unfastened the button and started to pull the zipper as there was another knock. "Shall I answer that, Master?"

"No, Erika, now would you please—"

She turned her head to face down the hall and shouted, "We're busy!" She gave me a smile, finished tugging her zipper down.

I went to the door, unlocking it as noisily as possible. Maybe a fear of embarrassment would keep her skirt on. I doubted it.

"You're busy?" Bridgett Logan asked me when the door opened. She looked like she should have been in bed.

"That wasn't me," I said, getting out of the way. I could smell her shampoo as she went past. "I've got a houseguest."

"So I gathered."

Erika was where I'd left her, the skirt still on but open at the back. She had black panties on and they didn't cover enough. Faded welts marked her skin. "Shall I serve her, too, Master?" Erika asked.

Bridgett looked at me for an explanation.

"Bridgett Logan, this is Erika Wyatt," I said. "Erika Wyatt, Bridgett Logan."

"Charmed," Bridgett said.

"Do I have permission to speak, Master?" Erika asked.

"Does she?" Bridgett asked.

"You're not helping," I told her.

"He's just beginning to discipline me," Erika told Bridgett proudly.

"Enough," I said, and reached down, taking her by one arm. She got to her feet, keeping her eyes on the floor. The skirt stayed on, clinging to her hips.

"Will you beat me, Master?" she asked, and there was hope in her voice. "Punish me? Have I disobeyed?"

Bridgett grinned, went to the refrigerator, and pulled out a beer. "I'll wait in the living room," she said, then went down the hall. "Take your time."

I guided Erika to my bedroom, and pointed her to a corner while I turned down the bed.

"That your girlfriend?" Erika asked.

"My friend," I said. Compared to the living room, the bedroom was crowded, and Erika positioned herself between my bureau and the closet door while I pulled back the sheets and turned on the nightstand lamp. There were three pillows on the bed, and I took one and a blanket from the closet. I've worked hard to void most of my Army-conditioned habits, but I still make a very neat bed. The extra pillows are a luxury.

"You going to join me when she's gone?"

"I'm going to sleep on the pathetic couch. There are towels in the bathroom, and you can help yourself to anything in the kitchen. We'll go out to breakfast tomorrow, if you like, but we're going to have a long talk."

She sat on the bed and started unlacing her boots. "Are you mad at me?"

"We'll talk tomorrow." I folded my blanket and went to the door.

"Hey, Atticus?"

I sighed. "What?"

"I've missed you."

"I'll see you in the morning. I've missed you, too," I told Diana's daughter.

Bridgett had placed herself in the same spot that Erika had chosen earlier, sunken back on the couch with her long legs fully extended to the floor. I took a second to look at her before coming the rest of the way into the room, enjoying the hum her presence set off in my stomach. She caught me at it and gave me a grin.

"Isn't she a bit young for you?"

"It's a long story."

"Well, I've got a story for you, too, actually, that's why I'm here. Why do *you* think I'm here, Atticus?"

"I think you're here because Burton called you from The Strap and said that the bouncer you told him to hire bugged out after a fight tonight," I said.

Bridgett tapped the hoop that ran through her left nostril and said, "On the nosey. Apparently your departure preceded an absolute flood toward the exits."

I sat back on the floor, in my corner by the radiator, putting the pillow and blanket beside me.

"Am I correct in assuming that your altercation at the club had something to do with the provocatively dressed nymphet who was offering herself to you when I arrived?" Bridgett asked.

"Yes."

She ran a hand through her glossy black hair and gave me a serious looking-over, so I returned it, because there are many things worse than looking at Bridgett. Bridgett is twenty-eight, my age, roughly the same height, but leaner, not as bulky as I am. Her face is a beautiful oval, with a small mouth and full lips, a stubborn jaw, and the bluest eyes I've ever seen. Both her ears are multiply pierced, hoops that run from the lobes to the high cartilage on each side. The hoop she wears through her left nostril is the thinnest and smallest of the bunch, and it somehow makes her face all the prettier. She's got another one through her navel, and the few times I've seen it, the effect on her torso is much the same. Bridgett was wearing gray sweatpants and a Stanford sweatshirt under her biker jacket, and a pair of Reebok high-tops, and I knew that Burton's call had gotten her out of bed.

She looked lovely anyway.

"He told me to tell you not to show up for work tomorrow night," Bridgett said finally.

"I'm fired?"

"Like a cannon." She rapped her fingernails on the brown glass of the beer bottle. I liked her hands; her fingers were long and slim. "You want me to talk to him?"

"Don't bother."

"What are you going to do for work?"

"I'll find something," I said.

Bridgett made a noise that was almost a snort.

"What?" I asked.

"Another bouncing job?"

"Maybe, if that's what I find."

"You're distressing me," Bridgett said. "Why aren't you out trying to drum up some real work, out there protecting people?"

"Because I don't feel like it."

"You're a PSA, and yet you haven't taken a job since Rubin died. Isn't it time you climbed back on the horse that threw you?" She was looking at the painting supplies when she said it.

"I'm just not interested in protecting anyone right now."

Bridgett shifted her eyes, now studying the double panels of the painting on the wall. "If this is some way of punishing yourself because he died, it's stupid."

"If it was, yes, it would be. But it isn't."

"No?"

"No."

She shook her head, not quite believing me, but not willing to call me a liar. "You leave the club because of her? Erika?"

"Yeah, she was trying to get back inside."

"I thought you were okay with this," Bridgett said. "That you didn't have a problem with the scene."

"I don't have a problem with the scene. She's fifteen. I don't know how she got past the door, but she was insistent about going back in, and I couldn't let her do that."

"Then you should have put her in a cab home, and gone back to work."

"Ease up," I said. "She won't go home. I didn't bug out because I wanted to. I've got a loyalty to Erika, and she needed my help."

Bridgett turned her head to look back at my bedroom. "Did you say fifteen?"

"Uh-huh."

"Doesn't look it."

"I know."

She looked back at me. "So, who is she?"

"Her father was a colonel at the Pentagon. I protected him and his family. Erika says he's retired now. She also tells me that he's molesting her, and that she's run away from home."

Bridgett raised her eyebrows. "Is he?"

"I don't know. The Colonel was a true son of a bitch, and we didn't get along, but I'm certain he never touched her when I was assigned to him. If Doug Wyatt is molesting her, it started after he divorced her mother."

"Where's her mother?"

"God knows. Erika says she doesn't know and doesn't care."

Bridgett finished the beer, examined the art on the label. "I know some people in Social Services. Also a really good children's advocate if you need names."

"I'll handle it. Figure she'll stay here until I find out what's going on."

"Sounds like a plan. You're certain you don't want me to talk to Burton?"

"I'm certain. I think he's overreacting, but then again, someone pulled a knife in his place tonight, so he's got a reason to be angry."

"Then I'll head home, go back to sleep."

Bridgett handed me the bottle, and after I'd disposed of the empty, I took her to the door. She stepped out into the hall, then turned and wrapped her arms around me, kissing me. It caught me by surprise, but I recovered quickly, and kissed back. Bridgett broke off, slid a fingertip over my nose and mouth.

"I'll call you tomorrow, stud," she said. "Maybe we can have dinner later this week?"

"I'd like that."

"I bet you would." She grinned, and I watched as she went to the top of the stairs. She gave me one last smile, then ran down the steps, her sneakers squeaking on the turns.

I fixed all the locks on the door, debated about looking in on Erika, and then went back to the living room, turning off lights as I went. The street illumination was enough to see by, and I made my bed, turned on the radiator, and took off my shoes and pants. It was risky, perhaps, but I didn't think Erika would see boxers as a sign of dominance. I put my glasses under the couch so I wouldn't step on them in the morning and lay down on my back.

The radiator hissed and banged, and I waited for sleep, thinking about how much I'd like to have dinner with Bridgett. We'd been close to becoming very close when Rubin died, and after the fire, I had stayed at her apartment until she had helped me find this place. Since then, we'd been trying to regain the ground his death had lost us, trying to discover what we meant to one another and what we wanted to mean.

Then I was remembering the Army, when I had met Erika, when I knew her mother and her father. I had served with some good people, one of them Rubin, and inevitably he dominated my thoughts again, like he had every night since he died, and once again I found myself missing him, wondering if I'd ever get over getting him killed.

CHAPTER THREE

She had left a message, scribbled on a piece of paper from my desk and left on the pillow that still held the memory of where she'd rested her head.

DID YOU FUCK HER??? the note read.

And if that's not a great way to start a day, I don't know what is.

I read the note a few more times, searching for hidden meanings, then crumpled it and dropped it in the trash. I cleaned up my room, then changed into my sweats and headed out to the East River jogging path. I ran for four miles, went home, did my sit-ups and push-ups and all the little things that were supposed to clear my head, although none did. When I showered, I checked the towels, and noted that none of them were wet. Erika had skipped bathing, maybe to keep from waking me.

I dressed and went down to the street, walking the half block to my bodega on the corner of Third Avenue. The bodega was run by a Korean family, and the youngest son, perhaps seventeen, was working the register. He gave me a thumbs-up and a grin, saying, "Plain bagel and coffee black, right?"

"Right," I said, giving him my money.

"Bitching cold out there today," he said. "Winter's coming early."

I nodded. "Did you see a girl this morning—pretty, blond hair? She would have been wearing a leather skirt and boots?"

He gave me my change, thinking, then said, "Really pretty?"

"Yeah."

"No. I would have remembered that."

I thanked him, took my coffee and bagel, and returned to the apartment building, doing my walk-through as I ate my breakfast. It was a four-story building wedged between two larger ones, and the three pretty much made up all the structures running between Second and Third Avenues. I didn't see any of the tenants or the super, and I saw no signs that the building had been broken into during the night. I checked the garage carefully, paying special attention to Bridgett's car. She owns a beautiful dark green Porsche 911, her pride and joy, and she uses my allotted parking space to keep from paying for one of her own. The extra security doesn't hurt, either. I don't mind, as I've no intention of ever buying a car; I hate cars.

I finished my walk on the roof, finishing the bagel at the same time. An empty bottle of Mad Dog 20/20, raspberry flavored, lay near an air vent, but nothing else. During the late summer, when I first moved in, some homeless people had camped up on the roof, having climbed down from a neighboring building. The roof was tar, and retained the summer heat, and I suppose it had been a pleasant and safe enough place to spend the night. I'd kicked them off anyway, feeling rotten about policy.

Since then, nobody had camped on the roof.

I threw the bottle in the recycling bin on the ground

floor, then went back up the four flights of stairs to my apartment, finished my coffee, and threw the cup out. My answering machine and telephone sat on a corner of the kitchen counter. There were no messages, but I hadn't expected any.

The bondage scene has slang for those who dominate and those who serve, calls them tops and bottoms. Last night at the club, and more so when I brought her home, Erika had been performing like a bottom. The maneuver in the kitchen spun that, turned her submission into a particularly subtle form of topping. It had been impossible for me to react without, in some way, validating her behavior. Sort of like asking the Senator if he's stopped beating his wife.

Now Erika had gone, leaving spite on my pillow for me to find. I wasn't certain if I was still playing her game or not; she was no fool, and she knew I would look for her.

Metro-North runs trains from Grand Central up the Hudson, and I caught an express to Poughkeepsie at a little before ten, taking a seat on the left side of the carriage to watch the river as we worked upstate. The sky was overcast and the tint of the windows made everything outside look gloomier, hinting that winter was closer than any of us mortals suspected. The coach was empty except for two elderly black women, seated side by side, reading paperbacks. I didn't have anything to read, so I just kept staring out the window.

According to NYNEX information there were three Wyatts in the Garrison phone book, and although there wasn't a Douglas listed, there was a "D." The operator had been kind enough to give me the address, and I appreciated that, because if she hadn't I would have had to go through the New York State DMV, and I didn't have an in there. That would have required calling Bridgett for help, which in turn would have led to her asserting her right to accompany me on this trip, no debate allowed.

I needed to see the Colonel alone.

Garrison sits on the opposite side of the Hudson River from West Point, maybe four stops south of Poughkeepsie. West Point rises from the river, steely and grim, as if it has always been there and always will be. The academy looks like what it is: a military school dedicated to the art of war, where cadets are turned into leaders devoted to country and God. I've never actually been inside, only seen it from a distance, but each time I do I feel the same strange twinge of history and foreboding. The place frankly gives me the creeps.

The train left me on the platform to get my bearings while zipping up my coat. The cold was working on my hands, and I felt my fingers resisting me slightly when I moved them. The platform itself looked more appropriate to a spaghetti western than to the Hudson River valley, with a closed restaurant and an information shack, both made out of wood. There was only the barest of covering to shelter under in case of rain or snow, and it didn't look like it would do much good. A display case hung on one side of the shack. Sun-faded copies of the Metro-North schedule and a street map of Garrison were tacked up inside. I checked the map against the address I had, then decided I could use the walk. It didn't look far.

It took twenty minutes, walking along the shoulder of the two-lane road that paralleled the river, keeping my hands deep in my pockets. The Hudson was a muddy gray, choppy, and there were no boats out. I passed a few houses, each spaced generously apart from its nearest neighbor. Smoke trickled from their chimneys, and the scent of burning wood made me wish I was indoors or, at least, warmer. Inside was comfort. Outside was solitude.

The house was two stories with a gravel driveway leading to the garage. The place looked beaten into submission by weather and age. A new Chevy pickup truck, navy-blue, was parked in the driveway, dusty and water-spotted. There was a chimney here, too, but no smoke, and looking at the windows, it was hard to tell if there was anyone at home. No lights shone from inside.

I crunched my way up the drive, crossed over the dead grass on the corner of the lawn, and knocked on the front door. My hand was cold enough that the contact hurt, and I shoved it back into a pocket so it could recover, thinking that a smart man would buy himself a pair of gloves, what with winter coming and all.

Nothing happened. I listened, and heard no noise from inside, only traffic in the distance and some gulls crying out overhead, and under it all the Hudson slapping the shore. I quite possibly had the wrong house. I considered peeking through one of the windows, and instead knocked again.

From inside came the sound of steps working slowly down the hall. They stopped at the door and I heard the bolts turning, two locks, one after the other. The door opened inward, swung back, and I saw Colonel Wyatt standing there, one hand still on the knob as if using it for support.

His other hand was pointed at my forehead, and in it he held a gun.

CHAPTER FOUR

CHAPTER FOUR

I think he was almost as surprised as I, his thumb back on the hammer and his finger resting on the tail of the trigger. When he got over being shocked, he relaxed, drawing his finger to the side of the barrel, not committed to the firing any longer.

"Sergeant Kodiak." The sound of his voice was surprising, hoarser than I remembered, almost wheezy. He didn't bother to move the gun.

"Colonel." The barrel looked deep and clean, and it wavered only fractionally in front of my eyes. It looked like a Colt .45, the traditional officer's side arm, although a lot of them now carry Berettas. I had been in the service when the debate had started as to which weapon was better, arguments about stopping power and reliability, and so on. Personally, I preferred the Beretta. The Colonel, it seemed, was a traditionalist.

Funny what you think about when someone's got a gun pointed at your face.

"She's not here," Wyatt said. "We're divorced."

"I know." His face looked drawn and yet flaccid, like he had lost a lot of weight and had lost it quickly, his skin sagging with the change, unable to keep up. Shadows hung tight to each cheek, and a white crust stuck to the corners of his mouth. I could see the same color on his tongue when he spoke.

"I'm wondering why I shouldn't drive a hollow point through that NCO brain of yours," Wyatt said. "Sort of like God's given me an opportunity to get some payback, that's what I'm thinking."

"I saw Erika last night."

He licked his lips again. "Where?"

"You want to lower the gun?"

"Where'd you see her?"

"In the city."

The Colonel brought the weapon down, flicked the safety, leaving it cocked but locked. The act seemed to tire him immensely. On the ring finger of his right hand was his class band from West Point, and it slid to his knuckle when he lowered the gun.

"Lock it behind you," he said, and turned away.

I stepped in and shut the door, threw the locks, then followed him down the hall. The rooms were dim, and Wyatt moved slowly, leading me into the kitchen. He stopped at the stove and picked up the kettle. Steam drifted from the spout. He stuck the gun in his waistband, then made himself a cup of tea, carefully pouring the water into a mug. He had been taller in my memory, and I realized that, in fact, I had as much as three inches on him. Both his pants and sweater looked too large, as if mimicking the skin around his skull. There was a smell, too, a little saccharine and cloying, tinged with vomit and urine, and it permeated the whole house. It was the smell hospitals try to disguise with bleach and air fresheners.

The place was very clean, but cramped, filled with all the items Wyatt and Diana and Erika had collected while moving through the years from post to post. A sunken den had been built beyond where the kitchen opened into a breakfast nook, and from the different shades of wood marking the spaces, I assumed the den was a recent addition. A couch and two easy chairs marked the space, facing the large window that ran across the wall. Through it I could see the unkempt backyard, then the Hudson, then The Point. Around one of the chairs were grouped three space heaters, their electric coils glowing orange.

Wyatt put lemon into the tea, then honey, then broke into a fit of coughing that required him to hold on to the counter for support. The coughs were dry and harsh, and when they ended he had to wipe tears from his eyes. He turned, leaving the mug, and walked past me into the den, saying, "Get that for me." He took the pistol out of his pants and set it on the folding metal television tray beside his easy chair. A red and black flannel blanket was draped over one arm, and he spread it out, covering his legs with it after sitting. Even from where I was, I could feel the warmth from the space heaters.

I brought him his tea.

"No, put it on the tray, Sergeant."

The television tray had the New York Giants logo on it, and I set the tea next to his gun.

"You want a fucking tip?" he said. "Sit down."

I unzipped my jacket and took the other chair, being careful not to kick any of the heaters. I was already beginning to sweat.

Colonel Wyatt took a sip, then cradled the mug in his hands against his chest, drawing in the steam. "Ask me if I'm enjoying retirement," he said.

"Are you enjoying retirement, Colonel?"

"No, but thank you for asking. And you? How are you?"

"I'm fine."

"You've been out for how long, now?"

"Three years."

"I always knew you would bug out."

"I wasn't a lifer, Colonel. Never pretended to be."

"I fucking hate retirement," Wyatt told his tea.

"What's with the gun?" I asked.

He looked at the weapon. "Fucking kids keep coming by, ringing the bell and running off. Thought I'd teach them a lesson."

I took off my jacket, wiped some sweat from my forehead.

"So you saw Erika," he said.

"Last night."

"Did you fuck her, too? Is that why you're here, you've come to gloat?"

"No." It was a cheap shot, but not entirely unexpected.

"No, you're not here to gloat? No, you didn't fuck her? No, *what*, Sergeant?"

He barked it out as if I were still in uniform, and I had to bite back the urge to respond appropriately. It was difficult enough to not add "sir" to everything that came out of my mouth; three years free and the conditioning was still in place. Instead, I asked, "Do you know where she is?"

Wyatt looked into his tea again. "She's gone down to Manhattan to stay with some friends."

"When was the last time you saw her, Colonel?"

"Tuesday. She'll be back by the weekend, usually is. Why are you asking me this?"

"I was bouncing at a club last night. A place called The Strap. It's a bondage club—"

Wyatt laughed. "No shit? Well, it's rough all over, isn't it, Sergeant? My mighty security officer reduced to baby-sitting perverts while they party. I like that, I like that a lot."

"—that's where I found her," I finished.

He didn't find that quite as amusing. "You're full of shit."

"Why would I lie to you?"

"Because you always lied to me, Sergeant."

"She told me she'd run away from home, Colonel. I

watched a man pull a knife on her because she wouldn't play with him.''

His gaze was level, and he thought before saying it. "You are a goddamn liar."

I shook my head, looked out the window. If it didn't get warmer, it'd be snowing by nightfall.

"She goes to visit friends," the Colonel said. "She doesn't want to be around here, and I don't blame her."

"She's homeless," I said. "She's turning tricks in exchange for a place to sleep."

"Shut up, you shut up," he ordered, and it started him coughing again, strangling, rasping barks. The mug swung in his hands, hot tea splashing over the lip. I got up and took it from him, and Wyatt was coughing too hard to even resent my help. I set the mug down, picked up his gun and unloaded it, making it safe. I didn't think he would shoot me, but I didn't know how he would react to my next statement. I put the gun down, but didn't move from beside his seat.

The coughing ended, leaving him drained, his head back against the chair, his eyes staring at me. "I never liked you, Sergeant. Even before you slept with my wife, I never liked you. You're arrogant and you're too damn proud for your own good."

I nodded. It wasn't a unique observation. "Erika tells me that you're molesting her," I said.

His eyes had held steel when I knew him in D.C., when I worked for him at the Pentagon. His eyes seemed so much smaller now, but steel came back to them all the same, and he started up from the chair, screaming, "You son of a bitch. You son of a bitch, how dare you?"

"Are you?"

The blanket dropped to the floor, and he punched at me slow, already winded. I let him land it, and he connected with the left side of my cheek like a drunken mosquito. There was no muscle behind it, only rage, and when the punch didn't move me, he prepared to throw another one, bringing his right back, then stopping. It was too much effort for too little result; we both knew it. He dropped his arm and relaxed his fists, turned away from me, looking out the window.

"She wouldn't say that," he said, finally.

"She said it."

"And that's why you're here? Because you figure I could be that kind of monster? You think I could hurt my daughter like that?"

"I don't know what goes on in your head, Colonel. I never did." My shirt was sticking from the heat.

He sat again, and it took effort for him to reach the blanket, but I knew better than to help. When he had covered himself once more he sagged back into the faded chair.

"Sit down," he said. When I had, he pointed to the corners of his mouth. "You know what this shit is, Sergeant? It's called thrush, that's what it is, and it's a fucking yeast infection, it's what women get in their cunts, except I've got it in my goddamn mouth. Do you know why I've got it in my mouth, Sergeant? Can you field that one?"

"You have AIDS," I said.

"That's right, I have AIDS. I can't fight off a fucking yeast infection, I've got shit in my mouth, my body is turning to crap, I need a nurse to come in every fucking day just to clean me. I am dying, do you understand, and it's as inevitable as the river out there. I am a walking dead man." He ran out of breath and stopped, his chest heaving, then reached for his mug. When his breathing had slowed, he sipped some of the tea.

I looked at his pistol, wondered why he hadn't used it on himself.

"Erika is my life," Wyatt told me. "Erika matters more to me than anything I've ever had. I would never hurt her. So, you're accusing me of infecting my daughter, murdering her, that's what you're accusing me of. How do I respond to that?"

"I don't know," I answered.

"You don't know." He laughed, and I expected him

to start coughing again, but he didn't. Sleet started to pelt the glass. Neither of us moved. The sleet and the river, it reduced the world to just us, just two men in this room on the Hudson, with three space heaters and a whole lot of history.

Erika had lied about her father. She had substituted incest for AIDS, and it made sense. No one would question her decision to run away from abuse; running away from someone who was terminally ill, that was a different story. The problem was, the lie threw everything she had said into question. One lie leads to another, and now I didn't know what to believe.

"They made me retire, because soldiers don't get a faggot's disease," Wyatt said softly. "It was easy, I got to keep my goodies. I left and bought this place so I could look at where it started, to look at The Point, and I brought my baby home because she's all I have left. She's out in the middle of nowhere, her father is broken and dying, her mother is fuck knows where, so why the hell she stay here? Why the hell should she sit in a dark house on a cold river with her dying father? Would you?"

"I had to ask."

"You had to ask . . . and you hoped it was true."

"I didn't."

"No? You never liked me, either, Sergeant, I know that."

I didn't say anything.

"Now Diana's gone, and I'm dying of AIDS."

"The irony hasn't escaped me."

"No, it wouldn't have," he said. "All of the fucking around I did, I guess this is how it caught up to me."

"Do you know how you caught it?"

"No. Could have been any one of a hundred women." He knuckled his eyes. "Don't think I gave it to Diana, though, so you're probably clear. Have you seen her?"

"No."

"Not once since then?"

"I heard about the divorce through the grapevine," I told him. "That's all I knew about you two."

He rubbed at the corners of his mouth, swore at the flakes that came away on his fingertips. "I would have thought with me out of the way, Diana would have gone straight to you."

"I haven't seen her," I said.

He took his mug again, finished the tea. "She left, and a year later filed for divorce, started fighting for money and Erika and everything else I had. Three years of fighting, and she didn't even try to see us, just let her lawyer do all the talking."

"She didn't see Erika at all?"

"Once or twice."

"She wouldn't do that," I said.

"You knew her that well?"

"Well enough."

"Get out of my house," he ordered.

I got to my feet and waited for him to rise, and as he did, we both heard the front door open. The thrush at his mouth cracked with his sudden smile, and he hurried past me to the hall, kicking over one of the space heaters, calling, "Erika?"

I bent and fixed the heater, heard her voice, and then another's, and the sound of the front door closing. I came down the hall to see Wyatt facing another man and Erika standing in the entranceway. She looked haggard, and it seemed to me frightened, but otherwise healthy.

"I told you not to," Wyatt was saying. "Dammit, Robert, I told you—"

"Easy, Colonel," the other man said, and his accent was British, and I was thinking that it couldn't be coincidence when I got a look at his face, and began to worry.

Not Trouble, not the man who had pulled the knife, but instead I was looking at one of the two men I'd seen enter before the fight at The Strap had started, the older of the two. His skin was a beautiful, rich brown, and his tight crew cut was peppered with gray. It was absolutely the same man from the night before. Maybe six feet tall, and with muscle, wearing a dark red polo shirt under his anorak and his very blue jeans.

"We just gave her a ride home," the man continued telling the Colonel. "Isn't that right, luv?"

"Is that true?" Wyatt asked his daughter.

"Yeah, that's right." Erika wouldn't look at any of us, staring at the baseboard. She still wore the miniskirt, stockings, and boots, but had covered her top with a gray sweatshirt that I recognized as mine. I wondered if she had taken anything else from my home.

"Robert Moore," the man said to me, extending a hand and a smile. "You a friend of the Colonel's?"

I shook his hand, saying, "Atticus Kodiak. I'm an acquaintance."

Moore went for strength in his grip, but not for the crush, smiling like he'd known me forever. If he recognized me at all, he was covering it well, but the smile never made his eyes, and they were professional, assessing me. When he had seen enough he dropped my hand, and I spotted the lump of a holster at his hip under the anorak. Like Trouble, Moore also had the same black tongue hanging over his pants pocket, also was carrying a knife.

"They're a great family," Robert Moore told me.

"Yes, they are."

"You close to them?"

"I was."

"Army?"

"Yes."

Moore nodded, then turned back to the Colonel, whose voice was controlled, but fraying, when he said, "Damn you. I told you not to do this."

Moore's eyes flicked to me, then went back to the Colonel. "Are you certain we want to talk about this here, sir?" he asked softly.

Wyatt coughed once into his hands, then looked at his daughter, who continued to look at the floor. He took a deep breath, and even where I stood I heard the rattle in his chest, like wind running through a field of weeds.

"Walk Atticus out," Wyatt told Erika.

Her posture changed slightly, all at once, and I knew her father had just let her down. She spun, went straight to the door. "Come on," she muttered.

"Take care of yourself," Moore said to me.

"I can stick around," I told the Colonel.

"You'll miss your train."

"I can get another."

Wyatt brushed his fingers through his hair, wiped the oil on his shirt. "You don't want to be late," he said.

"It's been a pleasure," Moore said.

"I'll see you," I told the Colonel, then stepped past Moore and out the door.

Erika came out behind me, shutting the door with a slam and then going straight to the porch railing. She crossed her arms and pressed her hands into her armpits for warmth.

I zipped up my jacket, wishing she would look at me. The wind was slapping the sleet down in cold gusts, but we were safe from the spray where we stood under the overhang. Erika began to shift from one foot to the other, doing a lazy hop to keep her legs warm.

"So, who is he?" I asked her.

"Some guy," she said. "Why are you here?"

"Just some guy?"

"Yeah, just some guy the Colonel knows."

"Where'd you meet him?"

"It's like he said, okay? They picked me up. I told you, Dad knows him." Erika uncrossed her arms and cupped her hands together, blowing on them.

"What does that mean, they picked you up? Off the street? At my place?"

"At the train station, okay? Jesus fucking Christ, it doesn't matter."

"It does matter."

"Why are you here?"

"I was looking for you."

"Yeah?" she asked, clearly not believing me. "Why were you looking for me?"

"You were gone when I got up," I said.

"So?"

"I was worried."

"You wanted me to leave."

"I never said that."

"You wanted to be alone with what's-her-face," Erika said.

"Bridgett, and no, I didn't say that, either." I didn't sound exasperated at all.

She shrugged, kept looking at the empty road and blowing on her hands. "You didn't say it, but you wanted to. You're in love with her. She totally wants you, too. She was dripping for you. She's a slut."

A black Cherokee was parked in the driveway, beside the Chevy. Moore's car, I assumed, and inside I could see two men, both sitting in the backseat, watching us through the sleet. There was no way to make out their faces, but I had an idea who they were. Trouble and the other man from the club, the young one, most likely. The plates were New York, and a rental tag was stuck in the corner of the front window.

They hadn't picked her up at the train station, I realized. She was dry and there had been no shelter to speak of at the platform. With the sleet coming down, she should have been soaked through.

Another lie.

"Who are they?" I asked, looking at the Cherokee.

"Friends of his."

"All Brits?"

"Sure."

"One of them the guy who pulled the knife last night?"

She looked honestly surprised. "No."

Neither of the men inside the car had moved, or even

acknowledged my gaze. They were waiting, and they were waiting like professionals—no fidgets, no shifting around in their seats. They didn't even appear to be talking to one another.

"I think you're lying to me," I said to Erika. "You lied to me last night and you're lying to me now."

"Yeah?"

"You lied about your father."

"So fucking what?" she asked.

I exhaled, watched the steam cloud and then whip away with a gust of wind. "It's a serious thing to accuse your father of doing."

Erika shrugged again and gave up on trying to warm her hands with her breath, instead rubbing her palms together.

"Erika."

"Okay," she said. "He's not fucking me. There. Okay? What more do you want?"

"What do I want? Jesus, Erika, I want to know that you're all right, that you're not sleeping in the streets or in strange beds, that you're not in trouble. I want to know if Moore hurt you. I want you to tell me the truth, dammit. What I want is a little of your trust."

Her head came around to look at me, chin out and mouth tight, full of anger. She was laughing at first, but tears were welling in her eyes, and as she spoke, the tears started spilling down her cheeks, and the laughing turned to crying. "You fucker! You motherfucker! Trust you? You want—you want me to—where were you, huh? Where were you? You said we were friends! You said I was like your sister, that you wouldn't forget, but you left, you left and you don't care, don't pretend that you do. It was all her, and when you couldn't fuck her anymore, you didn't care, so don't pretend—" And then the sobs caught up to her, and she was biting her lip to stop them, pressing both her palms to her eyes as if that would dam the tears.

I watched her, feeling small and embarrassed and

then, mostly, like a scoundrel who had been caught breaking into someone's heart.

The sobs racked Erika and I reached to hold her, but she flailed at my arm angrily and backed away until she was against the railing, saying, "Don't touch me, you don't fucking touch me. Go away, just go away, get out of our house." She put her back to me again, crying hard.

In my pocket I found my pen and the receipt for my train ticket and wrote my phone number on the back of the slip. I walked over to where she stood crying, held the paper out past her shoulder. She saw it and grabbed the paper with one hand, wiping her nose with the other while reading it.

"Call me if you need anything," I told her.

She crumpled the ticket and flung it away. The wind snatched it and blew it into a corner of the porch.

"I didn't know you knew," I said. "I'm sorry, Erika."

Then I turned up my collar, and started off the stoop to the road, walking past the Cherokee and the two men who were watching me go, beginning the long walk back to the train station.

CHAPTER FIVE

After ten minutes I was soaked and frozen and angry, and almost blind, fighting to keep my balance on the rapidly forming skin of ice, and swearing at the driver of the last car who hadn't bothered to avoid a puddle. My glasses were almost entirely coated with sleet, and I swiped at them with my fingers, clearing the lenses, as I heard another car coming behind me. I ducked my head to my chest, brought my arm up as a shield. Sure enough, another blast of ice and water hit me.

I swore and looked up and saw it was Moore's Cherokee, and that it was pulling onto the shoulder twenty yards ahead.

Fuck, I thought, and stopped.

None of the doors opened. The exhaust from the car clung to the asphalt where it trickled from the muffler.

I started forward again, and when I was even with the car, the passenger door swung open, and I could see Robert Moore leaning across the seat at me, dry and warm.

"Get in, mate," he said. "You're going hypothermic."

I swiped at the ice in my hair, looking into the backseat where the two other men were seated. The one behind Moore's seat I recognized as the young man who had been with him at The Strap, and the young man looked at me with a smile, then turned in his seat to look back down the road the way they had come. I decided he was twenty-one at the most.

The other one was taller, older, perhaps thirty, with brown hair and disconcerting eyes that were fixed patiently on mine. It took a second for me to realize exactly what was throwing me off—his right eye was blue; his left was brown.

Both were dressed similarly to Moore, comfortably and casually, jeans and sweaters and coats, and all were very neat, very healthy, and I realized it was a carload of soldiers.

A carload of British soldiers.

"You're letting the hot air out," Moore told me. "Come on, get in. We don't bite."

The one with different colored eyes laughed. "Denny does," he said.

Denny was the young one. He turned and slugged the speaker in the arm lightly. "Fuck you, Terry." He sounded as upset as any soldier gets at allegations of homosexuality.

"Don't think you're his type, though," Terry told me.

"You getting in or not?" Moore asked.

What the hell, I thought. Whoever they were, if they wanted me in the car, there were enough of them to make certain they got their way. And maybe they'd tell me what was going on.

"I'd wear the seat belt," Moore said after I'd closed the door. "These fucking roads, doesn't matter how good a driver you are, you know?"

I snapped the belt across my lap. The defroster was on full, blasting hot air, and the ice was already melting into cold trickles down my face and neck. I took a moment to clean off my glasses, searching for something dry to use as a towel, and settling for an almost dry corner of my shirt.

"Where you headed?" Moore asked.

"Train."

He looked over at me, almost adding a second question, then checked his mirrors and pulled back onto the road.

"Thanks," I said.

"Ah, it's not a problem. Soldiers have to look out for one another. The Colonel tells me you were his body-guard, that right?"

"That's right."

He nodded. "Fucking hard work, that. Muck that up, the brass comes down on you like a ton. Ever happen to you?"

"No."

"God bless you for it," Moore said. "Mind if I smoke?"

"It's your rental."

"That it is." He pulled a pack of red Dunhills from his pocket, fed one into his mouth. The car slid a bit on an easy turn, but he held the wheel with one hand, lighting up with the other. Behind me I heard Terry move, and the flick of another lighter. The defroster made the cigarette smoke tango.

"We can take you farther," Moore said, exhaling two streams from his nostrils. "Down to the city."

"The train is fine."

"Your choice, mate."

I looked in the rearview mirror, watching the reflection of Denny in the backseat. His eyes met mine, crinkled into a grin. He looked very friendly, so I turned around in my seat and looked at both men, saying, "Hi, I'm Atticus."

Moore said, "Fuck, where are my manners?"

"I was going to ask, boss," Denny said.

"Atticus Kodiak, the young fellow is Trooper Edward

Denny, and the man behind you is Trooper Terrence Knowles. Say hello to Atticus, boys.''

Both Denny and Knowles said hello, and we all shook hands. They were wearing guns, too, and had knives clipped to their pockets. Both were wearing Rolexes, and I tried to remember if I had seen one on Moore's wrist.

"Can I see your knife?'' I asked Denny.

He hesitated, and then Moore said, "What's he going to do with it, boy? You can hand it over.''

Denny shot me a sheepish look and handed over the knife. I turned back to face the road and examined it, and it was exactly what I thought it was, and that didn't make me happy at all.

Knives are fetish objects for most professional soldiers, and the higher trained the person, the more knife choice matters. It's not simply that they're looking for a knife that can cut well; it's a multipurpose tool that needs to be as rugged as, in theory, the soldier himself. What's the point of carrying a knife that won't open after you've slogged through a swamp, or rusts if you take it under water, or loses its edge once you've cut a throat to the bone?

The knife Denny had handed me, and the knife that Trouble had pulled at The Strap, and I assumed the knives that both Moore and Knowles were carrying, were all the same model, one called the Emerson CQC-6. CQC stands for "close quarter combat." It's a folding knife that can be opened with one hand. The blade is aggressive, very sharp, and the tanto point makes it ideal for cutting, thrusting, or chopping. Good for chopping kindling, or killing, depending on your preference.

It's a knife that the special forces community covets, the way they covet Rolex watches; they always want the best equipment. Like the Rolex, it's a lodge pin of sorts—you have one, you're a member of the club. You have both, you've been paying your dues.

So I was sitting in a car with three special forces–

trained soldiers. The only question was which group, and I already didn't like the answer to that one.

I closed the knife and handed it back to Denny, saying, " 'Who dares wins.' "

Denny reverted to his sheepish look. Knowles examined his cuticles.

"Figured it out, huh?" Moore asked.

"You're all SAS?" I asked, and there was no way the question could sound casual, but I tried anyway.

"Badged members in good standing."

I went back to looking out the window.

It meant a couple of things. It meant that if they wanted me dead, I was dead. There were three of them in the Cherokee, and they could take me with their bare hands without breaking a sweat. It explained why Trouble had been so gleeful at the thought of tearing me apart the previous night; on a good day, I might have given him a run for his money, but it was the challenge that he was responding to, and the odds would have been in his favor.

It explained a lot. But it raised a thousand other questions.

Moore slowed the car carefully for another easy turn, and I felt the wheels slip before finding traction again.

"You're a sergeant, too?" Denny asked.

"I *was* a sergeant," I said.

"Well, you never really leave it behind, do you?" Moore said, rolling his cigarette from the right corner of his mouth to the left.

I didn't answer.

Moore pulled the Cherokee carefully into the lot across from the train platform, shutting off the engine but keeping the defroster blowing. Even with the hot air being pushed out, the windows kept a steady blanket of condensation. The world outside of the car seemed to recede behind the mask of fog.

"Sure you don't want a ride into the city?" Moore asked.

"I'm sure."

"Well, we'll wait, if you like. Don't want you freezing your prick off in this weather."

"It's bad," I agreed.

"Fuck, yeah. Like maneuvers in the North Sea. Ever been out that way?"

"I did some exercises in Alaska," I said. "That's the nastiest weather I ever had to deal with."

"Now, that's fucking beautiful country," Knowles said from behind me.

"They're going to rape it blind, though," Moore added. "Just like the North Sea. They've got these fucking oil derricks out there now, blowing shit into water and ruining the view."

"Let me ask you a question, Sergeant Moore," I said.

"You can ask me whatever the fuck you like, but you'll have to call me Robert. They're the ones who have to call me Sergeant." He gestured toward the backseat.

Knowles said, "Among other things."

Denny laughed.

"Robert," I asked, "why is an SAS brick after Erika Wyatt?"

He let the cigarette dangle from his bottom lip, then took it between his fingers and crushed it out in the ashtray. "What do you mean?"

"I mean you picked her up outside of my apartment this morning, didn't you? Which means you followed us home last night. Both you and Denny were at The Strap, and that other fellow, the one who wanted to fight. What stopped him? Did you warn him off when my back was to you?"

But for the defroster, the car became very quiet.

"I don't think anybody followed you last night," Moore said evenly.

"So, you're saying that meeting her at the train was just good luck?"

"Yeah, I guess that's what I'm saying, Atticus."

I looked around the interior of the car, at the backseat, at where both Denny and Knowles were focused on me. Their friendliness had gone. Knowles was staring at my throat, probably wondering what it would look like with his hand through it.

Three SAS-trained men versus one fifteen-year-old girl. It wouldn't have been much of a contest. My memory didn't reveal any marks on Erika when she had stood on the porch, but there didn't have to be any. If they had wanted to hurt her, they could have done it without leaving so much as a blemish on the outside.

I looked back at Moore. Pissing off members of Britain's Special Air Service is never intelligent no matter how well trained you might be. The SAS is to Great Britain what the SEAL teams and Detachment Delta and the greenies are to the USA, although many would say they're even better. In 1980, the Iranian Embassy in London was taken over by terrorists opposed to the Ayatollah Ruholla Khomeini. After five days of negotiations, the terrorists killed a hostage, and the SAS went in, black balaclavas and all. It took them eleven minutes to clear the Embassy; they killed five of the six terrorists, and freed twenty-two hostages. All on national television.

Apparently, of the five terrorists killed, all had thrown down their weapons before being shot.

In the great pyramid of soldiering, if the SAS isn't the top, they're only one step down. They're hyper-trained, hyper-committed, and exceptionally gifted at all the arts of war.

Which only meant that Moore and Company could have grabbed Erika, put her through an emotional and physical wringer, and then brought her home to Daddy. To what end they would do such a thing, I had no idea.

In fact, I had no idea what was going on at all. I looked out the window again. Wyatt, Erika, Moore. They're all lying to me, I thought.

What the fuck does it matter anyway?

"Never mind," I said, reaching for the door handle.

"Erika's all right, though, isn't she?" Moore asked. "Home safe and sound?"

I got out of the car. "Thanks for the ride."

Moore nodded, pulling another cigarette out of his pack. "We'll see you around, mate."

"You probably will."

I slammed the door and went onto the platform, pressing myself under the tiny awning that hung over the board where I'd read the map earlier. The sleet kept coming down, and the shelter was useless. Moore's Cherokee pulled away, splashing through new puddles, then turning on the road and heading out of sight.

Both Denny and Knowles watched me as they went.

CHAPTER SIX

The sleet had stopped by the time I returned to the city, and I came out of Grand Central Terminal to see patches of blue sky. It was still cold, but the weather had turned docile, and I decided to walk back to my apartment in Murray Hill, arriving in time to catch the mail carrier filling the tenants' boxes. I waited until he was done, then took my mail with me upstairs.

There were a lot of bills.

I changed out of my damp clothes and into some dry ones, putting Moore and Wyatt and, most of all, Erika out of my mind with a more pressing concern: money. The insurance check from the fire had been robust enough when it had arrived, but now seemed positively anemic. The job at The Strap hadn't paid well, but it had paid enough to keep me warm and dry.

After some thought, I went to the living room and sorted through Rubin's old canvases, finding the painting of Natalie Trent. In my opinion, it was the best piece he'd ever done, about as far from the cartoon style of

Gun and Head as possible. He'd captured Natalie the way an artist is supposed to capture beauty, with passion and precision and hope. Her face was tilted skyward, toward her raised hands, kind and strong, framed by red hair like the corona around the sun.

When Rubin had died, I'd been working with two other bodyguards, Dale Matsui and Natalie Trent. Dale was another Army buddy, like myself a graduate of the JFK SpecWar Center's School for Executive Protection. We'd met doing the course, and had both been posted to the Pentagon at the same time, although Dale had covered a one-star who worked in the NATO office, and I'd covered Wyatt, who'd been appointed the President's Advisor on Far East Terrorism.

Natalie I knew through her father, who ran Manhattan's biggest security firm, Sentinel Guards. Elliot Trent was ex–Secret Service, and had worked the Presidential Detail for Carter and, for a while, Reagan. He'd trained Natalie, and she was damn good, my second whenever I needed someone to check my work and watch my back. Natalie had been my friend, and it was she who had introduced me to Bridgett.

Rubin I had trained myself. He'd never done the course at JFK, he'd never protected a president. He had been at the Pentagon, too, but as a driver for a light colonel who worked across the hall from Wyatt.

Rubin and Natalie had been in love.

His painting of her wasn't something I could look at for too long. I felt like a spy.

There was a poster tube among the supplies from the studio, so I slid the canvas inside and sealed it up, then grabbed my jacket and headed outside and uptown, to Sentinel Guards.

I made it to the offices on Madison, guarding the poster tube from pedestrians and other standard Manhattan street hazards. The blue sky had disappeared quickly, and it was gray above once more, threatening rain or perhaps more sleet. It took me twenty minutes, and I arrived a little after four, walking into the marble lobby of the building and striding boldly past the reception desk. One of the attendants called after me to stop.

I raised the tube so he could see it, and without breaking stride said, "Artistic License, we're on Forty-seventh. Delivery for Natalie Trent." I continued to the elevator, got in, and punched the button for the eighth floor, wondering if the attendant had any training at all.

He hadn't, it seemed, because when I got out on eight, no one waited for me. I went down the hall to the double glass doors and stepped into the reception room. The receptionist was a tiny blonde in her forties wearing a starched white blouse and lipstick so red it looked like a magnesium flare had gone off in her mouth. She frowned when she saw me, I suppose at the way I was dressed. Sentinel's clients are the Fortune 500 brigade, decked in Armani suits and Ferragamos. I was wearing dark green corduroys and a black sweater and my army jacket. Under the sweater was a T-shirt, but I didn't think the receptionist could see that. My feet were clad in Reebok high-tops, but I didn't think she could see those, either, from where she was seated. What she could see was that I stood a little over six feet with 190 pounds behind it and had two small hoops hanging from my left earlobe.

One of these things is not like the other, I thought.

"Atticus Kodiak," I told her. "I'm here to see Natalie Trent."

"Is Ms. Trent expecting you?"

"No."

The receptionist picked up her pen and made a small mark on her desktop blotter. "Ms. Trent's extremely busy."

"I'm a friend of hers. Would you tell her I'm here?"

She made another mark beside the first, and then a third, and I realized the receptionist was drawing herself a tic-tac-toe board. "She's in with a client, Mr. . . . ?"

"Kodiak," I said.

"Mr. Kodiak, yes. Ms. Trent is in with a client right now and has asked not to be disturbed."

"I'll wait until—"

From down the hall we heard someone shout, "Kodiak? Is that you?" Both the receptionist and I turned to see Yossi Sella coming at us, straightening his tie and grinning broadly. He looked sleek and handsome, with hair and eyes so brown they appear black. Yossi's a born-and-bred Israeli whom Natalie's father wooed away from the Shin Bet's Executive Protection Squad, and though his English is flawless, he speaks with the rich Israeli accent that sounds like gravel being sifted through silk.

He had his hand out and I transferred the tube to my left, giving him my right. The shake was firm, dry, and quick. "Are you slumming?" Yossi asked.

"I'm here to see Natalie," I said.

"We should have had you come in the service entrance."

"Probably."

He turned to the receptionist. "Mr. Kodiak's with me, Tina, don't worry about him."

"Certainly," Tina said, and gave me a glare, then logged my arrival and went back to her game of tic-tac-toe.

Yossi clapped my shoulder, guided me down the hall. The carpet was gray, thick enough to eat footsteps, and I felt like I was in a doctor's office, which is the way I always feel when visiting Sentinel. Natalie used to say that the decor was to project professionalism; to me, it projects sterility.

The door to his offices was oak, with an engraved brass nameplate centered on it that read MAJ. YOSSI SELLA and beneath it EXECUTIVE THREAT ANALYSIS.

"Major?" I said.

Yossi shrugged, opening the door. "Trent thinks it makes me sound more authoritative."

"And he would know."

That earned another chuckle, and he led me through

the front room past his secretary. "Peter, hold my calls," he said.

Peter was typing at a computer and didn't turn his head. "Consider them held."

Yossi grinned at me. "I love saying that."

"It shows."

"Don't you have work to do?" Peter asked, head still bent, fingers flying over the keyboard. He was a demon typist.

Yossi chuckled some more and held the door to the inner office open for me. "I have a secretary," he said, clearly delighted.

"I noticed."

"Peter's the best," Yossi said, pointing me to a chair. I sat and rested the tube against my knee. He closed the door, then went to the coffee machine and poured us two mugs. His office was nice, with a leather couch and solid wooden desk. The chairs were leather, too, the sort one imagines in a gentlemen's club. He had a computer on the desk, a telephone, and several manila folders with neatly typed labels. Three photographs hung on the wall, one of Yossi standing alone in uniform, one of him with his unit. The last one was smallest of the three, and showed Yossi shaking hands with Yitzhak Rabin. If you wanted to get Yossi in a fury, all you needed to do was mention the security around Rabin when the Israeli Prime Minister was assassinated.

"You take anything in your coffee?" he asked.

"Black as my heart," I said.

" 'And death will fear you, because you have the heart of a lion,' " he said, doctoring his mug with sugar and cream. "That's an Arab proverb, you know? I like that one."

"It's a good one."

He handed me my mug. It was a glossy black with the gold Sentinel Guards logo printed on it, a Roman soldier standing behind a tall buckler, looking fierce and possessive. Yossi sat behind the desk, opened a drawer on the side, and leaned back, resting his feet on the new extension. He tasted his coffee, then asked, "What can we do for you?"

I said, "I was thinking I should talk to Natalie."

He shook his head. "That's not so good, my friend. Natalie doesn't want much to do with you, I think."

"Is she here?"

"She's in the office today, yes. Some movie hotshot wants protection, Natalie's doing the interview." Yossi pointed at the tube. "That's for her?"

I nodded.

"I'm sorry about your friend," he said. "The doctor you were protecting, have you heard from her?"

"She's working in Florida. That's all I know."

"Brave woman." He assessed me some more, then asked, "Aside from Natalie, why are you here?"

"How do you know I want something more?"

"I didn't." He grinned, his teeth lightly yellowed from years of cigarettes and coffee. "Out with it." When I didn't immediately speak, he asked, "You looking for work?"

"Either you're reading my mind or my face, and I like to think I'm not such an open book in either case," I said.

Yossi chuckled some more, washed down his mirth with a deep drink of his sweetened coffee. "There are only two reasons for you to be here, Atticus. The first is to see Natalie. The second is to find employment. You've already admitted to the first, and you're still here."

"I could just be acting polite," I said.

"Sure, you could."

"If I were looking for some pickup work . . . ?"

"Can't promise anything. Trent's scaling back for the fiscal quarter, and there's a rumor floating about layoffs. I do wish I could tell you more. I'll certainly keep you in mind."

I shrugged. "That's all I ask."

His intercom buzzed as Yossi was about to apologize

further, and Peter said, "Your four-thirty is here, Major."

"I should take this," Yossi told me.

"Certainly, Major." I rose and saluted and he laughed. He took the mug from me and I retrieved the poster tube, and then Yossi again put a hand on my shoulder, walking me out.

A beautiful African-American woman was waiting by Peter's desk, dressed in shredded blue jeans showing long johns beneath, a black halter top, and two flannel shirts. Tina hadn't given her any flack, though, because she was also wearing a long rope of pearls looped twice about her neck. The pearls made it plain that this woman could wear whatever she liked, although she was more than attractive enough to wear tinfoil and make it work.

"I'll call you if something comes up," Yossi told me, taking the new arrival's hand. The charm was already in full force by the time the door closed, and I found myself grinning as I walked back to reception. Yossi could be very smooth, indeed.

Of course, it had to happen.

I was halfway down the hall to Tina's desk when the door to Natalie's office opened, and she came out laughing at something the man with her had said. I recognized him, too. Not quite an actor; more a movie star in the making. And it's true what they say: He was a lot shorter in person.

"Monday," Natalie told him. "You'll be picked up at the airport by two guards, then come back here, and we'll start the detail then."

He faced her, gazing intently. "I can hardly wait."

I don't know if he thought the attempted seduction would work or not, but I understood why he felt the need to try. If Bridgett is at the top of The Most Beautiful Women I Know list, Natalie runs a close second. Her hair is fire-red—not carrot, almost burgundy. She was wearing her professional clothes, a black cashmere blazer and black skirt, low-heeled shoes. Natalie paid her way through college on the money she had made modeling during high school, and it would probably still be a feasible career for her if she wasn't so old. She's twenty-seven, after all.

At the reception desk, Tina said, "Ms. Trent, that man is waiting to see you." She pointed an accusing pen at me.

Natalie turned, and her professional smile crumbled to a fixed line as her eyes met mine. I thought she'd react in some other way, move or speak, but she gave me nothing more. She just stared the cold stare she'd discovered over Rubin's body.

"I can hardly wait," the actor said again. Perhaps he thought she'd missed her cue.

Natalie's eyes were as gray as the sky outside.

The actor looked over at me, back to her, then shrugged and said, "Whatever. See you Monday."

After he was out the glass doors, I said, "Hey, Natalie."

Nothing.

I hefted the poster tube, then walked the ten feet between us until I was close enough to hand it over. "I've been meaning to give this to you."

She looked at the cardboard as if I were offering her nothing but air, then resumed staring at me.

"It was at the studio," I said.

Natalie licked her lips, then said, "Tina?"

From the desk, Tina said, "Yes, Ms. Trent?"

"Mr. Kyle will be needing an appointment on Monday, about three in the afternoon," Natalie said. She kept looking at me. "And tell Mossen and Herrera I'll want them to pick him up. He's flying into JFK on United from LAX, arriving at thirteen twenty-one hours."

There was a pause that I interpreted as Tina writing Natalie's orders down, and then Tina said, "I'll make sure they know."

"Thank you," Natalie said.

"He would have wanted you to have it, Natalie," I said.

Nothing.

I offered her the tube again. "Please. It was for you."

Natalie's eyes changed, shifted slightly as if she was finally, after all this time, focusing on me. Her mouth moved a fraction, making me think she would acknowledge me, either a curse or a greeting. Instead, she turned and went back into her office. The door closed gently after her.

CHAPTER SEVEN

"Happy birthday," Bridgett told me when she came through the door.

"It's not my birthday."

She kissed me fiercely, then handed over one of the two paper shopping bags she had brought with her. "No, but I missed your last one, so I'm making up for lost time. And you remembered mine, so this is karmic balancing, that's what this is."

"You didn't know me on my last birthday."

"You're a gracious bastard," Bridgett said, blowing past me to the living room. "You're holding the salad fixings."

"And you're holding?"

"You'll find out."

I took the bag she had handed me into the kitchen, placing its contents on the counter. After folding the bag and putting it away, I pulled my new colander off its hook by the fridge and began washing lettuce. Bridgett returned, sniffing the air.

"You baked bread."

I nodded.

"I love fresh bread," Bridgett said. Her lipstick was the brown of dried blood. "If it's any good, I may swoon."

"Oh, it's good, I promise. I learned from the best."

She elbowed me gently away from the sink, saying, "I'll do that."

I relinquished the colander and set the table, then opened us both a beer. She was still shredding and chopping when I had finished, so I sat down and watched her, listening to Joe Jackson playing on the stereo in my room. Today, Bridgett was wearing black tights and a short black pleated skirt and a black turtleneck under a black sweater, and her hair was loose, ink-black that reached for her shoulder blades. Gemstones of water shone in her hair from the rain that was pouring outside. The temperature had risen in the two days since I'd seen the Colonel, but the weather was still miserable, and my radio was forecasting snow by the end of the week.

When the salad was done she sat down and I checked the lasagna in the oven, then the bread.

"How we doing?" Bridgett asked.

"Another fifteen minutes."

She took a pull of beer from her bottle, pushed the unused chair from under the side of the table with the toe of her boot, and then swung her legs up. I sat back down and she asked me about Erika and what had happened, and I told her about the visit to Garrison, about Moore and Company showing up, about how I'd seen him and Denny at The Strap. I glossed over the conversation with Wyatt, since that would have required an explanation of my relationship with Diana, and I didn't want to slide down that slippery slope yet.

"She called me a slut?" Bridgett asked, amazed.

"A dripping slut."

She laughed. "What the hell's her problem with me?"

"You're a strong female. You threaten her."

"That must be it. You have any idea who the fuck Moore is? Not somebody from your jarhead days?"

"Those are marines. I was a grunt, sometimes called a swinging dick. No, never met him before. All I know is that he's SAS."

"*The* SAS?"

"All three of them. Trouble, too, probably."

"Bastards." She practically spat it.

"Don't much care for the Special Air Service?" I asked.

She didn't like the levity. "Let me tell you about the illustrious Special Air Service. They work undercover in Northern Ireland. They're suspected of running death squads there. They're suspected of employing a shoot-to-kill policy when dealing with the Irish."

"Any of that proven?"

She snorted. "Of course not. You think the British government is going to cop to that?"

"Your politics are showing," I told her. "If they're fighting the IRA, they're fighting a terrorist organization. You can't really condone one over the other."

"Watch me," Bridgett said. "I'll tell you a story. In 1988 the SAS gunned down three IRA members in Gibraltar. They thought they were planting a bomb, see? So the SAS starts following these three, and then one of the IRA turns around, looks right at some trooper. The trooper panics, figures he's been made, pulls out his Browning, and starts pumping bullets. His partner does the same thing to the other one, a woman, shoots her in the back. They fire something like twelve shots into these two. The third guy, young fellow named Sean Savage, understandably turns around at all the noise, he gets shot fifteen times by the guy who's following him. He shoots Savage fifteen times, and four of those shots are into his head once he's on the ground.

"The kicker is that none of the three were armed, none of the three had a detonator, and there was no bomb found anywhere on Gibraltar. Lo and behold, though, when the public finds out and the outcry starts, the SAS finds a car loaded with Semtex days later.''

"You think the car was planted?"

"I think the SAS enjoys firing their guns a little too much, that's what I think. They should have arrested the three, not have gunned them down." Bridgett rubbed her eyes. "That's only one incident, mind you. There are others." She sighed heavily enough to make her chair creak.

"And how was your day, honey?" I asked.

She winced at the "honey." "I closed the infidelity case I've been working. The client is coming in tomorrow at eleven, and I'll have a set of glossies for her." Bridgett ran fingers through her hair, separating wet strands. She'd been working for Agra & Donnovan Investigations for as long as she'd been licensed, and had plans of one day turning the firm into Agra, Donnovan & Logan Investigations.

"Glad it's over?"

Bridgett shrugged. "Some man or woman starts screwing around on the side, they don't have the courage to tell their significant other that it's going on, that's abuse, in my book."

"Depends why they're having the affair, doesn't it? Could be that they're in love with this new person, or that this new person is providing something their partner is denying them."

"In which case, they should tell the abused partner it's going on and not skulk around like high school kids. I'm not saying it isn't understandable, Atticus. I absolutely understand desire. There are times when I don't give a flying fuck who's cheating on who, both partners are rotten, and all I think is good riddance."

"This case isn't one of those."

Bridgett shook her head. "The problem with this case is that this woman is devoted to her husband." She stopped to drink some more of her beer and look out the window at the rain. The runoff gutter on this side of the roof was broken, and water was pouring into the alley with a steady slap.

Bridgett continued, "Sometimes, a client will come in, man or woman, doesn't matter, and they'll hem and haw and then say, 'I think my wife/husband/lover is having an affair. I need to know.' And the pain is so obvious. They *already* know. They just want the proof. And I always say, 'If you're right, and I find the proof, you know that won't solve the problem.'

"And they look in my eyes, and they nod, and they tell me to do it anyway." She turned away from the rain, faced me again. "That's what I get to do tomorrow."

"I can't tell if you don't like the work or the result."

"I don't like the pain."

The lasagna was done and I pulled it from the oven and set it on the counter to settle, served the salad with some of my freshly baked bread. When she tried the bread, Bridgett swooned theatrically. We each had another Anchor Steam and ate, and then Bridgett said, "I saw Natalie last night. We went out for dinner."

"How's she doing?"

"She's better. She told me you came by the office, tried to give her one of Rubin's paintings."

"I'm surprised she told you. She didn't speak word one to me, and we were face-to-face. She acted like I wasn't there."

"She told me she didn't know what to say to you."

" 'Hello' would have been nice for starters. 'How you been?' Any of the small-talk standards would have worked, instead of a silence that said 'Fuck off and die.' "

Bridgett tore the heel of the loaf in half, took a small bite. "I doubt that's what she was thinking."

"I'm pretty sure it was. I'm pretty sure she hates my guts."

"Natalie doesn't hate you, Atticus."

I gnawed on the other half of the heel before saying,

"She belted me at the funeral. She ignored me yesterday. She wouldn't even take the goddamn painting."

"And you can forgive that, can't you?" Bridgett asked. "Grief and all."

"She hasn't spoken to me once."

"You confronted her at work, in front of a client, as I understand it. Not the best timing. The phone works two ways, you know. You should have called her first, asked if you two could get together."

I took my empty plate to the sink, rinsed it quickly, and put it in the dish drainer. When I went back for Bridgett's, she put her hand on mine. "You're painful for her to be around, Atticus. You were his best friend, you two were a package. Natalie doesn't know how to know you without Rubin."

I nodded and she moved her hand, and I washed off her dish, then served the lasagna.

"It'll pass in time," Bridgett said. "You can't be impatient about this."

"Rubin's dying really fucked up my world," I said, and it came out far more bitter than I had intended.

After we cleaned up the table, we made a pot of coffee, and once we'd filled our mugs, Bridgett led me by the hand into the living room. Three boxes lay on the floor in front of the couch, gift-wrapped, one large and two small, laid out in descending order, right to left. Bridgett kissed my cheek, then stepped over the boxes and sat on the couch.

"You didn't have to do this," I said.

"You took me to dinner and a movie and you gave me a case of mixed Life Savers on my birthday," Bridgett said. "Just pretend this is yours, okay?"

"But I didn't get you anything."

"It's not *my* birthday."

"That's sort of my point."

Bridgett shook her head, playing exasperation. "Just

open them. This one first." She indicated the largest box.

I picked it up. The same paper decorated each box, cute bear cubs wearing pointed party hats and holding balloons. I gave the box an experimental turn, didn't hear anything shifting inside. It weighed maybe four pounds.

"What is it?" I asked.

"It's called 'a present.' You see, in some cultures, when one person likes another person, and they want to do something nice for said individual, they spend money on them in the form of commercial items for the sheer pleasure of giving the gift. It's an ancient and revered capitalist tradition."

"Thank you, Margaret Mead," I said.

She bounced her knees up and down impatiently, holding her coffee mug in both hands. "Come on, you're killing me here."

I found the seam where the paper had been joined, began working the first bit of tape free.

Bridgett started knocking her boot heels together. "Just rip the goddamn paper, dammit."

It was a toy X-wing fighter.

Bridgett laughed with glee. "Isn't it *great*?" she demanded. "Isn't it fucking great? Open that one next."

It was a Luke Skywalker doll.

Bridgett giggled, grabbed her jacket from where she'd left it on the arm of the couch, and took out a package of four AA batteries. "I saw them and I just couldn't resist."

"Uh," I said, because no words were springing to mind.

Bridgett gave me a wonderful smile. "I got you, didn't I? You *like* this."

I nodded, felt myself grinning without meaning to. "Should I open the last one?"

"Depends if you want to play with the X-wing first or not," she said mysteriously. "You open that one, there's no going back."

I picked up the smallest box. It was very light, roughly the width of a cassette tape, but longer and taller. Bridgett watched me for a moment, then shifted her attention to the toys.

"Cocaine?" I asked.

"Gift-wrapped. You got me." Her smile was broad and dazzling.

I tore the paper off, and found myself holding a package of thirty-six condoms.

"They're a little big for Luke," I said, indicating my new doll.

"I didn't buy them for Luke."

I turned the package in my hand. We'd been dancing around this moment forever.

"What do you think?" Bridgett asked.

"I think that you were right."

"Yeah?"

"There's no going back."

I stood, and Bridgett set her mug on the floor, then rose, too.

"Happy birthday," she said as she put her arms around me.

We didn't do a lot more talking after that.

The weather the next morning was fucking awful, rattling rain and sleet, and I decided to skip running to stay in bed with Bridgett. The box of condoms sat on my nightstand, and there were plenty left, so we made love again, taking our time, and then Bridgett said that she had to go to work, and I said that I'd make coffee, and she said that would be good. She didn't bother to reach for my robe when she got out of bed, just walked on out of the room and headed down the hall. I watched her go, looking at the tattoo of a rose on her left calf as she went.

Yet another discovery from the previous night.

I made coffee and, when Bridgett got out of the bathroom, went to take my turn, showering slowly. The muscles in my thighs trembled while I let the water run off me, and I liked the feeling. I liked everything I was feeling. I was very happy that Bridgett had stayed the night.

When I got out, I dried off, put my robe back on, and headed back to the kitchen.

Wyatt was seated at the table, scowling.

Before I could open my mouth he said, "Ditch the bitch, Sergeant. We need to talk."

CHAPTER EIGHT

Bridgett stood in the corner by the coffeemaker, and she calmly offered me a mug. Once I'd taken it, she asked me, "Can I shoot this arrogant cocksucker?"

I shook my head.

"Get rid of her, Sergeant," Wyatt ordered.

"You let him in?" I asked Bridgett.

"If I had known, I'd have made him wait outside."

"Yeah, yeah, yeah," Wyatt said. "You two can fuck anytime. I need to talk to him now."

Bridgett leaked air out of her mouth in a soft hiss, decompressing. Her eyes were closer to gray than blue now, and her lips were pressed together hard. But the question was there, clear.

"I'll walk you to the door," I told her.

She nodded, finished the contents of her mug.

"Nice meeting you," Wyatt said.

"Eat me," Bridgett told him.

I unlocked the door and she gave me a very nice kiss before stepping into the hall, and when she broke it to pull away, I tugged her back in, holding her close and tight. I held on to her for a good thirty seconds, pushing my face into her hair, feeling my heart beating, enjoying our new intimacy. I was falling in love with her hair.

"Thank you for a wonderful birthday," I whispered.

She laughed low in her throat, then sighed, kissed me again. "If you need help disposing of his body, call me at the office."

"I'll talk to you tonight."

I locked the door again, went into my room, and dressed quickly. As I pulled on my clothes, I could hear the Colonel moving in the kitchen, opening and closing the cupboard doors. When I came back into the kitchen, he was looking in the refrigerator, and I ignored him, went to the coffeemaker, and poured myself another mug. After a second to think about it, I put on a kettle for tea, too. No need to stoop to his level, I thought.

He shut the refrigerator door firmly, looked at me, then sat back down at the table. "Nice-looking cunt," Colonel Wyatt said.

I pivoted and covered the space between us. "You talk about Bridgett like that again, I'll throw you out the window, Colonel."

"You're a fucking hypocrite, Sergeant. You know that?" He smiled, and the yeast scent rose off him sweet and sticky.

"I'm not married."

"Is she?"

I shook my head and went back to the stove. "I'm not cheating on anyone. Must be hard for you to swallow that, huh?"

He muttered something I didn't catch, unwrapping his scarf from around his neck. He was wearing a fat down winter coat, unzipped, and beneath it I could see a thick navy-blue sweater, wool. A black stocking cap stuck from the pocket on the jacket's left side.

"You want tea?" I asked him.

"If you're going to the trouble."

I pulled a box of tea bags from a cupboard, got another mug out. "The water will take a few minutes."

"Thank you."

We looked at each other. Wyatt broke the stare to examine the calendar of jazz greats I had hanging on the wall. This month's picture was of Thelonius Monk. He shook his head, then checked his watch.

"Can I have a glass of water?" His tone made it seem like I'd already said no.

I filled a glass and put it on the table, and Colonel Wyatt pulled several bottles of pills from his pockets, opening them one at a time, laying out his dosages. I counted eight bottles before I went back to the stove, watched as he began putting pills in his mouth, shooting water down after them.

"What are you taking?" I asked.

"Every fucking drug they make." He grimaced, took another pill. "AZT, DDI, Bactrim, you name it. Vitamins, too. Fuckload of vitamins." He finished his last pill and emptied the glass.

"Are they helping?"

"Do you think they're helping, Sergeant? There's no cure for the disease, right? All they do is fuck with my system, that's it."

He held the empty glass for me to take, and I brought it to the sink, and had a paranoid fit that I should maybe throw the glass out instead of just washing it. But I wasn't going to get AIDS from Colonel Wyatt, not unless we ended up exchanging fluids somehow. I made certain the water was very hot, though, in spite of myself.

The kettle started to rattle, and I turned off the heat, poured the Colonel a cup, then brought the mug to the table with a bottle of honey and a spoon. I didn't have any lemon.

"I've got to go out of town for a while," the Colonel said after he had dropped a dollop of honey in his mug. The thrush at his mouth fell like snowflakes onto the tabletop as he spoke. "Johns Hopkins has an HIV program, they've got a treatment I've been selected for, and I'm leaving tomorrow. Could be gone for a week or two, I don't know. I want you to watch Erika while I'm gone."

"No."

"I was thinking she could stay here, with you," he continued, ignoring me. "I'll bring her down in the morning, before I go to the airport, and you can keep an eye on her, take her out, whatever. Just so she has somebody with her."

"I said no, Colonel."

"I heard what you said. I want you to watch her for me."

"I'm not a baby-sitter."

He turned in the chair, sighing. "You want me to fucking blow you, Sergeant? I need you to watch her. I don't have anyone else."

"You and Moore seem chummy," I said. "Why not ask him or some of his boys?"

"It's not their bag."

"And it's mine?"

"It's closer to what you do."

"I protect people, Colonel. You know that."

"When you're not bouncing, you mean."

I let it slide, dumped the remaining coffee in my mug down the drain.

"She needs to be protected," Wyatt said.

"Yeah?" I thought about the SAS, about Trouble and his knife. "From whom?"

I heard his down jacket rustle with a shrug, and turned back to see he was still facing me.

"I think your friend Moore and his crew are a little more than casually interested in your daughter," I said. "I think they've been following her, and that maybe they're prepping to grab her. I think that's why he brought her back to your place the other day, just to show you how easily he could do it."

"That's what you think?"

"It's a theory."

"Moore wouldn't hurt Erika," Wyatt told me. "He's a professional, like you and me."

"How do you know him?"

"Same way I know you. The Army."

"And?"

"And what, Sergeant?"

"And what's going on? What's your relationship with him? Why was he at the house? You can answer any of those."

Wyatt started to respond, then bent with a rapid series of coughs. These sounded thicker, wetter, than they had in Garrison, and it occurred to me that it was stupid for him to be out on a day like today, to have come into the city in weather like this. His system couldn't defend against the environment, and traveling in the wet and the cold would get him nothing but a quick and lethal case of pneumonia.

I waited.

Wyatt finally got enough breath back to say, "Moore's a good man, and a good soldier. He wouldn't hurt Erika."

"Somebody tried to."

"Then let her stay here while I'm gone, Sergeant. You can protect her. I know you can do that. I'm asking for your help."

I just looked at him, trying to think of a way to refuse.

"You owe me this," he said. "Diana left because of you—"

"Diana left because you were sticking your cock into any and every thing that moved. Diana left because you were a fucking awful husband, and you treated her like shit. Sir."

His eyes narrowed at me. People didn't talk to him like that, I knew, and he was contemplating his response. Finally, he decided to go on as if I hadn't spoken, saying, "And Erika, she was devoted to you. You abandoned her. You never wrote. You told her you would. You didn't. You never called. You betrayed my trust, and you betrayed the trust of my daughter. Now I'm asking you for help, here. I'm asking you for this, and I've never asked you for anything before. Do this for me, Sergeant. Watch her. Let her stay here with you."

This wasn't right. He should have upped and walked out by now. He should have thrown my insults right back at me. But instead he just sat in his huge coat, looking diminished, and his expression did nothing but support his words.

"What's going on?" I asked.

"I told you, I've got to go down to Baltimore for treatment."

"If you don't tell me what the threat is, I can't protect Erika," I said.

He almost smiled. I'd turned the corner, was on his street, now. He considered, then said, "Just keep an eye out for a rogue brick."

"I could use more information."

"That's all I can give you," he said. "I'll be by tomorrow before nine with Erika. I'll leave a number where you can reach me. How much do you charge?"

I hesitated.

"They're the SAS," Colonel Wyatt said. "You'll need help, and help will cost."

"A couple hundred will do."

He knew I was going low. "I don't want any of your fucking charity, Sergeant. I'll pay what you're worth." He got up, wrapping his scarf around his neck, and the discussion was obviously over. I walked him to the door, and he went on out without saying anything else, without looking back. His steps were slow going down the stairs, and the echoes rang back in my apartment, even after I had closed and locked the door.

I spent fifteen minutes cleaning up the apartment, the kitchen and my bedroom in particular, and when I caught a whiff of Bridgett on the bedsheets, my stomach did a quick flip, and I felt stupidly giddy. Then I put on my jacket and went to do my walk-through of the building.

A rogue brick, the Colonel had said. Watch out for a rogue brick, meaning watch out for a group of SAS. Or, watch out for Moore and his crew.

There are three regiments of the SAS, the 21, 22, and 23, though only the 22 is active military; the other two are reserve units. The 22 SAS is referred to as, simply, The Regiment, and has somewhere between 550 and 750 troopers assigned to it. Troopers are subsequently broken down into smaller units, or troops, and those troops are divided into bricks, which are units of three to eight men, normally assigned to specific functions—counterterrorism, mountain operations, vehicle operations, training, or whatever.

Unlike the United States military, where if you join the Rangers or the Green Berets, say, you stay, most SAS troopers are "temporary." Soldiers volunteer from other units, go through a hellish selection process, and then, if they're accepted, are badged as members of the regiment. They serve something like three years, and then return to their parent regiment. That's most of them; others are permanently badged, soldiers who are accepted into the SAS, and there they remain.

Moore had said they were all permanently badged, referring literally to the insignia that the regiment wears, and that meant these guys were on top of their game. No lag-time to dull the lessons they'd learned. If Moore was leading a brick, he could have as many as seven more highly trained soldiers at his beck and call. So far, including Trouble, I'd met four of them.

And they were rogue, which meant that whatever they were doing, they were doing it without sanction from their government. Possibly as mercenaries, possibly for motives entirely of their own.

It was enough to make me regret agreeing to watch Erika.

The Colonel had been absolutely correct; not only would I need help, I'd need a lot of it.

I spent the rest of the morning in my apartment, cleaning and installing, putting cup hooks in the bottom of one of my cupboard shelves. I consider my apartment pretty secure, but if I was going to keep Erika in it, it also had to be defensible, and that meant that I had more shopping to do. About noon I went out to a hardware store and bought supplies, including a new front door, and paid for same-day delivery and installation. The person who took my money told me they could have it at my place by four, but I'd be paying time-and-a-half if they had to stay past six for the installation. I smiled sweetly.

Next I went shopping for a cellular phone, and ended up buying a no-frills model for only seventy dollars, plus an additional activation fee. The phone was probably hot, but that didn't much matter to me. I was going to use it only in emergencies.

My last stop before returning home was at a furniture store, and I bought a queen-sized futon and frame that would fold up into a not unattractive couch. When the cashier ran my credit card through the reader, I winced, fully expecting the purchase to be bounced back. It went through, though, so I guess I wasn't over my limit yet.

I returned home, and set about hardening my defenses. This was mundane stuff for the most part, just installing another set of sliding dead bolts on the front door and getting the still-mostly-empty spare room ready for Erika. The futon and frame arrived first, and I had just finished putting it together when my intercom buzzed, telling me my front door was at my front door. I helped the delivery men bring it up, then directed them to the office.

"You want it here?" the older of the two asked. He was in his late fifties and looked cheerful, if confused.

"Right there. Take the other one out, put that one in."

He looked at the interior door, then at the new one leaning against the wall, then at me. "This is a front door," he said. "You know that, right?"

I nodded and he smiled at me, the way someone smiles at a dog they're not certain is going to bite them. I thought about explaining that I was trying to create a hard room, a place I could retreat to with Erika if the apartment was breached, but figured such information would only confuse him more.

I left them to their work and went to the phone in the kitchen, called Dale Matsui at his home. It took seven rings, and he answered with a "Yo?"

"Dale? It's Atticus."

"Atticus!" He sounded overjoyed. "Jesus, I was going to call you today, see if you wanted to go bar-hopping tonight, try to corrupt the youth of America."

I laughed. Since Rubin's funeral, I'd pretty much avoided everyone but Bridgett. Somehow, Dale made my guilt at avoidance irrelevant. "How you doing?" I asked him.

"Still got all my fingers and toes," he said. "So, what do you think about tonight?"

"Actually, I wanted to see if you could come over here around seven or eight," I told him. "I've got a job, and I need help."

"How long?"

"Looks like two weeks, maybe less. Local. Starts tomorrow."

"Is it glamorous?"

"It's watching a fifteen-year-old girl. Erika Wyatt."

"Colonel Doug 'If-It-Moves, Fuck-It' Wyatt's daughter?"

"You remember her?" I asked.

"Of course," Dale said. "How could I not? You were sleeping with her mom, for God's sake."

My pause said it all.

"You think I didn't know?"

"Yeah," I said, finding my voice again. "I thought you didn't know."

Dale got a good chuckle out of that. "Rubin told me about Diana. And I was out at the house a couple of times, don't forget. You had that family vibe when you were out there. And you and Mrs. Wyatt, watching you two practically required insulin."

"We weren't that bad."

"Maybe not around the Colonel, but yes, you were. I'm surprised the kid didn't know."

"Ah, well, it turns out she did."

"Everyone in the E-ring knew Wyatt was a horn-dog. I personally thought you had drawn a raw deal, having to protect him. I mean, how do you keep the man secure when he's sleeping with a different woman every night?"

"You don't," I said. "When I tried, he ordered me to leave him alone. That's how I met Diana—the Colonel ordered me to secure his home because he didn't want me following him on weekends. I can't believe Rubin told you."

"Well, he was happy for you, if a bit jealous of the time you were spending with her. Said you were in love." He said "in love" like he was Barry White crooning into a microphone.

"That's five years old," I said.

"Of course it is. And now you've got Bridgett, and that's moving up in the world, at least in my book."

"What?"

"You and Bridgett," Dale said patiently, and I imagined his self-satisfied grin, the one he wears when he knows he's got a secret.

"How'd you hear about that?"

"Bridgett called Natalie this morning, Nat called me."

"What'd she have to say about it?"

"Nat? She was happy for you."

Somehow I didn't believe that. "I have no secrets, do I?"

"None," Dale said, pleased. "I think it's great, by the way. You and Bridgett balance each other well."

"You think so?"

"Shit, yes. You're practically made for each other."

"Like oil and water."

"I was thinking like Stan and Ollie," Dale said. "So, why does Erika Wyatt need protection?"

"Some rogue SAS types have designs on her," I said.

There was a brief pause, and then Dale gave me the dum-de-dum-dum sting from *Dragnet*.

"Yeah," I said.

"Who else are you getting?" Dale asked.

"I'm going to call Yossi next, and Bridgett."

"That's it?"

"That'll be four, including me."

"You should call Natalie," he said, as if scolding a child.

"I'll think about it. How's eight tonight?"

"I'll be there with bells on," Dale said.

"Bring your gear. We're going to use my place as the safe house."

He said he'd be sure to, and we chitchatted for a couple more minutes, with Dale telling me about the work he was doing on his place. The storm windows on his house were giving him grief, but his garden was prepared for the winter. Before I got off the phone, he said, "It's good that you're working again."

I said thanks and hung up, wondering that if it was so good for me to be working again, why didn't I feel more confident about going up against the SAS.

CHAPTER NINE

By a quarter past eight, Dale, Yossi, and Bridgett were gathered in my living room, worshiping around pizza boxes. Yossi and Bridgett had taken the couch, and I sat by the radiator. Dale sat beneath the window, playing with the X-wing between bites of his slice. He's a big guy of Japanese descent, with about two inches on me and another forty pounds, all muscle. If you saw him coming at you down a dark alley, you'd swear you were a dead man. But that's his mask; in truth, Dale's one of the most gentle people I know. He had taken it visibly harder than any of us when Rubin died, and perhaps that was why he had seemed to recover sooner and faster.

"Give us the brief," Yossi said, when everyone had finished their last slice of pizza.

I laid it out, giving all the details I could, and trying to explain the situation as I knew it. None of them liked the fact that I was vague on the threat.

"They're trying to kidnap the girl?" Yossi asked.

"That's what it looks like."

"But it could be a hit," Dale said.

"It could be, but I doubt it."

"We better hope to God not," Yossi said. "If there's one thing those SAS boys know how to do, they know how to kill. They won't hesitate to put bullets into us to get to their target."

"We'll defend her to the best of our ability," I said. "It's just like any other operation."

"Where are you keeping her?" Bridgett asked.

"Here."

"You certain that's wise? If they picked Erika up outside of here, Moore knows where you live."

"It's a hardened location," Yossi interjected. "They can know she's here, doesn't mean they'll be able to breach the defenses. Better to keep your principal in a place that you know than one that you don't."

Bridgett looked at him, perhaps amused, perhaps alarmed, then switched back to me, saying, "Do you really want a firefight in your apartment?"

"If they want to come in after her, they'll have to do a recon," I said. "And we can make this place look pretty hard to crack. There are four of us, remember."

Dale pressed the button on the X-wing, and the sound effect of lasers squealed twice, then stopped abruptly. "Natalie said no?"

"I didn't call her."

All three of them looked at me. Dale made a scolding noise, and Yossi just shook his head.

Bridgett said, "Well, you're going to have to call her, stud. I've got to go to Jersey tomorrow with one of the bosses, and I'm going to be out of the city all day."

"We need at least four guards at all times," Yossi said. "And one of them should be a woman, so she can stick with the kid in the bathroom, and so on."

He sounded a little patronizing to me, and I almost responded to it before reason intervened. They were still all looking at me, and I realized they were absolutely right, that I would have to make my peace with Natalie.

"I'll talk to her tonight."

Everyone smiled, and Bridgett leaned forward and patted my knee. "That's my boy."

"He learns quick," Dale said.

"I understand he's actually quite bright," Yossi added.

"College boy."

"That so?"

"Sure. Cambridge, Yale, Harvard, all of the fancy ones."

"You're embarrassing him," Bridgett said.

I showed them all a tight smile.

"What are the positions?" Dale asked me.

"If Natalie agrees, she'll work my second, and we'll alternate close cover on Erika. You'll handle driving and egress routes, and Yossi will be the perimeter man. Bridgett can float when she's available."

"How many cars will we have?" Yossi asked.

"One," I answered. "We'll use Dale's."

Yossi shook his head. "We should have two. One to follow."

"He's right," Dale agreed.

"It's too easy to ambush a car," I objected.

"All the more reason to have two."

"I hate cars."

"Too bad."

"He hates cars?" Yossi asked Dale.

Dale just nodded.

Yossi looked at me for an explanation.

"I just don't like cars," I said.

"We can use mine. It's a company car, good for light work."

"That'll be fine."

"I'll bring it when I come over tomorrow," Yossi said.

"That'll be fine," I repeated. It occurred to me that I should say something about their challenging the authority of the team leader, but knew that wasn't really what was going on. If we were in the field, it would be different, but as of now, the protective effort had not officially begun.

We spent another hour going over details, checking the safe room and the rest of the apartment, and by ten everyone but Bridgett had left, saying they would be by tomorrow between seven and nine in the morning. As I ushered them out, Bridgett was using the phone. I traded my last good-byes with Yossi and Dale, shut the door, and bumped into Bridgett who was standing behind me, holding my coat.

"Going out?" I asked.

She shook her head. "You are. I called Natalie, she's expecting you."

"If I'm not back by midnight, she's killed me."

"If you're not back by midnight, it went exceptionally well, and you're reminiscing."

"You'll be here?"

"I'll be here."

I took the subway up to Eighty-sixth Street and headed for her apartment on East End Avenue. The doorman was pushing seventy, with two rows of brass buttons on his jacket running from throat to his bulging waist. I could see my face reflected in each of the buttons as I identified myself and asked him to ring Natalie Trent's apartment.

The doorman went to the house phone, dialed, and said I was downstairs. There was an interminable wait of only five seconds before he hung up again and said, "You can go up."

I went through the lobby to the elevators, pressed the button. There was a small marble-topped table with a pink flower arrangement opposite the elevator door, and behind it hung a mirror. The reflection made it seem as if I were holding the vase of flowers.

The car arrived and I rode it up to seventeen. Her hall

was empty and quiet, and I walked to her door, knocked twice. She opened it almost immediately, then turned and left me standing there.

I stepped inside and shut the door.

Natalie's apartment was big, almost unreasonably spacious for someone her age living in Manhattan, and the door opened into a living room with a hallway running from the left that led to the bedrooms and bath. The living room had two large windows through which you could admire the city, and a sliding-glass door that led onto a patio with a high railing. I could see scattered lights from other buildings, and as I looked, it started to snow.

Natalie went to the stereo and switched off the music, loud rock sung by an angry woman. Then she went to look out the patio door, maybe at the view, maybe at the snow, or maybe just my mute reflection in the glass.

A Persian rug covered the wood floor. Between bookcases on one wall was a display cabinet, with small statues arranged inside, some of bronze, others of crystal. Her books ranged from college editions of the classics to trades on security, electronics, and firearms to modern novels and short-story collections. On the seat of one of her chairs was a copy of Gerald Posner's *Case Closed*. The bookmark peeking out of it had a red tassel. She looked to be about halfway through.

Inside the display case, beside a miniature replica Degas sculpture, was a framed photograph, and at first I thought I was looking at Natalie, but the clothes were nearly twenty years out-of-date. The closer I looked the more I could see differences in the features, and I realized this was the first time I had seen a picture of Natalie's mother. Rubin had told me that she had died while Elliot Trent was still in the Secret Service. Natalie had been eleven or twelve at the time.

Natalie hadn't moved, and over her shoulder I could see three wooden planter boxes, arranged against the railing. I could also see her reflection, watching me, and I watched back, and so she turned and fixed the stare on me, folding her arms across her chest. Her hair was down and loose, and she wore a long-sleeved white T-shirt and blue jeans. She had lost some weight since Rubin died.

"Thanks for letting me come up," I said.

Natalie brushed some of her red hair behind her right ear, then crossed her arms again. Just as I was thinking she'd be giving me the same silent treatment, she said, "Could I have stopped you?"

It wasn't much of a question.

"I appreciate it," I said.

"I probably shouldn't have let you in."

"Yeah, but you did, and I'm here now."

"Yes, you are," Natalie said. After a second more, she went to a cabinet beneath the display case, opened it, pulled out a decanter and a lowball glass. She poured herself something golden and put the stopper back in the decanter hard, and the edge of it rang on the crystal, a low note. The sound depressed me.

"What do you want?" she asked.

"I need your help."

"Out of cannon fodder, are you? Need another corpse to cover your mistakes?"

I couldn't find a response that wouldn't make things worse.

"Help doing what?" Natalie asked when I didn't say anything.

"I've signed on to protect a kid, fifteen years old. She's got a rogue SAS brick after her."

"You are full of shit."

"I'm not making this up."

"The SAS is after this kid?"

"No, just one brick, maybe eight guys. They're rogue."

"Why are they after her?"

"I don't know."

She looked downright disgusted. "Who hired you?"

"Her father."

"And he didn't tell you?"

"No."

"They want to snatch or whack?"

"I think snatch. But both are possible."

"Who have you got?"

"Yossi, Dale, and Bridgett," I said. "But Bridgett's got to go out of town tomorrow, so we'll be short one."

"You're short anyway," Natalie said. "You can't defend against a brick with only four people."

"I could with five."

"No, you couldn't."

"What do you want me to say, Natalie?" I asked. "I'm here because I need your help."

Natalie looked down into her glass, decided she didn't want to take a drink just yet. "What would you want me to do?"

"Work as my second, provide close cover for Erika. I want somebody with her at all times, and that'd be a hell of a lot easier if one of the guards was female."

"You don't have any right to *ask* for my help," Natalie said. "I don't want anything to do with you."

"I let this girl down once. I can't do it again, and I can't protect her without you."

"So the burden is on me? I don't help you, you're fucked?"

"Yes."

Natalie set her glass on the shelf, gently, took three steps to where I stood, and punched me in the mouth. It was a good punch, and my vision blurred for a couple of seconds. My lip began leaking blood immediately, and my hand came away with a smear on my palm. I wiped the blood off on the thigh of my jeans, focusing on her again. She stayed in front of me, ready to throw another.

"You are a son of a bitch," Natalie said, and her voice shook. "How dare you lay any guilt on me, come into my home and unload that shit on me."

I checked my lip again. It'd start swelling soon. "I deserved that," I told her. "But only that. Nothing more."

"You deserve a lot more. You deserve shrapnel tearing open your back and snapping your spine."

"Is this about the girl or about Rubin?"

"It's about you. It's about you being negligent and dangerous, about how you let members of your team get killed."

"I didn't let Rubin get killed." I was trying not to shout. "He was doing his job, and it was a job he had volunteered to do. Nobody forced him into the detail, nobody ordered him to the front of the formation."

"He was an *artist*, for God's sake!" Natalie cried. "He wasn't a PSA, he never should have been a PSA. He shouldn't have been on scene in the first place."

"He was exactly where he should have been, doing exactly what he needed to do. He saved the principal's life, Natalie."

"You are responsible!"

"Yes, I am. I don't deny that. And I hate it that he's dead, and I feel guilt every time I think about it. But that doesn't make me guilty."

"You got him killed."

"What is it, Natalie? You have to blame me to find a way past this? You can't blame the guy who made the bomb, the guy who held the detonator?"

"You were in charge," she spat.

"You were my second. If you saw holes, why didn't you say so? If you're so certain it was my fault, why the fuck didn't you tell me we had a problem? If he shouldn't have been leading formation, why didn't you do something about it?"

Natalie's mouth went tight, and I knew that one had hit home and hit hard, and I figured she was going to punch me again. Instead, she went back to the shelf and I thought she was going for her drink, but she didn't, just dipped her head to look at the floor. Then her hand came up, pushing her fallen hair back, and with it, her head upright. To my reflection in the glass, she said, "Because I didn't think of it."

"None of us did."

"But we should have. You and I, we should have."

"The PSA's job is to protect their principal. The nature of what we do for a living is that people like us *do* lead the formation, that we're in the right place at the wrong time."

"I should have been leading."

"You were on the principal, where you were supposed to be. If anyone was out of formation, it was me, and that was because a madman had a gun pointed at my head."

Somewhere in the room I could hear the motor running on a clock, and the sounds of traffic on the street far below. It wasn't much past eleven, and yet it felt far later, as if we were pushing toward morning with no rest and no sleep.

"Tomorrow's a Friday, you know? We used to spend Friday nights at your place."

"You two used to kick me out to get some privacy," I said.

"Yeah." In the reflection on the window, I could see her eyes close, her breath condensing on the glass. "Where and when?"

"We're keeping her at my place, starting tomorrow," I said. "It's only supposed to take two weeks, tops. Yossi and Dale will be coming over by nine."

She nodded.

"Thanks, Natalie."

"You can thank me after," she said. "If no one dies."

CHAPTER TEN

Natalie and Yossi arrived together around eight, just as Bridgett was preparing to leave. We all said good morning, and Natalie kept her tone level, rather than sincere. Yossi and I unloaded their gear in the living room while the two women talked in the doorway. I couldn't hear what they were saying, and Yossi caught me straining to listen.

"Cut it out," he said. "You're worse than a kid in school."

"And if they were talking about you, you wouldn't want to know what they were saying?" I asked.

"Kid in school," Yossi repeated, opening one of the bags and removing four radio sets.

Bridgett called my name and I went down the hall, moving out of Natalie's way as she brushed past.

"I won't be back in the city until at least eight to-night," Bridgett told me. "You want to get together then?"

"If you're up to it, that'd be great."

"Then I'll call when I get in."

We kissed good-bye and I shut the door, went back into the living room to find Natalie loading a shotgun. "Where does this go?" she asked.

"In the spare room," I said.

"Show me," she said, and I realized this was the first time she'd been in my new apartment. I led her to the office, and she looked the room over carefully, checking the window and the view out onto the street, before setting the weapon in the corner by the door. She closed the door, threw the bolts, and then turned the knob and gave it a good sharp tug. The door didn't budge. She checked the spyhole next, then stepped back.

I waited, wondering if this was how Rubin had felt when a critic reviewed his work.

"Looks good," Natalie said, finally.

"I had it installed yesterday."

She searched the room again with her pro gaze, then put her hands on her hips. "Where's the secondary phone?"

I pulled the cellular from where I had stowed it under the futon.

"They can block that," she objected.

"There wasn't enough time to have NYNEX install another line. This was the best I could do."

"The first thing they'll do is cut the phone lines," Natalie said. "Then they'll cut the power. Then they'll blow through the front door or one of the interior walls."

"I know."

In fact, that was the entire motive for having purchased the cellular in the first place. The room we stood in served two purposes as far as the protective effort was concerned. Primarily it would serve as Erika's space, where she could keep her things and sleep at night. Its secondary purpose was as our room of Last Stand; if Moore and his men broke in, this was where we would retreat with Erika, and pray we could hold them at bay. The phone was simply for calling the police, in the hope that they could arrive in time.

"Visibility to the street is good," Natalie said. "At least we'll be able to see the cavalry if they ever arrive."

"Passive/aggressive behavior doesn't suit you," I said.

She whipped her head around at me, and her ponytail lashed out like blood in the air. "You want me to second you or not?" Natalie asked.

"I want you to second me, absolutely, but if you're going to sound that pessimistic when the principal arrives, I'd recommend keeping your mouth shut. You make it sound like she's already dead and buried."

"I'm pointing out potential problems and weaknesses in your security."

"And I'm telling you that I'm aware of them."

We stood and glared at each other, and then I heard the intercom buzz out in the hall. "That's them," I said.

Without a word, she took a step back, letting me unlock the door. I hurried down the hall, pressed the talk button on the intercom panel, and asked, "Yes?"

"We're here," the Colonel said. Through the grille, his voice sounded like it had gone through a food processor.

"Come on up," I said, and buzzed them through.

They took their time on the stairs, and I waited with the door open for almost three minutes before Erika appeared, her father right behind. He was clearly winded from the climb, and she looked half-asleep, in jeans and my sweatshirt.

"Morning," I said.

Erika ignored my greeting, walking straight to the living room with her duffel bag and backpack. I heard Yossi greet her, then Natalie, and she ignored them, too.

"We had an argument on the way down," Wyatt confided in me, handing over a thick plain white envelope.

"I don't need this much." I tried to hand it back.

"You don't know what it fucking is, Sergeant." He

had cleaned himself up, shaved, and the thrush around his mouth was diminished, but it still appeared on his tongue; his breath was still sweet and cloying.

"This is too much."

"No, it's not." He went after Erika, and I looked at the envelope in my hand, then dropped it on the kitchen table and followed.

Colonel Wyatt had finished shaking hands with Natalie and Yossi, and was now facing his daughter, saying, "I'm going now, sweetheart. I'll see you in a week or two. You listen to Atticus and his friends, do what they say, all right?"

Erika folded her arms across her chest and looked at her father, then at me. "Sure."

"I'll be in touch."

"Yeah."

Wyatt took another step toward her, put his hands on her shoulders. He looked large again, the way I had remembered him, with his hands like two mammoth paws on Erika. He kissed the top of her head lightly and awkwardly.

She unfolded her arms and wrapped them around his middle, hugging tight. Her fingers barely met at the small of his back.

Wyatt pulled away. "I left the number where I'll be staying in the envelope. You take care of her, Sergeant."

"I will."

"Good."

I locked the door after him, went into the kitchen, and opened the envelope. Inside was a piece of paper with a phone number written on it, and I recognized the area code for Baltimore. The rest of the envelope was stuffed with money, twenty thousand dollars by my quick count.

Too much money.

Erika had followed me. "She's not here, is she?" she asked.

"Who?"

"What's-her-name."

"Bridgett?"

"Yeah, slut-girl."

"Don't call her that, Erika."

She mocked a sharp intake of breath. "Is Atticus in love with the slut-girl? Did I hurt Atticus's feelings?"

"You don't know Bridgett well enough to be calling her names," I said.

"I know her. I see women like her all the time. She's trying to act tougher than she is. She's attitude and nothing else, Atticus."

I didn't say anything about pots and kettles.

"What about the redhead?" she asked. "Total babe, huh?"

"Let's put your stuff in your room," I said, and led her back into the living room. Yossi was seated with his back to the wall, his gym bag open beside him and its contents arrayed carefully on the floor. He had six spare magazines, two boxes of ammunition, two semiautomatic pistols, five grenades—smoke and CS—and an assault rifle. Yossi's position on the team was as the perimeter man, which meant he had to be quick, and he had to have the firepower to cover a retreat, or lay down suppression, if it was necessary. For that purpose he had chosen the civilian model of the M-16, the assault rifle the U.S. military normally uses.

"Holy fuck," Erika said.

I nodded. It was an awful lot of hardware, and even I found it somewhat disconcerting. Yossi grinned up at us, enjoying his work.

"You going to war?" Erika asked him.

"Anybody tries to hurt you, angel, you bet your cute ass."

I gave him a warning look, and Yossi shrugged, went back to loading his magazines. Charming or no, I didn't want him flirting with Erika, even in jest.

She stifled a laugh. "So if I get shoved on the subway, you're going to open fire?"

"If you get shoved on the subway, I'll shove back,"

Yossi answered without looking up. "Anybody tries to really hurt you . . . he's dead."

"Really hurt me how?"

"Points a gun at you," Natalie said. "Threatens your life."

Erika looked us all over, ending her pan on me. "You'd kill someone who pointed a gun at me?"

"We all would. Our first duty is to protect you," I said.

Erika watched Yossi load for several seconds longer. "He's crazy," she finally declared.

"He's an Israeli," Natalie explained. "He won't take any chances with you."

Erika examined Natalie before asking, "What about you?"

"Me? I get to be with you whenever Atticus isn't."

"Yeah?"

Natalie nodded, and there was a hint of a smile.

"What happens if I don't like you?"

"Then I get to be with you whenever Atticus isn't." The hint turned into a confirmation. "But I think you'll like me."

"Oh, yeah?"

"Yeah."

"How do you know?"

"My dad's a pain in my ass, too."

"What about your mom?"

"I don't have one."

"Bullshit. Everyone has a mom."

"She died when I was twelve."

"You lie."

"Absolutely not."

Erika went quiet, then glanced over to where Yossi was still clicking rounds into place. She brought her eyes to mine, said, "Show me my room."

We took her bags into the office, and after they were set down, Erika turned and went to the door, shutting it. She put her back against it and leaned, looking me over, then said, "They're all right."

"There's one other guy coming, too. Dale. He was at the Pentagon around the same time I was working for your father."

Her brow was a couple more years from having serious creases, but she furrowed it all the same, then said, "He protected General Vogt, right? Big Asian guy?"

"That's him."

"He was okay. What happened to your mouth?"

I touched the swollen lump from where Natalie had hit me the night before. "I got rapped in the mouth."

"Yeah? Who did it?"

"Natalie," I said.

"Liar."

I shook my head.

Erika looked over at the shotgun. "That for me?"

"No, you're not to touch that. It's loaded, and we need to keep it in here, in case there's trouble. Are you going to have a problem with that?"

"I know how to treat guns. Dad taught me."

"I want your word that you won't touch it, Erika. Otherwise I'm going to have to move it into another room."

She elaborately crossed her heart. "Hope to die," Erika said.

"You want me to help you unpack?"

"I can do it. Besides, if you stay in here much longer, they'll think we're fucking or something."

"I doubt it."

"You totally don't want me, do you?"

"I totally don't," I agreed.

Her gaze went past me, to the window, and her expression had turned neutral. Then she made the briefest nod, grabbed her backpack, and headed for the futon. "It's not like I have to stay in this room, is it?"

"No, you can have the whole apartment. If you want to go out or anything, though, we'll have to talk about that."

"I told Dad that you didn't have a television. He said he gave you enough money to buy one."

"When Dale gets here, I'll send someone out for one."

"And a VCR."

"Sure."

Erika removed a laptop computer and its power cables from her backpack, then began hunting for an outlet. I pointed her to the one beneath the desk, and she got down on her hands and knees to plug in the cord. Unlike the last time she had crawled on my floor, Erika was quite matter-of-fact about it.

"You seen Moore or any of his buddies?" I asked her when she was back on the futon.

"Not since you were at the house."

"Are you going to tell me what happened?"

"Nothing happened. They just picked me up, that's all."

"At the train station."

"That's what I said, isn't it?"

"You were awful dry for a lady who'd stood on that platform in a storm," I said.

"They had the heat turned way up in their car."

I sat beside her on the futon, rubbed my eyes behind my glasses. Erika tapped on the keyboard a couple of times, brought up a game of solitaire, and began to play. Down the hall the intercom sounded, and Natalie went to answer it. It was probably Dale. If it wasn't, she'd get me. I listened and didn't hear her come back down the hall, but I did hear her opening the front door. Definitely Dale, then.

"Did they hurt you?" I asked Erika.

She answered immediately without looking up from her game. "Would it matter?"

I needed a second before I could say, "Of course it would matter. Yossi isn't the only one who doesn't want to see you hurt."

"Yeah? Who else?"

"Your father, for one," I said. "Me."

"You?"

"Me."

She twisted her mouth as if chewing on lemon rind. "Sure."

"I should have been there for you, and I wasn't, and I'm sorry, Erika. I was a bad friend. All I can say is that I made a mistake, and I'm trying to earn a second chance at your trust."

Erika clicked the top of the computer shut and turned on the futon so she could look directly at me. "No," she said.

"Please," I said.

She smiled at me, and it was an old person's smile, sad and deeply tired. "I've given second chances, and it gets me nothing. Nothing fucking at all. I trusted you, Atticus, and you didn't even care. Mom's pussy ran dry so you forgot about me, you just forgot. No letter. No call. All the things you said you'd do, you didn't do them. You had your chance, and you fucked it up."

She had leaned forward, kept her voice low and gentle with the weary smile still in place as she spoke. This was worse than her tears on the porch, in a way, because she was so calm. I was guilty as she'd charged, and we both knew it, and although what she suspected were my motives and the truth were different, they weren't so different that her words didn't strike and stick.

I had been twenty-four, she had been eleven, and she was right; I'd thought of her as my baby sister, but I'd forgotten her when Diana turned me away.

Erika put her hands in her hair, pulling it up and away until she held strands like sheets of gold. Then she shook her head, as if dismissing the whole speech. She leaned back against the futon, staring out the window to where the snow that had started last night was still falling.

She said, "You know what the sick fucking thing is? Everyone does it. Everyone. Mom did it, the same thing, and she's supposed to love me, but instead she just left and never said another word.

"And then there's Dad, the lovely fucking Colonel

who was fucking everyone but his own wife, who sent me away to school after school because he didn't know what the hell to do with me. And then they had the nerve to fight over me, to each claim that they were the better parent. And when it was all over, and the Colonel had won, he said he wanted me home, wanted me near him, and I find out it was only because he's going to croak. It's not that easy, Atticus. You can't just undo it."

"I know."

"Then don't expect me to be like you, okay? 'Cause I'm not. I can't be."

"Like me?"

"You trust everybody. You trust me. You shouldn't, but you do. You trust Dad, and you shouldn't, but you do. Fuck, you should be in the bondage scene, you trust so much."

"Am I that bad?"

"Your best friend could have totally betrayed you, you would never have known it," Erika said. "Because you wouldn't even consider the possibility that he *could* betray you. He could've been a total fucking lying bastard, you would have just kept on going in total blissful ignorance."

"Rubin and I didn't keep secrets," I told her. "And I'd appreciate it if you didn't talk like that about him."

"That's exactly what I mean."

"I'm serious, Erika. That's enough."

"Fine." She picked up her computer and put it on the desk, then went back into the living room, leaving me alone. I could hear Natalie introducing her to Dale, and Erika said that she remembered him, and they all started chatting happily, like the best of friends. Even Yossi joined in, and between him and Dale, they had Erika in stitches.

I sat on the futon for another five minutes, thinking about what Erika had said, then decided I was being antisocial, and joined them in the living room. For the next hour, Dale, Yossi, Natalie, and I went over the security procedures with Erika, making certain she understood what each of us did, and what each of us wanted to do if things went bad. She was attentive, and made no visible reaction when I mentioned the possibility of Moore and his men trying to grab her, remaining carefully indifferent to her fate; Erika perked up when we started talking about vehicle operations, excited at the prospect of going out.

"When?" she asked.

"Maybe tomorrow," I said. "Where would you like to go?"

"Anywhere," she said, and then focused on Yossi's gym bag. "Can we go to a range?"

Yossi told her, "I like you."

"Can we?"

Natalie brushed stray strands into place while thinking it over, then asked me, "City Hall Rifle and Gun?"

I nodded.

"It's one of the more secure places in the city."

She was right. All of the ranges in Manhattan were exceptionally secure, and the City Hall Rifle and Gun Club was one of the best.

"You know how to shoot?" I asked Erika.

"The Colonel taught me, I already told you. After Mom left he tried to make it a father/daughter thing. When I was home on breaks he'd take me to the range."

"You'll have to behave."

Erika looked hurt. "I'm not stupid. I know how to treat guns." She shut her eyes and used her fingers to tick off points. "Treat every gun as loaded unless you have personally checked that it ain't; don't ever point a gun at anything you're not willing to destroy, ever; keep your finger away from the trigger until you're ready to shoot; always control where the weapon is pointing at all times; and never shoot at water or another hard surface, so you prevent ricochets." She opened her eyes as Dale and Yossi both gave her a small round of applause.

"Very good," Dale said.

"Please?" Erika asked me. "Can we go shooting?"

"All right, we'll go tomorrow."

That made Erika happy, and I left her alone with Dale and Yossi, taking Natalie with me on a walk of the building. We each took a radio so we could stay in contact, and we each took our personal weapon, for me my HK and for Nat her Glock. I doubted we were in any danger in the building, at least right now, but from the moment Erika had arrived, we were all obligated to be in full paranoia mode.

We started in the garage and worked up, staying silent for the most part, as we didn't have much to say to each other. Bridgett had taken her Porsche for the day, so my parking spot was empty. Dale, Natalie, and Yossi had all driven, but none of them had used the garage, which was probably just as well. If the building was being watched, then the garage was being watched, and there was only one way in and out of the space. Moore and Company would have no problem spotting any new cars. As it was, they were probably logging all the comings and goings from the building, putting us under surveillance and constructing a timetable, evaluating when would be the best time to strike.

"Which vehicles are we using tomorrow?" Natalie asked as we were checking the boiler-room door. It was locked, as were the other rooms in the basement, but we were checking each anyway.

"Your car is wired for communications?"

"Both Yossi and I are wired, handheld and vox," she answered.

"Then we'll use those. He's got a sedan, right?"

"Yeah."

"That'll be the principal's car."

Both Natalie and Yossi used their cars for business, and they had been modified accordingly. Most people imagine a protective vehicle as some sort of James Bond car—bulletproof everything with tear gas dispensers hidden in the boot. In fact, some are, but those are rare vehicles, and aside from the obvious expense such modifications require, there are downsides. Such vehicles are very heavy on the road, often sluggish to handle, and like all things, the more moving parts they contain, the greater the chance that something will go wrong. For their work with Sentinel Guards, Natalie and Yossi really only needed lights and sirens, a hands-free radio setup, and, perhaps, tire inserts to keep the wheels going if the rubber went flat.

We'd use Yossi's car to move Erika, with Dale driving. Either Natalie or myself would ride along, and then Natalie's car would follow, driven by whoever wasn't on top of Erika. Yossi would literally ride shotgun in the follow vehicle.

Natalie and I worked our way up to the roof, and stood in the falling snow for a minute, scanning the surrounding rooftops and the street. It felt in the high twenties, chilly enough to make me want to head back inside. The pack on the roof was undisturbed, which I took as a good sign; no one was lurking around above my apartment.

"I'm not seeing any watchers," Natalie told me.

Nothing looked out of the ordinary, just pedestrians walking below in the snow. As I watched, an elderly man slipped on the near corner of Third Avenue, by my bodega. A passerby saw the fall begin and shot out an arm as she went past, catching the man by the elbow and keeping him from hitting the concrete. Once the man was upright, each of them continued in their chosen directions. It didn't look like they exchanged any words.

Other than that, the traffic flow looked entirely normal. Cars were parked on the opposite side of the street, some covered with snow, others cleared off. I looked over the adjoining and opposite roofs once more, didn't see anything that looked like a surveillance blind. Still no movement.

"Neither am I," I said.

"I don't like your roof," Natalie announced. "It's too

easy to access from either of the neighboring buildings."

"You want to put someone up here?"

"I want to get a motion alarm, like they sell for travelers to use in hotel rooms. We should hang it off the inside of the door to the stairs. That way, if someone comes in from above, we'll hear it."

"Good idea."

She put her hands in her pockets, turned in a slow circle, scanning, and finally settled on me. "What's the plan for the rest of the day?"

"Keep Erika happy and occupied. When Bridgett gets back we'll talk about giving someone time off tonight."

"Bridgett's willing to come over and stay with Erika?"

"I don't know. You have plans for tonight?"

"Don't you?" Natalie asked.

"What?"

"Don't you have plans for tonight?"

"I'm planning on staying here," I said, slowly. "With my principal."

"Good." She was keeping her eyes on mine. "You ready to go back down?"

"After you."

I followed her back to the apartment, wondering if she really thought I would bag my watch to sneak off with Bridgett.

At two that afternoon, I sent Dale out with five hundred of the Colonel's dollars to do some grocery shopping, pick up a motion alarm, and purchase a television and VCR. Before he left, he asked Erika, Yossi, and Natalie if they wanted anything specific, and that led to Erika deciding she wanted to cook us hot sesame chicken salad for dinner. She went through my kitchen quickly, and gave Dale a list of all the ingredients she needed, which turned out to be everything but spaghetti. He told her he'd do his best, and I walked him down to the front door. Dale went off, and I scanned, thinking I'd just make a quick check, then head back up.

Trooper Edward Denny was sitting in a rented blue Chevy coupe across the street, seven cars down from my left.

I keyed my radio. "We've got a watcher," I said.

"How many?" Natalie came back immediately.

I checked the length of the block carefully. "Just the one."

"What do you want to do?"

Denny was eating a sandwich, and he looked over my way. After a pause, he made an apologetic shrug, and took another bite out of his meal.

"I'm going to talk to him," I said.

Natalie took a second. *"You want support?"*

"Negative. You guys stay put. I'll be in touch."

I stowed my radio and made my way across the street, avoiding the traffic that came slaloming past. Denny had his window rolled down, and when he was sure I was coming, he got out of the car and went around to the sidewalk, to wait for me.

"Good afternoon, Sergeant Kodiak," he said. He had black cargo pants on, an anorak much like Moore's, and a pair of black leather gloves. He offered me his hand and I ignored it.

"What are you doing?"

"Just watching your place." There was an almost innocent edge in Denny's voice, as if he wanted approval. "Not in the way, am I?"

"Well, actually, Mr. Denny—"

"Oh, you can call me Ed. Everyone calls me Ed. Except Terry, but Terry likes to tease, you know how people like that are."

"Actually, Ed, I'd like it if you moved," I said.

He rubbed his chin, as if checking his last shaving job. By my guess, he was a couple years away from having to worry about stubble.

"Can't," Denny said. "Sorry."

"Why not?"

"Orders."

"Why are you out here?"

He looked up at my building, and his jaw tightened a fraction, and I realized that most of what he was giving me had to be an act. The SAS is brutal to its recruits. Nobody who was as aw-shucks as all this would have ever survived their basic course.

"She's in there, is she?" Denny asked.

I sighed, scanned the street once more. No sign of Moore or Knowles or Trouble. He seemed to be entirely alone. I looked back at him, and he had put the smile on again, eager and friendly. "Either you move, or I'll call the police, and have you moved."

"Don't see how you can do that," Denny said.

I moved around him to get a look in the car. On the backseat was a large duffel bag, another smaller bag beside it. Then I took a look at the license plate of the car.

"Why don't you just go back inside, Sergeant? Get back to what you were doing," Denny suggested.

"No," I said. "See, Ed, what I'm going to do is call in this vehicle as stolen. And then the police will come and they'll arrest you—"

"They'll arrest you, too, filing a false report."

"No, they won't. Because when they arrest you, they'll find your gun and your knife and whatever else you've got stashed in the backseat, there, and I'm betting none of your guns are licensed."

He frowned.

"Criminal possession of a firearm is a felony in Manhattan," I said. "You'll be held at Rikers Island until trial. And when I'm questioned, I'll tell the police about Sergeant Moore and Trooper Knowles and Trooper I-Don't-Know-His-Name who pulled a knife on me, and you'll pretty much be shut down for a while."

Denny scratched his chin again, then kicked some snow, before heading back to the driver's side of the car. I watched him climb behind the wheel, and he started the engine. Before he pulled out, he said, "Well, look, you have a nice day all the same, all right, Sergeant?"

I smiled and waved good-bye. When he was out of sight, I keyed my radio. "Nat?"

"Problem?"

"None at all."

Dale was gone for almost two hours, during which time Erika played *Doom* on her laptop, the explosions, growls, and gunshots echoing out of the spare room. Natalie played with her for a while, while Yossi and I kept watch; then Yossi played, and Natalie and I kept watch. Erika invited me to play, and I tried to watch the first-person perspective as it blurred past, but discovered that it was making me motion sick, so instead kept an eye on the window and the snowy street down below.

Denny did not return, and no replacement appeared. At least, none that I could see.

Then Dale buzzed us from the lobby to say that he had returned victorious in his hunt for both electronics and ingredients, and would we please open the fucking door and let him in, his arms were killing him. Natalie went down to the lobby while Yossi and I waited with Erika, and they came up together in under two minutes, carrying a box with the Sony label on it, and two grocery bags. Natalie immediately found the motion alarm in one of the bags and went to set it up on the door to the roof.

I stayed with Erika as she proceeded to make a mess out of my kitchen, cutting, crushing, and spicing with abandon. Dale had purchased an integrated television-VCR unit, and he set it up quickly, then returned to the kitchen to tell us he had taken the liberty of renting some movies, and would Erika like to watch them after dinner. She told him yes, and we brought bowls to everybody in the living room. Yossi waited until we had finished before having his dinner. After everyone had eaten, Erika went from person to person making certain we liked her cooking. We assured her that was, indeed, the case. Dale started a movie on the VCR while I went to wash up, and Natalie took her radio and went on another walk-through.

It was five of ten when Bridgett called. "Sorry I'm late. Just got back into the city."

"I was beginning to wonder," I said. "Did you bring the car back?"

"No, I parked it at a garage by the office."

"How'd it go?"

"The agency took the job, and then Donnovan put me on it as lead. Should only take one day, but that means I can't lend a hand tomorrow." I heard her put a candy into her mouth, click it against her teeth. "How's your end?"

"We're settled. They're watching a film on our new television, and Erika seems content. She's been good all day."

"You lie."

"No," I said. "We're going to go out tomorrow, and I think that's made it easier on her. She and Natalie are getting along fine."

"And you and Nat?"

"We're getting along."

"Fine?" Bridgett asked.

I ignored the bait. "You coming over?"

"I was sort of hoping you could come over here, leave the baby with the sitter, stuff like that."

"I can't do that," I said.

"I thought I was going to see you tonight."

"I thought I was going to see you, too, but I can't leave here."

She crunched the candy. "Are you going to give any of them time off?"

"I'll probably send Yossi home for the night."

"So he gets to go off shift, but you're working twenty-four/seven."

"He has to be fresh tomorrow. Vehicle work is hardest on the perimeter man."

"And if not Yossi, you'll send Dale, or Nat, right?"

"Probably."

"Listen, stud, you and I both know that you're going to have to take a break at some point, or else you'll burn out."

"True," I said. "But I can't take one yet."

"Why not?"

From the living room, I could hear the movie playing on the VCR, the voices from the soundtrack. Erika, Natalie, Dale, Yossi, they were all quiet, listening—either to the movie or to me, I didn't know which.

If I was protecting anyone else but Erika, I'd happily take a night off for myself. I'd just work myself into the rotation along with the other members of the squad, and when my turn came, I'd get out of the way. It's what I would allow Yossi and Dale and Natalie to do. It's not simply an issue of kindness, either, Bridgett was correct: it's necessary to give all the guards time to do something other than guarding, to let the brain and body rest from the concentration that's been required. No PSA in his right mind stays on a long rotation without a break, for no other reason than that it ultimately does more harm than good. It's one of the reasons true protection requires teamwork.

But Erika had already said she didn't trust me, had said it point-blank, and I knew she meant it. If I left her alone with Natalie and Dale and Yossi she would probably be safe, but I'd have run out on her again. And, if I went to Bridgett's, that would be adding insult to injury.

In a week, perhaps, I could take a night off. But maybe not, and certainly not now, not on the first day of the job.

"Is it because of the nymphet?" Bridgett asked.

"In part."

I heard her put another candy in her mouth.

"I don't know what to tell you," I said.

"Yeah, well, I can't think of anything, either. I want to see you, you can't see me, and it sounds like this is going to be status quo until her shithead father gets back. I'll lump it, but you should know that I'm feeling a tad shafted here."

"I don't like it, either."

"Yes, but you're not willing to do anything about it. Two nights ago we started something that I'd like to continue."

"I would, too."

She didn't say anything.

"I don't have a choice, Bridie," I said. "I have to do it this way."

Her sigh was loud in my ear. "You know where I'll be. Call me if you have the time."

She hung up before I could respond.

CHAPTER ELEVEN

We took both cars downtown a little before eleven the next morning, Dale driving Yossi's blue Saab with me in the backseat beside Erika. Natalie drove her car behind us, a black Lexus sport coupe, with Yossi seated at her right in the front, his gym bag at his feet. We all had our side arms, and each car had its radio set to voice-operation, so Dale and Natalie could communicate. In addition to my pistol, I'd brought another bag with my range equipment.

We'd checked the street carefully before bussing out, and there had been no signs of an SAS presence. Of course, that meant nothing, and it made me nervous. If I'd had it my way, we wouldn't be going out at all, but Erika had made it plain she was going to make us miserable if she didn't get out of my apartment.

After getting off the phone with Bridgett, I'd sent Yossi home and told Natalie and Dale that they'd be spending the night at my place. Erika had taken that as tacit permission for a slumber party of sorts, and it was almost one before she had gone to bed, Dale and I following suit. Natalie had awakened me a little after five to spell her, and she had taken my bed after I'd showered and dressed. Yossi returned at eight, by which time Dale had risen, and the two of them watched the apartment while I went to make my rounds. Nothing had really changed, although the snow on the roof was now considerably deeper.

I'd returned to find Natalie showering, and Dale watching Erika sleep. I made everyone breakfast, and we kept our silent vigil until Erika woke up just before ten. She went through the morning ritual quickly, refusing breakfast, saying, "I want to go shoot."

So shooting we would go.

The traffic was normal for late-morning Manhattan, and the snow had stopped during the night, so visibility was good. Erika sat quietly while I tried to see everything around us as we went, convinced that I was missing more than I caught. Every PSA I've ever known has their own pet paranoia, something that worries them above all else when they're working, that gives them their nightmares. For some, like Natalie, it's snipers, and the knowledge of how hard it is to stop a man with a rifle if he knows what he's doing. For others, like Yossi, it's bombs, and the fear of a single sprung mind driving a truck loaded with two hundred pounds of TNT straight into a bus queue. Dale just hates crowds.

Every guard has his or her own ghost.

Mine's cars, or, more precisely, being ambushed in a car. Even before Rubin died, I didn't like them. Now, I felt more justified than ever in avoiding vehicles whenever possible. The way I see it, from a car, you have almost no control over your variables, over your environment. With a sniper, you can stay in cover, work in a tight formation, deny the shooter their shot. With a bomber, you can harden your target, misdirect, even jam or flood frequencies, trying to prevent detonation or cause a premature explosion. In a crowd, you close ranks, run surveillance, use decoys.

But there are just too many ways to take out a car. You can use a mine, or a rocket launcher, or a road-block, or another car. You can caltrop the road and blow out the tires, or put a bullet through the engine. You can scoot up on a Vespa, and just open fire with a submachine gun. And there are too many other fucking people on the road, and each of them is in their own little universe, oblivious of yours, just trying to get from A to B with all due speed. You're in their way, and that makes them mad.

Yet, if you need to move your principal, you must use a car. You can't really transfer the protective effort to a bus, or cab. So it's a necessary evil, and that makes me like it even less.

My tension must have rubbed off on Erika, and she was silent for the drive, listening to the communication between Dale and Natalie.

"You've got a cab coming up on your right, he's weaving," Natalie said.

"Got him."

I looked and saw the car speed past, brake hard, and then cut two lanes left to get to an opening behind another cab. Three people were crammed together in the backseat, and two of them looked terrified. Probably tourists.

"We're coming up on a yellow," Dale said. "I'm stopping."

"Right with you."

I put a hand on Erika's shoulder, ready to send her to the floorboards. Our back was covered by Natalie and Yossi, but our flank was badly exposed, and either of the neighboring vehicles could hold a threat. The only escape route would be forward, into the cross traffic, and that would probably get us killed.

But nothing happened, and the light changed, and Dale said, "Going."

"You're clear."

"Relax," Dale told me, glancing in his mirrors. "We're fine. Almost there."

I ignored him and kept watching the Mazda pickup that had turned onto the street behind us. It was hanging a couple cars back behind Natalie, and kept swerving slightly from side to side. Either looking for an opening, or the driver was drunk.

"There's a red Mazda pickup back there," I said to Dale. "I don't like it."

"You catch that, Nat?" Dale asked.

"Confirmed. You want me to close up?"

"No, keep your distance."

I heard Yossi start laughing over the radio, say something to Natalie that I couldn't understand. She chuckled, said, *"The Mazda's all right. Yossi says the driver is trying to change the cassette in his deck."*

"Nothing to worry about," Dale said.

"Shut up and drive," I said.

"Driving."

Dale dropped us off in front of the club entrance on Chambers Street, Natalie pulling in right behind, and then getting out. Yossi slid over to take the wheel, and then pulled away after Dale. They would park the cars together, and then stay with the vehicles while we were gone. When we were ready to leave the club, we'd radio them, and they'd drive back to get us.

The City Hall Rifle and Gun Club is all but unmarked, innocuous, and secure. New York City is reasonably paranoid about firearms, and the security at the Club is very tight. Access is controlled by a glass security door that leads into a foyer, another door beyond it. The glass is heavy ballistic stuff, made to take some savage punishment. A security camera in the foyer is pointed outside.

"This is a range?" Erika complained as we stood looking in through the door. "Doesn't look like much."

"It's a range," I assured her, pressing the bell and hearing nothing. After five seconds there was a buzz, and I pushed the first door open, guiding Erika past me, followed by Natalie, to the second. We went through it together, then down a flight of steps, walking side by side, into the hallway. There were no decorations on any of the walls, and there was almost no noise. Natalie took the lead at the next door, and we started down a second flight of stairs, this one very steep and very narrow. Erika stayed between Natalie and me.

We emptied into the outer room of the basement, and from behind the counter, I heard a man say, "Kodiak, Trent. You brought a guest."

"Lonny, this is Erika," Natalie said.

Lonny was leaning on the glass case, casting a shadow over the weapons on display. Lonny is five feet three, built like an oil drum, and entirely bald, but gets the height he needs for the shadow effect by standing on a footstool that he keeps behind the counter. He always carries a cocked and locked .45 on his right hip while working; like Colonel Wyatt, Lonny's a traditionalist.

Over his shoulder on the wall were three video monitors, one showing the view of the outside we'd been checked through on, one showing the first-floor landing, and one showing a view of the final set of stairs. The security was designed to turn that final flight into a fatal funnel if anyone was stupid or crazy enough to try to rob the place.

"Erika," Lonny said, extending a hand. She took it, then winced at his grip. "Nice to make your acquaintance."

"Nice to meet you, too."

I turned to look through the Plexiglas window, and noted that there was nobody on any of the shooting points. The range was empty.

"Slow day," Lonny told us. "How many points you all want?"

Natalie looked at me for an answer, so I said, "We'll take one."

"You're twenty-one, aren't you, Erika?" Lonny asked her.

"Turned twenty-one at the end of September," she said easily.

"Sure," Lonny said to me.

"She's responsible," I told him, getting out my wallet. "We need two sets of eyes and ears, and twenty-five Q targets."

Lonny raised an eyebrow, then grunted, took my money, and disappeared behind the counter. Erika looked happily from Natalie to me, and when Lonny came back up to hand them their eye and ear protectors, she thanked him.

"Pick your point," he told me, handing over the targets.

I led the way through the two sets of double doors, and then out onto the range, walking down to the last shooting point, eight. Erika stood with her back to the glass while I unpacked my goggles and ear protectors, but she came forward to help me load my spare magazines. When I was finished, Natalie prepped her gear, then hit the button on the side of the cubby. She clipped the first target onto the hanger, then sent it back out to ten yards. When that was done, Natalie stepped back.

I unloaded my gun, checked it, and then slipped in a magazine of the cheap ammunition. I set the gun on the counter, barrel pointing out, and stepped back, pulling on my ear protectors.

"Go ahead," I told Erika.

She glanced at me, then stepped up to the point, taking the gun carefully.

"There's no hammer," I told her. "You cock it by squeezing the lever in the grip. Keep it held down and fire away."

She nodded, and I heard the click as she raised the gun. Her stance was good, and she took her time before taking her first shot. Then the report came, and the target wavered, and I could see over her shoulder the hole she had put through the shaded paper.

"Good."

She nodded again, not looking away, and methodically fired off the rest of the magazine, one shot at a time. She missed once out of the thirteen shots, on the last one, but that was because she rushed. When the gun was empty, she set it down and looked back at me.

"It's different," Erika said. "I like it. It's fun."

"I'm glad. You want to shoot again?"

Erika looked at Natalie. "Can I try yours?"

"Certainly." Natalie waited until I reloaded, then checked her weapon. She handed the gun over and moved in behind Erika to give her pointers on the Glock. Erika fired like she had before, hitting the target cleanly, and when she was empty, she handed the weapon back to Natalie.

"You guys can go."

"We'll wait until you're done," I said.

"Can I shoot yours again?" she asked Natalie.

Natalie said yes, and handed her a fresh magazine. I took the spent ones and set about reloading while Erika continued to shoot. She went through another six magazines and another target, taking about thirty minutes to do so, having fun with it, but never getting sloppy. Her muzzle control was good, and I could see where the Colonel had drilled his respect for firearms into his daughter. She was a responsible shooter.

With her last magazine empty, she brought the target back and the three of us looked it over together.

"Nice groups," I told her.

"You think so? That's Dad. Taught me how to shoot and how to sleep around."

Natalie raised an eyebrow.

"Your placement is better than mine," I told Erika.

"Really?"

"Oh, yeah."

"It is," Natalie confirmed.

Erika looked at the target in her hands, then at us. "You're lying."

Natalie shook her head.

"You guys shoot. Then we'll compare." She stepped

back to watch as I put up a clean target and held the button down until it hung roughly seven yards away. The targets could be automatically sent out to the fixed distances of ten, twenty-five, and fifty yards, but since those fixed ranges weren't that relevant to my or Natalie's work, I didn't drill at them, and neither did she. Most engagements take place at seven yards or closer, and that's what I needed to be prepared for if things ever went so bad on a job I had to start shooting.

But if things ever got that bad, the odds were I wouldn't even get my weapon out.

Natalie and I took turns, and between us we fired off almost two hundred rounds in about an hour, doing our drills. We started with double-taps, firing two shots as fast as possible, then switched to vertical tracking where we would work our way up the target. We'd start with the gun either in its holster or in the hands at what's called the low-ready position. Then we switched to one-hand drills, first the strong hand, then the weak one, firing off shots again and again, five or six from each presentation position in each drill, and changing the targets for the different exercises.

When the papers would come back, we'd hand them over to Erika, asking her to circle where we'd missed the shading with a pen from my bag. The Q targets we were using are the same ones the FBI utilizes for qualifying work, and the shaded portion on them represents the human central nervous system. Shots to different areas net different results. In vertical tracking, for instance, the goal is to draw a line up the body, starting at the abdomen, with the hope of taking out the CNS. If it works, the target goes down and doesn't get up again. End of problem. Shots to the pelvic girdle, on the other hand, are motor shots, used to cripple a target, to keep him or her from moving. Shots to the cardiovascular system are bleed-out shots. They'll put the target down, but it can take up to fifteen minutes, sometimes longer. They're not much use in our line of work.

Natalie and I finished up by sending a target out to

fifty yards and taking some aimed shots with our good ammunition. When I'd emptied the magazine, I started to pull the target back in, but Erika stopped me.

"Can I try?"

"Sure," I said. I reloaded the magazine, set the gun down, and stepped back.

She made certain her goggles were in place and took the weapon, sighted, and cracked off a shot, looking back my way almost immediately. "What happened?"

"Different ammunition. You were firing some cheap stuff before. Now you're firing the stuff we use at work. It's a faster bullet."

"Kicks more."

"Yeah."

She readjusted, then emptied the gun. I cleared the weapon, reloaded it with the good stuff, then put it back in my holster while Erika called the target back from downrange and took it off its hanger. The three of us spent another ten minutes cleaning up, picking up our spent brass and dropping it in the buckets that were left for collection purposes.

We returned the eyes and ears to Lonny, and Erika thanked him again.

"You had fun?" he asked her.

"It was great."

"You can bring her back anytime," he told us. "She's a good little shooter."

We waited for Dale in the lobby, with Erika going over the targets while Natalie and I kept watch.

"You were right," Erika told us. "I did group better. Why is that? You guys shoot more often than I do."

"You're taking more time and you're using the sights more," Natalie said. "When we shoot, we're just trying to hit the target as best we can. We don't worry about the placement."

"The emphasis is on speed," I said.

"Don't you worry about where you hit, though? I

mean, you shoot some bad guy, you want him to fall down."

"Exactly," Natalie said. "We want him to fall down as soon as possible. So if Atticus can get two shots in, even if one of them just takes out his shoulder, he's probably going to fall down and go boom."

"Fall down and go boom?"

"That's the professional term," Natalie said. "All of us pros use it." Then her radio went off.

"*Ready*," Dale said.

"I want to ride with Natalie," Erika told me.

"You're sure?" I asked. It would mean I'd have to drive the Lexus, because Yossi couldn't do it and keep his hands free.

"Nothing personal," Erika said. "You're just way too fucking nervous."

"He's always nervous," Natalie said. "It's what he does."

"It's what I get paid to do," I said.

"Well, you can relax," Erika told me.

The SAS hit us twelve minutes later.

CHAPTER TWELVE

It was textbook perfect, a final exam A plus, and the only thing that saved our ass was that they didn't know there was a follow car.

We'd just cleared the transition on Third Avenue at Twenty-fourth, where the street changes from running two ways to only going one-way, north. They made their move in the flurry of cars trying to fill the new gap, coming up on either side, Gray on the left, Black on the right.

I caught the movement in the mirrors, radioed to Dale, saying, "Left and right."

"Got it," he said.

The gray car shot past, its passenger window open, and in the mirror I saw revealed a van, dark blue, following it. Delivery van, I thought.

"Van."

"Confirmed."

"Too much fucking traffic," Yossi said.

The window was open, I thought.

The two cars were already passing Dale as the van came parallel to me. I started to glance over when the brake lights flashed on the gray car, just a flicker of a foot on a pedal, and Yossi and I realized what was going on at the same time, but it was already too late, and all we could do was hold on as I started to brake.

Gray and Black had cleared the front of the Saab, the van coming along its left side. Then, perfectly synchronized, the two cars went right and left, slamming together and skidding into a stop that blocked all four lanes. It looked like a fender bender, it looked like two people trying to merge into the same lane at the same time. Dale's curse cracked over the radio, and he stomped on his brakes as we were coming to a stop. The Lexus skidded only slightly, and I felt the shoulder harness lock and hold me steady. The Saab slid farther, started to turn, but Dale got control of the skid, and they came to a halt just shy of the new roadblock. The van had braked also, and now was perfectly parallel with the Saab.

"It's a fucking stopper," Yossi said to me, already going into his gym bag.

Dale came over the radio, *"We're all right, we're all right—"*

Natalie's voice, saying, *"Fuck, oh, fuck, it's an ambush, we've got two men with MP5s, they're zeroed."*

"Don't move," I said.

"We're blocked on the left," she said.

"Don't fucking move!"

I saw Natalie shoving Erika down in the backseat. Other than that, both she and Dale were motionless. Beside me, Yossi was slamming the bolt back on his rifle. Then he began pulling spare magazines from the bag, stuffing them into his pockets.

Gray had turned in its collision with Black, so that the open window was now fronted toward the Saab. The driver was still seated, but I could see his weapon raised and steady, pointed at Dale. Gray was a white man, with curly black hair, but I couldn't make out his face.

From Black had emerged another man, also white, with brown hair tied in a ponytail, and he was edging along the side of his car to flank the Saab, his weapon leveled at Natalie.

Both men held submachine guns. Both men could hose the car with enough bullets to kill all three of its occupants. If either Dale or Natalie moved, tried to raise a weapon, it would be all over.

The side door of the van slid open, and over the radio, I heard Erika ask what was going on. Natalie silenced her.

Trouble came out of the van, sliding a gas mask over his face. He held a large canister in one hand with a hose that ran from the spout coiled in the other. Slung across his back was another MP5, and he had a pistol in the holster at his waist. Before the black rubber and plastic hid his expression, I saw the tic of his smile.

Over his shoulder, barely visible from my angle, was a fourth man, crouched, holding an automatic rifle steady on the Saab. The rifle looked like the same model Yossi had locked and loaded.

It was quiet, and I thought that Lexus made a very nice engine, that I could barely hear it, that I wasn't even certain we hadn't stalled out.

Ten seconds had passed, at the most. Behind us, in the stopped traffic, a couple of horns began sounding.

Whatever was in the canister, Trouble was going to pipe it into the Saab. Maybe tear gas, maybe pepper, it didn't matter. He'd just punch the needle through the seal around one of the windows, fill the car, and then, with Natalie and Dale out of the way, grab Erika and go.

"They're going to gas us out," Natalie said. *"They're going to gas us."* She sounded very calm, now, and I knew she was afraid.

"*Orders?*" Dale asked.

If they moved, they were dead.

Yossi shifted beside me.

"You have smoke?" I asked him, unfastening my seat belt. It would save me a second or two later, although I already knew I'd be paying for it.

Yossi nodded, and out of my peripheral vision, I saw his left hand open as he showed me the grenade.

"You know what to do?" My switchblade was in my coat pocket, and I got the knife out, held it tight in my hand.

"It's the only thing to do," he said.

Trouble was running one hand along the seam of the rear driver's side window, looking for a good spot.

"*Orders?*" Dale repeated.

Gray was steady and still. Black was edging closer to the Saab, his weapon canted to shoot down through the tinted windows.

Yossi had pulled the pin on the grenade. "See you on the other side."

Trouble was raising the needle to punch the seal.

We are going to die, I thought, moving the gearshift into first. The stick felt awkward under my palm, pressed against my knife.

"*Jesus, Atticus, what are our orders?*" Natalie asked.

"Now," I told Yossi, and he went, out the door, his rifle in one hand, throwing the grenade forward in the other, and I stomped on the gas, came off the clutch. "Brace for impact," I told the radio.

It took perhaps four seconds to cover the distance between myself and the Saab, and it was eternal, and I heard the shots, heard Natalie saying, Oh, fuck me, heard Dale shouting for everyone to hold on. Yossi was shooting somewhere behind me, firing his first volley at Gray, five shots that cracked back-to-back, and Black was breaking for cover, diving over the hood of his car. From the van, the man covering Trouble's back got off one shot, and a window in the Lexus broke, glass dancing onto the upholstery.

Stupid Things You Think When the Adrenaline Dumps #92: I hope Natalie's insured.

Then I rammed the back of the Saab.

The cars met with a crunch of metal, and the inertia went straight to me, throwing me forward, and just before I hit the dash, the airbag caught me, threw me back. My left knee hit the console and I thought it was louder than the sound of the metal twisting, of the glass breaking, of the shots. The windshield shattered, chunks of safety glass raining down as the hood buckled, and my head was aching, my neck sore, my left hand throbbing from deep in the bone. For a horrible second, I had no idea where I was, what I needed to do.

The smell of the smoke caught me, sweet in the throat, and I saw that we were through. Yossi's grenade was spilling a gray cloud out around the Saab.

Somehow, I'd held on to the knife. I popped the blade, then drove it into the bottom of the airbag, feeling the balloon collapse. I hit the switch again, put the blade away, and rolled out of the car.

The collision had spun both the gray and black cars almost 180 degrees. It was less than ten feet to the back of the Saab, and I broke cover and ran for it, hearing shots behind me. Each step with my left leg felt like my knee rested on splinters. To my right, on the ground, I could see Black, blood running from his head. His car must have hit him when the collision came, and all I thought was, good, maybe he'll stay down. Behind him, on the sidewalk, I could see people hiding in doorways, behind cars, trying to remain safe while trying to see what was happening before them.

I went down at the back of the car, drawing my gun and turning again to face the van. Yossi was firing another volley and Trouble had gone for cover inside the vehicle. The Cover Man with the rifle was returning fire, and I opened up with my pistol, trying to suppress.

It worked. The Cover Man pulled back, and Yossi dropped the magazine from his gun onto the ground, slapped in a replacement, and then began working his way toward me in a running crouch. I emptied my clip at the van, pulled back against the side of the Saab, and reloaded. I only had one spare left.

Yossi was crossing the line made by Gray and Black when the Cover Man ducked out of the van and lay down another return burst. He was firing on automatic, and the burst scattered off the wrecked Lexus as Yossi went past. I fired two double-taps as Yossi returned fire, and the Cover Man fell, and I saw that Yossi had gone down, too, and I was certain that both men were dead.

Then Yossi was scrambling to his feet again, blood running down his forehead, snapping shots at the van. On my left, I heard the side doors of the Saab open, Natalie shouting, "Get in, you bastard, get in!"

I waited until Yossi was inside, then followed, ending half on Natalie and facing the wrong way, out the rear window. Trouble was getting out of the van, and I saw him poke the Cover Man with his foot before Dale accelerated away, and the scene disappeared behind us in smoke.

Yossi was leaning low against his seat, reloading the rifle. Blood coursed down the side of his face, flowing heavily over his jaw, his neck, onto his white shirt. Erika had taken Dale's coat off the front seat and was applying it against Yossi's temple.

"Head for my place," Natalie told Dale, moving Erika out of the way to tend Yossi. She shot a glance over her shoulder my way, for confirmation, and I nodded, finished my reloading.

"No," Yossi said.

"We've had a strike," Natalie told him. "We can't go back to the primary location."

"We know his place," Yossi said. "We don't know yours. We know how to defend at the primary—"

"We're going to Natalie's," I said. "How's it look?"

"He got lucky," Natalie said. "A graze."

"Ricochet," Yossi said.

"He'll be all right?" Erika's voice was thick.

"I'll be fine, angel," Yossi told her. "I told you we'd shoot anyone who tried to hurt you."

Erika looked at me.

"He'll be fine," I assured her.

"Are you fine?" Erika asked me.

"I'm all right. Bumps and bruises, that's all."

"You want a hospital first?" Dale asked me.

"We secure the principal first," I said. "Then I'll take Yossi to the hospital."

"Confirmed."

I told Natalie, "When you get in, see if you can raise Bridgett, tell her what happened. Tell her we could use her help."

"I'll call the office, too," Natalie said. "See if I can get one or two of the guards on our roster to come over and assist."

"Good."

Everyone fell silent, then, with Dale driving quickly and carefully, and the four of us crammed into the backseat of the Saab, with the smell of blood, sweat, and gunpowder. The blood from Yossi's wound had slowed to a steady trickle. I was covered in a fine white powder, like sand, and I assumed it had come from the airbag. My index and middle fingers on my left hand were swollen, and already looked bruised, and I figured they were broken. My left knee felt like I'd rammed it into a brick wall.

Erika put her arms around me.

CHAPTER THIRTEEN

"What I don't like, see, is people shooting at each other on Third Avenue in broad daylight." Detective Third Grade Ellen Morgan was in her early thirties, five-eight at the most, with a leanness that made me think of a greyhound. Her hair was cut short and blunt, and she wore glasses with lenses so thin I wondered if she actually needed them. Her skin was the rich brown of dark beer.

I asked, "As opposed to shooting at each other in the dead of night?"

"Excuse me, do you think this is funny?"

"Sorry."

Morgan sat down in the chair opposite my end of the table. The interrogation room was NYPD-standard, probably built in the forties, and smelled of fear, cigarettes, Lysol. The mirror at the far end, behind her back, was smudged and dirty. I wondered who was watching us from the other side. Detective Morgan pulled a cigarette out of her pocket, lit it with a chrome

Zippo, all while consulting her notepad. By my watch, it was almost eight in the evening. Yossi and I had been in custody for almost three hours now.

"My attorney here yet?" I asked Morgan.

She didn't look up from her notes. "Not yet. You want to stop?"

I had waived my right to silence early; there was no sense in antagonizing Morgan and her partner. Our actions today had been defensible and, in my opinion, correct, but that didn't change the fact that shots had been exchanged in downtown, and somebody needed to be held accountable.

It also didn't change the fact that despite being certain I was in the clear, I was nervous as hell.

Morgan looked at me, and repeated, "Do you want to stop?" She kept it casual.

"No," I said. "Ask whatever you want."

We had hustled Erika inside at Natalie's place. I'd stuck around just long enough to make certain we were secure, before Natalie told me to get Yossi to the fucking hospital. I'd departed, driven the bullet-pocked and body-bent Saab over to Lenox Hill, and taken us both into the emergency room. Yossi had been lucid, but quiet.

It took over an hour before we were treated, I for my nasty bruises and two broken fingers, Yossi for his head wound. The doctor had wanted to put a cast on my arm, and I'd refused, forcing him to settle for a tape-up job with a metal splint. He'd had to do much the same on my knee, which was swollen, but functional.

Yossi didn't make it any easier on the man.

"What happened?" the doctor wanted to know.

"I was at a late lunch with clients," Yossi said. "You know the rich—they eat, they drink, they drink, and they drink some more. We were leaving the restaurant, there's a flight of stairs, and, well, all that snow and ice, whoops. Hell of a fall. Ouch." He turned his winning smile on. "Too many martinis."

The doctor sighed, nodded, and finished stitching up

the wound on Yossi's forehead. We left before the police arrived.

When we'd gotten back to the Saab, Yossi had pulled his cellular phone and handed it to me, saying, "You're in charge. The honor is yours."

I called the 13th Precinct, got a duty sergeant, and said, "A friend and I were involved in the shoot-out on Third Avenue around Twenty-fourth this afternoon. We'd like to come in and make a statement."

The duty sergeant could hardly contain his excitement, told me that would be great, and when could he expect us?

"Half an hour," I said, and hung up, dialed Natalie's apartment.

She answered after two rings, and I told her what we were going to do. "You'll need a lawyer," Natalie said.

"You're right." I gave her my attorney's number. "Call her and see if she's free for the evening."

"You make it sound like a date," Natalie said.

"They're going to hold us overnight, at the least. You have coverage?"

"Herrera from the office is here, and I touched base with Bridgett. She'll be over by eight. She wasn't happy."

"She's rarely happy," I said.

"I wouldn't know. Tell Yossi I'll have the house counsel meet you at the station. It's the One-Three, right?"

I handed the phone back to Yossi, and we got back into his Saab, with me once again driving. I went carefully, granting right of way, not taking chances. The drivetrain was off on the car, jarred by the collision, probably, and it handled like a drunk cat.

"You're going to have to get the car repaired," I told Yossi.

He was idly rubbing the gauze square that had been taped over his stitches. "No, no, no repairs. You owe me a new car."

For some reason, we both thought that was the funniest thing anyone had ever said, and we laughed for almost two minutes, amused at the brilliance of the line. Then our laughter died, and we heard the road, and the traffic, and the engine, and all of the sounds were distinct, as if set in relief against the rest of the world.

"Scared the hell out of me," Yossi finally said.

"Yes."

"How many did you count?"

"I only saw four, but there had to be one driving the van," I said. "Figure five."

"One went down."

"All right, four."

"Was that you or me?"

"I think it was you."

Yossi shut his eyes for a moment, and I saw him grimace. "Any of them that Moore fellow? Or the other one you saw?"

"Denny, and no. The one with the gas, though, I've seen him before." I tried to remember the faces, the bodies. "The gasser, he was the only one I recognized."

Yossi scratched the edge of the tape with his fingernail.

"Stop picking," I snapped.

He pulled his hand back with a guilty grin. "It itches," Yossi said. "They split the brick. Five men for the hit."

"That's how it looked."

"Where were the other three? On surveillance?"

"It's possible. Or securing their safe house, or preparing the escape route."

"SAS works eight-man teams, right?"

"I think it depends on the mission."

Yossi sighed, looking out his window at the Datsun passing us. The driver was a woman, maybe in her thirties, pretty. "If they had all been there, we would have died."

"I know."

"I appreciate what you did."

"It's mutual."

He turned his head back. "Sure, yeah, but it's something I feel the need to say, you know?"

I knew, and we didn't say anything more until we reached the precinct house. We were booked, our weapons taken, and then two uniforms escorted us up to the detectives' squad room to wait. The detectives were busy, we were told, working a crime scene out on Third Avenue. After fifteen minutes, Yossi's attorney showed up, and the two of them went off with the only detective present to have their interview. Twenty minutes after that, the Special Victim Squad was summoned, and Detectives Morgan and Hower arrived to take control of our interviews.

Ellen Morgan asked, "Where's her parents?"

"I don't know where her mother is. Erika's father is in Maryland, at Johns Hopkins. He left a number with me."

Morgan looked at me patiently.

"It's at home," I told her.

She nodded and wrote something in her notepad. "And these men, the SAS, they were going to do what to her?"

"Looked like a kidnapping attempt to me," I said.

"Why?"

"I don't know."

"Her father's not active military anymore, is he? You said he'd retired."

"That's correct."

"I've been working a lot, so maybe I missed this," Morgan said apologetically, and flicked ash onto the table. She used her fingernail on the filter, and the sound it made was like a cockroach crossing a kitchen floor. "We're not suddenly at war with that Green and Pleasant Land, are we?"

"They're rogue, I already said."

"Yeah, you said they were a, uh, 'rogue brick,' that right?"

"That's what I was told."

"By her father?"

"Yes."

Morgan took a drag and left her cigarette hanging in the corner of her mouth. She gave me a good look, head to toe, then flipped her notebook shut, got up, and went out of the room, saying, "I'll be right back."

"Right back" took fifteen minutes, and according to my watch, brought us to eight-oh-eight at night. She returned with my attorney.

"I'd like five minutes alone with him, if that's all right," Miranda Glaser told Detective Morgan.

Detective Morgan gave her a huge smile, and shut the door behind her as she left.

"What'd you do this time?" Miranda asked me.

"Hi to you, too," I said.

She shook her head, sat down in the chair that Morgan had used, one hand waving at the smoke that still hung in the air. Miranda's in her early thirties, slender, with short black hair and smart brown eyes that today were blue. She was wearing an ivory-colored turtleneck and burgundy-colored corduroys, and it was the most casual I'd ever seen her.

"Nice contacts," I said. "Blue suits you."

"I like them."

"Where were you?"

"I had a date."

"Dressed like that? Cheap date."

Miranda gave me the finger. "Spill it, Kodiak."

I spilled and she listened, her chin resting on her hands, her elbows parked on the edge of the table. She has an eidetic memory, and I've heard her quote entire conversations verbatim weeks after they occurred, much to the chagrin of other, opposing, attorneys. I like Miranda. She's always done well by me.

When I had finished, she said, "Good, it's a positive defense. You acted within your rights and according to the law. I'll be right back."

I sat at the table and looked at my left hand, tried to

move the fingers experimentally. The metal of the splint caught the light, and I tried to bounce the reflection onto the observation mirror at the far wall.

This time I was only alone six minutes, and Miranda returned with both Morgan and Hower in tow. Standing beside Morgan, Hower looked like a giant albino, with straw-blond hair framing a bald patch on his scalp, and watery blue eyes. He had a good twenty years on his partner, as well as seventy pounds, minimum.

"You and Mr. Sella are going to spend the night in custody," Miranda told me. "I just spoke to his attorney and with the detectives, here, and we all agree you and Mr. Sella acted within your rights. The D.A. will probably see it that way, too. But you'll have to stay in custody until your arraignment tomorrow."

"And then?" I asked.

"You'll enter a not-guilty, it'll go to the Grand Jury, and the case will be dismissed, because the Grand Jury won't indict."

"Sounds good," I said.

"It is good," Morgan said flatly.

"I need to use a phone."

"I'll call Miss Trent," Miranda told me. "Just give me the number."

I told her the number and Miranda went off to use the phone. Morgan resumed her seat at the table, with Hower looking at his reflection in the glass. After she had lit another cigarette, Morgan said, "We called Johns Hopkins. They have no record of Colonel Douglas Wyatt being admitted. In fact, they told me they have no special AIDS project at all. Just standard treatment."

That rat-fuck son of a bitch, I thought.

I shrugged.

"I thought you said he was verbal?" Hower asked his partner, and his voice was deep enough to make the table vibrate.

"He was verbal. You're scaring him," Morgan said.

"He lied to me," I said. "That's all I can tell you."

"Why would he do that?"

"I don't know."

"Do you know anything at all?" Hower asked.

"I know that five men tried to kidnap the teenage girl I've been hired to protect. I know that we barely got away. I know that a whole lot of shots were fired."

Morgan checked her pad. "And one man was killed."

"That's how it looked."

"Which of you did it?"

"Haven't the foggiest," I said.

"CSU found blood spatter at the scene," Detective Hower said, stroking his bald spot. "But no body. They probably put him back in the van."

"Did you get anything off the cars?" I asked.

Morgan enjoyed a drag off her cigarette before deciding to answer. "Both were stolen within the last twenty-four hours."

I nodded. No surprise in that. "What now?"

"Like your lawyer said, you go to Central Booking."

Hower turned around and leaned back against the glass, putting both big hands in his pockets. "Your buddy is a pain in the ass," he said.

"Yossi?"

"Went on and on about how in any other country but this one, what happened on Third Avenue today wouldn't be an issue."

"He was joking," I said, hoping he had been.

Hower grunted. "He showed me the stitches in his head, said he got it from a ricochet, said that I should appreciate the fact that he was the only professional there. Apparently, Mr. Sella was doing the citizens of New York City a great service by only firing those special bullets of his, those dynamite noble—"

"Dynamit-Nobel," I said.

"Whatever the fuck they are. Says they're training rounds?"

"That's right."

"So I should be grateful he's only killing people with training rounds?"

"Well, it's a range thing," I said. "The bullet is pretty much spent after a hundred feet or so."

Hower used both hands on his bald spot, as if polishing it. "Oh! I get it. He was only killing people in the twenty-four-hundred block. He didn't have enough bang to hit the twenty-five."

"Something like that."

Miranda returned, and said, "We're all set."

Somehow or other, perhaps because we had taken responsibility for the shooting and had made it relatively easy on the cops, Yossi and I got to share a cell at Central Booking. We handed over all our personal belongings, but they let me keep my earrings, for some reason. We received receipts, and were brought to a moldy cell in a noisy hall, where the winter chill seemed to work its way through the floor and walls, despite the strained heating system.

"That Hower fellow, he just doesn't understand brilliance," Yossi said. "No one got hit by one of *my* ricochets." I watched him tear the gauze from his forehead, then wad the cotton and tape into a ball and toss it at me, saying, "Catch!"

I caught the bandage.

"Want to play catch?"

"You're a sick, sick individual," I said, and threw the bandage back to him. "And you need professional help."

Yossi laughed, and we played catch until bedtime.

We were arraigned together the next morning, standing in the criminal court with an attorney flanking both of us. Miranda was all business today, power suit in place, and we were run through the system efficiently and according to plan. The judge asked for the charge, Miranda and Yossi's attorney entered our pleas, the A.D.A. said that as far as his office was concerned, we weren't a risk to ourselves or the community, and we were told we could go home.

"I'll get in touch with you before the Grand Jury date," Miranda told me, and then disappeared with Yossi's attorney to chat up the A.D.A.

Yossi and I went back to Central Booking to retrieve our things, and we checked them carefully against the receipts. Nothing was missing, although the NYPD hadn't finished testing our weapons. The guns would stay at the ballistics lab until they were certain neither had been used in another shooting. We'd get them back eventually.

We walked outside together, into a clear and cold day, with a bright blue sky and sunlight that bounced from the melting snow. I felt filthy and stiff, my fingers throbbing in time with my heartbeat. Yossi didn't look much better. The blood around his stitches had dried black and hard.

"I'm going home, get cleaned up," he told me. "Meet you at Nat's?"

My watch said it was ten of ten. "I'll see you there at two," I told him.

"You should shower. You smell."

"And you're a bouquet of roses."

Yossi grinned, clapped me hard and painfully on the shoulder, and then bounded to the street, hailing a cab.

I went for a pay phone and called Natalie's place. Dale answered.

"We're out," I told him. "How's it there?"

"Locked down. Erika just woke up."

"How is she?"

He paused. "Quiet. I think yesterday spooked her but good."

"Did me, too."

"When can we expect you?"

"Give me three hours. I want to head home, get some clean clothes and something to eat. Yossi's already gone off to do the same."

"We'll be waiting."

The shower was lovely, the clean clothes were better, and the bagel and coffee I grabbed at the bodega were downright divine. I went back to my place to finish eating, and found the number Wyatt had given me before he left. I dialed it and waited.

After two rings, a voice came on saying, "Hardee's, can I help you?"

You rat-fuck son of a bitch, I thought once more.

"Hello?" the voice said. "Is anybody there?"

"Yeah. Is Doug Wyatt there?"

"I'll check, hold on."

I held, and it took a minute before the voice returned to my ear, saying, "No, sorry."

"What's your address?" I asked.

"We're off Belair Road at I-695. Take exit 32." He hung up.

I dialed again, making certain I got the number Wyatt had given me correct. Benefit of the doubt, you know.

After one ring, the same voice answered, and I hung up before he could offer to help me.

The Colonel had known I'd recognize the Baltimore area code. So instead of just giving me a fake number, he went to the trouble of finding me a real one.

Yet another why. And I was getting tired of not knowing any of the becauses.

I went to my room and took out my spare HK, giving it a once-over. I loaded it and two extra magazines, put the gun in my holster on my hip, and the clips in the pocket of my army jacket. Then I made my way to Natalie's apartment, where the rotund doorman recognized me and waved me through.

By my watch, it was a quarter of twelve when I knocked on the door.

No answer.

I knocked again, harder.

Still no answer.

I listened, and heard nothing.

The air smelled of smoke.

I tried the knob. The door was unlocked.

My stomach began shrinking, and I drew my weapon while letting the door swing open. Of all the possible reasons to worry, this was the worst.

The door should absolutely not be unlocked.

Natalie never would have left the door unlocked.

I listened for another half a minute, then took a breath and went through the doorway.

From outside, I heard the wind whistling against the glass doors. Wisps of smoke hung in the air, turning gently, and the smell of a cooking fire flowed into my nose, down my throat.

Smells like bacon, I thought.

"Natalie?"

The main room was empty and quiet. The doors onto the patio were closed. On the dining table by the kitchen entrance, place mats, glasses, and utensils were laid out. More smoke drifted from the kitchen.

I heard the footsteps coming from the hall, several sets, running. I turned, bringing my weapon up, thinking that I didn't want to be shooting again, that there had been enough of guns already.

Natalie came into the doorway, Dale right behind her, and a third man I'd seen at Sentinel. Herrera, I thought.

I managed not to fire. "What the hell is—"

"She bolted," Natalie said.

CHAPTER FOURTEEN

"She wanted to make us breakfast," Natalie told me. "She wanted to make breakfast, so I went to shower, and Corry was setting the table, and Dale was in the kitchen with her."

"Eggs," Dale said. "I was beating the eggs."

"She was cooking the bacon," Natalie said. "And either it happened by accident or she started it herself, but there was a grease fire."

The four of us were in the main room, Natalie seated on the couch, Dale standing by the patio doors, and Corry Herrera in the reading chair. Herrera was short, handsome, with straight black hair and quick eyes, dressed in black jeans and a brown sweater. His face had the lines of a man who likes to smile.

"She meant to do it," Dale said. "She shrieked, and I saw the flames, and I thought she was trying to beat them out. She grabbed a glass of water she had filled—she was thirsty—and tossed half of it on the fire before I could stop her. By that time Corry had come in, and he got her out of the kitchen, then came back in with me. It took us a minute to get the flames out, and Corry went back to get Erika, told me she was gone."

"The door was wide open," Corry Herrera said softly. "She must have run the moment I left her to go back into the kitchen. Took the stairs, probably went out the back."

Natalie's mouth was shut tight, and her eyes were on mine. Strands of wet hair stuck to her cheeks and neck. Still heavy with water, it made the color closer to brown than red.

"We checked the building," Dale said. "No sign of her. Asked the doorman if he'd seen her, nothing."

"She could be anywhere," Corry said.

I nodded, still watching Natalie, waiting for her to speak. The silence was spreading like oil.

She clenched her fists at her sides. "I fucked up," Natalie said.

I nodded again.

"What do you want to do?" Dale asked me.

"We have to find her," I said. "And in this city, that's going to be next to impossible."

"We can get police help."

"I'll call Morgan and Hower," I said. "They'll be delighted. Did anything happen while I was gone?"

"Like what?"

"Like a fight. Like somebody maybe did or said something to upset her."

"I think the gunfight yesterday was probably enough to upset anyone," Natalie shot back at me.

"So that's a no?"

"Correct."

"Not even when Bridgett was here?" I asked.

Dale said, "They tossed some insults back and forth."

"Like?"

"Erika made a comment about Bridgett's relationship with you. Bridgett hit back."

"How hard?"

There was a moment for memory, or decision, and then Corry answered. "Logan said that Erika ought to get over having tits, and try having a brain, instead."

"She got us, Atticus," Dale said. "There was nothing we could do to stop her. No way we could have seen it coming."

Corry Herrera leaned forward in his seat and asked, "Do you have any idea where she would go? Maybe home?"

"Not home," I said. "She knows it isn't safe."

"We have to contact her father," Natalie said.

"We can't. I don't know where he is."

"He gave you a contact number."

"It's bullshit. It's the number of a Hardee's in Baltimore. NYPD tried to reach him through Johns Hopkins, came up empty."

"Why the hell did he do that?" Dale asked.

"I don't know, and it doesn't matter right now. What matters is finding Erika. We've got a city of eight million some odd, and she could be anywhere in it with an SAS brick coming after her, hard."

"Maybe she left the city," Corry suggested. "Her parents are divorced, right? Maybe she's looking for mom."

"It's possible," I said. "Check your wallets, see if you're short cash."

Dale and Corry both went to where their coats were hung on the stand near the door, and Natalie went to her room. I felt the tension coming off her, bottled and rising. She didn't like being made a fool of, and I suspected she liked it even less in my presence.

Dale said, "Motherfuck."

"She tapped you?"

"Cleaned me out, almost one hundred and fifty bucks," he said. "I had change from the shopping. She left my cards and papers, though."

"One-fifty, she could catch a bus or train, even a short flight," Corry said.

"She's still in the city," Natalie said tersely. "She won't leave the city."

"How do you know?" I asked.

"She won't leave the city," she repeated, and then headed for her coat. "I'll start checking the immediate area, see if she just ducked into a park, anything like that. Dale and Corry can check the terminals." Though Natalie had said their names, she directed the last at me.

"Check Grand Central, first," I told them. "I may be wrong. She might have decided to try going back to Garrison after all."

I waited while everyone got ready, and then we stepped out of the apartment. Natalie locked up, and we went down to the lobby in a silent group. When we hit the street, we split.

"Watch your back," I told them.

After two tries, I found a pay phone that worked, and got ahold of Detective Morgan, told her what had happened.

"Jesus Christ," Morgan said. "I'll have some units head over, do a search of the area. We'll have to report this to the local precinct."

"I appreciate it."

"She ran? She wasn't taken?"

"Ran."

"Why?"

"Hell if I know," I said.

"We'll notify you if we find her," Morgan told me, and hung up.

I dropped another quarter and caught Yossi before he left his apartment. He listened to the rundown, made the appropriate noises of frustration and concern, and then said he'd come by Natalie's and give her a hand.

"I'll bet she's livid," Yossi said.

"Natalie? Livid might describe it."

"And how are you?"

"I feel sick," I said.

"Erika will be all right. She's a smart kid."

I dialed Bridgett next, got her at her desk, and she sounded good.

"Hey, it's me," I said.

"Hey, you! I've been sitting here, having lascivious thoughts and hoping you'd call. Wazzup?"

"Erika bolted."

"What are you talking about?"

"A little before noon," I said, and explained what had happened.

"Clever maneuver," Bridgett said when I'd finished. "Didn't think she had it in her."

"Yeah, I heard about that."

She caught the tone. "Oh, come on. You can't seriously be blaming me for her running off."

"No, I can't, and I don't, but I don't think it was bright to antagonize her."

"Me?" Bridgett said, and I heard her chair creaking over the phone, could picture her straightening in her seat. "That nymphet has the manners of a spoiled cat. She's going to claw at me, I'm going to claw back, stud."

"She's fifteen."

"And should therefore know better. Don't come down on me because she ran away from you."

"That a singular or a plural 'you'?"

"Take your pick."

I took a breath, watched traffic whiz past. This was getting us nowhere, and I didn't want to fight. What I wanted was to find Erika, and fast. Most of all, I wanted the lump in my gut to disappear.

I said, "Natalie, Dale, and Corry Herrera are all out looking for her. Yossi's on his way over. I'm going to start poking around, but the problem is there's no reference point, nowhere to start."

"The bondage scene." Bridgett said it immediately.

"You think she's looking for some action?"

"Jesus, relax, Atticus. The kid's into the scene, then

that's what she knows in the city. She'll go to a club. The entire principle of bondage is trust. She figures she's safe there."

"That's a hell of an assumption," I said.

"It's the same assumption the SAS was making, you got to figure. Explains that guy with the knife." There was a moment's pause while she put something in her mouth. Probably a Life Saver. "That's where I'd look."

"The Strap," I said. "Can you lend a hand?"

She sucked on the candy in her mouth. "I'll meet you there at ten."

"I was hoping sooner."

"I can't sooner. I'm working."

"See you at ten, then."

"Good luck."

I hung up and it took a while, it took an hour of fruitless searching, with the panic in my gut rising, and no sign of Erika, before I realized that I was angry at Bridgett.

I wasn't sure why.

▰ CHAPTER FIFTEEN ▰

I was outside The Strap at a quarter to nine that night, alone. Our search party had reconvened at Natalie's apartment at seven to share results, and we'd each come up with the same nothing as everyone else had. Dale and Corry decided to drive to Garrison and check with the local police, just to be certain that Erika wasn't hiding at home, and after they left, Natalie got the idea to check the youth hostels in town. Yossi went with her. Everyone said they'd call me in the morning.

I'd gone home after that for food and some warmer clothes. The clear blue sky of the day had disappeared behind clouds even before sunset, and the temperature had taken a nosedive. I fixed myself a bowl of oatmeal, didn't eat it, put on my gun and my coat, and headed down to the street and started walking. After three blocks, it began to snow.

Jacob was working the door instead of the bar when I arrived, and he wouldn't let me in, saying, "Uh, no, Atticus. You've been banned. Burton's orders."

"I'll pay," I said. "Just like any other customer."

His face tightened in a pained expression, thinking, and I could see that Jacob wanted to let me in, but that he also wanted to keep his job. It was that last that did it for him, too, I think. After all, I'd been fired, so there was no question it couldn't happen to him.

Jacob shook his head. "Sorry, can't do it."

"Is Burton here?" I asked.

"He's up in the sound booth, setting up the tapes."

"Let me talk to him."

That he could do, and so Jacob turned and asked one of the cashiers at the door to fetch Burton, bring him down to the front. I backed off and waited beside the door, using the palm of my right hand to shield my glasses from the falling snow. There was a short line of people already waiting to get inside, most outfitted for light bondage and the rest dressed as if this was just another club, which, ultimately, I supposed it was. I saw a couple I recognized, a man and a woman who tended to play in a corner by themselves. A very pretty Hispanic woman with a small hoop through the left corner of her lower lip and wearing tight black leather pants gave me a careful sizing up, then a smile. She was wearing a bright orange quilted ski jacket, zipped, and was keeping her hands in her pockets for warmth. I tried to recall if I knew her or not. I didn't think so.

Burton stuck his head out the door. "What?"

"I need to get inside," I told him.

He folded his arms across his chest, and the gesture made me immediately think of Erika. Burton is an average-looking guy in all ways, and he dresses like a neat Connecticut preppy, pure WASP. You'd never know by looking at him that people paid Burton hundreds of dollars for the pleasure of being bound and beaten at his hands. Despite that, even Burton admits that his club is barely in the scene.

Burton surveyed me slowly, lingering on my swollen lip and splinted fingers before saying, "Absolutely not, Atticus."

"Will you hear me out?" I asked.

He nodded.

"A young woman I was taking care of ran away this afternoon. Her name is Erika. She's the girl that had the knife pulled on her last week, the night you fired me. She's got some hard people after her, one of them is the guy who pulled that knife."

"You think she's hiding here?" Burton asked, confused.

"No, but Bridgett thinks she's hiding in the scene, and there's a chance that somebody here might know Erika, maybe even know where she's gone. I just want to get inside and ask some questions. I'll be good, I promise."

Burton thought, putting his right thumbnail in his mouth and scraping it against his bottom teeth. Someone in the line greeted him—the Hispanic woman who had approved of my form, in fact—and he gave her a nod and smile, then stepped out of the doorway to get closer to me.

"You're putting me in a bad position," Burton said softly. "I believe you, I believe what you're saying, but I can't let you into the club, you've got to understand that."

"Why not?"

He put his hands together as if about to pray, pointing the steepled end in my direction. "I had a fight here a week ago. I had a man pull a knife on an employee *and* a customer. This is a sensitive scene, and I know you understand that. People were here that night, they saw what happened. How is it going to look if I let you back inside? They know you've been fired, they know why you've been fired. If I let you in, it looks like I'm going back on my word, that I'm not committed to protecting my clients."

"I think that puts more of the blame for the fight on my shoulders than I deserve," I said, carefully calm.

"It does. I know you didn't start it. But a knife came out in my establishment, was brandished openly, and that's the damage. If it's any consolation, I can assure you that neither the girl nor the guy who had the knife are in here tonight. They've been banned, too." He watched my reaction, hoping I understood. "I am sorry. It's not personal."

"I know." He was starting to head back in when I asked, "Will you let Bridie inside?"

When he smiled, he looked like a benevolent priest. "Yes, I'd let Bridgett inside."

It was almost ten-thirty when she arrived, and she was dressed for the scene, black jeans, black boots, and her biker jacket. Her top was black, too, but from the collar to the swell of her breasts was a thin mesh instead of solid fabric. It wasn't the cheap lace Erika had worn, more an expensive optical illusion, showing skin only if the light caught the cloth right. Bridgett's hair was pulled back, and she'd removed all of the studs from her ears, replacing each with surgical steel hoops. Her lipstick was burnt red.

"Cute," I said, and my anger came back as I said it.

"If I'm canvassing, I don't want to look out of place."

"Aren't you cold?"

"It's going to be hot inside."

"Burton won't let me in," I told her. "I'll wait out here."

"Where can I find you?"

"By the fire exit. I don't want to scare off business by standing out front."

"You can go home, you know."

"I'd prefer to wait here."

"This could take a while."

"I'll wait."

Bridgett dropped a red Life Saver in her mouth, then put the pack away in a jacket pocket. "Your choice. See you in a bit."

"Good luck," I said.

She headed past me and cut to the front of the line.

Before anyone could protest, Jacob had waved her through, and I watched her go out of sight, pushing through the black masking that had been hung inside the entrance to block the view.

I walked up to the alley and then turned left, going on until I reached the fire exit. Several cardboard boxes had been stacked by the Dumpster, and I discovered a couple that had yet to be touched by the snow. I experimented for a few minutes with placement, finally finding a way to stack them so they could hold my weight, and then sat down, putting my back to the wall.

The snow was falling more slowly, large and heavy flakes that floated like trim feathers. The ground had been clear and wet until now, but with this snowfall the dirty concrete and asphalt dissolved away under smooth fresh white. It would be pitted and brown by morning, polluted, frozen ice rather than soft powder. The temperature felt in the mid-twenties.

Through the wall I could feel more than hear the thud of the music playing in the club. I couldn't recognize the tune. There was noise from the street, traffic and voices, people coming and going. At the far end of the alley, yellow cabs were going in and out of their depot. I could hear the sounds of the cars being washed as cabbies went off shift. The cars would remain clean for maybe thirty seconds after they hit the street.

A hard winter, I thought.

Near eleven a group of people came through the fire exit, five of them, men and women, club-hoppers rather than scene players. They ignored me and moved like a rugby scrum toward Tenth Avenue, discussing where they should head next. One of them suggested his home, and that began a loud debate. They were out of earshot before reaching a conclusion.

A homeless man came my way forty minutes or so later. I gave him five dollars, and then he asked for my cardboard boxes. I handed them over, and he left happy.

That's me, Atticus Kodiak, harbinger of sweetness and light.

Bridgett came back out at seven after one, her arm around the waist of the Hispanic woman I'd seen earlier. Both were laughing, and I'd have thought that maybe both were drunk, too, but knew that wasn't possible. Burton's soda was potent, but not that potent.

"Atticus, this is Elana," Bridgett said, introducing me.

"Oh, so this is the guy," she said, grinning. "Elana Corres." She offered me her left hand. Her right remained around Bridgett's waist.

I took it and said hello. Corres was an attractive woman, and I put her close to my age, perhaps twenty-nine. Her hair was long and black, tied into a single braid that ran down her back. She had her orange ski jacket open, and aside from the leather pants, I could see she was wearing a black leather vest. The vest was short, showing cleavage at the top, and her navel at the bottom. She had a stud through her belly button, and I wondered if she knew that Bridgett wore a hoop through hers, too.

Elana Corres released my hand and then reached into an inside pocket, coming out with a long, thin cigar. Bridgett and she separated, and Elana took a double-bladed cutting tool from the same pocket, began to slice the end of the smoke.

Bridgett said, "Elana knows Erika."

"You do?"

Elana didn't look up from her work on the cigar. "In passing. Nice kid. Can't believe she's only fifteen."

"How do you know her?" I asked.

"Elana's a writer," Bridgett answered, leaning back against the wall. "Scribbles for a variety of magazines and journals, isn't that right?"

Elana blew on the cut end of her cigar. "I do all right,

cover the club scene for the *Free Press* and rags like that." She slid the cutter back in her pocket.

"And the *Voice*," Bridgett added.

"And the *Voice*." Elana lit up, rotating the cigar in her mouth until the end was going well. "I met Erika about a month ago, maybe," she said between puffs. "Kept seeing her at all these different clubs—Paddles, The Vault, Spankers—and we just started chatting one night. Smart girl. Real pretty."

"You take her home?" I asked, and that's when I was certain I was jealous.

Elana blew out smoke and laughed, stowing the lighter. Bridgett gave me a look that was more than a warning. I gave her one back that asked what was going on.

"No," Elana said. "I wasn't interested. She tried, though. She did try."

"You got another one of those?" Bridgett asked her.

Elana held up the cigar, then offered it to Bridgett, saying, "Certainly, pet."

Bridgett took it and began smoking, saying, "There's more. Tell him."

Elana took a second cigar out of her pocket, offering it to me. I shook my head, and she set to work on it, saying, "Well, Bridie says that you're also looking for some men, maybe men who have been lurking in clubs looking for—" She swung her head to look at Bridgett. "What is it you called her?"

"Lolita," Bridgett said, puffing.

"Like you've read Nabokov."

"Like you have."

"Bitch."

"Tramp."

Both of them laughed, and I shifted in the snow, glancing down to see it crushing beneath my shoes. My feet were cold.

"Yes, well," Elana said, glancing at me and acting more serious, "I haven't seen all of the men described, but I've seen one of them, I think. A Brit, about five feet ten, black hair, mean. Looks in his thirties?"

I nodded. Trouble.

"He was at Spankers two weeks ago, asking around about Lolita. Erika. Offering money. He got thrown out of the place."

"Have you seen him since then?" I asked.

She put the cigar in her mouth, saying, "Couple days ago he was at an underground club I sometimes hit, up in Harlem. Looked like his nose had been broken. He had modified the approach, but the vibe I got off him was that he was still on the prowl for your little girl."

"Anything else?"

Elana shook her head. "*Lo siento.*"

"I may need you to talk to the police, just have you tell them what you've told me," I said. "Would you be able to do that?"

"Sure." She lit her cigar, looked over at Bridgett, who was watching us, puffing quietly. "Rose there knows where to find me."

I thought of the red flower on Bridgett's left calf, didn't say anything. I switched my eyes over to Bridgett. She suddenly seemed unhappy, and I realized she wasn't looking at either of us anymore, but past us, down the alley. Then her eyes came to me, then to Elana, focusing.

"Thanks," Bridgett said.

"It's no problem. I hope you two find her. Like I said, she's a smart kid. I liked her." Elana checked her watch. "I've got to go." She turned and offered me her hand again, saying, "Nice meeting you, Atticus."

"Thanks for your help."

She smiled and turned back to Bridgett, leaned in to give her a kiss on the cheek, holding her cigar at arm's length. "See you around. Don't be a stranger."

"You, too."

We both watched as Elana walked down toward Tenth Avenue. When she made the turn, Bridgett sighed, looking down at the cigar in her hand. She dropped it in the snow, crushed the end with the heel of her boot. The odor from the tobacco intensified, sour.

"We used to go out," she told me.

"So I'd gathered."

"The rose comment gave it away?"

"That, and the fact that she calls you Bridie."

"We stopped seeing each other in May," Bridgett said.

"How long had you been going out?"

"Eight months."

"Serious?"

"I was in love with her." Bridgett zipped up her jacket. "You want to go get a drink or a cup of joe?"

"I was thinking I'd go home."

She heard the contrariness in my voice. "Does it bother you?"

"It doesn't bother me that you were involved with another woman, if that's what you're asking," I said. "I'd have preferred to find out you were bi another way, though."

"Oh, yeah? How? A threesome? You, me, and Elana, maybe?"

I watched my breath float away before I said, "You could have told me."

"You never asked, Atticus."

"She the last person you were involved with?"

"Yeah. I went from her to you. I'm just batting a thousand so far, aren't I?"

"What?"

"Nothing. Never mind," Bridgett said. "You think I should have told you about her?"

I nodded, knowing that even that was a mistake.

"Right. Sorry. I didn't realize that we had to do postmortems of all our past liaisons before we could sleep together. I mean, you've been so forthcoming and all about your past, for fuck's sake."

I still didn't say anything.

"I'm going home," Bridgett said. "You know where

you can find me." She looked at me for a second longer, and when I didn't move or speak, she turned and went.

The streets were as near to empty as they get in Manhattan, and the few people who were out had come to enjoy the weather, walking alone or in couples, watching the snowfall. It was a beautiful night, the island lit by a canopy of light reflected from the falling flakes. It was the sort of night to look up and open your mouth and catch what you could, and to be happy you could catch anything at all. It was a good night for children and lovers.

I didn't look up.

When Bridgett had introduced Elana to me, it'd seemed that she was getting some payback for our argument the night before last, and for the way I'd sounded when she'd arrived at The Strap this night. It was petty, but no more than I had been, and it should have been something from which we could both recover. Yet it had only gotten worse. When they had come outside together, I'd felt an inner alarm go off, but now I couldn't tell if I was honestly jealous about Elana or not. I'd told Bridgett the truth. Elana could have been a purple Amish woodsmith, and I wouldn't have cared. Love has always seemed like love to me—gender, race, religion, none of those things matter when on that playing field.

But I was bothered and, again, vaguely scared, and it wasn't until I was coming down Twenty-eighth Street that I realized why. It wasn't that she hadn't told me about Elana; it was that I sensed she'd deliberately withheld the information.

And that's when the guilt hit but good, because what the fuck was I doing, if not the exact same thing?

My shoes were soaked through and my toes and fingers felt like marble when I unlocked the door to the building. I went to the stairs, heading up to the sound of my feet going squish-squeak-squish. A spineless sound, I decided. Apropos.

I reached the top, fourth floor, and turned, and there was a rustle from outside my door, someone standing up in the shadow, and I thought, it's the SAS. Idiot, Atticus, idiot, so busy, so concerned, and your mind was elsewhere, and now they've got you dead to rights, and you're screwed, you're absolutely screwed.

My gun was clearing the holster when I realized it was a woman who was coming toward me, and I stopped and I stared.

"Atticus?" The light hit her, and it wasn't Bridgett.

It wasn't Erika, either.

No, this time, it was the real thing, and I felt my stomach tighten, the anxiety ache giving way to a different kind of nervousness entirely.

"It's not too late for you to invite me in for a cup of coffee, is it?" Diana Wyatt asked. "I've been waiting out here all night."

CHAPTER SIXTEEN

She looked lovely, a little older perhaps, and that made her more attractive. She was forty-one now, and the lines at her eyes and mouth had gone a tad deeper, more definite, but the face was the same, the body the same, the voice the same. Just seeing her was enough to take my breath and hide it, leaving me speechless.

Or maybe that was just the surprise.

Either way, I just stood there, trying to cope, one hand on my gun, gun in its holster. Jaw on the floor.

Diana stopped, amused, and then her arms came up and around me in a hug and the top of her head grazed my chin. She smelled just the same, and all of it came back with that, the memories, the emotions, and I almost didn't hear her saying, "It's good to see you. God, I've missed you. It's so good to see you."

"Diana," I said.

She tilted her head up, her smile wonderful, her arms still around me. "Atticus," she said easily, and that was the way she always said my name when we were alone, no Colonel, no Erika, just her and me, like I was comfortable, and hers.

Then we would kiss, and even as I thought it, I felt her hand sliding up my back, going to my neck. I let her tug me down, and I put my lips against her cheek, caught the scent of her perfume. She accepted the change, turned her mouth away, let the kiss rest where I set it, and then she pulled back.

"Late night?" Diana asked. "It's nearly two-thirty."

"Have you been waiting out here long?"

"A couple of hours," she said. "I should have called first, but I wanted to surprise you."

"You did," I said.

She laughed, following me into the apartment as I unlocked the door and turned on lights. I stopped in the kitchen, saw that the indicator on my answering machine was blinking red. The apartment was quiet, and looked undisturbed. Snow fell past my window.

"Do you really want coffee?" I asked.

"I'd really like a drink," Diana said.

"I've got beer and some harder stuff, that's about it."

"Scotch?"

"I have scotch."

"Neat, please."

I fixed her a drink, and she took it with a thank you, then began looking around the apartment as I poured myself a glass. When she was out of the kitchen, I hit the play button on the answering machine, hoping the message was good news.

It was Bridgett.

"Hi. I guess you're not home, yet. Wanted to talk. I'll . . . I'll try to reach you later. Maybe tomorrow." The machine beeped and clicked, and erased the message.

I removed my coat and gun, then went with my drink to find Diana. She was standing in the living room, examining Rubin's painting.

"Gruesome," Diana Wyatt said.

"I suppose."

"Hold this?" She offered me the glass of scotch, and I took it, watched while she took off her coat and draped it carefully over the arm of the sofa. It was made from lamb's wool, navy-blue, and beneath it she wore a ribbed mock turtleneck top the color of Spanish moss, and light gray wool pants. Her belt was thin and black, and her shoes were black, too, leather ankle boots that looked soft and expensive.

Diana sat on the couch and after I'd handed her drink back, she asked, "Surprised?"

"Stunned," I said.

"Pleasantly, though?"

I nodded.

"I got into town this evening," Diana said. "Somewhere I'd heard you were in New York, so I looked and there was your name in the book. It's been five years?"

"Four."

"Still too long." She took another small sip from the glass, caught me looking at her left hand. Smiling again, she wiggled her bare fingers at me. "Free at last, free at last."

"I noticed."

"Two years now," Diana said. "That goatfucker fought it every step of the way. Got himself a fancy lawyer, stuck me with nothing, and left me with less. I barely won visitation rights." Her eyes narrowed when she spoke of the Colonel, and the hazel there darkened to brown. "He won't even let me see my own daughter."

I nodded, but kept quiet, still not quite believing it was her. My stomach was beginning to settle, but the anxiety and excitement remained, and it was awkward, trying to determine what I still felt.

I took a seat against the wall, and we went silent. Finally, Diana asked, "Nothing to say?"

"I'm trying. I'm really trying."

"You can keep staring at me. I don't mind."

I laughed and looked away, saw the X-wing lying in a corner.

"How's Rubin?" Diana asked. "Did you two ever link up again after the service?"

"Yeah, we did," I said. "He died three months ago."

That surprised her, and she was quiet for several seconds, trying to think of what to say. When she spoke, she used the traditional "I'm very sorry."

I nodded. "What brings you to New York?"

"Not the weather."

"No."

"Doug has AIDS," Diana said.

"I know."

"You've seen him?"

"We've been in contact."

"I've been tested," she said quickly. "I'm clean."

"I'm glad to hear it."

"Not like I had much chance to get it from him. The last time he and I made love, Reagan was in his first term." The bitterness was sharp in her voice. "The son of a bitch deserves it. How long do you give him?"

"I don't know. He's not well. Maybe six months. Maybe more."

Diana almost smiled. "Then I'll finally get my daughter back."

"Is that why you're here?"

She looked surprised, but knocked it down. "I lied," Diana said. "Erika called me a couple days ago, said she was staying with you."

"Erika called you?"

Diana nodded.

"She told me she didn't know how to contact you," I said. "That she hadn't talked to you since the divorce."

"Then she lied, too," Diana explained. "Doug doesn't want her talking to me, Atticus. He's forbidden her from doing it, and you remember how he is when he gets in a rage. Erika called from his house once, while he was sleeping or out or something, and when the bill came, he discovered what she'd done. She told me he hit her. She's been calling from pay phones ever since. Is she here?"

"No," I said.

"Did she go back to Garrison?"

"What'd she say when she called you?" I asked.

She wanted me to answer first, but I kept quiet. Before the silence got entirely awkward, Diana said, "Just that she was staying with you while Doug went out of town and that everything was fine. I got off the phone and thought I'd fly out—I've been living in Chicago—and surprise the two of you. Finally have a chance to spend some time with my daughter, and maybe do some catching up with you. Bad idea?"

"You missed her," I said, thinking that somebody was lying, here. For the last three days, at least until this afternoon, Erika hadn't been alone long enough to make any calls, long distance or otherwise. She could have used the cellular I'd put in her room, but I doubted it; one of us would have heard her talking. It was just possible that she could have reached out to her mother after bolting from Natalie's, and perhaps, out of fear and with nowhere to go, that's what she had done. Diana could have rushed to catch the first flight available to come to her daughter's aid, but if that was the case, why was she here?

Just too much coincidence, Diana arriving the same day Erika ran away.

"Doug came and picked her up?" Diana asked.

"When did she call you?"

Diana looked at me, again wanting my answer first, and again I waited her out. "Yesterday evening," she said finally. "I flew out today after I got off work. Did she go back to Garrison with her father, Atticus?"

"She's staying at a friend's," I said.

"Do you have a number? I'd like to see her before Doug makes that impossible."

"I'll get it for you," I said, and headed back to the kitchen where I wrote a random number down on a pad. It wasn't much of a lie, but it would buy me enough time to think. The clock on the coffeemaker read twelve minutes past three. I doubted Diana would call to check tonight.

She followed me, carrying her coat. She put her empty glass in the sink and then took the sheet of paper from me, folding it precisely and putting it into her pocket.

"I'll call her tomorrow," Diana said. "We can plan something for the three of us."

"That'd be nice."

"It would," she said. "Time for bed?"

"I need to get some sleep."

"You look like it. What happened to your hand?"

"I got in a car accident."

Diana put a hand out to my face, slipped it down to the side of my neck. Her palm was warm. "I can stay," she said.

"I don't think you should."

"I've missed making love with you."

I shook my head, and after a second she removed her hand and grabbed her coat.

"I'll call you tomorrow," Diana said.

"Yes," I said. "You will."

CHAPTER SEVENTEEN

Sometime after four, I fell asleep. I was up again before seven.

It was still snowing.

After my walk-through, I made calls to Natalie, Yossi, and Dale. The calls were pretty much the same: no, I hadn't found her, and no, they hadn't either, and yes, we'd all keep looking. Natalie and Yossi were going to work Times Square, and Dale and Corry were going to try Port Authority. They said they'd call in the afternoon, after they met up again.

Good luck, I thought, knowing full well we wouldn't find Erika at any of those places.

I went down to the diner on the corner for breakfast. Diana would be calling before ten, I was certain, demanding to know what the hell I was playing at, and where her daughter was. I still didn't know what I would tell her. Gee, Di, great to see you, and by the way, until yesterday afternoon, I was protecting Erika from an SAS brick. Then she ran away. No, I have no idea where she is now. Yes, nice to see you, too.

I got myself a copy of the *Times*, ordered myself a bowl of oatmeal, and tried to clear my head over breakfast. I don't know how I got on the oatmeal kick; as a kid I'd hated the stuff, but the last few days, I'd been craving it. Maybe it had something to do with the change in the weather.

The bell over the door jingled, and I glanced up and saw Moore, Denny, and Knowles enter, all pulling off gloves and watch caps. The gloves and watch caps were black, but otherwise, they were dressed the same as when they'd given me a ride to the train station six days ago. They looked at me, and then Moore said something and the other two picked a booth against the wall so they could keep an eye on the door and on me. Moore came straight to my booth, smiling a greeting. I forced one out in return, then checked the street through the window. Traffic was moving normally. I didn't see the rest of the brick, but that meant nothing.

"Always sit with your back to a wall, do you?" Moore slid in on the vinyl seat, waved at the waiter, saying, "Coffee."

"What do you want?" I asked him.

"I was thinking breakfast. What's good?"

"I like their oatmeal."

"Porridge," he told the waiter, then explained, "oatmeal."

The waiter grunted.

Moore moved his cap and gloves from his hands into a pocket, then unzipped his anorak. I could see the edge of his gun in its holster, but if they had come to shoot, I'd have been dead already. In their booth, Denny and Knowles were examining the menu.

"What do you want, Sergeant?" I asked again.

"Did the Lady Wyatt visit you last night?"

"You're still watching my place?"

"Did she?"

"Where's Erika?"

"Don't you have her?" Moore asked. His smile was cheerful and condescending.

"Is she with you or not?"

"I don't have her."

"I don't think I believe you, Sergeant."

"Robert," he corrected. "You should. What did Diana tell you, mate?"

I ignored him, began looking at the sports page.

"Whatever she told you, ten to one she's lying, Atticus," Moore said. "I know you have a history with her, but if you're placing loyalty with that woman, it's a grand mistake. She ran out on her husband and her kid."

"She ran out on a miserable marriage," I said. "Colonel Wyatt was a rotten spouse, and I saw that firsthand."

"Every kid needs a mother."

"You should run for office," I told him. "Family values are very vogue right now, what with the millennium coming and all."

"I'm not on about the decline of western morality," Moore said. "I just want to know what she said to you and where she is."

"You didn't follow her when she left?"

"Let's say we had a run of bad luck and lost her, shall we?"

"That sucks, Robert. Sorry to hear it."

"Traffic in this city is a bitch."

I put the paper down. "Do you have Erika?"

"No."

The waiter came, set the bowl of oatmeal and coffee on the table. "Same check?"

"Sure," I said.

When the waiter had retreated, Moore grinned. "I like you, Atticus. You don't trust me, you don't even like me, and you're willing to front me breakfast."

"You're paying," I said, and went back to the paper.

He chuckled, and I heard him pouring sugar into his coffee, the clink of the spoon as he stirred. Moore asked, "You know what it is that I really like about you?"

"My ability to fire three rounds a minute in any weather?"

That earned a full-bore laugh, loud enough to draw attention. Both Denny and Knowles looked our way, and they raised their hands to me in greeting. I waved back. We were a polite bunch of killers, and Moore certainly didn't seem worried about being spotted with me.

"No, it's that you're a professional like me," Moore said easily, answering his own question. "You're still carrying the burdens of your rank, your honor, your sense of loyalty."

His eyes were on mine, crow's-feet crinkling with his smile. It seemed to me that if he thought I was so honorable and so loyal, he didn't know the full story about Diana. He certainly didn't know about Bridgett.

"But your loyalty's misplaced," he went on. "The Lady Diana don't deserve it. Come on, now, tell me what she said to you last night."

"Why is an SAS brick after Erika Wyatt?"

Moore sighed. "An SAS brick isn't after Erika Wyatt, Atticus. You've got to believe me. I mean little Erika no ill will. She's safe with me, as far as that goes. I've no interest in her whatsoever. It's her mother I'm concerned with."

"If you're so sweet on Erika, why'd you have some of your boys try to snatch her away from me and my people two days ago?"

"I didn't."

"Yes, you did, Robert. I know you did. I was there. I've got the broken fingers and the knee brace to prove it."

We stared at each other for a full fifteen seconds before he turned his head, looked out the window onto the snowy street. Denny and Knowles were both eating their breakfasts, shoveling food as if they were in a mess tent.

"I don't want to go toe-to-toe with you," Robert Moore said. "I could take you, and I know that sure as the sun rises, but it wouldn't be easy, and we could do one another a lot of hurt before it was over. We don't have to be at odds, mate. I'd prefer to work this out amenably."

"I would have, too," I said. "But that passed when five of your boys started shooting at me and mine."

"And if the boys who shot weren't mine at all? If Erika is in absolutely no danger from me? If she's safe?"

"Then I want to know who they were, and I want to know where she is."

"What did Lady Di say to you?"

"Do you have Erika?"

"You tell me where Diana Wyatt is, you tell me what she said to you, I'll give you an answer."

"No," I said. "I want Erika. That's all I want. I want to know where she is, if she's all right, if she's safe. If you've got her, I want her back. If you don't give her back, I'll find a way to take her back. And until she's with me I've got nothing more to say to you."

"Atticus—"

"I'm not finished," I said. "If you or any of your boys harm her in any way, I will kill you."

"You know what you're saying?"

"I know perfectly what I'm saying. And who I'm saying it to."

"We don't have to do it this way," Moore said.

I folded the paper and slid it over to him, getting up. "Thanks for breakfast. If you've got the time, there's a nice article on A-12 about special-forces involvement in Korea."

"Don't do this, Atticus."

"You have a good day, Robert."

While I was unlocking my door, the phone in the kitchen started ringing. By the time I was inside and reaching for the receiver, the answering machine had picked up, and when that happened, the caller disconnected. The indicator light was blinking rapidly, and I hit play, listened to the string of messages. Four of them, all from Diana, all wanting me to call her.

As the last message ended, the phone rang again.

"The number you gave me was wrong," Diana said. She didn't say hello. She sounded frustrated.

"Good morning, Diana. I know."

"Where's Erika? I want to talk to my daughter."

"We need to meet," I said.

"You lied to me last night, didn't you?" Diana asked in a hot rush. "You lied to me. Why'd you do that?"

"It's a long story. We meet, we can talk it over."

"I'm at the Bonnaventure," she said. "Registered as Diana Bourne. Come over."

"False name?" I asked.

"Maiden name."

"It'll be at least an hour, maybe more," I told her.

"Just get over here and tell me where my daughter is."

The Bonnaventure is off the Avenue of the Americas, near Rockefeller Plaza. From my apartment, it normally takes upward of fifteen minutes to get to the hotel, closer to thirty if you walk. I took two hours, foot, cab, train, and bus, until I was certain that none of Moore's company was dogging my trail. I didn't know why Moore wanted Diana so badly, but for once I felt I had the advantage, knew something that he didn't, and I wasn't about to blow it.

Big mistake.

It was noon when I reached the house phone and asked the operator for the room of Diana Bourne.

"What the hell kept you?" she asked.

"I wanted to make certain I wasn't followed. You want me to come up?"

"Room eleven thirty-three."

"Be right there."

The snow I'd accumulated on my clothes and in my hair was melting by the time I reached the elevators. The bandage around my splint was soggy, and my broken fingers ached from the cold. My knee was acting up, too, irritated by all the running around I'd been doing. I unzipped my coat, unwrapped my scarf, and, on the eleventh floor, made my way to room 1133. The dark green carpet was spongy and my shoes sank with each step. The hall was empty.

I knocked and Diana said, "Atticus?"

"It's me."

"Come on in."

The room was nice as far as hotels go, and large, with a window that afforded a view of skyscrapers to the west, and then, through the cracks that were the streets, a shiny sliver of the Hudson River. The bathroom was on the left as I came in, a closet on the right, and both doors were shut. Diana stood at the foot of her bed, wearing a black sweater and ocean-blue corduroy pants, no makeup.

I shut the door, then headed into the room, and as I came around the corner of the bathroom, Trouble hit me in the stomach. The strike caught me completely, and I felt my air blow out my mouth and nose, my gorge rise even as he yanked me upright again. There was another one, the man with curly black hair who had driven the gray car. The skin on the right side of his neck was puckered and discolored, like a cancer had grown there once upon a time. As Trouble pulled me up, the other man put two more quick rights into my stomach, then a last left to my jaw.

Then there was disorientation and pain, and I felt hands on me, and heard Diana saying that was enough, that was more than enough, to leave me alone, and I was being dragged to my feet.

Trouble had my gun, and I watched while he worked the slide, ejected each bullet unspent onto the carpet.

When the gun was empty he tossed it at Diana, saying, "Hold on to that."

She caught the pistol, shoved it into the waistband of her pants, and then pulled her pretty sweater down over it.

"Hold him still, Glenn," Trouble said. "He's liable to elbow you something fierce."

Glenn pulled me up a little higher, his grip around my throat tight. I felt my breakfast spasm and try to climb out, but managed to keep it down. Somehow, my glasses had remained on my face.

Diana kept watching all of us, her arms folded across her chest, and her face drawn.

"Where's the girl, then?" Trouble asked me.

I didn't say anything, mostly because I didn't have the air required.

Trouble pointed to his nose. "I owe you for this, see. You tapped me, and I don't like that. You made me lose my knife, and I don't like that either. You slotted one of my boys, and I like that least of all. Now, where's the fucking girl?"

I wanted to sound defiant when I said, "Rot in hell." Instead, I sounded weak and tired.

Trouble looked at Glenn, and Glenn slammed my head against the wall. It hurt. A lot.

"What I will like, though," Trouble informed me, "is beating you bloody."

Clever guy, I thought.

"That's enough, Mark," Diana said.

Trouble looked back at her. "He knows where your kid is."

"Let me talk to him."

"He already lied to you once."

"He didn't know what was going on," Diana told him. "Let me talk to him. Let him go, Glenn."

I couldn't see Glenn's reaction, but Mark—Trouble—gave him a nod, and the pressure around my neck went away, and I tried to keep my feet, and instead fell forward, coughing. The oatmeal came up, too.

"You're not good," Mark told me. "You're not even lucky."

Very clever, I thought.

"Go. Let me talk to him," Diana repeated.

Mark cleared his throat and spat on the back of my head, then said, "Come on." Glenn followed him out the door.

My breath was coming back, now, and with it my orientation, and Diana gave me a hand, helped me up and around onto the far side of the queen-sized bed. Out the window, the city was pewter, snow falling like sugar from a shaker. It still felt as if Glenn had his hand around my throat. Diana went into the bathroom, and I heard her running water. I straightened my spectacles, got myself upright as she returned and handed me a glass.

"I'm sorry about that," Diana said. She went back to the bureau by the television, took my gun from her waistband. She considered what to do with it for a moment, finally dropping it next to the ice bucket.

I drank the water and looked at her. The sour taste melted slightly, but my throat still felt tight. I put the glass on the nightstand. The nightstand had a digital clock on it. Another nightstand, on the other side of the bed, had a telephone.

"They work for me," she said. "I hired them to get Erika away from her father. I guess he hired you to keep me from doing that."

"I guess so."

"He's brainwashed her, Atticus. He's made my own daughter hate me. This was my only choice."

"Bullshit," I said.

"They're rough men."

"Hadn't noticed." My stomach trembled with the water, but didn't rise.

"They were out of line. Sterritt's angry at you. He says you killed one of his partners. Mark gets rougher than the rest," Diana said, as if that would apologize for the beating, explain away the pain.

"You know who they are?" I asked.

Diana nodded.

"You know they're SAS?"

"Former, but yes." She was matter-of-fact about it, as if there was no difference between SAS and PTA.

"These are very bad men, Di. Hard men. These are not men you want near your daughter."

"This is the only option I have left."

I shook my head.

Diana frowned. "I don't like using them. If I had a choice, I wouldn't. But Doug's taken every other option away from me. He's turned my own daughter against me, made her hate me. I can't get close to her. And he's going to keep her until he dies, and that's torture. He hates me so much he's willing to torture Erika. This is the only way I can get her back."

I would have laughed, but didn't trust my stomach enough to try. "How's it going?"

"Poorly. Doug hired you to protect Erika, didn't he?"

I nodded.

"He figured it out, I don't know how, but he figured out that I had hired Sterritt and his people, so he hired you to protect Erika. You see what he's done? Now he's turned us—you and me—against each other. We're fighting each other."

"Maybe," I said. "How many men does Sterritt have?"

"Three others. He had four, but your people killed one of them." Diana pulled an attaché case from the floor and set it on the bureau, opening it. The case was black and elegant, and inside I could see a lot of money. She took a stack of bills and held them for me to see.

"This is ten thousand dollars," Diana said. "Un-marked, untraceable, tax-free legal tender." She dropped the bundle back into the case, but left it open, to make certain I could see.

"A lot of green."

"There's two hundred thousand dollars right here," she said. "I can get you another three hundred thousand in stones, diamonds and emeralds. You can have it all if you take me to my daughter."

"Where'd you get the money?" I asked.

"It's not important."

I looked down the hallway at the door to the room. Sterritt and Glenn were probably standing right outside, listening as best they could. At least two more men were lurking nearby, too. SAS-trained mercenaries. They would be very expensive. Very expensive indeed.

"I'm offering you five hundred thousand dollars, Atticus. It's money for nothing. You don't owe Doug anything. He split us up. It was you and me and Erika, and he destroyed that like he destroyed our marriage."

"If I don't tell you?" I asked. "What then? You hand me back to Sterritt and let him finish his beating?"

"They'll torture you."

"And you'd let them."

"I want my daughter back."

I rubbed my neck, felt the soreness around my Adam's apple. "I don't know where she is," I said.

Diana pushed air through her nose. "Don't lie to me again. You lied to me last night, don't do it again. I don't have time."

"I don't know where she is, Di," I said. "Honest to God. She ran away from me and my people yesterday afternoon."

"I don't believe you."

"Then we have a problem, because they won't either, and I don't fancy getting tortured."

Diana reached into the attaché case and came out this time with a gun. It was a small gun, a holdout weapon, exactly the kind of pistol designed to be concealed in a case full of money.

She pointed the gun at my head.

"Don't do that," I said. It looked like a Beretta. Maybe the Jetfire.

She cocked the gun.

I could feel my pulse throbbing in my broken fingers. "You're going to shoot me?" I asked.

"Atticus, tell me where you're keeping my daughter." She adjusted her grip on the gun, supporting it with both hands. In her fingers it looked ridiculously small.

"You're really going to shoot me, Di?"

"Goddammit, Atticus, you tell me where she is!"

"I don't know."

"Stop fucking lying to me!" She was almost screaming. "Damn you! Damn you, I will shoot you, do you understand? I will shoot you if you don't tell me!"

"I don't know!" I shouted back. "Ask Moore. Maybe he's got her."

That stopped her.

"She ran away from us, Di," I said. "She could be anywhere."

"Moore?" The gun dipped slightly, but not enough to keep me from being hit if she decided to fire.

"Sergeant Robert Moore, of the 22 SAS. Didn't your pal Mark tell you about him? I assumed they were all *mates.*"

"Were you followed here?" she asked. She was very pale.

"I don't know. I don't think so."

"You don't know?"

"Moore and a couple of his men leaned on me at breakfast, wanted to know where you were."

Diana shouted, "Mark!"

The door opened immediately, and Sterritt came in, Glenn right behind him. Both men had their Brownings drawn.

"Moore's here," Diana told them. "He's got men with him."

"Yeah, I know," Sterritt said, eyefucking me all the while. "Knowles and some new brat. Looking for us."

"You *knew*?"

Sterritt nodded. "Figured they followed the paper. It's all right, they're way behind us."

"You idiot," Diana snapped. "Moore had breakfast with him this morning." She used the pistol to indicate me. "He might have been followed."

They didn't like that. "We're fucking leaving now," Sterritt said. "Get the boys."

Glenn went to get the boys.

"You're packed?" Sterritt asked Diana.

"Yes."

"Kill him," Sterritt said.

"What?"

"You have to kill him. He can connect all of us. If he tells Moore or the Feds, it's all over."

"We can take him with us."

Sterritt grinned. "Nah, we can't. Too dangerous, isn't it? We've got to leave him here."

Diana began to shake her head.

"You don't fucking do it, I will," Sterritt said, and he started to bring the Browning in his hand up, and I figured if I was going to die, I'd rather go with my fingers in his skull, and I moved, and then there was the shot, and my legs cut out, as if they no longer existed. I hit the bed, saw the red stain from where my middle had hit the mattress, and then my knees were on the floor. I had swallowed fire, it was living inside me, starting to catch and spread, and I fell back, felt the glass of the window icy cold on my head.

Both of them were looking at me. Mark Sterritt had let his gun drop to his side, and his mouth was wide with a smile.

Diana still had the gun pointed at me.

I tried to say something and it felt as if Glenn had his hands at my throat once more. I tried to move, and my legs just didn't listen.

Diana took three steps to where I was propped against the wall, and with her right foot, she pushed me over, onto my back, and I was lying between the bed and the window, and I thought it was a strange grave.

"Good," I heard Sterritt saying. "Put one in his head and make damn sure."

She stepped in beside me and looked down, and her eyes were empty and far away. Her hair fell along her face, a light brown with yellow. It made her seem far away, too. Diana raised the gun once more, in both hands, and the barrel was over my right eye.

"Don't," I said.

Then she pulled the trigger.

CHAPTER EIGHTEEN

I waited, and it was the hardest thing I've ever done, and I don't know how much time I lost, I don't know when the pain made me go away, or when it made me come back.

They're gone now, I thought. Time to get up. Rise and shine.

I took a breath and tried to sit, and the world pirouetted, flipped, and any sense of direction or gravity went with the dance. The fire in my stomach burst into open flame, and I went back hard, gasping for air, suddenly queasy, and managed to turn before I started puking. The heaves were dry, and each one hurt my gut, and when the fit passed, I was fetal on my side, my hands around my abdomen, looking at where the last shot had gone.

The bullet hole in the carpet was neat and small. It didn't look like a hole that size could do much, really. Not much at all.

Except if Diana had put that hole in my head, I wouldn't be around to wonder at it.

Tears had filled my eyes, and I tried to wipe them away, saw my hands wet and red. My shirt and jeans were sodden with blood, and I realized I was lying in it, and that it was my own.

She'd hit once, though. She'd gut-shot me.

My legs hurt, muscle-sore, and now that I remembered, the pain in my abdomen cut loose, rolling free, and I stayed on my side, trying to keep control. My legs were shaking, and I could hear a keening that was either myself or the winter wind.

I hoped to God it was the wind.

I thought I could hear my blood falling.

All those shots. Someone will be here. Someone will come. It's a hotel, after all, and you never can get the privacy you want in a hotel.

I'm losing blood. I'm dying, here.

Moore's on his way. He'll find me. He and smiling young Trooper Denny and old Trooper Knowles, they'll find me.

Dead.

How professional of me. How honorable, how loyal. Yeah, I'm a fucking sterling troop, that's me. I'm doing what soldiers have always been trained to do. I'm dying.

The nightstand was above me, dark wood with shiny handles and a lamp on high that shone too bright. I reached, and the muscles in my belly tore, and I stopped reaching.

Where was the phone? Which nightstand? This one?

The other one. The one on the other side of the bed.

Might as well be in Tahiti.

I'm bleeding, I thought.

Gut wounds are the worst. You die so slow, you die with a perforated bowel and shit filling your stomach, touring in your blood. For fuck's sake, if she had to shoot me, why couldn't she have done it right? Why couldn't she have shot me through the eye?

Oh.

Right.

For fuck's sake. Jesus, I sound like Bridie, here.

I realized I was talking out loud, and decided that that was good, that meant I was still conscious.

A muscle spasmed in my belly, and I brought my legs in tight, my arms back around, driving my teeth together to stay silent. The muscles stopped, and I relaxed again, wheezing for air.

Male.

Stupid bullshit asshole male.

Go ahead and scream. People will hear.

People will hear you and come.

I think I shouted for help.

I think time passed, and no one came.

Figure only four, five hundred feet to the top of the bed. The bedspread was a washed-out blue with randomly spaced squares of green on it. The pattern stung my eyes. I reached for it with my left, used it to pull myself sitting, making noise as I went up.

Nothing.

Go.

It took both hands and my legs to make it up on the bed, and my broken fingers hardly mattered, because I was crying by that time from the pain in my middle. I made it to the top, twisting as I sprawled across, trying to shield my stomach. Tears had fallen from my eyes onto my glasses, warping my vision.

Go.

Go, dammit. At least don't die on the bed. How will that look?

And then Dale will tell Bridie about Diana, and Bridie will think I was fucking Diana, that I didn't care. Bridie will think that I didn't care, and that I didn't trust her, and that I died that way.

Go for the phone, asshole. It's not that far away.

Nice mattress. Firm. Comfortable.

I'm bleeding all over the bedspread.

That'll never come out. They'll have to bill Di and Mark and Glenn. They'll have to bill Di and Mark and

Glenn and then they'll pay in diamonds and emeralds and other precious stones.

Go. Go go go go don't stop. Don't rest. Go.

It's actually quite nice here, on the bed.

No, it's not nice.

Quit fucking slacking and pull yourself to the other nightstand, and get the damn phone. Go on, get the phone.

Go.

The receiver slipped out of my hand when I pulled it from its cradle. There should have been noise when it banged against the nightstand, when it fell to the floor. I didn't hear any.

Oops.

Dropped it.

Just forget about the receiver for now, no, don't reach for it, don't stretch, you still have to dial. Dial first, then you get the receiver. Dialing first, receiving later.

Go, asshole.

Press zero. The one at the bottom, in the middle. Zero.

Okay.

Now, off the bed. Just roll off the bed.

Right.

Atticus, meet gravity. Gravity, meet Atticus.

Atticus, meet floor.

Go.

Get the receiver.

Go.

Say, "I've been shot and I don't want to die, please. I really don't want to die."

Stop.

CHAPTER NINETEEN

I came up for air to find Detectives Morgan and Hower waiting for me. She came to my side, leaning in. Her features were pleasantly fuzzy and kind, and then she slid my glasses on me, and her expression resolved, and I saw that it was neither of those things. Angry and tired, perhaps; not fuzzy, and most definitely not kind.

"You rotten little shit," Detective Morgan said, by way of greeting. "Ben, he's awake."

Hower looked down on me. "Howdy," he said, drawing it out. "How you doing, cowboy?"

I croaked at them. My throat was stripped raw, and my stomach felt full of broken glass. But all my fingers and toes seemed in place, even the broken ones. I decided I was alive.

"He probably wants water," Hower said. "The anesthetic dries you out."

"That so?" Morgan said, sounding genuinely curious.

"Absolutely. Plus the blood loss, this guy is probably

one desiccated husk of a citizen. That's why he's on two IVs, see, because he's so damn drained."

"Desiccated. That's a nice word."

"Yeah, I like it. It was on my calendar this morning." They both looked down at me some more.

"You should offer him a cup of water, something like that," Hower told Morgan.

"Not my job. Besides, let him desiccate away, I don't give a fuck."

"Yeah, but if you want him to talk, he's going to need some sort of, ah, lubrication for his vocal cords."

"I doubt he's got anything to say."

"Well, you won't know until you ask him."

Morgan considered that, pursing her lips. She leaned in so she was directly over my face, and asked, "You got something to say to us?" Her voice seemed very loud.

I winced.

"See?" Hower said. "Give the poor cowboy some water."

"You do it. I don't want to have to touch him."

Hower buffed his bald spot, then moved to the stand beside the bed, poured water from the supplied pitcher into a plastic cup. Both the cup and the pitcher were an ugly brown. Hower took the cup, helped me sit, and put the drink in my hands. The tubes running from my IVs had been taped to my arms, and my splint had been removed and replaced with a new one, nice and shiny and tight, and it made my left hand all but useless. I had to support the cup from its bottom. There was a tightness in my gut, too, a strange soreness as if I had over-extended my abdominals. I tried a swallow, felt the tepid water slide past a lump in my throat, or maybe it was a grapefruit.

"That better?" Hower asked.

I winced again.

"Thought you said he wanted to talk to us," Morgan said. "He's making faces, Ben. That's not verbal communication."

"You're the one who said he was verbal."

"So I was wrong. Shoot me."

I finished the water, and the grapefruit shrank to an orange. Hower took the cup, and I lay back again.

"Give him a second, Ellen," Hower said.

Ellen Morgan looked at her watch, then down at me. She said, "Okay, talk."

"Fuck you." My voice skidded over sandpaper before coming out.

"I'm going to kill him," Detective Morgan said to Detective Hower. "I'm going to kill him right here."

"Well, see, he's irritable, now. He got shot, after all."

"Oh, that's right. He got shot. I forgot. Funny how that happened, what with him and his friends running through my city, shooting at people in my streets, leaving bodies that have no papers or names for us to find."

I had started to drift during her monologue, but that hooked me and yanked me back. "Bodies?" I croaked.

"Just the one," Hower said. "John Doe, found in the back of a bullet-riddled van near the Riverside Parkway. That's what the papers called it, 'bullet-riddled.' Guy was shot with your buddy's fancy bullets. Those training rounds kill pretty good, don't they?"

"That's all?" I asked, getting anxious.

"Well, there could be more," Morgan said. "We just haven't found them yet."

Not Erika. Not Diana. Not the Colonel.

I closed my eyes.

"Where're you going?" Morgan snarled.

"He's tired. Let him sleep."

"Where am I?" I asked, my eyes still closed.

"Roosevelt," Hower said. "You came out of surgery four hours ago."

"How . . . ?"

"How, what?"

"He wants to know how he got here," Morgan said. "Isn't that right?"

I nodded. At least, I think I nodded.

"Apparently, you called the front desk at the Bonnaventure Hotel and asked for an ambulance."

I didn't remember doing it.

"Who is Diana Bourne?" Morgan asked.

"Her mother," I said. I had to say it twice, because the first time it didn't sound like English.

"Erika's mother?"

"Yes."

"Who shot you, Atticus?" Hower was doing the asking.

"Her mother."

"Erika's mother? The kid's mother?"

"Yes-s-s . . . I think so. . . ."

"Can you give us a description?"

I was fading fast. They had to ask me about her hair color three times, and finally, I felt my glasses being tugged off, and heard Morgan gripe, "Jesus, you're useless. Just heal, would you? We'll be back tomorrow."

I was out again before they left the room.

It was light when I opened my eyes again. An analog clock hung over the door, and it read either shortly after ten or eleven. I couldn't tell without my glasses. I tried to roll and reach for the nightstand, when I heard Bridgett ask, "What are you doing?"

She was seated in the far corner of the room, long legs extended, slouching in her jacket. She pushed herself up using the armrests, saying, "I'll get it. You after water?"

"My glasses," I said.

Bridgett handed my glasses to me, and once I'd taken them, moved her hand, pressing her fingertips against my forearm. It was a light touch, and it seemed to embarrass her, and by the time I'd put my spectacles on my face, she had started for the door.

"I'll call a nurse," she said.

"I think I'm okay."

"Yeah, you're great, but I'll get a nurse anyway."

The door squeaked shut, and I lay on my back, taking inventory. The IV in my left arm had been removed, and the bandage over the incision itched. I thought about scratching it, wondered how Yossi was doing with his stitches. My head felt much clearer, but it seemed there was nothing wrong with lying in bed, admiring the acoustic tile above me, maybe never moving ever again.

It took twelve minutes for Bridgett to return, leading a slender nurse in her fifties who reminded me of my grandmother. The nurse checked my chart while Bridgett went back to the chair in the corner and began popping Life Savers.

"Mr. Kodiak, I'm Renee. How are you feeling?"

"Sore."

Renee the nurse nodded. "Dr. Vollath will be by later on his rounds, and you can talk to him then. How's your head?"

"Sore."

Renee nodded again, apparently pleased by this response. When she checked the stitching in my belly I winced, but got my first look at the wound. The line of sutures was black. Renee checked my eyes, my blood pressure, my pulse, my breathing, and my orientation. After I had told her what year it was and the name of the President, she patted my arm.

"Get your rest." To Bridgett, she said, "Don't tire him out."

"Shucks," Bridgett said dryly, then waited for the door to close. Once it had, she said, "You stupid fucking idiot."

I fumbled around for the controls to the bed, raised myself up so I could get a better look at her. Bridgett had left the chair and was now pushing the curtains away from the window. The curtains were a bleached light blue. I couldn't see the view from the window.

"I'm not certain how to apologize for getting shot," I said. "It wasn't something I meant to do."

"Morgan and Hower, neither of them will tell me what's going on." She was keeping her voice low and level, and I knew her well enough to know she was very angry. "I asked Nat and Dale, and they don't know either. You were supposed to meet them yesterday afternoon, you never showed."

"I was detained."

"Oh, that's funny, that's really very funny," she said, turning to look at me. "Did those SAS fucks do this to you?"

"No . . . I don't think so."

She waited for an explanation.

"I need you to do something for me," I said.

"Who shot you?"

"Erika's mother. Diana."

"When did Diana enter the picture?"

"She was waiting for me when I got back from The Strap, night before last. I went to meet Diana yesterday at the hotel she was staying at, and it all went downhill from there."

"She shot you?"

"Yes."

"What the fuck were you thinking? Why didn't you have backup? Dale, or Natalie? Or, heaven forbid, even me?"

"I didn't think of it."

She snorted.

I went to rub my eyes, hit the lenses with my splint, realized there was no way I could use my left hand for the task, gave it up. "It looks like there are two teams of these SAS guys. One of them is working for Diana. She's paid them to get Erika away from the Colonel. She says her ex-husband has brainwashed their daughter into hating her, and this is the only way to save Erika. She said it was torture to permit Erika to live with the Colonel until he died."

"And hiring killers to kidnap the girl isn't?"

"She wasn't rational."

"No kidding. Two teams?"

"I think Moore's leading one, and the guy who pulled the knife, his name is Sterritt. Mark Sterritt. He's in charge of the other group. Sterritt's working for Diana."

"They're mercenaries? This woman hired mercenaries to grab her own kid?"

"She's got a lot of money, and I don't know how she got it, but she's willing to spend it. She offered me five hundred grand to take her to Erika."

Bridgett came over to the bed, sat on the end. She was careful not to touch me. "Colonel Bad Attitude knew this?"

"I think that's why he hired me."

She snorted. "That whole family needs to be put against a wall and shot."

"Not Erika."

"No, Lolita just needs therapy. A couple decades of it."

"She's a good kid," I said. "She's confused and she's being yanked from all sides. Cut her some slack."

Bridgett started to retort, but instead grabbed for the roll of Life Savers in her pocket. She put a red one in her mouth, and then, after a thought, took a second one, green, off the roll with her fingers and handed it to me.

"I need you to do something for me," I said again.

"Find Lolita?"

"Yes."

"Sort of figured that would be the next move."

"Get Natalie and Dale and everyone, tell them to give you a hand. Moore told me that he didn't want Erika, that he wouldn't hurt her. Even if he is telling the truth, if Sterritt and Diana get to Erika first, we'll probably never see her again. We need to find her."

Bridgett moved the red Life Saver around with her tongue, and I could see the shape pressed against her lips, then cheek. "All right. They're pretty steamed at you, too, you know. Natalie went ballistic."

"Probably angry she didn't get to do it herself," I said.

"Knock it off," Bridgett said. "We'll start searching

the scene tonight. It's going to be impossible to find her."

"Call your friend Elana. Maybe she'll help," I said.

"Maybe I will." Bridgett rose.

"Have fun."

She looked at me, angry, and I saw that I'd spiked a nerve. Before I could apologize, she was out of the room.

I slept until mid-afternoon, only to be awakened by the arrival of Dr. Vollath. He didn't look much older than I, sporting a neatly trimmed black beard that failed to make him look either older or more distinguished. He checked my chart, prodded my belly, listened to my chest, sighed deeply, and then explained why I was the luckiest man in Manhattan.

"You exercise, don't you? Sit-ups, run maybe?"

"Yes."

He nodded. "Saved your life. You were shot with a twenty-five, and it didn't have enough energy to break the muscle wall. If it had penetrated to the bowel we'd have lost you. Even if we hadn't, you'd have been fitted for a colostomy bag."

That was an image I didn't want to pursue. "So when can I go?"

"We want you to stay here another day or two, at least. After that you can go on home, get some rest. You're going to be muscle-sore for a while. If you don't push yourself, you should be fine."

"Can I leave tomorrow?"

"Two days," Dr. Vollath said. "And don't try to figure out how to leave sooner. We don't want any complications. You tear your bowel, you'll be in septic shock before the end of the week."

I promised I'd be a good patient, and Dr. Vollath told me not to lie to him, he knew a good patient when he saw one, and I clearly didn't qualify. He left, saying he'd be back to check on me sometime tomorrow.

Morgan and Hower returned just after dark to have me go over the story once more, and to bring me up to speed. There wasn't a lot to say, really, only that Erika was still missing, and that they had found no signs of her, her mother, or the men who'd worked me over. The detectives took their frustration with them when they went, and left me with my fear.

I tried calling Dale, then Natalie, then Yossi, and then, finally, Bridgett, and not one of them was home. I left messages, and no one called back.

All I could think was that I'd let Erika down, again, that she was gone, either on her own or with her mother. Neither option was good, and neither made it easy to lie still and memorize the holes in the acoustic tile while the night passed.

Once again, Erika was lost.

CHAPTER TWENTY

Neither Renee nor Dr. Vollath liked the fact that I was discharging myself.

"I knew you would do this." Vollath tugged at his beard, saddened by my predictability.

"I didn't want to disappoint you."

"You go easy. Nothing strenuous or you'll tear that wound open again."

"I'm going to go home and sleep," I told him.

"Liar," he said as Renee handed me a pile of forms to sign. When I had finished, Vollath added, "You have any seepage, any infection, you get your fanny back here, pronto."

"Pronto," I repeated. Now he was reminding me of my grandmother.

Renee gave me what was left of my clothes. My pants were intact and clean, having been sent through the hospital wash, but my coat was bloodstained. There was no sign of the shirt I'd been wearing. They'd probably cut it off me when I arrived in the ER.

Getting my shoes on proved difficult, and I took my time with them, bending slowly. My abdomen was tight and sore. I struggled with the shoelaces, too, my splinted fingers getting in the way. It took me twenty minutes to get everything on and tied, and I was zipping up my coat when Bridgett came in, smelling like an ashtray that someone had filled with beer. Her eyes were puffy, and her black hair tangled, and she looked very pale, very tired. She was wearing a T-shirt and leather pants, both in her traditional black, and held her jacket in one hand.

"I'll give you a ride home," she said, then turned on her heel and left the room, returning in under a minute with a wheelchair from the nurse's station.

I got into the chair carefully, and Bridgett pushed me out of the room and down the hall to the elevator. While we waited for the doors to open, she took a stub of mint Life Savers from a coat pocket, crunched down three of them. That was the closest we came to conversation.

When we reached the garage, Bridgett rolled me to the side of the Porsche, took her keys from one of her pockets, and the alarm chirped on the car. I tried to stand, using the Porsche as support, and managed to get upright without undue pain. She returned the wheelchair to a rack by the elevator, and as she came back, I asked, "You get any sleep?"

"No," Bridgett said. She opened my door, then headed for hers while I climbed inside. Getting into the seat wasn't one of my smoother performances, but I was having less pain from the movement than I'd have thought.

She buckled up, started the car, and pulled out. It was snowing again, and the roads were dusted with slush and powder.

"How you doing?" I asked.

"I spent all night looking for your little Lolita in places where questions are unwelcome at best." Bridgett didn't look at me when she answered. "Ten clubs in twelve hours, wading through smoke, sweat, and drama, and I come back here to find you're on your way out the door. How do you think I'm doing? I haven't been home in days, I haven't been to sleep, I feel like shit, and I smell like the bottom of a very sleazy bar."

"I'm sorry."

"I don't want your damn apology. Not for that, at least." She floored the Porsche suddenly, scooting us around a moving van parked on an angle on Forty-second Street. The Porsche slid only slightly, shooting spray away from the sides of the car.

"Elana help you out?" I asked.

"Elana knows what Erika looks like. We don't have a photo of her, remember? Of course she helped me out."

"How are things with her?"

Bridgett stopped hard at a light. "The same. If you're worried about something happening between me and her, you can stop. We broke up."

"So you said."

The light changed, and she shifted up, racing past an NYPD sector car on the right. If she was afraid of getting a ticket, it didn't show. "She was cheating on me."

That muzzled me.

"We'd been going out eight months," Bridgett continued. "I thought we were serious about each other. And then I found out she'd been cheating on me for three of those eight. Maybe even longer. This was shortly after Da died, and I didn't take it well."

"Bridgett," I said. "I'm sorry."

"You and your damn apologies. I don't get involved lightly, do you understand that? Whatever is going on between us, however much of an asshole you've been or I've been, I've made a commitment here, and I'm not planning on bugging out."

My stomach hurt, and it wasn't the stitches, and I didn't open my stupid mouth again until we'd reached my apartment building and Bridgett had pulled the

Porsche into its slot. I watched her hand as she killed the engine, pulling the keys out and then rattling them in her palm.

"What you said yesterday. You're right. I was a stupid fucking idiot," I said.

"You've been that a lot lately."

"I had an affair with her, when I was in the Army. When I was working for her husband."

She used the mirror to look at my face. Her eyes were very blue, waiting.

"Wyatt was cheating on her. Everyone at the Pentagon knew it. It's one of the reasons he never rose past Colonel. The Army likes their officers to be good family folk, and Wyatt didn't even pretend."

"So you figured it was all right to jump on that train?"

"He used to go out, pick up women. I'd try to cover him, and it just wasn't possible. I told him what I thought and he told me to leave him the fuck alone, I was getting in the way of his fun. So I ended up at his house, watching Diana and Erika. That's how it happened."

She kept silent. Nothing changed in her eyes.

"I was twenty-three, twenty-four, and I thought I was in love. After six months Wyatt found out, and I got transferred. Overseas for a while, then to the CID."

"You ever see her again?"

"Four days ago was the first time I'd seen her since then."

She looked away from me, from the mirror, rattling the keys in her palm. "Love."

"At the time."

"When she was at your door the night I introduced you to Elana, did you invite her in?"

"Yes."

"Did you sleep with her?"

"No."

Bridgett looked at the keys in her hand. "So," she said.

"Yeah."

She got out of the car, and after a time, I did, too. She came around to the passenger's side, leaned against the car's body.

"I should have told you about Diana earlier," I said. "I should have told you when Erika first showed up."

"Maybe." Her voice was hard to hear. "I didn't tell you about Elana."

"It's not the same."

"Sure it is. We both have secrets. It's a question of trusting one another enough to share them," Bridgett said. "Let's get you upstairs and back into bed. You shouldn't be up and around yet."

"We need to find Erika."

"We've got nowhere to go until night falls. The clubs are all closed."

"We're past this?" I asked.

She let her breath out in a little hiss. "Do you want to be?"

"Yes."

"Then we're past this. Now you should kiss me."

So I kissed her.

We slept half of the daylight away, wrapped side by side for warmth. I woke twice briefly, each time surprised Bridgett was still beside me, and the second time my fear for Erika was so strong I couldn't get back to sleep. I'd dreamt about her, I realized, and as I worked myself upright and out of bed, pulling my glasses on, I remembered that in my dream, Erika had died.

I had turned on the heat and started making tea when Bridgett emerged from the bedroom. She was in her underwear and T-shirt, and I was about to ask if she was cold, when the intercom buzzed. She was nearer the grille than I, and so she turned and punched the button and asked, "What?"

The Colonel's voice came through the grille, demanding that we let him inside.

_____

"You're supposed to be looking for my daughter, not fucking your whore." Colonel Wyatt pushed past me before I could respond, and that was just as well, because AIDS or no, I believe I would have punched him had he stopped moving.

I shut and locked the front door, followed him into the kitchen where Bridgett was fixing herself a mug of tea at the counter. She had pulled on her leather pants, and the Colonel took a seat at the table, looking her over. "I'll take one of those, sweetheart."

She smiled benignly at him and began fixing another cup of tea while I asked, "Where the hell have you been?"

Colonel Wyatt began unwrapping the scarf from around his neck. "Chicago. Baltimore." He heaped the scarf on the table, still watching Bridgett. "Like I said before, Sergeant, you've got taste."

"He means you," I told Bridgett.

"Go figure," she said, turning to offer me the mug of tea she'd finished preparing. To Wyatt, she said, "I'm looking forward to the day you finally die." Her smile was still in place.

Wyatt searched for a retort, failed, and went to the standard backup. "Fuck you."

Bridgett pouted her lips like a little girl. Then she laughed at him.

Wyatt turned to me and said, "So the bitch shot you." His voice was reedier than before. The wet weather was probably wreaking havoc on his system.

"If you mean Diana, yes."

To Bridgett, he said, "He was fucking my wife. You know that?"

Bridgett nodded.

He looked surprised that I'd ruined his surprise. "Watch yourself. He'll fuck you over, too."

"Why didn't you tell me where you were going?" I asked the Colonel.

"Because I was looking for Diana, dipshit. You're fine?"

"I got lucky."

"Purple Heart." He sounded disgusted.

"Erika's gone," I said. "She ran away."

"I know."

"How?"

"You're a fucking moron, Sergeant. Moore has her. She's all right."

"Moore's working for you?" Bridgett asked.

"With me. He's got his own agenda."

"You should have told me what was going on," I said.

"If I had told you my ex-wife—your ex-fuck—had hired mercs to snatch my daughter, would you have believed me? Until that two-faced cunt tried to cap your ass, you were still in love with her." He turned his head down to the floor and coughed, covering his mouth.

I looked at Bridgett. She was staring at the top of Wyatt's bent head, mouth curled in disgust.

When the fit had passed, the Colonel wiped his hands on his scarf, but said nothing.

"I want an explanation," I said.

"Of what, Sergeant?"

"Diana shouldn't be hiring mercs, Colonel. She shouldn't know how to contact them, let alone afford them. There's an SAS brick running around downtown, and it looks like you and Diana are right in the middle of it. What's really going on here?"

He rasped air. "What makes you think I know?"

Bridgett laughed curtly. "You are *such* an asshole."

Wyatt stabbed a finger at Bridgett. "She doesn't need to hear this."

"Yes, she does," I said.

Bridgett leaned back against the counter and looked satisfied.

He scratched at the corner of his mouth with a fingernail, deciding. Then he grunted. "Maybe five years before you came on at the Pentagon, I put together an intelligence op with some boys from the SAS. Moore was one of them. This was just after I'd started as the PAOFET—"

"PAOFET?" Bridgett asked.

"President's Advisor on Far East Terrorism," Wyatt and I said at once.

"Ah."

"Can I continue?" Wyatt asked her.

"If you've got the air, be my guest."

The Colonel grunted again, eyes cold. "There was a need to gather hard intelligence on terrorist groups in the Far East. You know how terrorists are, they'll sell their own dicks if the price is right. So Moore and his brick handled recruitment, located contacts, offered them pretty paychecks and whatever goodies got them all hard, then brought them in and baby-sat during debriefing. All the contacts had to do was provide good intel."

Wyatt had been PAOFET for several years before I'd arrived at the Pentagon to protect him. That dated him to the early eighties, after the failed attempt by Detachment Delta to rescue the hostages in Iran. One of the things that failure had created was a military within the military, an environment where Oliver North could exist, and where soldiers could take actions that the public, and the Congress, never even heard whispered about.

"Superblack," I said.

"Of course. Off the books. Entirely unauthorized. No oversight committees, no receipts. No paper at all."

"Illegal."

He held out his right hand, tilted it from side to side as if balancing scales. "It was off the books. We were acting in the country's best interest."

"How in heaven's sweet name can you say that if the country didn't know about it?" Bridgett asked.

He shot her a look that said women should be seen and never heard. "You don't understand."

"I don't understand that arrogance," she agreed. "So clearly, I don't understand you."

"Is she going to shut up?" Wyatt asked me.

"Where'd you get the funding?" I asked him.

"Wherever we could, through a slush fund. Standard skimming, you know. It was an expensive op. We were handing out six, seven million dollars a year for a while. Not just cash. Some of these guys got paid in dope, weapons, cars. Whatever. You following?"

"Jesus," Bridgett muttered. The disgust was rolling off her like waves.

"I'm following," I told the Colonel. I was, too, and beginning to get nervous at the thought of where this road was going.

"Set all this up in the States, you understand. We couldn't keep the money and dope in a bank, and besides, we needed safe houses for debriefing, and so on. The SAS didn't have anybody they were willing to use at the start. They wanted to keep it as quiet as we did, and they didn't want to get hit by the shit if it went wrong. But I knew it wouldn't go wrong, you see?"

It was like being shot again, and Bridgett hit it as I did, and she said, "You used your wife?"

The Colonel cracked a smile that gave us both a good look at the thrush on his teeth and tongue. "Think about it. I was a full bird. I couldn't be seen hopping around, flying here and there, signing leases and contracts under false names. Would have been fucking unbecoming of an officer. But Diana was high speed."

"You used your own wife to set up a superblack intelligence operation," I said.

"Yeah." He was smug, either with the memory of his brilliance, or with our reactions. Probably with both. "She had travel clearance, could go anywhere, no questions asked, or, at least, no questions asked that couldn't be reasonably answered. Erika was a kid. All Diana had to do was leave her with a sitter and take the next flight to Switzerland. It took some work, but between Moore and myself, we turned her into a pretty fine spook. She couriered for us, messages and merchandise, set up the safe houses. We had places all along the Eastern Seaboard. There was a great place in Providence, right on the water. Always impressed the ladies."

Bridgett muttered something I didn't catch, and Wyatt's smile grew.

"She set up your cache?" I asked.

"We had a place in Baltimore that we used," Wyatt confirmed. "One of those high-tech operations where the storage rooms move around underground."

"Diana knew where your slush fund was?" Bridgett asked.

Colonel Wyatt nodded.

"And that's why you were in Baltimore," I said. "To check on the cache."

The Colonel nodded again.

"And?"

"I'll get to it. Thing is, by the time you came on board, Sergeant, the operation had been running nice and smooth for a while. We weren't using Diana anymore. We didn't need her. So we cut her out."

I thought about Diana, at their home in Gaithersburg, alone while an eleven-year-old Erika was at school, while her husband was at the Pentagon. How had she felt knowing that the Colonel was bedding yet another nameless woman in an apartment that Diana herself had rented? Knowing she had been a convenient tool, nothing more.

"Then we had a change of presidents," Wyatt went on. "New administration, new agenda, and we shut the whole thing down."

"But you kept the money," Bridgett said, and she made certain the Colonel heard the contempt in her voice.

"What the fuck was I supposed to do with it? Give it back? Nobody fucking even knew it was gone. I figured to hold on to it, and when I got sick, I used it to buy the house. The rest is for Erika, to make sure she goes to college, gets the life she deserves.''

It was clear, finally, the lies all falling away at last to reveal a tiny truth, hard and sharp.

"How much did she take?" I asked.

"Two million in cash," the Colonel said. "Another four million in gold and platinum. Left the dope and guns.''

"Any gems?"

"No. You take a loss on the exchange. We stuck with metals.''

"You're certain?"

"It was my fucking cache, of course I'm fucking certain. We never used stones. Why?"

"Curiosity," I said. She'd offered me gems, and showed me cash, and that meant either Diana had lied or she was converting the metal for transport. Even at roughly four hundred dollars an ounce, four million dollars in gold would be too heavy to move quickly or easily. "Does Moore know about the money?" I asked.

"Moore doesn't care. That's not why he's here. He's after Sterritt and the rest of those fucks. They were all the same brick, you see? Moore was Sterritt's sergeant.''

"And that's how Diana knows Sterritt."

"Right.''

"So Sterritt knows about the six million?"

"Probably.''

"Why didn't you move it?" Bridgett asked.

Wyatt coughed instead of answering. This was a rough bout, and it made me remember Diana asking how long I thought her husband had left. Less than before, time forfeited by trips to Chicago and Baltimore, by coming here now.

"When your wife left, why didn't you empty the cache out, find a new location?"

"I made a mistake," the Colonel finally admitted. "I never figured she'd go there. I'd convinced myself that she'd forgotten she was ever part of the op.''

Bridgett rolled her eyes at me, reeling from the Colonel's arrogance.

"Bit me in the ass. She's got me, now."

We went into silence, thinking. I thought about how Wyatt had destroyed Diana. I thought about how she knew where to get the money to fund her revenge. I heard a television snap on in the apartment below mine, the rumble of reproduced voices. "Why are you telling me this now?" I asked.

"I want you and your people to take over my daughter's protection," the Colonel said. "Free Moore up to resume his hunt."

"What about your wife?"

"I don't give a flying fuck about my wife."

Liar, I thought. "Have you explained this to Erika? That her mother has hired mercenaries to kidnap her?"

"No."

"Not at all?"

"Moore explained the situation to her."

"Jesus," I said, feeling disgusted.

"Will you do it?" the Colonel asked.

Something ugly reared inside me, opening its eyes. "You haven't thought about your daughter once in all of this, have you? Not once. You haven't stopped to consider Erika."

Wyatt began to growl a response, then choked. His face stayed bone-white, and he lurched from the chair, spat into the sink. Bridgett moved to one side, never taking her eyes from him.

"It's like it was in Gaithersburg," I said. "You and Diana still slicing pieces out of one another. Still using Erika as the sharp edge."

"No, not anymore," the Colonel said. "Not anymore. I've changed. That's what Di's trying to do, but it's not my game."

"Bullshit," I said.

He faced me, made certain I was looking in his eyes. "I was a rotten father, I admit that, but I've changed, Sergeant. My time's running out. I'm doing all this for

Erika, don't you see? The money was always for her, all of this is for her. I can't let her go with her mother."

"Hey, dumbfuck," Bridgett said. "You're dying, remember? What happens after you croak? What does your daughter do then? What if she wants to go with her mother then?"

"Then that's her choice. I just hope she'll choose better." The Colonel's voice was sour. "All that bitch had to do was wait, a year at the most, and Diana could have had Erika all to herself. But instead she does this, she buys mercs and fucking declares war. Well, I'm not going down without a fight."

The Battle for Erika. Not something they teach at West Point.

"You've got the whole story, now," Wyatt said, when I stayed silent. "Will you protect my daughter, let Moore take Sterritt down?"

I wished I could actually think about what he was asking me to do, that I could justify deliberating. But there was no decision to make, really. It didn't matter if the Colonel was telling me the truth, if I could trust him, if he had changed, if he did this for his daughter or for himself. At the core, I didn't care what he wanted, what Moore wanted. And what Diana wanted had nearly killed me.

"Where's Erika?" I asked.

Wyatt went back to the table for his scarf, saying, "Get your coat. I'll take you to her."

"No," I said. "You're going home. Give me the address and a phone number, I'll call Moore and tell him I'm coming over with my people, but you're going to stay the hell out of the way."

"I'm involved in this, Sergeant."

"You show up at the safe house, I'll have one of my people carry you all the way back to Garrison if I have to," I told him. "You're going to stay out of my way."

He stood by the table, holding his scarf, glaring at me. Then he reached into his pocket and pulled out a folded square of paper, which he threw on the table. "She's my wife. You can't cut me out."

"She *was* your wife. And I can and I will. You're sick, Colonel."

"Of course I'm sick. What sort of shithead observation is that?"

"We'll notify you if anything happens," I said.

Colonel Wyatt wheezed into his hands, his skin going papery. "I know what I'm doing, Sergeant."

"So do I," I said. "You're trying to get yourself killed, but you're not willing to take the responsibility for it. You never took responsibility for your actions. You're hoping the weather or maybe Sterritt will do it for you. You go home, or I won't take the job."

Color began to leach into the Colonel's cheeks, and he drew one ragged breath after another while we stood face-to-face and Bridgett watched. And then the Colonel shoved past me, to the door, and I watched him snap the locks back, yank on the handle. He stormed to the stairs, and I could hear his coughs echo down the hall as he disappeared.

Bridgett said, "You know he won't go home."

"I know," I said, and went to the phone to make the calls that would tell Natalie, Dale, and Yossi that we were back in business.

CHAPTER TWENTY-ONE

The safe house was off Christopher Street in the Village, a quiet block with quiet homes. Bridgett parked the Porsche around the corner, and together we walked back, each of us carrying one of the bags Erika had left at my apartment. It was shortly after three, and the snow that was falling was thin and light, abused by the wind, and hard to see in the fading light.

A short set of concrete steps led to the front door, a hardwood monster with a spyhole set high in its center. Windows onto the street were positioned on the left and right, the curtains drawn. The house looked empty.

"We the first to show?" Bridgett asked me.

"Dale and Natalie should've arrived here an hour ago." I'd reached each of them immediately after the Colonel had left my apartment, my calls dragging them from their rest. I'd told them where to go and who to see, asked them to contact Yossi and Corry. Then I'd called Moore.

"I'm coming in to take over the security," I told him.

"About bloody time," he said. "Don't be followed."

I'd taken the admonition to heart. Of all the people involved, I was the one most likely to be tailed. If there was any way to possibly help it, I wasn't going to be the man to lead Sterritt to Erika. Bridgett and I had left my apartment separately, I on foot and she in her car, each of us heading in our different directions, and after an hour we'd met up outside the main branch of the public library. We'd been clean then, but spent another thirty minutes making certain before coming the rest of the way to Christopher Street.

I rang the bell, and after he was certain it was me, Corry unlocked the door and let me inside. Dale stood at the far end of the hall, his weapon out, and he holstered it with a goofy grin, as if apologizing for being careful.

"Who's here?" I asked him.

"All of us but Yossi," Corry answered without looking away from the street.

"Moore?"

"He went out after we got here, to join the others. On the hunt." He shrugged.

"Where's Erika?"

"She's in her room," Dale said. "Napping. Nat's watching the door. I get the impression the kid hasn't been getting a lot of sleep."

"Show me around, then," I said.

Dale walked Bridgett and me through the house. Someone had done a good job of locking the place down, and the space was secure, although not a fortress. The furniture was mixed, with a butler's table that looked authentically antique, and a fair number of what could only be described as disposable pieces put together with a screwdriver and some white glue. The walls had movie posters tacked up, B films I'd never heard of, and, inexplicably, a poster from the last Cézanne exhibit at the Met. In the living room, someone had hung a picture of the centerfold from this year's *Sports Illustrated* swimsuit issue.

"That's lovely," Bridgett said, not meaning it.

"It was here when we arrived," Dale said. "One of Moore's boys must've put it up."

"Moore picked the place?" I asked, dropping Erika's bag on the couch. The room smelled of Chinese food and cigarettes. The ashtray on the coffee table had several butts in it, Dunhills.

"Through a rental agency, yeah," Dale confirmed. "He assured me there's no paper trail for the Bad Men to follow."

Bridgett took the pinup off the wall, and looked around. Not finding a trash can, she dropped it on the floor and nudged it under the couch with her toe.

"What does Nat think?" I asked.

"She likes it for the most part," Dale answered. "Thinks that the street's too quiet, and I agree with her there, but otherwise, we've got a nice view on all sides."

"Did Moore say when they'd be back?"

"Sometime tonight, depending." He showed us into the kitchen, offered us coffee. We each took a mug, and he said, "I'll go relieve Natalie and you guys can brief."

"I'll go," Bridgett said. "After all, you three are the security pros. I'm just a lowly P.I."

Dale shrugged and looked at me and I said, "Don't antagonize Erika. She's having a rough time."

"I'll be Emily Post," Bridgett told me.

I tried my coffee and wished I hadn't. It was industrial stuff, and I figured it had been sitting on the burner for most of the day. I dumped the mug down the drain and turned off the pot, began cleaning it out. "Has Erika said anything about her mother and father?" I asked Dale.

"Nothing at all. She doesn't know that Mrs. Wyatt shot you, either, FYI." He smiled softly. "We didn't want to scare her any more than she already is."

"When's Yossi coming in?"

"He was working at Sentinel today. Figure he'll be

here by six tonight. Natalie wants to send Corry home when Yossi comes on post."

"How's he working out?"

"Corry? He knows his stuff. Young, though."

"Pedigree?"

"Sentinel. Been with them about a year."

"One of Trent's," I said.

"One of Trent's what?" Natalie asked, coming into the room.

"We're talking about Corry," I said.

"Is there a problem?"

"I don't think so," Dale replied.

Natalie looked at me.

"I just asked how he's working out," I said.

"He knows his stuff. Dad trained him."

"Then there's no problem. Let's brief."

Dale propped himself against the wall by the oven, and Natalie remained standing, and we spent the next half hour talking about the situation as we knew it. Bridgett had relayed most of the information about the shooting already, and between what Wyatt had told me, and what Moore had told them, the picture was now pretty complete. Neither Natalie nor Dale had anything to say about my getting shot.

"Do you believe him?" Natalie asked me when I was done.

"Wyatt? I'm not sure. The superblack story is all too possible, and it does explain Diana's connection to Sterritt, Moore, and the money."

"But you don't believe Wyatt?"

"I think Wyatt's got his own agenda, and I'm afraid his daughter is incidental to it, at best."

"Special Agent Dude?" Dale suggested. He meant Scott Fowler.

Natalie almost smiled, then caught herself.

"Yeah," I said. "I'm thinking I'll reach out to him today, see what he thinks."

"You think Moore's going to be happy you're contacting the FBI?" Natalie asked.

"No," I said. "Neither will Wyatt."

"So you're going behind their backs."

"Our concern is Erika's safety. Everyone and everything else can go screw."

Natalie folded her arms across her chest, and considered before asking, "When?"

"I'll call Scott when we're done, see if he'll meet with me," I said. "How are we here?"

"Fine. I don't want to go lower than three guards at any time, though."

"I agree. Dale said you wanted to send Corry home?"

"He was up all last night, like the rest of us," Natalie said, "looking for Erika."

"When Erika wakes up, he can go."

"She's up already. She was getting into the shower when Bridgett relieved me."

"Then let Corry walk, have him back by ten tonight. That way one of you can get some sleep."

"I'll stay," Natalie said.

Dale shrugged. "No skin off my nose. I like sleep."

"There's one last thing," I said. "I need a gun."

They both looked at me as if I'd said I needed clean underwear. Dale asked, "What happened to yours?"

"I lost my backup when I got shot," I said.

"Any flavor in particular?"

"What have we got?"

Dale looked over at Natalie, and she pushed hair back behind her shoulders, sighing. "There's a Smith & Wesson in my bag," she said.

"Be right back," Dale said, and went to fetch the gun. When he went through the door back to the living room, I heard a snatch of voices, probably the television.

Natalie said, "Don't worry about Corry."

"I'm not. If you say he's good, he's good."

She pushed off from the counter, where she had been resting, and her expression was flat. "He is."

"I trust you."

Natalie thought that over, then headed out the door, saying, "I'll tell Corry he's free."

I made a fresh pot of coffee, thinking that while the stuff may be the water of life for the protective effort, Natalie ought to cut down a little. I trusted her absolutely. If she didn't believe me when I said as much, there was nothing I could do about it.

When the coffee began dripping, I made a call to the FBI offices in Manhattan, asking for Special Agent Fowler. I was told Fowler was out of the office for the day, but I could leave a message. I did so, asking that he call me as soon as he got a chance.

Erika was on the couch in the living room, her legs tucked beneath her, her backpack in her lap. Dale sat beside her, clicking bullets into a clip. Bridgett had pulled one of the chairs from the dining table by the far wall and was straddling it, watching both of them. The television against the wall had been tuned to a shopping network, and a middle-aged man was hawking food dehydrators from the screen. Erika looked fine, clean and healthy, wearing blue jeans and my sweatshirt. She finally looked her age, too; just a kid watching TV.

She saw me enter and knocked the backpack off her lap, hitting Dale with it, then popped off the couch as if she'd been sitting on springs. She didn't say anything at first, just came straight to me and then stopped short. She put her right hand out to touch me.

"You're okay?" she asked.

I looked over her to Bridgett, wondering if she had spilled the beans, and she made a slight shake of her head. "I'm all right," I told Erika.

"I was scared stiff about you."

"Is that why you ran from Natalie's place?"

That earned a nod.

"You scared us pretty good," I said.

"You fucking scared me first! I thought you were going to die, Atticus. And then Yossi got shot, and you were both in the car, and then . . ." She shook her head. "You scared me first."

"I know."

"Well, that's why I ran, okay?"

"How'd you find Moore?"

Erika went back to the couch slowly, tugging the sleeves of the sweatshirt down into her palms and balling her fists. "He told me something might happen, that these men were going to try to get me, maybe, and I thought he was just trying to scare me. He gave me a number and told me to call him if I got in trouble. So I called him after I left Natalie's apartment."

"When did you talk to him?"

Her look clearly questioned my intelligence. "They gave me a ride that day," Erika said. "You know? The day you were at the house when I got home?"

Dale slipped the full clip into the pistol on the coffee table, then held the loaded weapon out for me. I took it, put it into my holster. It was a double-action semi, no safety, just point and shoot. I wondered briefly how long I'd be able to hold on to this one.

"They're going to try for me again, aren't they?" Erika asked, watching me stow the gun.

"Maybe," Bridgett said.

"You're a rotten liar," Erika told her without turning her head. To me, she repeated, "They're going to try again."

"Yes," I said.

Erika sank back against the cushions of the couch, stared at the television screen, and didn't say anything more.

CHAPTER TWENTY-TWO

Yossi arrived at half past six. Bridgett headed home for a shower and a change of clothes, saying she'd be back by eight. Erika watched her departure closely, and I couldn't read her expression. As far as I'd observed, they'd had nothing to say to each other.

Neither Moore nor his men returned, and at seven I cut Dale loose, standing post by the door with Yossi while Natalie and Erika played Scrabble in the living room. We checked the windows, trying to stay aware of what was happening beyond our four walls. The stitches on Yossi's forehead had been cleaned up, and the line looked neat, the skin pink and healthy. I showed him my scar.

"Mine's better," he told me.

"Everything's a competition with you."

"I'm just saying, mine's better."

From the living room came the sound of something clattering onto the floor. Erika shouted, "Quit it!"

I told Yossi to stay put and went to find Erika on the

couch, knees drawn to her chest, Natalie in the chair opposite her looking stunned. The Scrabble board was facedown on the floor, tiles scattered as far as the wall.

"You're cheating," Erika said. Her breathing was fast, and she looked at Natalie as if she hated her.

"I'm not—"

"You're throwing the fucking game, you're fucking cheating. I don't want to play if you're going to fucking cheat."

Natalie looked at me, shaking her head slightly.

"Stand with Yossi," I told her.

Natalie left the room. Erika didn't move.

I waited a couple of seconds, then picked up the board and began collecting tiles. "What happened?"

"She was cheating. She was letting me win."

"How do you know?"

"She played 'tomb' and then she played 'tone' and there was only one square between them, and it was a triple-word-score."

"Were they legal?"

"Of course they were legal! But she knew I had an 's,' okay? She knew I had it and she set it up anyway!"

I dropped a handful of tiles into the draw bag. "Maybe she didn't realize what she'd given you."

"She knew."

I pulled the drawstring and shut the bag, then sat in the chair Natalie had used.

"I'm not stupid," Erika said through a clenched jaw. "I know what's going on."

"No, you're not stupid."

"Mom hired those men," Erika declared. "Because she wants me back."

"Yes."

"It's the same thing, see? Like I don't have a choice, like I can't make a decision on my own, like I don't *know*. It's the same thing as trying to make me spell 'tombstone,' like I can't handle myself, make my own fucking moves."

"It would have been a nice play," I said.

Erika swore.

"You don't want to go with your mother?" I asked.

"Do you?"

"No."

"Even if she wanted you back?"

"No," I said.

"Not even if she said she still loved you?"

"No."

Erika was silent.

Bridgett returned at seven after eight with a case of soda and six sandwiches from the deli near her place.

"Hey, slut," Erika said when Bridgett came in.

I tensed.

"Hey, brat," Bridgett responded.

Erika smiled, and it occurred to me then that neither of them meant what they had just said. Erika followed Bridgett into the kitchen, and I heard them trading insults, and then I heard them both laugh.

"What just happened?" I asked Natalie.

She answered with a look that said there were mysteries between women I'd never understand.

"You want to head home?" I asked her.

"I can stay," she replied.

"How long you been awake?"

"Since yesterday. I'm fine."

Yossi made clucking noises with his tongue. Natalie glared at him.

"I want you to go home," I told her. "Get some rest. Come back tomorrow around ten."

"I can stand."

"I know you can stand, but now's a good time to rest. Go home. Be fresh tomorrow."

Natalie wavered, and I was afraid she'd fight me on this, too, but then she nodded. "I'll be back at eight."

"Fine."

She scribbled Corry's number on a slip of paper, stuck her head into the kitchen to say good night, and then went to the door. Yossi and I covered her exit, waited until she was off the street, and then went back to post. After that, Erika and Bridgett came out of the kitchen, and all of us had sandwiches and soda. I put on more coffee after the meal, and Bridgett left Erika to watch television, following me into the kitchen where we snuck a kiss.

"Been a while since we did that," she said.

"At least ten hours," I said. "What's with you and Erika?"

"We're getting along a little better."

"So I see. Who called the truce?"

"When we got here this morning and I went to watch her room, she started snipping at me, so we had it out. I told her everything I didn't like about her, and she told me everything she didn't like about me. She thinks I'm a poseur, you know that?"

"She'd mentioned something to that effect."

Bridgett took a tin of Altoids out of her pocket, giving the container a shake. The mints rattled against the tin. "I'm a poseur and a fake, and I'm all attitude. The attitude bit I don't dispute." She opened the box and put four or five of the mints into her mouth.

"What'd you say about her?"

"That she was selfish, self-pitying, way too interested in her power as a sexual creature, and that if she was jealous of my relationship with you, too fucking bad, because she's fifteen and I'm not."

"And because of that you two are trading insults like endearments?"

"It's taken her all day to decide, but, what can I say? Honesty is the best policy."

Around nine Bridgett asked if Erika wanted to play Scrabble, and Erika said yes. Corry returned at ten, and we were about to discuss arrangements for the rest of the night when Yossi drew his pistol and said, "Car pulling up. Two exiting, driver still set."

Corry drew and moved without a word to cover at the end of the hall, and I pulled back to find Bridgett putting an arm around Erika.

"Where does she go?" Bridgett asked me.

"The bathroom."

"It's just Sergeant Moore," Erika protested.

I nodded and told Bridgett to take Erika to the bathroom anyway.

Corry was using a corner of the wall as a brace, setting up his shot with both hands, and I went past him, saw Yossi waiting off to the side, near one of the windows looking out. There was a pounding on the door, a clenched fist, rapid. Yossi held up a hand and I nodded, drew my gun, and went to the door, being careful to stay out of the line of sight from the spyhole. Whoever was outside probably couldn't see us inside, but if I blocked the light to the hole, he or she would know where I was standing. All it would take then would be a trigger pull.

The Smith & Wesson felt big, its butt thicker than I was used to. I held it in both hands, my splinted fingers only getting in the way. I really didn't want to have to shoot. Yossi was still watching me, waiting on my signal. Doors are funny things, and people universally treat them the same way. Ask a question from behind a closed one, and the responder will direct their answer straight to it.

"Who is it?" I asked.

"It's Moore, damn you. I've got Denny with me. Open up."

I nodded to Yossi, and he took the glance past the curtains.

"Fucking let us in, we're in a hurry."

Yossi nodded at me, lowered his gun.

I threw the locks back and stepped away, saying, "It's open."

The door swung inside, and Sergeant Robert Moore came in right after it, Trooper Denny on his heels. Outside, I could see the Cherokee parked at the curb, lights off, Knowles waiting behind the wheel. Denny bolted down the hall, ignoring Corry and his weapon. Moore turned to me, his features sharp with excitement. "We found the bastards," he said.

"Where?"

"They're staying at an apartment in TriBeCa, one of those short-term places. We're going to take them down." He said the last with a smile verging on glee.

"You're certain?"

"Wyatt did a recce, says that Diana and—"

I shook my head. "Wyatt?"

"Yeah, I don't know how he did it, but he found them, and gave me a call."

Denny came back, two large duffel bags slung over his shoulders. "All set, boss."

"Put it in the car," Moore told him. "You and Knowles check and load."

Denny nodded, hustled out of the house. He was smiling, too.

"Wyatt still there?"

Moore nodded. "He's sitting on them, making certain they don't take air."

"And Diana's there?"

"They're all fucking there! Sterritt, Perkins, Cox, Hardy, Diana, it's bloody pay dirt, Atticus." He said it impatiently, like I was being thick.

Shit, I thought.

Moore was turning to go, already out the door, and I looked at Yossi, and he just shook his head, because he knew what was going to happen. Moore and Denny and Knowles would infiltrate the building, find the apartment, wait until everyone was in the nest. Then they'd blow the door and go in firing. And they'd kill everyone they found.

Including Diana, and I couldn't let that happen to Erika's mother.

"Call Dale, get him down here," I told Yossi. "Keep Erika secure. Anybody you don't know tries to get in, shoot them."

Then I ran after Moore.

CHAPTER TWENTY-THREE

A film of mucus shone between the Colonel's nose and upper lip, shining in the streetlight. The night turned his pallor cyanotic, and he kept coughing and wheezing to catch his breath. But if his physical condition was sapping him, he was wired emotionally, sitting impatiently in the back of the Cherokee while Knowles, Denny, and Moore quickly set their gear and loaded their weapons.

The apartment building was a big one, thirty floors with a doorman and a manned security desk, both visible when Knowles had made his initial drive-by. A sign over the awning advertised executive suites—a home away from home for weary business travelers. Long-term rates were posted for single, double, and triple occupancy rooms, all expensive. We were parked a block away, in the shadows, but Colonel Wyatt hadn't taken his eyes from the building, proud of himself, still watching the entrance, still bragging.

"I got the bitch. I got her. You asked me if we had

any gems, and the only reason you would've asked me that was if that cunt had some, if she had been selling off the metal. She had to be converting them. I called around. Fucking direct hit with Credit Suisse on Broadway. See, she had to use her name, she had to use her real name so they could cut her the check, and she had to warn them she was coming, or else the exchange would've taken forever. So the stupid cooze told them she was coming, and they told me. Fucking showed up at three with two of the mercs and a fucking hand truck. I followed them from the bank. They thought they were clean."

"Or they made you and are trying to reel us all in," I pointed out.

Moore looked up momentarily from where he was stripping his Browning, and cast a glance at Wyatt.

The Colonel shook his head violently. "The fuck they did. I was careful and I was slow, and they didn't look back once. They split up after the bank, and I stayed on the slut, and she led me right back here. Couple hours later, the other two returned. Nobody's been in or out since."

"How many exits to the building?" I asked.

"Two."

"Then you don't know if they're all in there, you don't even know which floor they're fucking on."

"Twenty-six," the Colonel said immediately. "I saw Diana take the elevator."

Moore had gone back to assembling his gun, and I watched him slip a clip into the Browning and rack the slide.

"You can't be serious about this," I said to him. "You don't even know which apartment you need to hit."

"Fucking pussy," the Colonel told me, wiping his nose.

Moore ignored us both, turning to Knowles. "I'm giving you twenty minutes," he told him. "Set the line cutters to take out the phones and lights at 2340, not a bloody moment before. We'll meet you on twenty-five at 2335."

"They won't even know I was there, boss," Knowles said, and then he and his duffel bag were out of the Cherokee and disappearing into the cold shadows across the street.

Denny was singing softly to himself, contented.

Moore turned in the front seat to face me. "You're going to get us inside," he said.

I said nothing, knowing my silence was saying it all.

"They're rental suites, for businessmen," Moore said. "Turnover has to be high, then, doesn't it? Means the fucking doorman hasn't a fuckin' clue who's supposed to be there and who isn't. But the bloke at the security desk, now he's supposed to know faces, so you're going to lead us in like you belong there, and he'll be a good puppy and not bark."

"You don't need me for that," I said.

"Both Denny and I got the wrong skin color," Moore said. "Security will stop us as a matter of course. We need your white face to do this. Once we're on twenty-five, we'll break out the weapons, get to work."

"Have you not heard a thing I've said?" I asked him. "This is not Prince's Gate. You don't know what apartment they're in, you don't know if they've made the Colonel or not, you don't even know if they're all fucking there, Robert."

"This is not an extraction, this is a hit," Moore said, patiently. "We just find them, point, and go to work."

"You're planning on going room to room?"

Moore smiled wide. "No, I'm planning on watching you use a little social engineering. You're a fucking bodyguard, Atticus, you're a professional sneaky bugger. You'll figure out a way to get the information."

I pushed my glasses back up my nose, knowing that he was right. I could think of at least three ways to get the guy on the security desk talking. It wasn't that hard to do. It didn't matter that I didn't want to do it.

"And we find the room, and you three start killing," I said.

"Right."

"Including Diana?"

Moore hesitated, and in that space the Colonel broke in, saying, "Fucking pussy bullshit limp-dick crapola. Leave him in the fucking car, Robert, I'll get you through the door."

"You're staying here," Moore told Wyatt.

"You can't trust Kodiak. He's still popping chubbies over my wife, you don't want him covering your back."

Moore appraised me for a second, then looked back at the Colonel. "She tried to slot him. I figure that pretty much ended the relationship."

"I need to be there," the Colonel wheezed, angry and choking up.

"You'll fucking wait in the car," Moore bellowed, and I suddenly knew how he must've sounded while training his troops. "You're sick, you're slow, and you're bloody useless to us. If I had my way, I wouldn't use either of you, you're both fucking sub-par. But I need Atticus to get inside, and he's coming with us."

"You can't trust him," Wyatt insisted.

Moore looked at me when he answered. "Yes, I can. I figure he doesn't want to get shot again."

It was depressingly easy to get into the building, as Moore had predicted. We left an angry Wyatt in the Cherokee, hailed a cab, and had it take us around the block and drop us in front of the building. The trip cost twenty dollars, and the cabby thought twenty was more than enough to make up for any weirdness in our request. The doorman looked us all over as we got out, me leading, Moore carrying the duffel bag right behind me, Denny at his side.

Before we were all out of the cab, the doorman had opened the doors for us, and the three of us walked into a large open foyer with linoleum on the floor that was supposed to look like marble. In the center of the foyer was the security desk, a black plastic crescent shape with its points directed to the back of the space, at the elevators. The man behind the console was maybe in his early twenties, wearing a navy blazer with the building's logo over his heart. As we approached I could see the telephones and monitors mounted on the console, but the guard hadn't been paying attention to those; he'd been watching one of the late night talk shows on a small portable television.

He saw us enter, though, and I headed his way before he could rise.

"Excuse—"

"Jesus, I was so hammered last night," I told him. "I don't even remember—" and I turned my head to Moore and said, "Bobby, who the hell did those guys work for?"

"London CompCom," Moore said, and he pushed his accent, and he didn't miss a beat.

"Oh, yeah, the Brits," the guard told me. "They're in twenty-six oh-eight."

"Thanks." I slowed down to let Denny and Moore pass me on the way to the elevator, then leaned in to the guard and gave him my best virile male smile. "You know that babe last night?"

His eyes flickered, desperate for a memory.

"Did her."

"Yeah, she was sweet," the guard agreed.

There were two cars for the elevator, and one of them had been parked on the ground floor, because the door was opening as I joined Moore and Denny. We got into the car, and Moore hit the button for 26, then for 25. The doors slid shut.

"Brilliant," Moore said, patting me on the back.

Denny, who had yet to stop singing to himself, raised the volume a bit, and gave me a wink. I could finally make out the lyrics. He was singing "Born in the USA."

"This is not going to work," I said.

"Sure it will," Moore soothed, checking his watch. "We've got eight minutes, still."

The car stopped, and the doors whispered open.

"Hold the car," Moore told Denny, and stepped out onto the hall carpet. It was wall-to-wall, light blue with red checks. Denny reached for the DOOR OPEN button and held it down, and we waited. I wondered if the guard downstairs was watching the elevators, if he'd noticed we were on the wrong floor. It didn't matter; even if he did spot the discrepancy, he'd just think we'd hit the wrong button by mistake.

Moore was back in ten seconds, saying, "Okay, we get out here." He pulled the duffel bag halfway out into the hall, so it would block the elevator doors, then moved aside to let us out.

The hall was quiet, and wide enough for the three of us to stand abreast if we wanted to. The door to the stairs was marked with an EXIT sign and emergency lights, and on the wall beside it was a fire alarm and extinguisher. There were eight other doors on the hall, leading to different apartments, and it took a moment for my ears to make out the muted sounds of a stereo playing in one of the nearby rooms.

Denny unzipped the duffel and both men removed their jackets, then began grabbing gear. Moore told Denny, "The stairway doors are all one way, so we'll have to ride the elevator up to 26."

Denny nodded, producing one HK MP5 from the duffel bag. He checked the weapon quickly, slapped the bolt down, and slung it over his shoulder. "Does he get one?" he asked Moore. He didn't look at me. I might have been part of the wall-to-wall carpet.

Moore nodded. Denny removed a second machine gun from the bag, handed it to me. It was an identical model, banana clip already in place, with a second clip inverted and duct-taped to the first to make for a faster reload.

"Robert, I can't let you kill Diana," I said.

He didn't look up from where he was busying himself

with the duffel bag. "Jesus, don't tell me the Colonel was right. You're not still harboring hopes of dipping your wick, are you?"

"The only hope I'm harboring is for Erika. I can't let you murder her mother."

Moore straightened up, adjusting the MP5 on his shoulder. He checked his watch, then jerked his thumb toward the door to the stairway. Denny went wordlessly, I assumed to wait for Knowles.

"Listen to me, Atticus," Moore said. "If the woman's in the way when the bullets start, I'm sorry, too fucking bad, it's the price she pays for picking the wrong team. I'm here to do a job, and I'm going to bloody well do it."

"I can't let you—"

His hands came up fast and grabbed my jacket, and then I was being pinned against the wall. His voice was steady, and the hint of the smile had returned. He said, "Yes you can let me, because you've only got two choices. Either I trust you to cover our asses and not fucking interfere, or I put a bullet in you here and now. Makes no difference to me either way, lad. No difference at all. Understand?"

Denny was opening the door to the stairway, and I could just make out Knowles as he emerged. Denny closed the door carefully, and together the two of them trotted lightly down the hall to us. They made no noise as they came.

"You understand?" Moore repeated.

I nodded.

He made a clicking noise with his tongue and released me. Denny handed me a gas mask.

"You may need it, Sarge," he said. "The wankers'll pop the CS if we give them the chance."

"Thanks," I muttered.

Denny resumed singing. Knowles was telling Moore something about the cutters, that they'd be going off in four minutes. "I set two on each line," Knowles said. "Just in case one of them misfires."

"That's my boy," Moore said. "Let's get to work."

We all got into the elevator and Denny pulled the duffel back into the car, pressed the still-illuminated twenty-six, and the doors slid shut.

We're four men standing in a Manhattan elevator with machine guns and gas masks, I thought. Ding. Twenty-fifth floor, guns, ammo, SAS. Ding. Twenty-sixth floor, mayhem, blood, murder.

Everybody out.

Moore turned to me after the doors opened, saying, "Take the bag, put it against the wall. When we go in, if any of them make it past us, I expect you to take care of it."

The layout was identical to 25, with 2608 at the opposite end of the hall from the stairway. I dropped the duffel against the wall between the elevator doors. Denny tapped my shoulder and motioned me to pull my mask down, and as I did, I saw the up arrow mounted on the wall for the second car light up, and I pointed. All three men dropped into a crouch, pulling their masks into place and unslinging their weapons, moving to surround the door when it opened.

There was another soft ding as the car arrived, and I thought, oh fuck, it's one of them, it's Sterritt or Hardy or whoever, come back from searching for Erika. They're doing what we were doing, they're hitting the clubs, they're working at night.

Then I saw the gun, the cocked and locked Colt, and I knew it was the Colonel.

CHAPTER TWENTY-FOUR

"Get the fuck out of here," Moore hissed at the Colonel. Through the mask, his whisper sounded ethereal and frightening.

"Go screw yourself," the Colonel spat back. "I'm part of this action, I'm involved, and I'm going to be here to see it through. You wouldn't be here if it wasn't for me."

Moore started to respond, but Knowles caught his eye by tapping his watch. Moore nodded, the mask bobbing strangely.

"I'll hang back," the Colonel said. "You go in, do whatever you need. I'll hang back."

It was too late to get rid of him, I realized. We could put the Colonel back in the elevator, but it wouldn't matter, because when the power went out, he'd be caught between floors. We could try to send him down the stairs, but unless one of us went with him, there was no way to guarantee he wouldn't just double back. His timing couldn't have been worse. Or better.

Moore realized the same thing. "Stay the fuck out of the way," he said.

Wyatt grinned and took up position opposite me, holding his Colt. Moore began leading his men down the hall, again in their crouch.

They were almost at the door when Wyatt started coughing, and I glanced over to see him fighting it, his face white as a bleached bone. Moore, Denny, and Knowles froze.

Room 2608 knows we're here, I thought.

The Colonel swallowed hard, but didn't make any other noise. Trapped in the gas mask, I could hear my own breathing, too loud, feel the way the rubber was sticking to my skin. Sweat had already started down my face, slicking the bridge of my nose.

Great, I thought. My glasses slide down my face and I won't be able to see. I adjusted the MP5, trying to grip it firmly with my good hand, only using my splinted one for support.

They had reached the end of the hall, passing 2606 on their right. Outside the door to 2608, Moore and Denny went to the left of the doorway, Knowles to the right. Moore held up a fist.

And the lights went out, and the whole world went black.

All around us, in all of the apartments, people began to move.

The emergency lights clicked on, dim and ineffective illumination filling the hall, and Moore's fist came down, and Knowles's boot hit the door, and for a moment there was nothing to do but watch and appreciate the beauty of it all. They had rehearsed this entry a thousand times, perhaps a hundred thousand times, and all three of them moved in a special-forces ballet, with each of them knowing their place and their duty, and doing it flawlessly.

Knowles put the sole of his boot just above the doorknob, and the blow shattered the plate, the door snapping back on its hinges with a pop and a crack, the security chain jangling as it broke free from its housing. And even as Knowles was stepping back from his kick, turning again to get out of the doorway, Denny was moving in, slipping low in a crouch across the threshold, crossing from outside on the left to inside on the right, the MP5 steady before him. Before he had come to a stop, Moore followed suit, staying tight on the wall, his left shoulder against the door frame as he swiveled around from the hallway to the apartment.

Cross buttonhook, I thought, very nice, and I waited for Knowles to finish the move by filling the gap, waited for the shooting to begin.

But Wyatt ruined it all, lurching forward before Knowles could move, rushing past the three men and into the darkened apartment, screaming for someone to fucking take a pop at him, for the cunt to give him her best shot.

I was aware of the noise from the apartment, aware that the door to 2606 was opening as I went forward, but I didn't stop and I didn't think. I just sprinted full and jumped for the Colonel, feeling the stitches in my belly pull and tear. He was screaming that his wife was a slut, that she should fucking kill him now, and I got my hands on his shoulders, and I rode him all the way down, hitting furniture, hearing him still shouting, and then hearing gunfire.

The apartment was barely lit and I rolled onto my back, looking for the threat, and saw the shapes of Moore and Knowles diving down for cover in the apartment, and a muzzle flash beyond the doorway coming from the hall. Denny had managed to pivot in cover, and he fired back as a second burst cut loose and I heard Moore swear. Glass above and behind me shattered, and in the emergency lights shining above the door to the stairway, I saw Diana being shoved into the well by Hardy. Sterritt was covering their retreat and I tried to bring my weapon to bear as he fired again, but the Colonel caught my arm, cursing, wheezing, clubbing me with his free hand. I saw Sterritt reach for the fire alarm, tug the bar down, and the klaxons filled the building, painfully loud.

And Sterritt was through the door and they were gone.

CHAPTER TWENTY-FIVE

The building was in mayhem, and that's the only reason we got out without being stopped, arrested, or shot. With the rush of people for the exits, we'd been able to stow the gear back in the duffel bag and join the crowd on our way out. In making good their escape, Sterritt had made it easy on us. Not that any of that mattered to Moore; all he knew was that when we reached the street Sterritt and the rest had gone, and with them, Moore's best chance at bringing them down.

For a second, among the crowd in the lobby, Moore pulled up, saying curtly, "We need to separate."

"I'll stick with you," the Colonel told him.

The rage in his voice was impossible to hide. "You'll fucking not," Moore said. "Terry, take the Colonel to the train, and fucking ride with him all the way fucking home. Make sure he stays there. If he gives you any trouble, blow the slag's bloody kneecaps off."

Terry put a hand on the Colonel's shoulder. "See you tomorrow, then," he told Moore.

We watched them slip into the stream, make for the front door. Denny went next, turning left onto the street. The security guard looked directly at Moore and me as we passed his station, his phone to his ear, and he nodded an acknowledgment to us.

Wonderful night, I had to agree.

We broke track outside, heading away from where the Cherokee had been parked and walking in a five-block loop back to the vehicle. Moore carried the duffel bag with him, and he didn't say a word until we were in sight of the car. Then he stopped short, dropping the duffel bag and grabbing for my jacket to pull me back.

"You didn't fucking tip them off somehow, did you, Atticus?" he asked. His right hand was on his hip, resting on the butt of the Browning.

"How would I have done that, Robert?" I asked.

He searched my eyes. Then he let go of me, let his hand drop from where he wore his gun. "No, you couldn't have done."

"They were adjoining apartments," I said. "There's no way we could have known they had free access to both."

"Better intel."

I didn't say anything to that. None of us had gotten a good look at the space, but the one thing we'd all been able to determine was that 2608 and 2606 were adjoining apartments. The spaces were rented to suits in town on prolonged business, after all, so it was only logical that the layout would be something akin to a hotel's. If we'd taken more time before going in, one of us would have realized that fact.

But we hadn't, and Moore knew that was where we'd stepped wrong; or, rather, that was one of the places we had stepped wrong.

It was five minutes to one when we got back. Dale was on the door, and he let us in with Yossi covering from the far end of the hall. Denny went straight for the room he, Moore, and Knowles had been using for their quarters. Moore and I went into the living room, to find Bridgett and Erika there, facing off over the Scrabble board. Erika was setting down the tiles for "sleazy" with a blank for the "z."

"How'd it go?" Bridgett asked.

I just shook my head while Moore smiled benevolently at Erika, then gave Bridgett a long looking-over. I realized that this was the first time they'd met.

"Sergeant Robert Moore," he told her. "A pleasure."

"SAS?" Bridgett asked sweetly.

No, not tonight, I thought.

"Yes, ma'am."

"Go step on a mine." Bridgett shook the tile bag and offered it to Erika. "Draw."

Moore looked at me, so I said, "This is Bridgett Logan. She's helping us out."

"Logan," Moore said. "Irish?"

"Irish," she said.

"Ah, fuck. It's not true, whatever you've heard."

"What have I heard?"

"All the bullshit about the Regiment slotting their way around Ireland," Moore said, rubbing his eyes. "It's shit, it's just propaganda."

"No kidding?" Bridgett said. "God, I am relieved to hear you say that. So, Gibraltar was just propaganda, too?"

"Gibraltar was unfortunate."

"Loughall?"

"The IRA was trying to blow up a police station," Moore said, and the edge he'd used on Wyatt came back a bit. I wanted to tell him that it wouldn't work on Bridgett, but knew it wouldn't do any good.

Bridgett dropped her smile and said, to me, "The 'Regiment' killed nine people that day. One of them was some poor son of a bitch motorist who just happened to be driving by."

"They had a fucking bulldozer loaded with explosives, darling," Moore said, and I could see Bridgett's shoulders tense at the endearment. "Five hundred fucking pounds, and they slammed it into the RUC station. The plan was to send those constables straight to fucking heaven."

"It was an ambush," Bridgett said, still talking to me. "They evacuated the police station, had forty-some-odd men with guns hiding in the fields. They waited until the bulldozer hit the police station before even moving, and when they did, it was a bloodbath. Ten minutes of shooting everything in sight." When she said "they," it was clear she meant Moore. "Easier to execute those men than to arrest them."

Erika turned her head to Moore, waiting for his response. She was listening closely with a handful of tiles, not certain if she should be alarmed.

"I'll not fucking talk about this," Moore said. "Your kind is all the same. The poor fucking IRA. What about the poor fucking men and women you'd murdered that year, or the years before, or the years since? Or maybe you think the '84 bombing in Brighton was justified politically, or maybe you think mortar attacks on Royal Ulster Constabulary are reasonable? Maybe killing innocent people doesn't bother you at all?"

"Explain to me the difference between what the SAS did in Loughall and what you condemn the IRA for," Bridgett retorted, color climbing her cheeks.

Moore looked at me for help. "Who the fuck is this woman?"

Bridgett said, "Explain to me how death squads are any better than what you're calling terrorism?"

It was as if she'd verbally kicked him between the legs. "There are no death squads!"

Bridgett smiled at him, the face of a murderous angel. Erika quietly began pulling tiles from the letter bag. There was the sound of a car passing on the street, and I heard Yossi telling Dale that everything looked clear.

Moore pivoted with a sharp squeak of his boot and went into the kitchen, shutting the door with a slam that made the Scrabble tiles jump.

"I win," Bridgett told me, pleased with herself.

"Congratulations. Now do me a favor and cut him some slack."

She shook her head. "We can work together, I'll swallow that, but I will not be on the same side as that son of a bitch."

"If you can't get along with him, you're going to have to leave," I said.

The pleasure of victory dissipated some. "I'm not going to kiss up."

"I'm not asking you to kiss up, Bridie. I'm asking you to work together."

Erika had finished placing her tiles in her rack. "I'd like it if you stayed," she said, pushing the bag across the board. "It's your turn."

"Fine," Bridgett said. Whether it was to me or to Erika, I wasn't certain, but I decided to take it as both, and headed into the kitchen after Moore. As I left, I heard Erika asking what exactly Loughall was.

"Loughall is the reason to never trust the SAS," I heard Bridgett say.

Sergeant Moore had opened himself a beer and was drinking it while looking in the sink. The sink, as far as I could tell, was empty. Moore had removed his anorak and bundled it onto the counter. Gun and knife were still in place.

"Fucking bitch," he said to me.

"I think of her as spirited."

"It's bullshit, you know that?"

"What is?"

"Death squads."

"She doesn't think so."

"Nobody fucking thinks so. There's this son of a bitch in England, wrote a book, and in it he claims he was a member of the Regiment, and that he'd been part of some secret death squad in Northern Ireland. Detailed all of these murders he and others in the squad had committed in the early seventies. And the book becomes a fucking bestseller, and everyone is jumping up and down saying look what the SAS has done. Regimental command is screaming that it's all bullshit, nobody fucking listens. Seven months this book is out there, and then finally the Royal Ulster Constabulary arrests this guy, the one who wrote it, and they bring him up to Belfast, and they sit him down, and they say, listen, mate, if it's true, you're going to be done for murder.

"And this guy, he immediately says, nah, it's not true, none of it's true. Made the whole thing up, see?" Moore looked at me. "And none of the book fucking checks out. He's got bits in there where he's detailing the date and time he's offing someone, and the RUC finds out that, in fact, he wasn't in fucking Belfast at all, but down at the dentist's in Dorset, some such. So none of it's true, not one word."

Moore finished the beer, set the bottle by the sink, began pushing it in a circle with his fingers. The countertop was an aquamarine tile, and the glass bottle left a smear of condensation that made the green seem darker.

"I've been SAS for over twenty years," Moore said. "I was in the Falklands, on the ground, blowing supply lines and aircraft. I was on the second pagoda team at Prince's Gate. We're the best damn soldiers in the fucking world."

"The SAS summarily executed five unarmed terrorists at Prince's Gate," I said. I didn't add that Moore had almost pulled a repeat of that move tonight.

"Tell me you don't know how that happened, that you can't imagine what it was like in there."

"That's what the government wanted?"

"Soldiers are an instrument of politics. Soldiers do what they're told. That's all I can say."

Not all soldiers, I thought.

"And then there're bastards like Mark Sterritt, and they take our good name and they take the skills we taught them, and they drag it all down into the shit, so deep you can't even see it."

"There's a huge difference between SAS and ex-SAS," I said.

"You think so? You really think if the press knew all about Sterritt, they'd not care that he and his boys all learned their killing at my knee?"

"Maybe not."

"Maybe not. But probably so. Just another nail in the coffin of the SAS."

The kitchen door opened, and Erika came in, saying, "Do we have any popcorn?"

Moore said, "Denny bought some of that microwave kind, it's in the pantry." He sounded sullen.

"You two should come back out," Erika said, opening the pantry door. "You're being antisocial."

"You should go to bed," I said.

She stuck her tongue out at me. "What're you doing?"

"We were talking," I said.

"Duh." She found the popcorn and put it in the microwave. "It's more fun if there's more of us out there."

"You think this is supposed to be fun?"

"Look, I'm the one who's stuck here. If I want to try and have fun, you should be helping me out." She was patient with her explanation, as if giving me a basic lesson in maturity.

"She's got you there," Moore told me.

"You, too," Erika said to him. "Bridgett will be nice. I had a talk with her." She absently reached for her left earlobe, and I saw she now had two hoops hanging there.

"She gave you those?" I asked.

Erika grinned. "Said I could borrow them." To Moore, she added, "Bridgett just wanted to let you know where she stood, that's all."

"She did that just fine," Moore said.

"Then quit hiding in here and come out. Bring the popcorn."

We watched her go out of the kitchen. The microwave beeped at us and Moore moved to fetch the bag.

"You go on point," he said. "That way I can dive for cover."

I found a bowl to serve the popcorn in, and we returned to the living room. Yossi and Dale were still on the door, and I heard one of them murmur something about the smell of hot popcorn. Bridgett greeted Moore with a look cut from the ice outside, and as I set the bowl down on the table, she transferred the look to my middle.

"Atticus," she said softly.

It took me a second, and then I looked down at my stomach, saw the bloodstain on my T-shirt from where my stitches had torn during my dive for the Colonel. "It's minor," I said.

"What?" Erika asked, and then she saw it, and she said, "Oh my God, you're bleeding. Why are you bleeding, what happened?"

"It's nothing."

"What do you mean it's nothing, your stomach is bleeding, that's not nothing."

"Oh, come on," Moore said. "It's not like he got shot again."

We all heard the penny drop.

Erika's face went flat. "Again?" She asked it softly.

"It's okay," I said.

She slid off the couch and walked over to me. "You got shot? When? Tonight?"

"Couple of days ago."

"And no one told me?"

"We didn't want to worry you," Bridgett said, glaring at Moore.

Erika ignored her. "Why didn't you tell me?" She kept her voice soft, asking a reasonable question. "Don't lie to me, Atticus."

"I'm all right," I said, and right after I said it, I saw her make the leap, put together the pieces we'd let slip.

"Mom shot you?" Her hands stayed at her sides, fingers curled into her palms. "It was my mom who did this?"

I didn't say anything, but that was enough for her. She knew.

"Let me see," Erika said.

I looked over at Bridgett, who shook her head slightly. Easy for her to say. I pulled up my shirt, thinking about Lyndon Johnson and feeling embarrassed. The bruising was beginning to fade around my stitches, and the bleeding had already stopped, but it didn't look pretty.

Erika didn't move.

I lowered my shirt, tucking it back in, and the movement made my stitches itch.

"That bitch," Erika said. "That bitch."

"I agree," Bridgett said.

Erika turned on her. "You don't know! You don't fucking know! She shot him! My mom shot him!"

Down the hall, I heard Yossi and Corry responding to the shouting, and I held up a hand, waving them back to their posts.

"Do you know what that means?" Erika was demanding shrilly.

"It means I got lucky," I said. "She could have killed me."

Erika spun back around, and now I could see her rage, and it was frightening. "Lucky! Because she didn't kill you? Everything else she did to you, and you think you're lucky? She's a fucking *liar,* she's a goddamn fucking *liar* and she shoots you and you think you're *lucky*?"

"Sterritt wanted her to kill—"

"*Lucky*? You let her keep hurting you and hurting you and you call that *lucky*?"

"It's not the—"

"She just fucking steps all over you and you call that *lucky*? When she was fucking Rubin, did you call that *lucky,* too?"

I thought, no, I didn't hear that right.

Erika slammed her mouth shut as if she'd swallowed a bug.

The whole house was silent.

I thought: She's lying again. She is lying to you, again, the way she lied about her father molesting her, about how Moore and Denny and Knowles didn't pick her up that day in the city. She's angry and she's upset and she feels betrayed again, and she's just going for the reaction. That's what she's after, the reaction. This is a lie.

Her expression had changed, and she was sucking at the air rapidly, avoiding my eyes. She had bitten her bottom lip so hard I could see teeth marks. "I'm sorry, I didn't mean that, I'm lying, I didn't mean that."

And then I knew she was telling the absolute truth.

Erika turned, put her face in her hands, and started crying.

Without thought, I put my arms around her. I brushed her hair back, stroked it, holding her the way I had in Gaithersburg, when she was eleven, and I was twenty-four, and desperately in love with her mother.

CHAPTER TWENTY-SIX

"The thing is," I told Bridgett, "it makes sense. It makes such perfect fucking sense. I'm a goddamn fool. I can look back, and I can see all the things that I read the wrong way, all the things I used to ignore—my evasions, his lame lies. It was goddamn fucking obvious, right under my nose, and I denied it because he would have told me. He was my best friend, and he would have told me."

Bridgett sat watching me from her chair, silent. Listening.

I looked around the room, down the hall at where Moore and Dale were standing post. It was quiet. Erika was maybe asleep in her chosen room, Yossi outside her door. It was just Bridgett and me, with me trying to explain why I was so angry.

"He knew," I said. "That's the thing that gets me, right now, that's the thing that makes me want to dig him up and spit on him. He knew I was seeing Diana, he knew how I felt, and he was screwing her anyway."

Bridgett nodded.

"He made a choice. He made a choice to betray me. And he took this little secret of his to the grave."

"Are you angry that he did it? Or that he never told you?"

"Who the fuck cares which one I'm angry about?"

She nodded again, and I wished she would stop doing that. It made me feel as if I were talking to a paid therapist.

"He left the Army before I did, you know? And when I was getting out, it was Rubin's idea for me to move in with him, for us to live in New York together. His idea. He was the best friend I ever had, he was the person I told everything to, every fucking little thing. And he didn't tell me. He turned our friendship into a sham."

"But it wasn't a sham," Bridgett said. "I didn't know him long, but I knew enough about the two of you to know that your friendship was mutual."

"Then why not tell me about her? Why hide it?"

"Fear, maybe. If he thought you would take it badly, if he thought it would threaten the friendship. He didn't have many people, did he?"

"I can understand him not saying anything when I first moved in. I can accept fear as a reason to be silent. But he died never having told me, Bridie. He died hoping it would never come out, that I would never know. And that's cowardice. It's unbecoming of him. It's fucking unbecoming."

"But you don't know what would have happened if he had lived," she insisted. "I've lost people before, too, and I've learned one thing from it if nothing else. You can't look back and speak to the things the dead didn't do. It's pointless, it gets you nowhere. You can have your own regrets, but you can't know what Rubin would have done had he lived, Atticus."

I stayed quiet, my throat raw with angry tears I was never going to shed.

"Everybody betrays us, in the end," Bridgett said. "Make your peace with it, Atticus. Grow up."

I couldn't answer that, and we sat in silence while I tried to sort my thoughts and feelings. But there was no clarity, everything in a jumble.

I got up, grabbed my coat. "I'm going home," I said. "I'm no fucking good here right now, I'm going to be in the way, and I need some time for myself. Give Natalie a call, have her come in."

"You want to wait until she gets here? I can go with you."

"No. No, I think I really need to be alone."

"All right. I'll make the call. Are you going to be okay?"

"Oh, yeah. I'm going to walk in the general direction of my apartment, hope that somebody tries to start something. Then I'll beat the fuck out of them. That's my plan."

"Take a cab."

"Go to hell," I said, and left.

In the Army, Rubin could get anything.

Early on he had discovered the hidden market, had mastered the barter system and become one of the long line of soldiers who could play the game of supply-and-demand as an expert. When we were on maneuvers during Advanced Infantry Training, he was the guy who got us beer in the field. When another soldier we both knew was getting short, Rubin made him a military ID that wouldn't expire until the next century. He'd create false identities for sport, with credit card applications and forged transfer letters from the New York State DMV. He had copies of every official form he had ever laid eyes on, and if you gave him a photocopier, he could create a letter that you would swear was signed by the Provost Marshal himself. It was what he did, and while it was often illegal, it was rarely harmful. He had been billeted to the Pentagon as a driver at about the same time I'd been assigned to Colonel Wyatt, but that was just Rubin's work.

His job was making deals, earning favors and then calling them in. And his first law was, "In this man's Army, you never get something for nothing."

His second law was, "And I'm the man who can get anything for anyone."

"Here," Rubin said, handing me an envelope. "Diana called last week, asked me to get this for Erika's birthday."

I was packing for a weekend at the house in Gaithersburg. The Colonel was off on another of his fuck-and-suck missions, and the only reason it was especially appalling this time was that Erika was turning eleven on Sunday. He had already told her and his wife that he wouldn't be back in time. A conference, he had claimed, but both Diana and I knew otherwise.

"What is it?" I asked, slipping the envelope into a pocket.

Rubin grinned. "You'll find out. See you Sunday night. Try not to get any hickeys."

"You're a crass motherfucker," I said.

Erika was at the door when I pulled up and she came down the driveway, running to the driver's side door and pressing her face against the window. With her features mashed against the glass, she looked like a demented Muppet. She made a face and I made one in return, and Erika was giggling when I got out of the car.

"Need help?" she asked, motioning to my bag.

"No, I think I got it."

She indicated the wrapped present on the passenger seat. "That for me?"

"Maybe."

She eyed the box while I picked it up, then said, "Mom told me we're going to a movie tonight. Is she lying?"

"Would your mother lie to you?"

Erika gave me a look that said my answer was totally beside the point. "Are we?"

"Lying?"

"Stupid." She made another face, this one a direct and unfavorable assessment of my intellect. "No. Going to a movie, doof."

"We are going to a movie." I started up the walk, hefting my duffel over my shoulder, the present under my arm. Diana stood at the open door, watching us both, looking amused.

Erika ran past me and came to a screeching halt in front of her mother, saying, "Atticus says we *are* going to a movie."

"After we go for pizza," Diana said.

"I'm gonna get my coat." Erika scooted past her mother and I heard her running up the stairs to her room.

Diana led me to the guest room. I dropped my bag on the floor, set the gift on the bed, and she kissed me, her hands on my chest. I returned the kiss in kind, my libido kicking like crazy. She pulled back when we heard Erika's feet pounding on the floor overhead as she ran for the stairs again.

"Rubin gave me an envelope, said you called and asked for it," I told Diana.

"Good, he got them."

"What?"

"Hopefully, exactly what Erika wants for her birthday."

We fetched her daughter, then, and went out for pizza and a movie. Erika talked throughout dinner, telling me about her week in detail, describing at length a particular boy in her class named Ryan that she classified as stuck-up.

"When he plays football, when he scores, he walks around with his hands on his hips in front of all the girls," she told us. "He thinks he's so hot."

We got back to the house near ten, and Diana hustled

Erika off to bed, then came back downstairs to join me on the sofa in the living room.

"That kid's got a crush on you," Diana told me.

"How can you tell?"

Diana toyed with the edge of my sleeve, where the fabric ended at my wrist. "Why do you think she kept talking about Ryan at dinner? She wants you to know she's looking at boys."

We kissed, and I very softly assured her that Erika posed no lethal threat to our relationship. We made love in the guest room, quiet and intense, and Diana left me lying there when we were through, returning to her bed upstairs without a word.

Erika's birthday party was attended by six or seven kids, most of them the children of other officers posted to the Pentagon or Quantico or any of the many bases in the D.C. area. The much-talked-about Ryan was in attendance as well, and he didn't seem like such a bad sort to me. Certainly shy. He was, after all, the only boy who had been invited to the party.

Diana had made tacos for lunch, and it was followed with a small cake, purely for the ceremony of song and candles, and then an ice cream sundae buffet, which was an enormous hit. Erika fixed herself a mountain of chocolate and vanilla, soaked in butterscotch and wrapped in whipped cream, crowned with what must have been half the contents from a bottle of maraschino cherries.

"This is going to be hell to clean up," Diana murmured to me while the kids were eating. "But I swear to God it's worth it. Look at her."

"She's going to be sick," I said.

Diana laughed and told me to stop acting like a parent, that I was stealing her thunder.

With the sundaes finished, Erika declared the time had come to open her presents. She began with those brought by her guests, and I remember them as gifts of the day, impersonal for the most part, most likely selected by the other kids' parents; a CD by the Pet Shop Boys; another by U2; a Breyer model horse; a cheap Walkman. Ryan gave her a stuffed plush dragon, purple and blue, and Erika seemed to like it, but also seemed to not want Ryan to know that fact.

The presents from her peers unwrapped and examined, she switched to those gifts coming from the adults. Her father's present first, a set of pearl earrings. The pearls were tiny but real, and a couple of Erika's guests made a big fuss over the jewelry.

"You like them?" Erika asked one girl. "You can have them. Here."

She started to hand them over but Diana moved to intercept, saying firmly, "I'll hold on to these."

Erika shrugged, opening her next present, which was from me. She took her time with the card and the wrapping paper. I'd bought her the boxed set of Madeleine L'Engle books, and she gave me a big smile, saying, "Cool. I can't wait to read these." She set them aside next to the plush dragon.

Finally, Diana handed her daughter the envelope Rubin had asked me to bring.

"What is this?" Erika demanded.

Diana was smiling, made a gesture of keeping her mouth zipped shut.

"Money," one of the guests said. "It's money."

Erika held the envelope to the light. "It better not be a gift certificate, Mom." She tore the envelope open, and out fell four concert tickets. A babble of voices started, asking what show they were for, and Erika gathered them up, reading in disbelief.

Then she let out an almighty shriek of delight, jumping to her feet and dancing in place, chanting, "Joshua Tree, Joshua Tree, Joshua Tree!"

"No way!" one of the girls said.

Erika shoved the tickets in her face. "Take a look! Four tickets to the Joshua Tree tour at RFK Stadium! I'm going to see U2, I'm going to see Bono and the

Edge and Adam and Larry! I'm going to see U2!" She pulled the tickets to her breast, protecting them, spinning, and then headed for her mother, exclaiming, "Thank you, thank you! You're the best, Mom, you're the absolute best!"

"You're sure you like them?" Diana asked, teasing.

"I love them!"

"Because if you don't, we can always return them—"

"I love them, I told you, I love them!" She danced about some more, stepping on wrapping paper, and, incidentally, the dragon Ryan had given her. "How did you get them? The whole tour sold out the day the tickets went on sale."

"I have my ways," Diana said.

Erika hugged her mother. "Thank you so much! This is the best present, the absolute best."

"I love you, baby."

"I love you, too, Mom." Erika studied the tickets once more, then handed them to Diana, saying, "Hold on to them, please."

The party pretty much died after that, with many of the kids gripped by a powerful envy concerning what a great mother Erika Wyatt had. Parents arrived to take their children home, good-byes were made, and Erika ultimately went up to her room to play her new U2 CD very loud. I helped Diana clean up.

"Tell Rubin I said thank you," she said as we were washing dishes. "He must have traded some heavy favors for those tickets."

"I'm sure he did," I said. The Joshua Tree tour tickets were scalping at one hundred dollars a pop, and those were for the nosebleed seats. "How'd you know to go through Rubin?"

"You told me, remember? 'Rubin can get anything for anyone.' That's what you said."

"I said that?"

She kissed me on my nose. Her breath smelled of ice cream and cherries. "Yes, you did."

"I was right."

"I know. Like I said, tell Rubin thank you. I owe him."

"You made Erika Wyatt the most popular kid at her school," I told Rubin when I saw him Sunday night. We were in our apartment in D.C., and he was sprawled across the sofa, working with one of his sketch pads. I was sitting on the coffee table, watching him draw. He was working on an idea for a comic book, one featuring a six-gun-wielding young woman who roamed the United States like a cross between Shane and The Man With No Name.

"I'll bet," he said, not looking up from his sketch pad.

"I can't imagine what you had to promise to get those tickets."

"Too much, I'll tell you that."

"You selling missile codes to the Libyans again?"

Rubin capped his pen, rolled onto his side to look at me. "Hey, I can get anything."

"You can't get me a ride on Air Force One to Paris. You can't get me a date with Mary Stuart Masterson."

"Well, I might've been able to until now," he mused. "Those tickets pretty much tapped me."

"Fibber."

"Fibber?" Rubin shook his head. "Nope. Got nothing out of this one. So if you're needing a favor anytime soon, I may not be able to provide, sorry."

"And here I was hoping you could get me some claymores to wire around the Washington Monument."

"You and your penis fixation," he said. "Like you're not getting any."

"Like you are."

He waggled his eyebrows at me, and I laughed, and that was pretty much the last I thought of it.

———

Until tonight.

I had introduced Rubin to Diana. I had even talked to her about his wheeling and dealing.

But I'd never said he could get anything for anyone. I had never said that.

It was an arrogant holdout on my part, and the only reason I refuted his claim was because I didn't believe it. He *couldn't* get me a ride on Air Force One to Paris; he *couldn't* get me a date with Mary Stuart Masterson. Stupid, perhaps, but I wasn't willing to stroke his ego like that, and it hadn't really ever mattered. He would say he could get anything for anyone, and I would always try to trump him, come up with something that was beyond the pale, and that was how it went. It was one of our games, one of the ways we communicated.

"Rubin can get anything for anyone," Diana had said.

She hadn't heard it from me.

And the thing that galled me most now, as I walked down the wet, snowy street to my apartment, as I fumbled my key into the lock, was that I had known something was going on the moment Rubin had handed me that envelope. And I'd ignored it.

Because, ultimately, what right did I have to be jealous? I was having an affair with a married woman. I'd taken a stance on the issue of fidelity, and it certainly wasn't pro the sanctity of marriage.

How could I condemn Rubin for doing to me what I was doing to Colonel Douglas Wyatt?

CHAPTER TWENTY-SEVEN

My coffeemaker told me that it was twenty-seven minutes past two in the morning when I got in, and I didn't bother with the lights, going straight to the radiator in the kitchen and twisting the knob with my good hand until I heard the steam hissing into the pipes. I pulled a chair from the table, tugged off my wet shoes and socks, purposefully bending too far, trying to enjoy the pain that came from my wound. My answering machine was telling me I had a message waiting, and I told my answering machine that it could go fuck itself, by ignoring the little red light.

I removed my coat and gun, then got up and found the bottle of Glenlivet and a clean glass. I poured myself about three fingers, and drank. For a moment, I wished I smoked.

New snowfall, and I watched it spiral past my window, heavy and fast. I poured more scotch. Rubin had loved vodka. Once, he brought me a case of Glenfiddich for covering his ass during a spot inspection. I told him I didn't want it, that he was my friend, and that he would have done the same for me.

"You're right, I would," he said. "But since I didn't, I stole you scotch instead."

It struck me then, dull points seated behind my eyes that made me realize, whatever else I was feeling, that I missed him horribly.

Right now what I wanted was Rubin, here, in this new apartment that I shared with no one but myself. I wanted to read him the riot act, ask what the hell he had thought when he first started seeing Diana. I wanted to ask if he had been in love with her, too, and was he still. I wanted him to tell me why he had kept this secret, and what other secrets he'd taken down with him. I wanted him to tell me if my trust in him was deserved, or if I was as gullible as Erika had called me over a week ago. I wanted to ask if Bridgett was right about my need to grow up.

I wanted to get shit-faced drunk with him, and tell bad jokes about the SAS and getting shot, to try to hide fear and guilt and repeated failure.

I wanted my friend back.

The intercom in the hall buzzed, and I looked at the clock, saw it was almost a quarter to four. There was another buzz, more tentative, and, as I started up from the kitchen table, a third, more insistent. The floor was very cold, and I shifted from one bare foot to the other as I pressed the speaker button. "Who is it?"

"Natalie," the intercom crackled.

I blinked a couple of times, thinking that perhaps I'd had more scotch than I thought. "Nat?"

"God, look, I'm sorry, I thought you were up." Her voice sounded pressured, as if it were being forced through the wires and out the intercom grille.

"No, I was up. I'll buzz you in."

I leaned on the button to unlock the door, counted to three, then came off it and leaned against the opposite wall instead. My feet were still cold, though, so I went to my room for slippers, and had pulled them on when I heard her knock. I checked through the spyhole first, confirmed that I was looking at Natalie Trent outside my door, and unfastened the locks.

"I'm sorry," Natalie said. "I didn't mean to wake you."

"You didn't. I was up. I've been drinking."

"You, too?" she asked. "The bars are closed."

I chuckled, led her inside, flipping the light switch on the kitchen wall as I headed for the cupboard. I had to squint while finding her a glass, but by the time I turned back to face her, my vision had adjusted, and I got a good look at her.

Natalie stood by the table, wearing jeans and a thick wool sweater, her gray pea coat on, but open. She had no gloves, no hat, and her hair was soaked from the snow. Flakes melted down her forehead and cheeks. Her eyes were red, and I thought it was irritation, but the rest of her face didn't sell it.

"Hey," I said. "Hey, what's the matter, Nat?"

Her mouth moved a fraction, as if she couldn't control it. She shook her head. She shut her eyes.

I put the glass on the table. "Natalie?"

When she opened her eyes, they were wet.

"I miss him," Natalie said.

It was still dark and still snowing when we finished the Glenlivet and moved on to the Maker's Mark, and by that time I had told her all about my night, about Rubin's affair with Diana and my affair with Diana and the whole damn thing. She had listened closely, getting good and angry along with me, then launching into a tirade about what a rotten bastard he'd been, and how he had made her miserable by dying. It had to be nearing five in the morning, now, but the only clock in the living room was the one on the TV/VCR Dale had bought, and he hadn't bothered to set it. As far as Sony was concerned, it was always an insistent midnight.

On the floor, unrolled, was Rubin's painting of Natalie, and she stood looking down at it, bourbon in her hand. He had painted her nude, on one knee, her arms above her head, fingers splayed, palms flat, reaching for something that either wasn't supposed to be there, or hadn't yet been painted. The muscles in her arms and legs were taut, and I wondered how much of her had been imagined and idealized in Rubin's mind.

"I hate it," Natalie whispered, staring at it.

"No, you don't. It's one of the best he ever did, ever."

"I hate it. I hate it absolutely." Her enunciation became precise.

I drank from my glass, watching as she tried to kneel on the floor. She had to put her left hand out for support, and ended up placing it smack on top of the X-wing. She yelped, yanked her hand back, and ended up on her rear.

All without spilling her drink.

"Bridgett gave you this?" Natalie asked, poking the toy.

"For my birthday."

"I missed your birthday?"

I waved a hand to dismiss her concern. "It's pretty cool, though. It makes noise."

"Noise is good," Natalie decided. She pushed the X-wing along the floor with her index finger. "I thought maybe you'd be over there. At Bridgett's, I mean."

"Not tonight."

She made a silent "oh," then asked, "How's your mouth?"

"My mouth?"

"Your lip."

I reached to check, surprised myself with the coldness of the splint. The swelling had gone down almost entirely. "It's fine."

"I hit you," she said.

"I remember."

"It's fine?"

"Yeah. I forgot about it."

She drank some more, then glanced back at the painting. "I hate him."

"I do, too," I said.

Her hair fell across her face when she tried to look at me. Natalie blew at it to clear her vision. "You don't really hate him."

"No," I agreed. "I lied."

She pointed her glass at me. "I *do*. I really really do."

"Why?"

Natalie looked back at the painting, evaluating it carefully. "Because he made me look fat."

I laughed, and Natalie began laughing, too, getting to her feet and coming back to join me on the couch. She flopped down, finishing her bourbon and then reaching for the bottle. I handed it over, and she refilled her glass, then refilled mine.

"They're looking for them?" Natalie asked, out of the blue.

"Who?"

"Moore."

"Tomorrow."

"I hope they find them."

"I do, too."

"Yeah. And those other ones. And Diana."

"Sure."

"They should find them."

"They should," I agreed, not entirely certain what we were talking about. There was only an inch left of the bourbon.

"And then we can protect Erika," Natalie said. "What time is it?"

I checked my watch, realized I'd taken it off. "Watch's in the kitchen," I told her. "Hold on."

"I'll come with you," she suggested.

Each of us emptied our glasses down the kitchen

drain. The coffeemaker clock read twenty-two minutes past five.

"I should go home and get some sleep," Natalie sighed. "I have to be at the safe house at eight."

"Yeah, me, too," I said.

She reached for her coat and I realized she'd left the painting in the living room, so I asked her to wait and went back for it, rolling the canvas quickly and slipping it into its poster tube.

"You almost forgot this," I said, trying to hand her the tube.

"I don't want it."

"Sure you do. Just to have it. You don't have to hang it anywhere or anything like that, but it's yours, and you should have it. He loved you."

Natalie looked at the tube in my hand, and there was an odd expression on her face, like for a moment she'd forgotten where she was, and then her breath got ragged, like something inside her had just broken.

I rested the tube against the wall, went to hold her. She pressed her face against my shoulder, and I could feel her cheek on my neck, her skin hot and flushed against mine, her face slick with tears. She put her arms around me, tight, shaking. She snuffled at the air, trying to clear her nose, and her hands turned against my back, her short nails digging through my shirt.

"I hate him," Natalie sobbed.

I put my good hand on her head, my fingers slipping through her hair, and the other on her back. She shifted against my body, and as Natalie moved I became aware of exactly how she felt against me, of the way her legs rubbed against mine, the press of her breasts to my chest. She turned her head in from my shoulder, and her breath hit my throat, and I could feel her tears on me, and she pushed harder against me. Her back felt strong, and I moved my hand, could feel the muscles that Rubin had painted.

Natalie tilted her head to see me looking at her, to see my expression. Her eyelashes were matted, tears shiny on her face. She said my name and her hands moved up my back, and she drew me in as I leaned to her.

Her mouth, like her skin, was hot, salty, and we were pulling at each other, trying to climb, to make one body. I felt a hand leave my neck, pulling at my shirt, and then her other hand followed it, and her fingers were on my skin. We were pulling at clothes, our lips still together, separating just long enough to remove our shirts, wanting to feel more of each other. I put my mouth to her shoulder, then lower, moving over her chest, and Natalie gripped my head with both hands, guiding and driving. She said my name again, and she was still crying, but that had changed, too, a different pitch, a different kind of flood. She pushed my head back with one hand, the other trailing down my chest, skimming over the stitches on my belly, until she reached my belt and began tugging it free.

Our remaining clothes landed on the floor near the shirts, and we put our arms around each other again, and I felt wonderful skin, soft and hot. She gasped when the splint touched her, laughed, pressed herself back against me. I couldn't get enough of her, I couldn't feel enough of her. I knew what was going on, I knew I could stop it, that I could pull away, that I could quit, but I didn't. I didn't want to.

And so neither of us did.

CHAPTER TWENTY-EIGHT

The phone woke me, the third ring before the answering machine clicked on, and I pulled myself out of bed, my stomach muscles throbbing when I sat up, the headache kicking in immediately. Natalie pulled the covers back over her, still asleep, and I stumbled to the machine to turn it off, but by then the beep had come, and Scott Fowler's voice filled the room.

"Atticus, call me. Call me. Call me now. Call me as soon as you get this message."

I stumbled back into my room for my robe and glasses, stepping over the clothes we had strewn in the hall. Natalie's bra was twisted on top of one of my slippers. The bra was a pearl-gray color, silk, very simple, very pretty. I imagined Natalie looked very nice in it, but I couldn't quite remember. She hadn't moved, eyes closed, breathing even and deep. My alarm clock said it was exactly nine in the morning.

I drank two glasses of water back to back, then swallowed four aspirin and a vitamin C with a third. My stomach felt stable, the muscle ache on the outside rather than within. I started coffee brewing, picked up our clothes, brought them back into my room. I put mine in the laundry bag. I folded hers, and set them on top of my bureau. She had rolled onto her stomach, and I watched her sleep for a while before heading back to the kitchen and calling Scott.

He answered immediately, asking, "Don't you ever check your messages?"

"We need to talk," I told him.

"I know," he said.

"You know?"

"I read the papers, Atticus. You have a shootout in downtown, you expect the city not to notice?"

"It made the papers?"

Scott expired air into the phone. "Are you at your place?"

"Yeah."

"I'll be there in twenty."

"Give me an hour."

"One hour," he said, and hung up.

Natalie woke at ten of ten, and came out in my robe to find me seated in the kitchen, dressed, drinking coffee and staring at Thelonius Monk. I pointed to where I had filled a glass of water for her beside the bottle of aspirin, and she went to it, then saw the clock and said, "Shit. Did you call them?"

"No," I said.

She reached for the phone, dialed. "Bridgett? Hi, it's Nat . . . yes, I know . . . I know, how's it look? . . . I overslept . . . Very funny. Give me an hour . . ." She looked at me. "No, I haven't talked to him . . . Fine . . . we're . . . Bridgett, we're getting along fine . . . I'll talk to you when I get there."

She hung up, took the glass and the aspirin, and went into the bathroom, carrying them. She showered quickly, emerged once more wearing my robe, headed back into my room. I got up and fixed her a cup of coffee, considered bringing it to her.

Better to wait until she was dressed.

I went back to the table, and she came out again, sitting in the other chair, her hands going to the mug, then to where I had laid the poster tube on the table.

"What do you want to tell her?" she asked finally.

"The truth." My mouth felt filled with broken glass.

"I don't know what I was thinking last night. I didn't mean—"

"I know. Neither did I." I drank some of my coffee. My head felt too small for my brain, but the aspirin was finally kicking in.

"We can just forget it ever happened," Natalie said.

"Is that what you want?"

"We were drunk, we were grieving. Why make it more than that?" Natalie looked at me, then repeated, "Why make it more than that?"

"That's all it was?"

"That's all it should have been."

Both of us had nothing to say, then.

"Rubin's wake," I said.

Natalie turned on a small smile. "Well, we never did have one, did we?"

"No."

"I'll talk to Bridgett, tell her what happened," Natalie said. "All of it."

"I should do it."

"No, let me. I'm her friend, I've been her friend for a long time. Let me tell her. You can talk to her after."

It wouldn't matter which one of us it came from, I knew. The damage was done. Either a friend or a lover had betrayed her. I gave Natalie a nod.

She emptied her mug and got up, saying, "I'll tell her when I get there. Maybe you . . ."

"I've got to wait here for Fowler to come by," I said. "It'll be at least another hour before I get to the safe house. That should give you enough time."

I was out of the shower and dressed when Scott buzzed, and I told him I'd be right down. I pulled on my jacket and my gun, locked up, and took the stairs as fast as I could without exacerbating my stomach. My abdominals were killing me.

"Dude," Scott said as I came outside. "You look like shit."

"Thank you, Scott. And might I say, the new earring suits you."

He smoothed his tie and then brought the same hand to his left ear to twist the new stud. It was a small gold stem, set a quarter of an inch above his old earring. "Prepping for undercover work," Special Agent Fowler said.

"They must hate you down at the Bureau."

"Most of them think I'm queer." He grinned. "They haze me out, I'll sue their asses for discrimination."

I laughed, and it only made my stomach hurt more. I considered Scott Fowler a friend. He'd been there when Rubin died, working the Federal side of the job. We got along, perhaps because he seems determined not to appear as what he is—a competent and professional agent of the FBI. He is three or four years older than me, and always manages to look like a California surfer, even in his conservative suits. It didn't matter that we were bearing into a vicious winter, he was still evenly tanned. His hair is the color of dried straw, and his eyes are blue. He was wearing contacts today, instead of his glasses.

Rubin used to call him Special Agent Dude, or SAD for short.

Thinking about it made me smile.

"It wasn't that funny," Scott chided.

"Something else entirely."

The smile faded to a more serious appraisal. "So, where we going?"

"Let's walk," I said, and started for Lexington Avenue.

Scott reached into his pockets for a pair of black leather gloves, and slipped them on as we began walking. The pedestrian traffic was light. Not many people wanted to be walking in the falling snow today, it seemed.

"How you doing?" Scott asked.

"Aside from being shot?"

"In spite of being shot. Why'd you call me?"

"What do you know about the SAS?" I asked, and then told him all of it. He listened, occasionally trying to catch snow in his gloved hands, and we were down to Twelfth Street before I'd finished.

"That fits with what we've got," Scott said.

"Which is?"

"I need you to put me in touch with Moore."

"I doubt he'll want to talk to you."

"He doesn't want to talk to me. He's avoiding me."

"Why?"

"What Wyatt told you is correct, to a point. Moore's here officially, with Knowles and Denny, to help bring down Sterritt."

"It's official?"

"To a point. It was the Brits who told us Sterritt and his crew were in New York, but their condition on sharing that information was that we allow Moore to assist us in the pursuit and arrest. The State Department said okey dokey, told Justice, Justice told us, and we swallowed it. Problem is, the moment Moore and his two hit the dirt, they were running, and they left us in the dust. He doesn't want to share with the FBI."

"How is it Sterritt warrants such special treatment from both governments?" I asked. "What's he done?"

Scott stopped, tilted his head back to catch some snow in his mouth. After he'd caught a few flakes, he said, "Tastes like shit."

"That's the sulfuric acid," I said. "You going to answer my question?"

"Yeah, Sterritt and his team, they've been in business since the late eighties, when they got booted from the SAS. They've been connected with three abductions in Italy between 1989 and '90, nine throughout the rest of Europe, mostly in the former Soviet states, and then a whole spate of them in Colombia lasting until a year ago."

I knocked snow out of my hair. "But why the FBI?"

"Three of the snatches were of American foreign nationals." Scott scooped up snow and began packing it into a ball between his palms. "They work for themselves, and they take contracts. Rumor is you get the squad for a flat million. If ransom's involved, there's probably a cut of that, too. Their record isn't very pretty."

"How many returns?" I asked.

"Less than twenty percent. Victims who make it back tend to need immediate medical care. Women fare much worse than men. Sexual abuse. Torture." He scowled at his snowball, then threw it to the ground, where it burst. "Those who come back go straight to therapy."

"And the rest?"

"The bodies aren't always recovered."

And these are the people Diana has hired to kidnap her daughter, I thought.

"Where's Moore?" Scott asked.

"Right now, I honestly don't know. Maybe at the safe house."

"Can you take me to him?"

"I need to pave the way," I said.

"Atticus, I've got to talk to Moore. We'd lost him, you understand? The first proof we had that any of them were still around was when the NYPD found Ennis's body in that van."

"Ennis?"

"One of Sterritt's crew. There are three others—Glenn Hardy, Evan Cox, and Michael Perkins. The one Yossi capped was Paul Ennis. According to the paper

the Brits sent over, they're all hard-core bastards."
Scott stopped, facing me. "Moore fucked us over good
when he ditched us. Like I said, we had squat, and then
Ennis turns up, the NYPD is telling me about an attempted kidnapping on Third Avenue, and all of a sudden, I'm looking at connections to my good friend
Atticus, who hasn't been returning my calls."

"Sorry about that."

"Uh-huh. Where were you last night?"

"The safe house, then my place."

"I called your place. You didn't answer."

"I didn't get in until late."

Scott shook his head, sad that I wasn't telling him the
truth. "You didn't go with Moore and his boys to a
building in TriBeCa last night, did you?"

"Why?"

"These men are dangerous, Atticus. You're going to
need help if you want to keep your principal safe, and
that means my help."

I had to agree. "I'll talk to Moore, see if I can put you
two together."

"Do that. Your principal, Erika. How secure is she?"

"Normally I'd say very, but they're SAS-trained, and
they know how to infiltrate. As long as Sterritt can't
find her, we'll be all right."

"Don't be counting on Moore to help you protect
her."

"He seems straight."

Scott stuck out his arm to hail a cab, and we stepped
back from the curb as one jerked over, spitting up slush
and water from beneath its wheels. "Moore wants Sterritt and the others, and he wants them so bad he can
taste it. Your principal is incidental to him, at best."

"He's done a good job protecting Erika so far," I
argued.

"That's because Erika's his bait." Scott climbed into
the back of the cab.

I said nothing.

"You make damn sure Moore calls me." He pulled his door closed, and the cab pulled away.

I watched it go, then made for the subway station at Union Square, wondering how I could convince Moore to talk to the FBI. He wouldn't listen to me, I knew. What he wanted was Sterritt, hell or high water, as the previous night had proven, and Scott Fowler would only get in the way of that.

Erika was his bait, Fowler had said.

And bait gets eaten.

CHAPTER TWENTY-NINE

Bridgett had left for work when I arrived at the safe house, Dale and Natalie letting me inside. I was informed that Moore, Knowles, and Denny had all departed before dawn, and that Yossi had gone in search of his bed soon after. Corry sat with Erika in the living room, both reading magazines, or pretending to. Natalie led me in and then gave me a slight shake of the head, and I knew what it meant, I knew she hadn't told Bridgett. I gave her the rundown on my meeting with Scott, and we each took up our posts.

The morning passed without incident, the house filling with a localized tension that was for the most part invisible. It showed only in paranoia, sensitivity to noise; the way we all tensed up when we heard a car sliding down the snowy street; the way Erika jumped when I dropped the remote control out of my splinted hand.

"When are they coming for me?" Erika asked at one point.

"I don't know."

"But they'll come?"

"There are a lot of people looking for them," I said. "The NYPD, the FBI."

"Looking for Mom?"

"And Sterritt and his guys."

Erika tugged the sleeves of my sweatshirt down around her hands, balling the fabric in her fists. "I hate this," she said. "It's making my stomach hurt."

"Mine, too," I said, truthfully, and then my pager went off, and both of us jumped. I silenced it, checked the number.

"Who is it?" Erika asked. "Is it my father?"

I shook my head. "A fellow I know at the FBI."

"Oh."

I got up to go to the phone, then stopped. "The Colonel still hasn't talked to you?"

"No."

"You want me to call him?"

"I don't care."

"I'll be right back," I said, and headed into the kitchen to find Natalie on her way out. I went to the phone, and she touched the back of my hand before returning to the living room.

Just a touch.

I called Scott.

"What's going on?" Fowler demanded.

"They haven't come back."

"When do you expect them?"

"I don't know," I said.

"I've got brass all over my back. Not to mention two detectives from the NYPD that you might remember from the Special Victim Squad," Scott said. "I need to talk to Moore."

"Are you tracing this call?" I asked.

"Are you kidding?"

"Well, pretend you are," I said, and gave him the address of the safe house. "Moore and his people are not here right now, but if you want to come over this evening, you'll probably find one of them."

"See you tonight," Fowler said, and hung up.

I called the Colonel next, and he was coughing when he answered the phone, and continued to cough for almost a minute longer after we were connected. He sounded awful, and the coughs, even over the phone, were savage and ineffective. When he finally spoke, I could barely make him out.

"What the fuck's happened?" he rasped.

"Nothing more. They've resumed the search."

"I've been waiting to hear from you. Where the hell are you?"

"The safe house."

"Still secure?"

"For now. They'll find us eventually."

"If Moore doesn't find them first."

"It's a big if, Colonel."

"How's Erika?"

"She's scared," I told him. "She's holding out. You ought to talk to her."

"No."

"She'd like to hear from you, Colonel."

"It's not necessary."

"For you, maybe."

He raised his voice, what might have been a shout not too long ago. "I've got nothing to say to her."

"Talk to your daughter, Colonel," I said. "At least let her know you're worried for her."

"She's not with the cunt, that's all that matters."

"You're a son of a bitch," I said, hearing my voice climb. "I almost believed you, you know that? But you're still the same selfish rat-fuck son of a bitch you were four years ago."

"Just do your job, Sergeant. Keep my daughter secure." He hung up.

I slammed down the phone, turned, and saw Erika in the doorway. I knew from her face that she had heard the whole thing.

"I just wanted a Coke," she said softly.

"He's worried about you," I said.

She took a can of soda from the refrigerator, closed the door quietly. "Sure."

"He told me to tell you he loves you."

"You don't have to lie for him. He's not paying you for that."

"He's sick and he's scared, Erika," I said. "He doesn't like being out of control. He doesn't like not being here with you."

"Sure," she said tonelessly, and went back to the couch and her unread magazine.

At two I sent Corry home, telling him to be back before midnight, and at four Yossi returned, so I cut Dale loose, giving him until the next morning. None of Moore's crew returned or called, either, but I didn't expect them to. I told Yossi and Natalie to keep an eye open for Fowler, and not to panic if they saw him lurking in the street.

Shortly after six, Bridgett arrived with two pizza boxes and a gym bag, and her appearance sparked Erika, lifting the gloom that had filled the house during the day. It was her manner, mostly, but the effect was immediate, and it made me very glad to see her.

"Hey, brat!"

Erika didn't miss a beat. "Hey, slut!"

Bridgett dropped the pizzas on the coffee table, turned into my arms, and gave me a kiss. It was hard and brief and unexpectedly sweet and she let me go quickly, but not before the guilt kicked me hard below my heart. She flopped down on the couch beside Erika and began opening her gym bag. "Figure I'll be spending the night here again, so I brought some stuff to keep us from going fucking nuts."

"Anything good?"

"Probably not," Bridgett said, reaching into the bag

and pulling out paperback books. "I wasn't certain you could read, you know?"

"Eat me," Erika said.

"Not on your life. See if there's anything you like and leave the rest for me." Bridgett pushed the duffel onto the floor, grabbed the pizzas, and went into the kitchen, saying, "I'll start serving up."

The kitchen door swung shut, and Erika began going through the books. I thought about telling Natalie she was free to go, then wondered if that was honestly what I needed to do, or just an attempt to assuage my guilt.

"Hey, look at this." Erika held up a copy of *A Wrinkle in Time.* "You gave me this for my birthday one year."

"I remember," I said.

"I'm a little old for it." She tossed the book carelessly onto the table. "Everybody else gave me crap that year, but I remember you gave me the whole series."

"Your mother gave you U2 tickets," I reminded her.

It took her a second, and then Erika said, "Shit, right. That was the Joshua Tree tour."

"How was the show?"

"I didn't go."

"What? You went crazy over those tickets, I remember."

"I know. I wanted to, but there were all these people who knew I had tickets, and they kept asking if I'd take them. There was a boy I liked, his name was Ryan, I think, and I wanted to go with him and you and Mom. And that was just before you left, and then Mom said she was too busy that night, so I ended up giving them away."

She shrugged, then said, "I didn't even tell her I hadn't gone. I remember that. I'd been over at somebody's house instead, and when I got home Mom asked how the show was and I totally lied, told her that it was amazing, and that I'd done pot and fooled around with some guy I'd met during the concert." Erika laughed. "She grounded me for a month."

"I'll bet."

Bridgett stuck her head out of the kitchen and asked, "Should I bring Nat and Yossi slices or should they come in here?"

"You can bring it to them," I said. "Just stay with them while they eat."

"No problem. You two might want to grab some food before it gets cold."

Erika and I went to get our slices while Bridgett took two plates to the front. I heard Natalie saying thank you, and everything sounded normal and fine, and I was certain she felt as guilty as I.

"You want a pepperoni slice?" Erika asked me.

"I'm not hungry."

"What's the deal with you and Natalie?"

She reads minds, I thought. "What do you mean?"

"I mean, what's going on between the two of you? Why have you been trying not to look at each other all day?"

"You don't miss much," I said.

She shook her head, agreeing with me, then licking pizza grease from her fingers.

I thought about denying it. Instead, I said, "Natalie and Rubin were going out when he died. When I got home last night, she came by, and we started talking about him. I was pretty upset because of what you'd told me. We had a lot to drink, and we ended up sleeping together." I wondered if this was the kind of confession you should make to a fifteen-year-old. I wondered whose questions I was answering in telling her.

Erika lowered her voice and raised her eyebrows. "You mean fucking?"

I hesitated before answering. The voices from the front were low, and I couldn't make out words, only tone. The tone sounded comfortable. I nodded.

Erika frowned, considering this revelation. "Was it an accident?"

"I don't know. We could have stopped, we knew exactly what we were doing, but we didn't. In part we were lashing out at Rubin, I think."

"In part?"

I took a moment to try to articulate some of what I was feeling.

"Natalie and Bridgett are friends, aren't they?" Erika asked, when I didn't answer. "They talk like they've known each other a long time."

"They're friends. Natalie introduced me to Bridgett."

The kitchen door swung open and Bridgett came back in, saying, "They want soda. Do we have any left?"

"In the fridge," Erika said.

Bridgett stopped and looked at us. "What are you two plotting?"

"Nothing," Erika said.

"Nothing?" Bridgett asked me.

"We're admiring your choice in pizzas," I said.

She went to the fridge and got three cans of soda, saying, "You two had better behave."

We were quiet until we heard the voices at the end of the hall start again. I shouldn't be doing this, I thought. Bridgett's distracting them from their posts.

"You're in trouble," Erika said in a soft playground singsong.

"I know."

"You haven't told her, have you?"

"Not yet."

Erika folded her slice and looked at it, not me. "Natalie's better for you," she said.

I didn't say anything.

"Well, she is," Erika said, as if I'd spoken, as if her reasons were obvious. "I mean, you don't have to prove anything with her, do you? She's like you, in a way."

"You get all this from having known Natalie for how long?"

"One week. And I don't miss much, remember. That's what you said. Right?"

"Right. I forgot."

She brought her head back around with a frown. "I won't tell Bridgett, if that's what you're worried about. That would be totally cruel, so don't think I'd do that, because I wouldn't."

"Bridgett told me that you two are getting along now."

"She's still a pain, but she's not really such a bitch as I thought she was." She picked up her plate. "We'd better go back out there. She'll wonder what we're up to."

"She already does," I said.

Moore and Knowles returned a little past eight, and the two of them finished the remaining pizza and soda. I'd sent Natalie home after dinner, and we'd exchanged silent looks that commiserated in guilt and anxiety, and desire. It was the desire that confused me most of all, that made the guilt worse. That she was feeling it too didn't help matters any.

Knowles went to join Yossi at the door after eating, leaving Moore, Bridgett, Erika, and me in the living room. Erika was reading on the couch, Bridgett beside her, listening to my conversation with Moore at the dining table. There had been no sign of Fowler on the street, and if he was out there, he was being either very patient or very discreet. Or perhaps he wanted all three of them—Moore, Knowles, and Denny.

"We're heading out again in an hour or so," Moore told me.

"Where?"

"We've chased paper to the Bronx, think they may be holed up there."

"The Bronx is a big place."

"So I've heard." Moore rubbed his eyes, and I could see the redness around his corneas. "Have you heard from Denny?"

"No."

"We split up this morning. He was trying to figure

where Sterritt's getting his gear, got a lead on a fellow in Brooklyn. If he calls or comes by, tell him to hold tight here. I don't like splitting the brick this way."

"You can wait until he shows," I said.

Moore shook his head, dismissing the suggestion.

"I talked to the Colonel this afternoon about contacting the FBI," I lied.

"No," Moore said. "No way. This is mine, this hunt is mine."

"I know the lead Fed on this end," I said. "He's a good guy, stand-up. He won't cut you out."

"Fuck that, Atticus. Sterritt's mine, they're all mine. I don't want to have to explain it to some stuffed-shirt civil servant limp-dick who's worried about puckering up to his superior's arse."

"Fowler's not like that."

"That his name? Fowler? I don't care what—"

Then the explosions started.

CHAPTER THIRTY

There were two of them, one on top of the other, terrifyingly loud, and maybe I heard the glass breaking before the explosions, but maybe that was just my mind filling in the sounds I'd missed. The flashes were brilliant and blinding, pure white, caught in my periphery down the hall, and my ears were already ringing. I heard Yossi yelling, inarticulate, in pain, and perhaps Knowles, too, but I was in motion already, going for Erika.

Grenades. They'd come with grenades. Stun grenades, probably, flash bang, and if that was all they were using, we were lucky, because that meant that Yossi and Knowles were still alive.

Bridgett had already grabbed Erika in her arms, and I heard the shots next as we went to the hand-off, pulling Erika to me with my bad left hand. I caught a whiff of explosive powder from down the hall.

The front door came down hard onto the floor of the hallway, the impact echoing down the hall, and I heard the sound of a spoon flying from another grenade. I wrapped my arms around Erika and dropped to the deck, hearing Moore shouting out, hearing the sound of something small and heavy hitting the floor and then, immediately, another detonation, loud enough to shake the room.

From behind the couch, I saw Bridgett fall with a cry, and my heart stopped as rubber shot ricocheted off the walls and ceiling, raining down, stinging me through my clothes.

My gun was in my right hand, I didn't even remember drawing it.

Erika was trembling beneath me.

I rolled, and came around to see the muzzle of a submachine gun pointed at my face. The man holding it was tall, broad-shouldered, wearing a black balaclava. A Browning was on his hip, and the Emerson knife was clipped to his left pocket. Too tall to be Sterritt. Maybe Hardy.

Beyond him, on the floor against the wall, Moore was doubled over in the fetal position, whimpering.

"Lose the gun," Hardy said.

I could hear Bridgett moaning in pain.

They had come with masks and stun grenades. They had thrown a stinger when they could have thrown a frag.

They didn't want to kill us. And that meant that all of us were still alive, in pain, maybe, but still alive. Because if one of us died, they wouldn't hesitate to pull the trigger on the rest. The difference between one count of felony murder and six counts felony murder is academic; after all, the State can only execute you once.

If I started shooting, even if I managed to get a bead and fire before he pumped thirty bullets into me, the others would kill us all.

It was simple, really.

They'd already won.

I put the gun on the floor.

"Push it away," he said.

I gave the Smith & Wesson a good shove, and it slid into the wall, scattering pellets of rubber buckshot as it went.

"Over here," he said, and motioned me off Erika. "Let me have a turn with her."

I hesitated, but it didn't matter, because another one came around from the other side and yanked Erika to her feet, threw her over the edge of the couch. She didn't make any noise when he moved her, and I could look into her face from where I was on the floor.

Whatever she saw in my eyes, it made her start to cry.

"Here, now," the other one said, and I knew the voice, and I knew it was Sterritt. "None of that."

The one on me motioned me back and up, saying, "Slowly."

"We'll treat you nice," Sterritt was saying. "You may even decide you like me." He'd pulled a roll of duct tape from somewhere on his person, and was done wrapping Erika's ankles, and apparently he had found another Emerson knife, because he was using it to cut the strips. He bound her arms behind her back, then took a handful of hair to pull her head up, and placed one last strip over her mouth.

Erika kept crying, kept looking at me.

The last piece of tape in place, Sterritt shoved the roll back into his jacket, folded his knife and slipped it back into his pocket, and then pushed Erika down over the back of the couch once more. "How we doing back there?" he shouted.

"Clear!"

"Take her," he told the one who'd been covering me, and the two changed positions quickly, giving me no chance, no opening.

Hardy hefted Erika over his shoulder. She was limp, not resisting, but she held her head so she could still see me. I thought she was going to hyperventilate, if she kept crying like that, what with the duct tape over her mouth. Her wet eyes pleaded with me to help her, to do something.

"I'll find you," I said to her.

She was carried down the hall, out the door.

Bridgett tried to move, then gave up, doubling herself over. Red welts were on her face and hands. Some bled. Moore had the same marks, caught by the direct blast from the last grenade, and he continued to rock in his fetal position, blood streaking his face, teeth clenched, eyes watching.

Sterritt looked down at me. "You're supposed to be dead."

"I got lucky," I said.

From behind the balaclava, he laughed sourly.

Down the hall, one of the men shouted, "Let's go!"

"Coming!" Sterritt looked at the submachine gun in his hands, then back at me. "Sarge told us never to do this, but I owe you, so here goes."

The muzzle hit me on the right side of my cheek, catching my glasses and knocking them off my face, the metal tearing into my skin. The blow was stunningly painful, and I went down on my hands and knees, my vision liquid and unsteady.

"Don't try to come after us," he said, and then he put his foot in my stomach, and I felt my stitches pop and tear, and I was on my back, on rubber shot, and he was gone.

I rolled the rest of the way onto my stomach, tried to use my hands to get up. I heard Bridgett and Moore getting to their feet, and they each gave me a hand, and then we were standing behind the couch, looking down the hall. Two men, both clad in black, balaclavas in place, were ushering Knowles and Yossi into the living room. They gave them a good shove, then began backing away. Yossi and Knowles managed to keep their footing, but they were unsteady, deafened from the blasts, still having trouble with their vision.

The last two men backed to the front door. One pulled another grenade from his belt. "Nice meeting you all," he said, then pulled the pin, tossed the grenade underhand at us.

Both Moore and Bridgett let go of me, diving for Knowles and Yossi respectively, and I saw them go down as I fell again, heard the jingle of the spoon hitting the ground, and then the pop of primer.

There was no explosion, and I thought, strange, there should be a boom, a really big boom.

The odor that poured into the family room was sweet and sticky.

"Smoker," I heard Moore say.

The smoke billowed into the room, dense and white and thick like smog and foul exhaust. I tried to get up again, heard either Bridgett or Moore moving, and then the burning started, and my head felt sealed in a plastic bag, and I tried to pull deeper and deeper breaths, and it only got worse, my whole chest contracting with pressure from all sides, cinders flying into my lungs and eyes and mouth, a sharp pain pushing straight to my heart. I coughed, crawled, felt something snap and break under my right knee, and knew I'd just destroyed my glasses. Something was running down my face, and my skin stung everywhere, eyes, lips, hands, neck—everything hurt, and I just didn't want to be hurt anymore.

Bridgett choked out my name, and I tried to locate the sound. Liquid ran down over my mouth, salty, and I thought it was blood and swiped at it. My fingers came back sticky and coated with mucus.

I felt a hand on my arm, and I reached, caught her, and she pulled me toward her. Through the tears and smoke I could barely make her out, and she looked like shit, snot running in thick streams from her nose, tears tracking down her face.

"Ah fuck, this hurts," Bridgett managed, coughing.

She reached up to my face, pulled herself in closer, and then gave up.

I did, too.

————

The first cops who arrived came in a sector car that was summoned by the neighbors, scared shitless by all of the noise. Two officers blundered blindly in through the smoke and got taken down just as we all had been. The cloud had spread through the whole house by then, and when Bridgett and I weren't coughing or spitting up snot, I could hear Moore or Knowles or Yossi fighting the effects of the tear gas, too.

It took forever to make it outside, suffering all the way, with Bridgett leading me along on hands and knees until we hit the fresh night air, cold and almost painfully clean, falling into the snow that had gathered on the steps. We lay there, tangled together, leaking blood and mucus.

Two EMTs found us that way, leaned down to help us up, and Bridgett croaked out, "There are others inside."

I couldn't speak.

One of them nodded, went back for his mask, while the remaining technician helped us to the rear of their rig, and began giving us oxygen. We sat with blankets around our shoulders, masks on our faces, while the tech tried to stop the bleeding from my cheek. He went through three gauze pads, and on the fourth I remembered something about facial wounds bleeding a lot, and tried to take comfort in that.

Then the tech saw my shirt and said, "Holy shit." He moved me up onto the gurney, and got out a pair of clothing shears and all I could think was that I didn't want to lose another shirt. I have no idea why I thought that; it was just a gray T-shirt, but I was adamant he not cut it off. He tried to bring the scissors in and I pushed him away, struggled to get my shirt off myself, and finally, with his help, succeeded.

The incision in my abdomen had opened, the stitches tearing through healthy skin to create another injury altogether. The tech tried to question me about the stitches, but I was still finding it difficult to breathe, let alone speak. The tear gas had pretty much cleared

Bridgett's system by then, though, and she offered answers as best she could.

Another rig arrived, then another police car, their lights painting the street and flashing bright inside the ambulance. I heard Yossi and the others being brought out, heard officers asking technicians what had happened, if the house was clear. Bridgett leaned down to look at me, past the technician's shoulder, and she had removed her mask, and I thought she was the most wonderful woman I had ever seen.

I said, "I'm sorry."

The mask kept my voice far away.

"Hey, don't worry," Bridgett said. Her voice sounded raw. "I'm going to talk to the cops, fill them in. Okay?"

I nodded and she gave my head a pat, then hopped out of the rig as the tech left my side, began hooking up a bag of ringers. He used a pocketknife on a nasal cannula, then attached the air line to the IV, turning it into a makeshift eyewash. It helped, and for some reason, that made it easier to breathe.

Eventually, I heard voices I recognized, though it took me a moment. Then Detective Hower was stooping to fit into the rig, saying, "Jesus, cowboy, you do like your punishment, don't you?" He looked at the tech. "Where you taking him?"

"Vincent's," the EMT said.

"How's he doing?"

"It's mostly superficial. The gas got him good, whatever it was."

"Tear gas," I managed.

The tech didn't hear me, saying, "He needs his right cheek stitched up, and the wound in his abdomen."

"We'll see you there," Hower said. "The lady wants to ride with him."

"All aboard."

The ambulance ride and the police presence guaranteed a quick trip to St. Vincent's emergency room. I was put on an examination bed at a suture station and had a moment to glance around me, to see the motion and count heads to determine that all were present and accounted for, before the privacy curtain was drawn around me. I'd been in St. Vincent's ER once before, with Rubin, after a bar fight that he had started by calling a racist Guido from Queens a racist Guido from Queens.

The memory of that and of him gave way to the full realization of what had happened.

The last time I'd been in an ER, it had been at Bellevue, and one of my principals had died. Now I'd lost another.

But Erika wasn't dead, not yet. If Sterritt honored his deals, she was already with her mother.

If he didn't honor his deals, the chances were high nobody would ever see her again.

Nothing good ever comes from visiting the ER, I decided.

Bridgett stood by the bed, checking her wounds. Some of the welts seemed to be fading, but I knew others would stay with her for a while. I was off the oxygen, now, and my vision had reverted to the familiar blur of no corrective lenses.

"That was mean," Bridgett said, her voice still raspy. She blew her nose on some Kleenex. "That was just mean."

"It got them what they wanted." My throat still burned, but I sounded clear to my ears.

"Hurt like a motherfuck. I thought we were dead."

"They didn't want to kill us."

"So they used riot grenades and smoke."

"And tear gas."

She took some fresh Kleenex from the box. "Talk about overkill."

"They threw it after the smoker so we wouldn't know it was there. The tear gas bonds to the smoke, hides it perfectly. It's a military trick. You have no idea what you're running into until it's too late."

She blew her nose again. "Like I said, it's mean."

"It gives us hope. They didn't want any bodies."

"You think they'll hurt her?"

I didn't say anything.

"Do you think they'll hurt Erika?" Bridgett asked again, and she was insistent.

"She's no good to them dead," I said.

"That's not what I meant."

We both knew what she meant.

A doctor rolled back the privacy curtain around us and came in, followed by Morgan and Hower. She gave me a local in my stomach, and that hurt, too, and then started sewing there while the Q&A began with Morgan and Hower. They had gotten a lot of what they were after from the others already. I was just a courtesy interview, used to verify descriptions and accounts. Moore had been able to identify both of the men who'd entered the living room by their voices, and Morgan confirmed it was Mark Sterritt and Glenn Hardy.

"Have you called Colonel Wyatt?" I asked.

Hower grunted. "We've sent a unit up to Garrison to get him. Didn't want to give him the news over the phone. Where do you think they've taken the kid?"

"Hopefully, to her mother."

"Hopefully?" Morgan asked. "If she's with her mother, they're already out of the city."

"If she's with her mother, she's safe, Detective," I said.

"You think those guys are planning to double-cross Diana Wyatt?"

"Maybe."

"As I understand it, the way these contracts work, they've only received half of their money so far. If they want the rest, they have to hand over the girl."

"If that's all they want," Bridgett said.

"What more is there?" Morgan demanded, like she knew we'd been keeping secrets from her.

Bridgett shrugged, so the detectives looked at me. I decided I didn't want to get into slush funds and super-blacks right now, so I shrugged, too. "Where the hell is Fowler?" I asked. "He was supposed to be watching the safe house, waiting for a chance to talk to Moore."

"Oh, was he?" Hower sniped. "Was the pretty Fed trying to cut us out?"

"All I know is that we talked today," I said. "Fowler wanted to see Moore, and I figured the best way for him to do that would be to come by."

"Nice to be in the loop," Morgan muttered.

The doctor was tying off on my stomach, and because of the local, it felt very strange, as if she were tugging on skin that had fallen asleep. She seemed entirely oblivious to, or uninterested in, our conversation, just dropped the needle she had used in the biohazard bin and then moved her stool over so she could work on my face.

"You want a local for your cheek?" she asked.

"Will he be able to talk?" Hower asked.

"If he wants me to punch through to his mouth, sure."

"I'll take the local," I said.

Morgan and Hower said they'd talk to me some more when the doctor was done.

Bridgett had been alert enough to grab my T-shirt out of the rig, and after I was sewed up I put it back on, then went with her and a couple of officers to the 6th Precinct. Morgan and Hower rode along separately, with Yossi, Moore, and Knowles all shipped in other cars. It took a good hour and a half for Morgan and Hower to square everything with the local detectives, then we all went through the night again, this time with forms being filled out. I caught some time with no one asking me questions, found a phone, and called Dale.

"I'm not supposed to be there until midnight," he said after I identified myself.

"We lost her," I told him.

"Oh, God, no. What happened?"

I ran it down in shorthand, then asked Dale to call Corry and Natalie. "Tell them the cops may be calling, just to get all the facts."

"I'll tell them. What are we going to do?"

"Hell if I know," I said, and hung up.

Coming up the precinct stairs was Colonel Wyatt, followed by two officers. He was bundled up for warmth, a dark red scarf around his throat, and his chin was sunk deep into the fabric. Without my glasses, he looked almost cuddly to me. Neither cop offered him assistance as he struggled with the stairs. Both looked like they'd probably learned the hard way how he responded to such treatment. When he finally reached the landing one of the cops detached, went to look for a detective, and Wyatt saw me.

"You pussy-fucking cocksucker," he spat. "First last night, now this. You've ruined everything." It was a blatant accusation, and although he wasn't very clear, or even very loud, I heard everything he put into the statement. "You lost her."

"Yes."

"I knew you couldn't be trusted. What were you doing, huh? Getting a tongue-bath from your girlfriend? You're fucking worthless, Sergeant. You're no damn fucking good at all."

I had nothing to say to that.

"Now Diana has her, so now Diana wins, and you helped her do it. I knew I shouldn't have trusted you with her." He made his way to an old wooden bench along the wall, sat down hard. The skin around his mouth looked coated with a white blur, as if someone had applied correction fluid there, but not enough.

There's one ultimate truth of protection, and that truth is, simply, it's impossible to protect anyone absolutely. It just can't be done. All a bodyguard can do is reduce the odds, take precautions, and try to be sneakier than the opposition. That's it. Because, in the end, time and everything else is on the side of the other team. They can wait, they can plan, they can invest time and money, research and people that the protective effort will never be able to muster, and that, when it's all done, that's what will make the difference.

I knew that. I knew that there was no way I'd win going up against the SAS. I knew that the moment Sterritt and Hardy had come through the door, it had been all over.

It didn't make me feel better.

All of the knowledge, the rationalizations, the reasoning aside, I felt that Colonel Wyatt was right, and because of that, I felt like shit.

Detective Morgan appeared, introduced herself to Wyatt. She gave him space to let him stand up, then led him away, saying, "We need to go over what happened tonight, Colonel. Maybe you can help us."

"Diana won, that's what happened," Wyatt told her. He was looking at me. "Diana won."

Fowler arrived just before eleven, bags growing beneath his eyes, his perfect tan looking sallow in the precinct lights. He cut past me quickly, barely giving me time to ask where the fuck he'd been, why he hadn't shown up. His only response was a look over his shoulder at me, and his eyes were cold and tired, and I realized the rest of him probably was, too. Scott took a second, then motioned me and Bridgett to follow him. He found Moore, then an empty interrogation room, and when all of us were inside, he introduced himself to Moore.

"Nice to finally meet you," Scott said. He didn't sound like he meant it.

Moore looked him over. "You're a Fed? You don't fucking look like a Fed."

"Yeah, I'm a Fed."

"Piss off," Moore said. "Atticus, who is this guy?"

"He's the FBI agent I was telling you about."

"Yes, I'm the FBI agent he was telling you about," Scott said. "And I'm too tired to play the aren't-you-a-little-young, aren't-you-a-little-tan, what's-with-the-earrings-are-you-queer games, Sergeant. If you had fucking honored your agreement with our government, I wouldn't have to be here."

Moore leaned back in his chair and glared at Scott, and for a moment I thought it was a ludicrous situation. Physically, Moore was a monster compared to Scott. He certainly looked like he could tear the younger man in two. "Don't fucking blow hard on me, boy."

"You had two other men with you when you arrived," Scott told him. "One of them's here. Where's the other one?"

"Denny's been out of touch all day. And if you're thinking it was an inside job and he set us up, you're a fucking idiot. Denny's a good troop."

Scott reached into his coat pocket and removed three Polaroids. He set the photographs on the table in front of Moore, but both Bridgett and I could see them.

"Mother of God," Bridgett murmured.

The photographs were crime scene shots of a body, stuffed naked into the trunk of a car. A line of lacerated flesh ran in what looked like a circle about the dead man's scalp, where skin had been peeled up. His face showed serious bruising, shattered teeth, a broken nose, set on a head that wasn't quite centered on the neck. Another of the shots showed his right hand, three fingers missing after the second knuckle. The flash on the camera had made the photos studies of light and dark, but the wounds on Denny's body were clear and devastating.

"Is that Edward Denny?" Fowler asked. There was a strain in his voice that I'd never heard before.

"Oh, Jesus," Moore said.

"Is that him?"

Moore picked up the photographs one at a time, looking at each picture hard and long, boring the image into his memory. Then he handed them back to Scott. "That's Eddy," Moore said.

"The body was discovered around six this evening," Scott said.

"That's how they found the safe house." Bridgett said it softly. "They tortured him."

"The autopsy hasn't been completed, yet, but the preliminary evaluation is that the injuries were all inflicted prior to death."

"How'd he die?" Moore asked. "They know that, don't they? They know how he died?"

"We can't be certain, but it looks like they broke his neck."

Moore closed his eyes, preserving the pictures in his mind.

"I'll leave you alone," Scott told him. "You might want to tell your other man."

Moore moved his head in a nod.

We started out of the room, me following behind Fowler and Bridgett, and as I was reaching the door, Moore said, "Kodiak—I want to talk to you."

I told the others I'd catch up.

"Close the door."

I closed the door.

When I turned, Moore's face had gone to its battle mask, hard and cruel. It was a disturbing look.

"We find them," he said quietly, "Sterritt's mine."

I held his look. "Erika comes first," I said. "We get her back, you can do whatever you like with Sterritt. Erika has to come first."

Moore nodded, saying, "Of course," and I knew he was lying to me.

CHAPTER THIRTY-ONE

They cut us loose at one that morning, sending Colonel Wyatt to a hotel and the rest of us home. Moore and Knowles left together, after another long meeting with Fowler. There wasn't much anyone could say at that point, no new information to be revealed, and I left the precinct feeling empty and numb, Bridgett beside me. There'd been no word of Erika. She'd been gone five hours. The NYPD had retrieved some of our gear from the safe house. I asked about the Smith & Wesson, and was told that it was being held for its owner, Natalie Trent.

Third gun down, I thought.

We didn't talk about it, just went back to my apartment together, and after I'd locked us inside, Bridgett put her gym bag in my room and started undressing, saying that she wanted a shower. I took out my spare set of glasses, and with the world back in focus, made my way to the phone and checked the messages on my machine. There were two, both from Natalie, sounding concerned, saying that Dale had called her and asking if I knew where Bridgett was, asking me to call when I got in.

I put the kettle on, then went through the apartment, turning on the heat. By the time the water was boiling, Bridgett was out of the shower and back in my room, and I was pouring into two mugs when she emerged, dressed, and the phone rang.

"Should I get that?" Bridgett asked.

I nodded.

It was Natalie. They only talked for five minutes or so, during which time I settled at the table with my mug. The tea tasted bitter, and I wondered if I'd steeped the leaves for too long.

"No, we're both fine," Bridgett was saying. "I look like I've been attacked by rabid ball bearings, and Atticus looks like crap, but everybody came through in one piece . . . I don't know. . . . You want to talk to him? . . . I'll tell him . . . probably tomorrow. We'll call you . . . you, too."

"How is she?" I asked when Bridgett had hung up.

"She's worried, sounds guilty as hell. I think she thinks she should have been there." Bridgett took her mug and joined me at the table. "I asked if she wanted to talk to you, she said no."

The look she gave me was sympathetic, and I realized she thought Natalie and I still weren't getting along. I wanted to tell her then, took a breath to do just that, and then Bridgett was getting up from the table, dumping her mug down the drain.

"I'm fucking exhausted," she said. "And you are, too. Let's get some sleep. We'll need it tomorrow."

"And what are we doing tomorrow?"

"Finding Erika, boy-o."

For a very long time I found I couldn't sleep, and ended up just looking at her beside me. Bridgett breathed softly, the blankets pulled to her shoulders.

When she slept, her face relaxed, and her mouth hinted at a smile. She cradled the pillow to her head like a child holding on to a parent, and at the crook of her left arm, near me, I could see a scar on her skin, what looked like a skin graft. She'd stripped to just T-shirt and underwear, and I could feel the warmth coming off her skin. The radiator hissed, banged erratically, and the noise didn't touch her, and it was easy to imagine that nothing could.

But I knew better.

It was after ten when I awoke, could hear Bridgett moving in the kitchen. I got myself out of bed, made my way to the shower, and bathed quickly. I thought about shaving, decided that it would be an exercise in futility and pain. One hand and one cheek, I could almost see the blood flying.

I dressed, made my way back to the kitchen, and found Bridgett reading the paper.

"Coffee's on," she said.

I mumbled thanks and poured myself a mug.

"Scott called," Bridgett said. "An hour ago."

I'd never heard the phone ring. "What'd he say?"

"That they've got squat. He left a number for Moore, though. It's a service. I called and left a message. Hopefully he'll call back."

I drank my coffee, looking out the window. It was clear outside, and looked cold. Most of the snow had been cleaned from the streets. I sat down at the table.

"How'd you sleep?" she asked.

"Like shit."

"Yeah, I sort of figured."

"I've got something I need to tell you," I said. My voice sounded slighter, more distant, and my stomach-ache returned.

She put down the paper. "This sounds ominous." She smiled.

I nodded, tried to find my voice. Watching me,

Bridgett sensed it, then saw that something was coming, and her smile faded. "What?"

"I slept with Natalie," I told her. "Night before last, she came over after I got home, and we were drinking, and we ended up in bed together."

The skin at the outside of her eyes crinkled, and her mouth moved slightly, lips coming tighter together. Then her jaw started to relax, and I knew what she was thinking, could hear the excuse she was forming for me, and I had to stop her before she said it, I had to get there first.

"I knew what I was doing," I said. "I wanted to do it."

She breathed slowly.

"I wanted to do it," I repeated.

"You son of a bitch," she said.

I nodded.

Bridgett's face changed, the muscles going slack. Her chest rose and fell with her breath, and then she got up, went to the sink, then pivoted on her heel and looked back at me. Her look was as accusatory as the Colonel's had been the night before, as hard, and in it I saw pain. She held the look until it snapped, then turned her head away, tilting her chin down, letting her hair conceal her face. When she spoke, the anger in her voice was cold. "You no-good bastard."

I nodded again, knowing she wouldn't see it.

"That hurts. That really hurts," she said softly. I saw the muscles in her jaw flex as she bit against her teeth. "You knew about Elana, you knew how I felt about things like this."

I couldn't have hurt her more if I had tried, and I knew that was exactly what I had done. Tried to get out of the relationship before I wanted to stay in it, tried to get out before she could hurt me, before another Elana fell in love with her, before she could go away and break my heart.

So I'd done it myself, instead.

All I wanted was to take the pain away, to not hurt

her anymore, to never hurt her again. I would have given anything to do that.

"Why?" Bridgett asked.

It took me a while to answer. "Because I'm a fool. Because I'm terrified of being with you."

Her head bent down, her black hair almost touching the rim of the sink, and then she jerked her head back, her hands coming up, and she rounded on me, and she laughed, bitter and loud. "Bastard."

"I'm sorry, Bridgett," I said. "I know it's worth nothing, but I am sorry."

The floor creaked as she moved, stepping closer to me. "You can keep your fucking apology," she said softly. "You can give it to Natalie, you can give it to Rubin's memory, whoever the fuck you like, but don't try to hand it to me. I trusted you with something I've given only to two other people in my life, and you broke it, you just fucking broke it."

Her face was close to mine, and when I tried to meet her eyes, she moved away again, denying me, going to grab her jacket from the hook on the wall. Her left arm caught in the sleeve, and she tugged hard, twice, before getting it through.

In the alley below, I heard somebody laughing.

"I was afraid I'd lose you," I said.

"You have."

I closed my eyes, remembered to breathe. I made each word as clear as possible when I spoke. "You are precious to me," I said. "And I have lost precious things. A fire took the objects. A bomb took a friend. It took me too long to realize what you mean to me, and when I did, the thought of another loss, that loss . . . I didn't want that again."

I opened my eyes. Bridgett had a roll of Life Savers in her hand, was picking at the foil.

"Why didn't you trust me?" she asked. "Why didn't you tell me?"

"I didn't know what I felt. And then, when I did, when I knew, it was too late. I'd done the damage."

She looked down at the roll of candy in her hand, then flung it hard into the wall. The Life Savers shattered, flew free of their wrapping, pelting the floor.

"I gave you my heart," she said.

I was silent.

"We're no longer lovers," Bridgett said, finally. "We may not even be friends. I can't trust you with anything but business now. I can't trust you, do you understand?"

"Yes," I said.

"We see this out, that's it. I don't want to talk to you anymore. I don't want to know you for a while. I don't think I want to know you at all."

She looked past me, her mouth closed and jaw set, and the hurt I'd inflicted was so clear, and there was nothing I could do about it. She was right. There was nothing more to say, not even that I'd never loved her more.

Then the intercom went off, and Diana was begging me to let her inside.

CHAPTER THIRTY-TWO

We could hear her running up the stairs, and a second later she came off the landing, making straight for us in the doorway. It wasn't an all-out run, closer to a stagger, but when she saw us she came faster, saying, "God, I didn't know if you'd be here, I didn't know where to go."

I moved back, let her into the apartment, and Diana came inside, ignoring Bridgett, just stopping in the hall. I shut the door and looked at her. She had black corduroy pants on and a blue crewneck beneath her coat. The cold had brought a flush to her cheeks, but aside from that, she was almost bone-pale.

She was holding a brown cardboard box, not bigger than a loaf of bread.

"I got it this morning, it was delivered to my room, some girl just handed it to me and left." She was breathless, and not from exertion.

I took the box. It was unmarked, clean, just a strip of clear strapping tape running over the flaps at the top.

The tape had already been cut. When I opened the box, Diana turned away.

Inside, on cracked salt, was a piece of meat and cartilage with metal hoops through it. It took another second before I realized the hoops were earrings, and I recognized them, and I wanted to scream.

The bottom half of Erika's left ear.

Bridgett made a choking sound beside me, but didn't move. I felt my pulse kicking at my wrists and temples, and I felt light-headed.

Beneath the piece of ear was a folded sheet of white paper, speckled with blood.

Without a word, I went to the kitchen table and set the box down. Diana stayed still, standing motionless in the hall, as if the power that propelled her had been suddenly switched off.

When I removed the paper, I could hear the chunks of salt falling onto the tabletop and the floor.

The instructions had been typed. They were very simple. There was a time in military notation: 2000 hours. There was a location: a spot on the Harlem River in the South Bronx. There was a demand: four million dollars. There was a caution: no police, no Moore, no SAS, nobody but Diana.

And there was an ultimatum:

Do not call the police, or the Feds, or your husband, or anyone at all.

Money at 2000 and she's in your arms at 2001.

Fuck with us, and she's dead.

Bridgett turned on Diana, grabbed her by the shoulder, snarling, "Were you followed?"

"I don't know."

"Fuck, motherfuck." Bridgett pulled her gun and headed to the door, saying, "I'm going down to check. Don't go anywhere without me."

I folded the note again, put it back in the box, covering the ear. Then I took hold of Diana and put her in one of the chairs at the table. She let me move her without resistance, but her eyes went to the box the moment she was seated, and they stayed there.

"We need to call the police," I said.

Diana shook her head.

"Diana, we have to call the police. It's the only way."

"I can get the money," she said quietly. "It's all I have. I'll give it to them and they'll give her back."

"No, they won't. There's nothing to stop them from killing you and her if you go to the drop."

"They'll kill her if we go to the police!"

"Listen to me," I said. "They are going to kill her anyway. The only way to get Erika back alive is with help."

"I know that! I know that, that's why I'm here!"

To ask me for help. Jesus, Erika was right, I thought. I'm a gullible fool, and I do it with my eyes wide open. "I can't do it alone," I told Diana.

She shook her head, still looking at the box.

I knelt down beside the table, so I could catch her eyes. For an instant she met my gaze, and I took it, speaking softly. "You must trust me. You must let me do this how I think best. There's still a chance to help Erika, to stop them. You have to trust me."

She just stared at me. Finally, she nodded, once.

"Where's the money now?" I asked.

"In storage," Diana said. "A place in Queens."

"Do they know it's there? Sterritt and Hardy?"

"No."

"You're sure?"

"I paid them out of the place in Baltimore and Credit Suisse downtown. Then I moved the money. I moved it, I didn't want them robbing me."

"Okay, you're going to have to go out there and get it, Diana. Go out to Queens, get the damn money, and come back here."

"But—"

"Now," I said. "I'll be here. Just get it and come back."

She shook her head like she was trying to wake up,

focused on me again. Her eyes were dull, as if she hadn't heard anything I'd told her.

"Then we'll go to the drop together," I said.

Diana got up. Her glance snagged one last time on the box. Bridgett was coming back down the hall as I let Diana out.

"It looks clear," Bridgett reported.

"Come right back," I told Diana. "Don't stop anywhere."

"I get her," Diana said suddenly, her voice brittle with hope. "When Erika's back and safe, I get her, right?"

Bridgett looked at me, and her eyes were accusing.

"When she's back and safe," I told Diana, "she's yours."

Diana accepted that with a nod, then continued on. We watched her go to the stairs, and when she was out of sight, I went back into the apartment, heading for the phone.

"Where's she going?"

"To get the money," I said. "I'm going to call Fowler, let him know, see if we can catch the bastards at the drop."

"You're going to let her make the exchange? You're going to let her leave with Erika?"

"I'm going to get Erika back. Then it'll be her decision."

"She won't be in any condition to make that choice," Bridgett said. "You can't let her mother be there, Erika won't be able to say no."

I put down the phone. "We don't even know if we'll be *able* to get her back," I said. "Who she goes with isn't even an issue, yet."

"It is, it's a huge issue. That girl is being bandied between parents like stock options." Bridgett's face was white with anger.

"What do you want me to do?"

"Cut Wyatt in."

"And how do I do that?"

"Tell Fowler that Wyatt has to be at the drop. He can come in after we've got Erika back. Let her make her choice."

"She won't be in any condition to make a choice, you just said so yourself."

"Then Wyatt has to be there, or else it's just another kidnapping under another name." She said it stubbornly.

"You bring him in, then."

"Fine."

I went into my room, fumbled through my stuff, and found my radios. Bridgett stood in the doorway watching me while I took out my two sets. These were my work radios, small units that could be affixed to a belt, with three leads running off them, one to the palm to transmit, one to the lapel as the mike, and one to the ear as the speaker. I hooked all the wires up for one of them, turned it on, and gave it a squelch. The charge looked good, so I shut it off and turned to hand it over to Bridgett.

She was looking at the box of condoms.

"Here, take this," I said, tossing the radio onto the bed. "Don't turn it on until after we've got Erika, or you'll run the battery down. I'll call you when it's clear to bring the Colonel in."

Bridgett picked up the radio without a word, putting it inside her jacket, beside her holstered gun. Then she started out to the front door.

"Where are you going?"

"None of your fucking business. I'll get Wyatt, I'll have him at the drop. That's all you need to know."

"You're just going to leave?"

Bridgett's boot heel left a mark on the floor when she spun to face me. "Yes. I am just going to leave. I don't want to be around you right now. I told you that. I'll call Fowler in a couple of hours, make certain that I know all those important details you won't want ignored."

And then she left.

———

It took two hours of phone tag to get everything together, starting with the call to Fowler. Scott listened to me very carefully, and he made it plain that he thought bringing the Colonel out was a bad idea.

"If it goes wrong, and he's there, he could end up seeing his daughter killed," Scott said.

"Then let's hope it doesn't go wrong."

There was a moment's pause, and then he said, "Time's working against us, Atticus. If they've half a brain, they'll already have staked the drop site out, in anticipation of this sort of maneuver."

"I'm trying to reach Moore. He trained them. He knows how they'll be thinking. He can help you position your people."

"If he gets in touch with you."

"He will. He wants to be there for the takedown, now more than ever. I'll steer him your way."

"You're going to ride out there with her? Mrs. Wyatt?"

"Yes."

"That could tip the whole thing."

"No, I don't think so. Sterritt knows that Diana and I have a history. He'll accept that she went to me for help."

Fowler sighed. Then he said, "I'll call Morgan and Hower, let them know what's happening. They'll want to be involved."

"Whose people will you use?"

"Probably theirs."

"Make sure they know what's going on," I said. "I don't want a sniper shooting too early, or putting a bullet in my back."

"Hell, you've already been shot once in the front," Scott said. "Do you figure another wound will stop you?"

"I don't want to find out."

We made arrangements for someone to come over

and get the box for evidence, and the courier had just left my apartment when the phone started ringing again.

"Go," Moore said when I picked up.

"We've got a swap," I said.

"The son of a whore tried a double cross, didn't he?"

"This morning. He sent the ultimatum to Diana at her hotel room. He wants four million dollars or Erika's dead."

"Was that all he sent?"

"No," I said, remembering the hoops, how small they had looked.

"A finger."

"Her left ear," I said. "I suppose that was kind."

"He won't be able to die enough," Moore said.

"You need to call Fowler right now," I said. "He's going to contact NYPD about getting coverage, but if they try to move in without knowing what they're up against, it could blow the whole thing."

"They haven't sent anyone out to the drop, have they?" he asked, and the alarm was loud in his voice.

"Not yet. Not that I know of."

"Jesus God, they had better not. What's his number?"

I gave him Scott's number. "Call him now," I said.

"I will, I will," Moore said, and I thought he would hang up, but he didn't, and there was just line silence for a couple of seconds. Then Moore asked, "You remember what I said last night?"

"Yes."

"Can I count on you?"

"Erika first."

"Erika first," Moore confirmed.

I thought about what he was asking, about everything that had happened, about how he had acted the night before, and the night before that. About the cracked salt that was still spilt on my kitchen table.

"Once we get Erika clear, he's all yours," I said.

"See you tonight," Robert Moore said, and he hung up.

Diana didn't return to my apartment until almost two that afternoon, buzzing from outside. I came down to meet her, stuffing my radio into my jacket pocket as I went down the stairs. She was waiting for me at the door, and she looked marginally better, with more color to her skin, more certainty to her movements.

"Where are you parked?" I asked.

She indicated her car, a rented Taurus, dark red, parked down the block. Some kids were lurking in the doorways near the vehicle, and I thought that would just be brilliant, for three street kids to boost a car loaded with four million dollars. I grabbed Diana's elbow and began walking to the Taurus, and she yanked her arm free, almost slipping on the ice. The kids pulled back when we approached.

"Keys," I said to Diana.

"I can drive."

"You'll drive tonight. Give me the keys."

She handed over the keys, and I unlocked the doors, waited until she was inside before sliding behind the wheel myself. My stomach got surly at the motion, and I went slow.

"Buckle up," I said.

Diana complied without objection, and I started the car, pulled out carefully onto the street. Traffic was heavy. A cab shot past us as we did so, and I swore.

"I thought you didn't like to drive," Diana said.

"I don't. What took you so long?"

She produced two plane tickets from her coat pocket. "I had to stop and get these. We're flying out of JFK at ten."

"Where's the money?"

"They won't get to leave with it, will they? I need it. It's for Erika and me."

"No, they won't get to leave with it," I said.

"It's in the trunk, in a briefcase."

Four million dollars in one briefcase, I wondered, and then I remembered her offer at the Bonnaventure, before she had shot me. Diamonds and emeralds. "You converted all of it?"

"Most of it," Diana said. Under her breath, so low I almost missed it, she added, "Just like they taught me."

"What about this car? How'd you get it?"

"Why are you asking all these questions?"

"How'd you rent the car, Di?"

"I used a credit card. Don't worry, it's fake. Mark never saw it."

"Have a lot of fake cards, do you?"

"I've got enough for an emergency."

"Rubin teach you that?"

She looked over at me.

"Yeah," I said. "I know."

"How?"

"Erika told me."

"Erika knew?"

"Erika knew, Di. Erika knew every last detail. You and me, you and Rubin, the Colonel and his whores. She knew it all." I stopped at a light, checking the mirrors. I didn't think we were being followed, but there was no way I could be certain with all of the afternoon traffic. I hoped not. Where we were going, I most certainly hoped not.

"She's a smart young lady," Diana said. She sounded proud.

"Then maybe you ought to let her decide for herself who she wants to be with, you or the Colonel."

Diana laughed. "Smart, I said, not invulnerable. Doug's twisted her mind around, the child can't possibly know what she wants."

"And you do?"

"I know," Diana said.

"Have you talked to her at all?"

"I know."

"Have you?"

"Yes."

"When?"

"A couple of weeks ago."

"She said it'd been a couple of years."

"She lied to you."

"Or you're lying to me."

That set her off. "It doesn't matter when I talked to her!" Diana shouted. "Doug shouldn't have her, Atticus! I'm her mother. I'm the better parent, I'm the one she needs, the one who cared for her, the one who isn't dying because he couldn't keep his dick in his pants!"

She fell silent, maybe because she'd said too much, or because she realized where we had stopped. She looked at all the squad cars lined up outside the 13th Precinct. I turned off the engine, began getting out of the car.

"What the hell are you doing?" Diana demanded.

I just shook my head.

"You said you were going to just call them." She made it sound as if I had been the one to cut off Erika's ear.

"Come on."

"Absolutely not. There's an APB out on me. I'm wanted, remember?"

"Oddly enough, I do. They won't arrest you."

"I'm not going in there."

And that was it, and without warning I heard myself shouting at her. "Get out of the fucking car and get inside the fucking station, now, Diana!"

She blinked, startled, and I realized it was the first time I'd ever raised my voice in her presence, the first time she had ever heard me shout. Diana said softly, "I just want to know—"

"Get out of the fucking car, now!"

Diana got out of the car, her boots sinking into the dirty snow.

"Thank you," I told her.

———

"There's an Emergency Services Unit team already been deployed," Detective Morgan told me. "Fowler, Moore, and Knowles are with them. They've been setting up for the last two hours. ESU is taking advice from Moore, so we should be covered on that end."

"The swap's set for when?" Hower asked.

"Eight tonight," I said.

He checked his watch, whistled softly. "Can you imagine what it must be like to have to stay perfectly still under cover for eight hours?"

I nodded, and he raised an eyebrow, so I said, "I was in the Army."

"So was I. Never had to do that, though."

I shrugged, found a pencil on the desk they had seated me at, and a piece of paper. "Tic-tac-toe?" I asked, drawing the board.

"I'll kick your cowboy ass," Hower said.

"Does she want some coffee?" Morgan asked me, motioning to Diana with her lit cigarette. Some of the ash flicked off when she pointed. "You can answer me, ma'am. It won't be used against you."

Hower chuckled and I looked over at Diana. She was seated beside another detective's desk, staring at me. She hadn't spoken since we'd gone into the station, and although she was well within earshot, hadn't contributed to our conversation. Occasionally, she would check her watch, but otherwise, she'd said nothing.

"Do you want some coffee?" I asked her, handing the pencil to Hower. "It's pretty bad stuff."

"Just bias her, why don't you," Hower grumbled. He considered my opening move, and put an "O" in the upper left corner, then handed the pencil back.

"No," Diana said.

"You ought to try and relax," Detective Morgan told her.

Diana said, "It's not your daughter."

Morgan knocked ash onto the floor, crushed it with her shoe. "No, I guess it isn't."

"Then don't tell me to relax."

The detective sighed, turned back to me and asked, "Where's the money? We need to mark the bills."

"It's at my apartment," I said, passing the pencil back once more. "I didn't want to bring it, leave it in the car."

Diana tilted her chin slightly, almost smiled. I was protecting her investment, after all.

"Your car is not going to get jacked up in front of the One-Three." Hower marked another "O."

"Says you. I've lived in this city for a while now. Stranger things have happened."

He handed the pencil back to me. "You're losing. You had the first move, in the center of the board, and you've managed to lose at tic-tac-toe. I'm truly impressed."

I crossed out the board and began writing on the pad. "How about Hangman?"

Hower looked at what I had written and said, "Sure."

"I'm going to use the bathroom first," I said. "Which way is it?"

Hower gave me directions, and I excused myself, went to the men's room. I used the sink to wash my face, dried off, then took off my shirt and began hooking up my radio. I only used two of the leads, the mike and the transmit button, because I could conceal both of those from Diana. If I ran the speaker to my ear, she'd spot that, and I didn't want her to know that the Colonel had been invited to the party.

It took him five minutes, and then Hower came in with another bundle of wires. "We were going to suggest this, anyway," he said. "Why are you so anxious to wear it?"

"Insurance," I said.

Hower paused to check his bald spot, see if it was still naked and in place.

"I don't know what's going to happen out there tonight. I want a record of it," I said. "And I don't want Diana to know that I'm wired."

He began unwrapping the set, then looked me over and asked, "Two radios?"

"One of them's to keep in touch with Moore. He's on a different frequency."

"He's going to be on the ESU channel. We all will be."

"Moore's SAS," I said. "He's got a different channel for himself and Knowles."

Detective Hower hesitated, his blond eyebrows knitting together, then he began wrapping the new radio around my middle.

"Watch the stitches."

"Yeah, yeah," he muttered. "You're a fucking disaster, you know that? I've seen better-looking bodies after an autopsy."

"At least you don't have to shave my chest," I said.

"Lucky me. You normally go so smooth?"

"They shaved me for the surgery, asshole."

Hower laughed, handed me the new microphone, and helped me tape it to my chest. I pulled on my shirt, then ran my other wires, putting the transmitter down my right arm and wrapping it around my wrist, and finally pinning the mike to the inside of my collar.

"You are just way too technical," Hower said. "We should get back, or Mrs. Wyatt will become nervous."

"Will you be recording?" I asked.

"Anything that plays off our wire will go to tape. You are now acting as an agent of the NYPD."

"I'm a snitch?"

"In a word."

"I need one other thing," I said. "My gun, the one that you guys took after the shoot-out on the street. Can I get that back?"

"You planning on shooting anyone, cowboy?"

I didn't answer.

CHAPTER THIRTY-THREE

Diana stayed silent while she guided the Taurus through the heavy traffic on the Grand Central Parkway, making our way to the Harlem River. I kept my eyes on the mirrors, checking the other vehicles. We were clear.

It was just the two of us, now. Morgan and Hower were following along a different route entirely, and would take up a holding position a good five blocks from the site. The last we heard, Moore and Fowler and the rest were holding steady. Apparently, they hadn't been made.

We were passing Yankee Stadium when Diana asked, abruptly, "Do you remember when he found out about us?"

"The Colonel?"

She nodded, then signaled a lane change. She was a cautious driver; Bridgett would have called her timid, or worse.

"Yes," I said.

"Do you remember what he said?"

"He said he'd ruin me. He chewed me out in the middle of your living room, in front of you, and he said he would have me dishonorably discharged, and that he'd make the rest of my life hell."

She cracked a grin. "And I said, 'You do, and I'll tell everyone in this town that I was fucking him.' He looked like I'd kicked him in the teeth."

"I don't think he expected you to react that way."

"No, he didn't. He thought I was just like him, and that you were nothing to me. And then Doug offered you a posting, anywhere you wanted, and you were gone by the end of the month."

"Is that when you took up with Rubin?"

She cast a glance my way, then went back to looking at the road. "No."

"You'd been seeing him before that." It wasn't a question.

"After you left, we became exclusive. Doug never found out about Rubin."

"Why?" I asked. "I mean, I know this sounds horribly naïve, but I thought you loved me. Was I wrong? Was it Rubin you loved?"

She didn't say anything for the next mile or so. I listened to the engine and the road, felt the tires bumping over the salt and sand and asphalt. The transmitter for my radio was digging into my back, and I tried to ignore it. My stitches itched, and the wire taped to my chest made it hard to breathe.

"Yes and no," Diana finally answered. "I loved you both, and I didn't love either of you."

"Nice paradox."

"I was lonely. You were what I needed, both of you."

"It's good to be needed," I said.

Diana fell silent, turning off the expressway and onto 167th Street. We were now heading toward the water. The digital clock on the radio read 7:43.

"Where will you go?" I asked her.

"California. I've always wanted to live in California," she said. "Which way?"

"Right, here."

She signaled and turned, and we were heading north again. After a mile I told her to make a left, and we ran west for another mile or so, and each block we passed seemed more devastated than the previous one. Economics in the Bronx had led to endless abandoned buildings, and they stood now in decay, waiting in vain for money and interest. It would never happen.

The clock now read 7:50, and Diana stopped for a light. I looked at her, but she kept her eyes on the road.

The light went to green and we started forward once more, and after another two minutes, the Harlem River came into view. The road curved north, following the bend of the choppy water. Along our left were empty lots, abandoned buildings, the whole terrain suddenly looking more like downtown Sarajevo than New York.

It made me scared, not only for myself, but for Erika. Until now, I hadn't allowed myself to believe we were too late, that she might be dead already, but suddenly the possibility was forcing itself to the fore. Sterritt could have killed Erika, assuming that Diana would bring the money to the swap all the same. Once she was on his ground, there was no reason to honor the deal. He could just hope to shoot her, take the money, and run.

Only decency, honor, or caution would keep him from doing so. And I knew he wasn't decent, and I knew he wasn't honorable. But he had seemed cautious, if cocksure, and my hope was that he had kept Erika alive to ensure that the money would come to him. After it was in his hands, then he'd be willing to kill her, but not before, not when she was still good insurance.

The logic seemed fine, but it didn't make me feel better. Sterritt had chosen a site out in the middle of nowhere, away from witnesses and prying eyes. The only reason to pick such a place was if he planned on a lot of killing.

I hoped to God that Moore knew what he was doing, that I could trust him.

"Slow down," I told Diana, and began scanning for the cross street. Cars had been abandoned along the side of the road, and I knew they would make good hiding places for a sneaky SAS bastard to stay in cover and perform recon. This side of the river looked like a junkyard, with trash and machinery left to rot and rust. Crisp snow clung to everything, reflecting light, and making the shadows long and blue.

The lot Sterritt had picked was another four hundred yards north, and as Diana turned into it the headlights lit a form, lumpy and twisted, and for a moment I panicked, thought the whole night was blown, that the ESU and Moore and Fowler and all the cops in the tri-state area had been made.

It was a snowman.

A pathetic-looking, malformed, lumpy snowman, with an empty bottle of some kind of liquor in its right hand.

The clock read 7:59, and as we stopped, it flicked to 8:00.

"Where is he?" Diana asked, not certain if she should panic.

"He's here. He's watching."

She killed the engine, leaving the headlights on. The beams made the snowman look as if he had been frozen in midmelt. I unwrapped the tape from the splint around my fingers, removed the metal, dropped the pieces on the car floor. My fingers hurt when I moved them, but I could use the hand if I had to, and that was what mattered.

"Now what?" Diana asked.

"Now we get out," I said. "And you get the money out of the trunk."

I took my time, going slower than I needed to. One of Sterritt's men would be lookout, I was sure, set somewhere in cover with a radio and a pair of binoculars. If he thought I was below par, that I was slow and no threat, so much the better.

I heard Diana slam the trunk shut, felt the car rock slightly as I got out. She came around to my side as I closed the door. The briefcase was brown leather, with brass clasps and fittings, expensive.

I scanned the surrounding area, looking at the line of buildings and the darkness. The river was audible, barely, flowing fast and nearby. Farther away I could hear traffic, and a distant siren, and then I heard the engine, saw the lights stream over the broken chunks of concrete as it came out of the darkness from across the street and came at us, fast, water and snow sluicing away from its wheels.

Diana and I stepped back, against the side of the Taurus, and the new car came around in a slide, then braked on the opposite side of the snowman, its head-lights blinding us.

I winced and thought, nice entrance.

We heard the doors opening, and then they got out, three of them. Hardy had been driving, and he stood behind his opened door, both hands out of sight. In the space between the ground and the bottom of the car door, I saw a piece of fabric dangling, the strap to his submachine gun.

From the passenger side door came another man, the one who had been driving the other car in the shoot-out, the one with the ponytail. He looked young, and I tried to remember the descriptions Scott had given me, figured it was Perkins. He kept his hands out of sight, too, but it wasn't as if I couldn't guess what he was holding.

And from the back came Mark Sterritt, holding Erika in a headlock against his chest. He had his Browning to her head.

She looked terrible, still wearing the clothes she had been taken in, the blue jeans and my sweatshirt, and I could see the dark stains of blood on the left shoulder, where it had run down the sleeve and front. A strip of duct tape covered her mouth, and her nostrils were flared as she tried to breathe. Another strip had been wrapped around her wrists, and a third to bind her arms to her body. The bloody bandage over her left ear looked black in the night, sodden and useless.

Three of them and Erika. Sterritt, Hardy, and Perkins. Which meant that somewhere out in the darkness lurked Cox with his radio, his binoculars, and probably a high-powered rifle.

Again, I prayed that Moore knew what he was doing, that I could buy enough time for everyone to get into position.

"Hey, Lucky, didn't think we'd be seeing you again," Mark Sterritt called to me.

"Bad luck," I said.

"For you." He took his time looking around, checking the surroundings. "Moore hiding out here, is he?"

"Moore doesn't know we're here," I answered.

"That right? Diana, is that right?"

"That's right," she said. Her voice could have frozen out a furnace.

Sterritt made a noise that sounded like a chuckle, then moved the Browning from Erika to us and then to the snowman. He fired two shots, and snow exploded from the shape, flew away from the malformed head, and the bottle dropped from the frozen hand.

Nothing else.

"Just checking," Sterritt said tightly. He came forward carefully, with Erika still gripped tight, the gun steady under her chin. Hardy and Perkins eased away from the car as he came forward, and I saw the submachine guns in their hands, the MP5s they had used at the safe house. Their move kept Sterritt from blocking their line of fire, and I thought that they were very well trained, indeed.

When Sterritt had reached the front of their Buick, he stopped. Erika's eyes were wide and clear. Good, I thought. She's with us, she's aware. If they had doped her up it would have only made things worse, but instead of drugs to control her, they had relied on fear, and that meant that if she could remember to think, we had another advantage.

Diana took a couple of steps forward, saying, "Baby?"

"Don't. Don't move," Sterritt chided, and made a big show of casually adjusting the position of the barrel beneath Erika's chin. "She's fine, you can see that."

"She's not fine," Diana spat. "She's not fine at all. This wasn't what I paid you for."

"So we modified the arrangement, sue us," Sterritt said.

"I paid you already."

"And we incurred more expenses, and then Lucky there killed one of my men. Think of this as hazard pay. I assume that's the money you're holding in your pretty little hands?"

"Yes."

"Four million?"

"Yes. Cash and jewels."

Sterritt nodded. "Cash and jewels. I love the way that sounds, cash and jewels." He looked over his shoulder, first at Hardy, then at Perkins. "Don't you love the way that sounds, boys?"

Neither answered.

"Toss it over here," Sterritt told Diana.

"Let her go, first," I said, trying to buy time, trying to think of a way to get Erika clear.

Sterritt thought that was very funny. "You figure you're in position to give orders, here?"

Gibraltar, I remembered.

"Can I show you something?" I asked.

"I don't know. Is it small and shriveled?"

I held out my right hand, palm up, so he could see it.

"Don't read palms," Sterritt said.

I held up my left hand, palm out, so he could see that, too.

"Don't do sign language, either."

I moved my left hand to my right wrist, and tugged

the transmit button into my palm. Hardy was on the ball, and he zeroed his MP5 on me, and I said, "I wouldn't."

Sterritt looked at Hardy, then to me, and asked, "Why the fuck not?"

"Because what I just put in my palm is a detonator," I said. "And what I put in our Taurus is fifteen pounds of plastique, give or take an ounce. Just to keep you honest, you understand."

"You're shitting me."

"I'm happy to push the button, let you find out."

Sterritt thought for a moment, readjusting his hold slightly on Erika. Her eyes moved from her mother to me and back, and I knew she was following us, that she was hearing it all.

At my left, Diana was looking at me as if I were crazy. I don't know if she believed me or not, if she thought that I had somehow managed to load explosives into the car, but it didn't matter as long as she didn't blow the bluff.

Sterritt said, "No. No, I don't believe you. You're not that hard. You won't kill the girl."

"If she's going to die anyway," I said, "I'm happier if it's at my hands."

"You're not that good."

"Maybe not, but I am a fast learner."

He thought for another second. "How do I know she hasn't filled that briefcase there with rocks?"

I held out my left hand to Diana, said, "Give me the case."

She hesitated, and I almost asked again, and then she handed me the briefcase. It was heavy, and the pressure of the handle on my sore fingers made it feel as if I had needles pushing into my hand.

"Meet you at the snowman," I told Sterritt.

"Glenn, make the swap." Sterritt said it sharply.

Hardy slid out his Browning, came around the front of the car to Erika's side. He handed the MP5 to Sterritt, who stepped back, then Hardy put his Browning against Erika's ribs, took her shoulder in his free hand.

With Hardy now holding on to their prisoner, Sterritt stepped back, gun trained. "You and Glenn," he told me.

I started forward and Glenn Hardy started forward, and it took each of us about ten paces to be within reaching distance of each other. The snowman, head missing from stubby body, stood to my left like a referee at the start of a nightmarish basketball game.

"Open it," Hardy told me.

I set the briefcase down in the snow, keeping my right hand curled around the button in my palm. I knelt, eyes on Hardy, on the position of his gun. I used my left hand to feel for the clasps, to hit the release tabs, and when both had sprung open, I pulled back the lid.

Hardy looked down, and the gun came away from Erika's side, and then his knees buckled, and he started to fall. The sound followed the bullet, the report echoing across the lot and the concrete and the water, and I was launching already, my gun in my hand. Erika pitched forward, and I caught her on my left shoulder, wrapped my arm around her, and brought her to the ground, firing two shots blind at where Perkins had been standing, and then we were in the snow, me rolling over Erika, covering her with my body. I heard Diana's garbled shouts, the chatter of Sterritt's submachine gun, and more snow spat as the snowman took the shots for us.

I raised my head and my gun, saw that Perkins was already down. Sterritt was backing away from the car. He fired another burst that pinged off the concrete and the vehicles. There was motion on all sides, voices, and pressing Erika down I tried to bead on Sterritt as he retreated into the shadows, when one of the shadows burst out of the snow, and Moore had him by the throat. Sterritt tried to raise the MP5, tried to slam it like a club against his former teacher.

He never had a chance. Moore broke his neck before Sterritt had even begun the downswing.

And it was suddenly deeply quiet, and I realized that I was laughing, and I holstered my gun and pulled Erika up into my arms and said, "This'll hurt," and then tore the tape from her mouth, and she didn't yelp, didn't scream.

She said, "I believed you."

I held on to her with my left, and with my right began feeling over Hardy's body, found his knife in his pocket, where I knew it would be. I snapped the blade out with my thumb, began cutting the tape around her wrists and body, and she winced as I pulled it away, but she put her arms around me when she was free, and I helped her up, my arms around her, and Erika kept saying, "I believed you, I believed you."

She wouldn't let go of me, and I didn't mind that at all, just held her and watched as Fowler and the ESU began clearing the scene, moving around Erika and me as if we were the eye of some human hurricane. Emergency lights appeared, and official vehicles, and an ambulance, and people were talking on radios and to each other, and their words didn't matter. Fowler told me they had caught Cox, that he had surrendered, and that Perkins would live. Sterritt and Hardy were both dead. Scott told me I could relax, and let Erika go. I didn't. He moved off, saying nothing.

Then Diana cleared her throat, and I saw that she was standing over Hardy, and she said, "Erika?"

Erika didn't answer.

"Honey?"

Erika moved her head cautiously, so that her wounded ear wouldn't rest against me, and looked at her mother. The bandage was loose, and I could see the piece of her ear that remained, and it looked painful and infected, thick with dried blood.

"Honey, I want you to come home with me," Diana said. "I want you to come and live with me."

Erika looked up at my face, and in her eyes there was

the question, and the only answer I could think of was to press my transmit button and say softly, "Bring him in."

The Porsche pulled up within seconds, and Erika and I turned to see Bridgett stop the car beside the ESU van. After a moment, Colonel Wyatt climbed out from the passenger side, and then Bridgett emerged. From where he had been standing by Fowler, I saw Moore react to the arrival. He began jogging over to us.

I heard Diana saying, "She's coming with me, Doug. You had her already, now she's mine."

The Colonel ignored his wife, standing slumped beside the car, encased in his winter clothes. Only his face was visible, the rest of his body wrapped in flannel, wool, and Polarfleece. He was breathing heavily, like he was wounded.

"Erika," he said. "Stay with me."

Erika looked from him, to me, to her mother. "No," she said, but I was the only one who heard her, and I understood exactly what she meant.

"I'm taking her with me," Diana said. She was still talking to Wyatt.

"You stupid fucking cunt." Saliva gleamed on the Colonel's chin.

"She's mine. She wants to be with me."

"She wants to be with you so fucking much you had to hire mercs to steal her away from me?"

"To save her!" Diana said it with quiet ferocity.

"Yeah, they did a nice job of that."

"You don't deserve her! You got everything else, but not her, you can't have her!"

"You stupid fucking cunt. You have nothing. You're getting nothing from me. Give it the fuck up. What else can you do?"

She can go for a gun, I thought, and even as I did, Diana was bending to Hardy's body, coming up with his Browning in her hand.

"This," she said.

CHAPTER THIRTY-FOUR

"Are you out of your fucking mind?" Bridgett demanded.

Diana steadied the gun with both hands, put the sight on the Colonel's forehead.

"What are you going to do? Shoot all of us?"

"Just whoever gets in my way." Diana said it flatly.

"Shut up," the Colonel told Bridgett without looking away from his wife. He was grinning.

No, I thought. Not in front of your daughter. No. "Colonel," I said.

"Stay the fuck out of this, Sergeant. It's between her and me."

Bridgett and Moore were still. Erika was staring at her parents, arms still around my waist, and she had started to tremble. Farther off, Fowler and Morgan and Hower were in a tête-à-tête with Knowles and the ESU commander. The ambulance had gone, but the ESU van still remained, and around it milled several of the team personnel, joking and waiting. Their helmets were off, their guns slung, celebrating a job well done.

Not quite.

"Maybe you haven't noticed?" Bridgett said to Diana. "But this place is crawling with cops."

"I noticed," Diana said.

"Everybody shut up!" the Colonel shouted, a command, like in the old days. He began walking toward his wife, ignoring the gun.

The chatting stopped, the joking went dead. It took a second for the team to realize what they were seeing, just a heartbeat, and then people were moving through the snow, and I heard the radios crackle once more, heard orders sent down the line as the ESU quickly redeployed. The river continued its contented burble. I heard Fowler demanding that people hold tight, that they hold their fire.

"Don't move any closer," Diana told her husband.

"What're you going to do?" He didn't break stride. "Shoot me?"

"I hate them," Erika hissed. Talking to herself, maybe just thinking out loud.

The Colonel stopped directly in front of his wife, braced his legs. Diana held the Browning steady, and the hate that ran between the two seemed to melt the snow at their feet.

Colonel Wyatt put his forehead against the barrel of the gun, and told Diana, "I shit on you, you're nothing, you're worthless."

"Dad—" Erika said.

"Less than nothing. I used you, and you let me. I ran you, I made you, and I broke you. Get your payback, whore. Pull the trigger. Get your payback."

Erika jerked forward, and I reached to pull her back to me but she kept going, straight to her parents.

Despite the cold I could see Diana sweating, motionless, staring at her husband, at the end of the gun.

"Colonel," I said. "Stand down."

"What are you waiting for?" he taunted. "Go ahead,

do it. Do something right. Just once, do something right."

The ESU were forming a perimeter around us, with Morgan and Hower and the rest. Guns were out once more, held in the low-ready, sights canted to the ground. It had gone quiet, even the radios were dead. I could hear the river water clearly at my back, and the dry scrape of Bridgett's boots shifting in the snow.

Erika said, "Please stop." It wasn't clear which parent she was addressing.

"Stay out of this, Erika." The Colonel didn't turn his head. His eyes stayed on Diana.

"Daddy, please—"

"I said stay the fuck out of this, little girl!"

Erika took a step back, and one of the ESU men began inching forward, perhaps to reach out and draw Erika away from the line of fire, but it was a mistake, because Diana moved for the first time, cocked the gun. "Don't," she said. "Don't. Anybody moves, I'll blow his head off."

The circle rippled as weapons went from low-ready to zero, as sights locked on to Diana. Fowler told everyone that he wanted them alive, to hold their fire.

"Erika, stay here." Diana's voice was strained and low, and the condensation when she spoke drifted out past the gun, around the Colonel's face.

The Colonel coughed. He moved slightly, as if to turn away. Then he spat into his wife's face.

Diana didn't flinch.

ESU hadn't fired, no one had fired, and that meant they'd made a choice, I knew. It all came down to Erika. She was the goal, she was the reason, hers was the life they had to save, and if she could keep her parents alive, they'd give her the chance.

It all comes down to her.

Erika seemed to know that, and she turned away from her parents, and began heading back to me.

She had gone five feet when her mother said, "Erika, get back here."

"Keep her out of this," the Colonel said. "This time it's just you and me. Leave her out of this."

"Get back here right now!" Diana's voice was thin and a little shrill. "You're coming with me!"

"No," Erika said.

"I'll kill him," Diana said.

Erika stopped, and the look on her face reminded me of her mother, when Diana had stood over me, and not put a bullet in my head.

"Good," Diana whispered, and she moved her left leg back for support. I saw the Colonel brace himself for her shot. "Get the case and bring it over here. Get the case and bring it to me, honey."

Erika spun in the snow, shouting, "Fuck you!" Her voice cracked, then, and the words told me how very young she was.

"Don't you dare talk to me like that!"

"Or what? You'll shoot Dad? You'll shoot me? Why not shoot Atticus again?"

"You get the case right now. You're coming with me, young lady."

"Don't you move, little girl," the Colonel ordered. "Don't you fucking listen to that whore."

Erika's eyes went from her father to her mother, then around the guns on the perimeter.

I wondered if the sniper who had shot Hardy was still in position, if he was setting his sight on the base of Diana's skull.

"This is what I want, Erika," the Colonel said.

Quietly, Erika asked, "What you want?"

"Yes."

She stared at her father.

"This has nothing to do with you. It's what I want."

"I understand."

I heard the anger rattling in her reply.

Erika nodded, then knelt, began closing the clasps on the briefcase. The sound was loud in the silence, like gunfire. When it was shut, she rose once more, taking the case in both hands, holding it in front of her like an oversized lunch pail.

"Is this what *you* want?" Erika asked her mother.

"That's a good girl," Diana said. "Bring it over here, honey, by me. Then we'll go to the car together."

Erika nodded, and the Colonel bit out a curse, and then saw that his daughter was backing away from them. When she reached me, Erika put her right hand out for my left arm, and I felt her fingers grip tight. She continued stepping backward, slow paces to make certain of her footing, the case now in one hand, me held with the other. I went with her.

"What are you doing?" Diana demanded, and I saw her fingers tighten around the Browning. "Bring that over here!"

In my peripheral vision, I saw Erika shake her head. The river was louder now, behind us. Or maybe the silence was just deeper.

"Get over here right now!" Diana shrieked.

Colonel Wyatt laughed at his wife.

Erika stopped, and we were at the water, and she let go of my arm and began unfastening the clasps to the briefcase.

"Get over here or I'll kill him! I swear I'll kill him, I'll do it right now!"

"Go ahead," Erika said, loud and deliberate, and she lifted the case, holding it shut, and dangled it over the water. The strain showed in her face, her neck muscles taut, her jaw clenched. "Go ahead, Mom."

Diana glanced at us, and understood what her daughter was going to do, and at that instant, so did I.

"Don't," I told Erika.

"Yeah," she murmured. "Sorry."

My hand went to my gun.

"No!" Diana screamed.

"This is what *I* want," Erika said, and she let the case fall open, and the diamonds and the emeralds cascaded into the dark water, and the bills took to the air.

Erika looked us all over, ending her pan on me. "You'd kill someone who pointed a gun at me?"

Diana turned, bringing the Browning to bear, crying for Erika to stop as I shoved her daughter down with my left hand, brought my weapon up in my right. Wyatt was diving for the ground.

"We all would. Our first duty is to protect you," I said.

I hit her with two double-taps, a clean vertical track, the first bullet in the solar plexus, the last just above her chin.

The ESU personnel who'd had clear shots each fired once, and hit her seven times more.

All it took was one.

The bullets tore into and through her, and Diana crumpled into snow that was instantly black with her blood and her flesh.

I heard a radio crackle. Morgan ran forward to take Diana's pulse. I knew she wouldn't find one.

A diamond glittered at Erika's feet.

Erika began walking to where her father was pulling himself up in the snow. With him on his knees, they were almost eye-to-eye. Erika dropped the empty briefcase in front of him.

"You ruined it," the Colonel said. "You ruined everything."

"Yes, I did."

"I don't know you. You're nothing. Just like your goddamn mother. Don't bother coming home."

Erika shrugged and went to Bridgett's Porsche. Moore and Knowles began helping the Colonel to his feet, and Fowler was guiding the three of them away. Engines were starting up, cars beginning to pull out.

Erika opened the passenger door and climbed inside, fastened her seat belt. Then she sat, still and calm, looking out over the hood at all of us, finally looking at me. Her gaze was strong, level, unapologetic. I hoped I saw a little sadness there, for herself, or her mother, or for me. Perhaps it was just my imagination.

She knew what she'd done. She knew what she'd made me do.

Then Erika turned her head away.

Bridgett came over to where I stood, still holding my gun. "I'll get her to a hospital. You want me to tell her anything?"

"Tell her I'll be in touch."

"All right." She held out her hand, and I realized she was offering me the radio set I'd given her, not comfort. I took it, put it into a pocket.

Bridgett looked at Diana's body for a moment. Then she made her way to the car without turning back, and then the engine growled to life, and she and Erika were gone.

The lot felt empty once more. Not for long, I knew. Detectives would descend, soon, and the Crime Scene Unit, with their flashlights and their cameras. The money and the stones would be recovered, if possible, then catalogued. Statements would be taken, interviews conducted. Reports would be filed, all telling the story of what happened here tonight, and none of them getting it quite right.

I turned around and looked at the ground, where Diana lay, waiting for attention. A hundred-dollar bill had caught in the wind, and was pinned against her body.

Tracks in the snow ran across the lot, and they stretched undisturbed ahead of me, almost out of sight to the empty road. I walked forward, then stopped, looking back at the path I had made, the signs of two feet, but no person. Just a ghost or memory or history, a solitary trail.

I resumed heading for the road, wishing that Rubin were with me, or Bridgett; just someone to walk with.

If you enjoyed Greg Rucka's FINDER, you won't want to miss any of the suspense novels starring Atticus Kodiak.

Turn the page for an exciting preview of SMOKER, Greg Rucka's latest thriller, available in hardcover from Bantam Books in November 1998. And look for SMOKER at your favorite bookstore.

SMOKER

by

GREG RUCKA

CHAPTER ONE

I'd been waiting for forty minutes in the Oak Bar of the Plaza Hotel. Outside, coachmen smoked cigarettes and made jokes about the weather while their horses shifted in the heat, anticipating the order to drag another tourist couple around Central Park. I was wearing blue jeans, white sneakers, a white oxford shirt, a gray and blue tie, and a dust-colored linen jacket. My glasses were clean, and the two small surgical steel hoops in my left earlobe sparkled. It was the fourth day of July, and instead of fighting my jet lag or enjoying a holiday barbecue, I was nursing a club soda and wondering why Elliot Trent was late.

For the most part, I like the Oak Room. It stirs cultural memories of the alcoholic idle rich, the Roaring Twenties, and makes me think of literary giants like F. Scott Fitzgerald and Hemingway's movable feast.

But after a while I start to think about the rest of it—the complacency, the arrogance . . . basically, everything that Fitzgerald talks about in *The Great Gatsby*.

My watch agreed that I'd been waiting forty-two minutes. I figured to make it a round forty-five before calling it quits. Trent hadn't said why I should meet him, only that it was "extremely urgent." That, in and of itself, was barely enough to draw me out. But there was a chance he wanted to talk about Natalie, and although I didn't think Elliot Trent knew the extent of my relationship with his daughter, I'd been wrong before.

I was reaching for the check when Trent arrived. He looked unhurried and cool, his summer-style business suit marking him over-dressed, even in the Oak Bar of the Plaza Hotel. It may have been the Fourth of July, but according to Trent's clothes, this was a business day like any other. He made me in my booth and took his time heading over, even stopping to order drinks from the waiter by the bar. If Trent thought he was late, you couldn't tell by looking at him.

He had company, too, a man in his mid-twenties who followed a few steps behind. The man was very pretty, strong featured, with dark eyes and black hair cropped and styled in the same fashion almost every man had worn in prime time this last television season. The combination of looks and dress made him seem familiar, the way, after a while, every magazine model seems familiar, and I decided I didn't like him on principle. I also decided I was in a bad mood.

"I ordered you another of the same." Trent reached my table and waited for the other man to take a chair before seating himself. "I hope that's all right."

"It might go to my head," I said. "I've been drinking for a while."

Trent frowned. He has a good frown, with creases in the right places and the silver hair above it to make it all look distinguished. The other man smiled. The smile, too, was out of a magazine.

"Carter Dean," Trent said, "Atticus Kodiak. Atticus, this is Carter Dean."

"Of the Greenwich Deans?" I asked.

Carter Dean looked vaguely alarmed. "No," he said.

"Good. Can't stand the Greenwich Deans." To Trent I said, "I've been here for forty-five minutes."

"I was held up at my office," Trent said, and that was all he was going to give me by way of an apology. In one sense, it was an adequate explanation: Elliot Trent runs Sentinel Guards, one of the biggest security firms in Manhattan. Over sixty men and women on the regular payroll, with an additional stable of part-timers for when the going gets really rough, covering everything from personal protection to corporate security. Trent himself is ex–Secret Service, and had worked the presidential detail for Carter and, briefly, for Reagan.

The waiter brought our drinks. When he had

gone, Trent said, "I've been trying to reach you all week. Erika said you were out of town."

"I got back today," I said.

"Working?"

"Yes."

"Not local," Trent declared.

"Los Angeles. I know a couple people out there."

"I didn't think it was local." Trent reached for his drink. "What were you doing?"

"Auditing. A Saudi princess is starting at UCLA in the fall. You know the story."

"So you weren't actually guarding."

"Nope."

"I'd imagine business has been rough. Not a lot of work."

"There's been enough."

"Really?" His creases went a little deeper in concern. "Even considering everything that's happened?"

I just looked at him, wondering what he was playing at. Pulling this shit in front of a client—if that's what Carter Dean was—made no sense.

"That whole SAS business, I mean." Trent shook his silver head. "And before that, the doctor, you remember. The one whose daughter was murdered."

"I remember."

"You were guarding them both, weren't you? The doctor and her daughter." He kept his gaze on me as he spoke, kept his voice wrapped in fatherly tones. His eyes are hazel.

I looked at Carter Dean. Carter Dean looked out the window. Out the window, one of the coachmen was tucking an octogenarian couple into his carriage for a ride around the park. The couple were holding hands.

"You know damn well I was," I told Trent. He also knew the rest, that one of the guards in the detail had died, and that the guard in question had been his daughter Natalie's lover and my best friend.

Elliot Trent took a sip of his drink, then wiped his fingers on the cocktail napkin. He glanced at Dean. Dean took that as his cue.

"I'm looking for some protection," Carter Dean said. He said "protection" like he was Al Pacino and Trent was Marlon Brando. I didn't want to know who that made me.

"Why?"

Trent answered for him. "Mr. Dean has just ended a relationship with a woman several years his junior. Of legal age, but young nonetheless. The lady in question has brothers. Irate brothers, who are unhappy with the disposition of the affair."

Dean made a face, probably at Trent's choice of words. "They feel I should have married her," he told me. "That just wasn't going to happen, and Liz understood that. They didn't. They don't. They're pretty angry right now."

"Wonder why," I said.

"I've told Mr. Dean there's probably nothing to worry about," Trent said, commiserating with me. "But he is insistent. Apparently, both of the Thayer brothers own guns."

"You're offering this to me?" I asked Trent.

"We're short staffed at Sentinel right now. I

can supply guards for Mr. Dean, but I have nobody free who can run the detail. So, yes, I'm offering it to you."

"It's not a detail," I said. "It's babysitting."

Trent stood up, and I thought the interview was over, but instead he just moved out of the way to let Dean pass. "Will you give us a few minutes alone?" Trent asked him.

Dean nodded, and I watched him head to the bar.

"I know it's babysitting." Trent sat down again. "You know it's babysitting. The threat is minimal, at best. Neither of the brothers—Joseph and James—has a record. I've already tried to dissuade Dean, but he's after the peace of mind, and he's willing to pay for it."

"You can't really be so busy at Sentinel you don't have anyone to spare," I said.

"We're running a major operation upstate, and it's taking all of my resources." Trent leaned back in the booth to appraise me. I don't imagine he liked what he saw, but I couldn't argue with that; lately, I didn't like what I saw in the mirror either. It wasn't just the need for a haircut, or the scar that ran along my right cheek from temple to jaw. It was the suspicion that the whole Atticus Kodiak looking back at me wasn't much of a package.

"It's an easy job, Atticus. We plant Dean at the Orsini Hotel, button him up there for two weeks, tops. Two thousand dollars for the work, and you don't even have to sit on him twenty-four/seven. I'll supply three or four other guards to make him feel safe, you'll all keep him company, and everyone will be happy."

"I'm wondering if I should be insulted," I said.

"The word is out." Trent said it gently. "Some people in our business—in this city, at least—don't want anything to do with you. After the death of that little girl, after the death of Rubin Febres, after the whole mess this last winter with the SAS, they figure you're dangerous. It's not hard to see why. You've had gun battles in downtown, for God's sake."

"Just the one," I said.

"There have been similar situations, but all right. Just the one." He smiled again, and I decided this smile was more condescending than paternal. "But the fact remains that another mishap will get you blackballed in our business. Right now, you're poison. If you do this job for me and you do it right, I'll see what I can do about restoring your reputation. I'll send more work your way, help you get back into the fold."

I stood up, found my wallet, and dropped a couple of bills. "I'll pass," I said.

"Atticus, don't be stubborn."

"I'm not interested."

"You owe me. I could call in my marker."

"If you want to waste it on this, go right ahead. But remember, I'm poisonous and I'm dangerous, and you probably don't want a man like that around the lovely Carter Dean."

"That's your answer?"

"My answer is no," I said, and headed for the

lobby. At the bar Dean shot me a smile and I shot back with a glare and pushed my way through the revolving door and onto the street, wondering if Trent would have called that last exchange a "battle."

And in the Oak Bar at the Plaza Hotel. Nick Carroway would've plotzed.

It was just shy of six when I got back to my apartment, unlocking the door to hit a wall of industrial music blasting from the stereo. I fought the subwoofers down the hall and lowered the volume, then doubled back and found Erika leaning out of her doorway.

"You get a job?" she demanded.

"Passed on it."

"You serious?"

"Perpetually."

"Yeah, I noticed that." She made a little grimace, then added, "I made plans to go over to Bridgett's tonight, to watch the fireworks. I can call her and cancel."

"No, don't do that," I said, but it took me a second, and she caught it.

"I didn't think you were getting back until tomorrow," Erika explained.

"It's not a problem."

"You're certain?"

"Absolutely."

Erika shook her head at me, then turned and went back into her room, leaving the door open. "You should phone her," she called, sounding fifty instead of sixteen.

I followed, watched as Erika stuffed clothes

into her backpack. She was wearing olive shorts, sneakers without socks, and a black tank shirt with a silver ankh stenciled on the front. When she straightened, she smoothed her hair reflexively to cover her left ear. Her hair is the gold of unstained oak, and her left ear is missing most of its cartilage and lobe from where a man named Sterritt had cut it off just to prove he was serious.

When Elliot Trent referred to "that SAS business" he was referring to Erika, to her mother and father who had gone to war over her. Her father had died in the spring, taken by AIDS in the form of viral pneumonia. Her mother had died in the winter when I'd shot her four times.

That was almost nine months ago, now, and in that time Erika and I had rebuilt a relationship I'd all but destroyed five years back. Technically, I'm Erika Wyatt's legal guardian, but neither of us see it that way; we're like siblings, and after squandering my first chance at being her big brother, I'm grateful for another try.

Erika doesn't talk about what had happened with her parents—at least, not to me, and most likely not to Bridgett. She'd been seeing a therapist twice a week until her father died, and then it had become once a week, and now only once a month. We'd attended Colonel Douglas Wyatt's funeral together, and when his ashes were scattered on the Hudson River opposite West Point, she'd cried. But that was all.

Erika repeated, "You should call Bridgett."

"I can't."

"You're both being really stupid about this."

"Probably."

"The longer you avoid each other, the worse it gets, and you're not fooling anyone into thinking it doesn't matter. I mean, you haven't spoken since November, and you're still hung up on each other."

I nodded, but couldn't add anything more.

Erika hoisted the backpack onto one shoulder, cocked her head. "You want me to stay?"

"It's okay, I've got plans. You should hustle if you want to get there before dark." I moved out of her way, followed her down the hall. If she knew I was lying, she gave no sign of it. "When should I expect you back?"

"Tomorrow afternoon, probably," Erika said, opening the door. "I'll call if I'm going to be late."

"I'd appreciate it."

She gave me a kiss on the cheek. Her cheek was soft and warm, and smelled of Noxzema. "You want me to tell her anything?"

"There's nothing I can say."

"Yes there is," Erika said. "You can call her and say 'I love you and I'm sorry.' That's what you can say."

"No," I said. "I can't."

I fixed myself a dinner of pasta with a homemade pesto sauce, then decided I was masochist enough to bake a loaf of bread. My sourdough starter was still alive, the yeast thriving in their earthenware home, and I pounded and kneaded and worked myself into a sweat for a bit. I took a shower while the bread rose, then sat back with a book and a beer. From my window I could see the flashes of early fireworks, glowing airbursts that made brief halos in the darkening sky. It wasn't full night yet and the effect was lost, but it's always that way on the Fourth of July; somebody always loses their patience, and the result is an unsatisfying and depressing show.

Wherever Bridgett and Erika were, I hoped they were watching a better spectacle.

At ten I picked up the phone and called Natalie Trent's apartment, knowing that I shouldn't, and hoping that she wouldn't answer. When I got her machine I hung up without leaving a message. It was probably just as well.

The phone rang almost ten minutes later, and Carter Dean said, "Mr. Kodiak, why won't you protect me?"

I said, "How'd you get my number?"

"I asked Trent for it. Answer my question. Why won't you take the job?"

"You don't need me," I told him. "I don't think you need Trent, either. If you're worried about angry brothers, take a two-week trip to France. It'll cost you less than what Sentinel is charging."

"I don't have a passport."

"Go to Canada, then."

Dean thought that was funny, and gave me a chuckle. Somebody on a nearby roof set off a string of firecrackers. They sounded a little like gunfire, but not much.

"This is what I'm thinking," Carter Dean said. "I want protection, and Sentinel is going to provide it. They're getting my money whether you're on the job or not. Given that I don't much like Elliot Trent, I'd prefer to give some of that money to you."

"If you don't like Trent, use another firm."

"Would another firm hire you?"

"I doubt it."

"I want you."

"Why?"

He was silent for a second. "I'd prefer to be dealing with someone closer to my own age, frankly. Trent's too old for my taste—I think he resents me being both young and wealthy."

Not to mention pretty, I thought. "So you're wealthy."

"I got lucky. Designed a computer game while in college, and the game was a hit. *Ferocious.* Maybe you've heard of it?"

"No."

"Well, trust me, most people who own a PC have," Dean said. "Look, I don't know what's going on between you and Trent, what that whole conversation at the Plaza was about. But you seem like a fair guy, a nice guy, and if I'm going to be spending two weeks locked up at the Orsini Hotel with bodyguards on me the whole time, I'd like at least one of those guards to be a fellow I can get along with."

"You don't need to get along with your bodyguards," I said. "All you have to do is listen to them."

"Then I want to listen to someone I respect," Carter Dean said. "I'd like that person to be you."

I almost laughed at him. Respect was something in short supply on my end. If Carter Dean had it for me, he hadn't been listening very closely to Trent.

"Please," Dean urged. "It would give me peace of mind."

I thought about it. The only reason I'd refused is that Trent had gotten me sore. I wasn't desperate for cash, but there was no question I could use the money. Erika was looking to start college in the next year, and as it was, she'd be traveling on student loans all the way. Two thousand dollars would lessen the burden just a little bit more.

A couple of booms like distant thunder went off overhead, and falling lights of red, white, and blue. Then another salvo, and another. One of the big fireworks displays had started.

"All right," I told Dean. "I'll do it."

PHILLIP MARGOLIN

The *New York Times* bestselling author

THE BURNING MAN
_____57495-7 $6.99/$8.99 Canada

AFTER DARK
_____56908-2 $6.99/$8.99 Canada

THE LAST INNOCENT MAN
_____56979-1 $6.99/$8.99 Canada

HEARTSTONE
_____56978-3 $6.99/$8.99 Canada

GONE, BUT NOT FORGOTTEN
_____56903-1 $6.99/$8.99 Canada